The Complete Moorigad Dragon Collection

DEBRA KRISTI

Moorigad Dragon Collection, Parts 1 - 3 Copyright © 2017 by Debra Kristi

All rights reserved under the International and Pan-American Copyright Conventions. Published in the United States by Ghost Girl Publishing, LLC. www.GhostGirlPublishing.com

This is a work of fiction. Names, characters, places, and incidents either are the product of the author's imagination or are used fictitiously. Any resemblance to actual persons, living or dead, events, or locales is entirely coincidental.

Warning: the unauthorized reproduction or distribution of this copyrighted work is illegal. Criminal copyright infringement, including infringement without monetary gain, is investigated by the FBI and is punishable by up to 5 years in prison and a fine of $250,000.

eBook ISBN: 978-1-942191-12-4 / Paperback ISBN: 978-1-942191-13-1
Hardback ISBN: 978-1-942191-20-9

Library of Congress Control Number: 2016930642

Cover wrap design artwork by Adara Rosalie
Perfect bound design by Ghost Girl Publishing
Editor: Eden Plantz

Moorigad / Debra Kristi. – 2nd ed.
Young Adult—Fiction. Paranormal—Fiction. Romance—Fiction
Visit the author: http://www.debrakristi.com/

Created with Vellum

ALSO BY DEBRA KRISTI:

THE BALANCE BRINGER CHRONICLES:

Becoming: The Balance Bringer

Awakening: The Balance Bringer

Empowering: The Balance Bringer

Igniting: The Balance Bringer

Uniting: The Balance Bringer

THE BALANCE BRINGER ORIGINS:

The Mystic Maker

The First Balance Bringer

The Would Be Queen

GIFTED GIRLS SERIES:

Magical Miri, Book One

Bewitching Belle, Book Two

Nowhere Nara, Book Three

Clever Chloe, Book Four

Fatal Freya, Book Five

MOORIGAD DRAGON COLLECTION:

The Moorigad Dragon, Part One Moorigad Collection

Reap Not the Dragon, Part Two Moorigad Collection

Plight of the Dragon, Part Three Moorigad Collection

Moorigad, Parts One–Three

CURSED ANGEL COLLECTION:

Blood Promise: Cursed Angel Blood Promise

MYSTIC'S CARNIVAL

Welcome!

Step inside and let the adventure begin!

MYSTIC CARNIVAL

Dragons · Shape-Shifters · Reapers · Magic · Tarot · Creatures of all races

CARNIES WANTED - APPLY WITHIN

Admit One

CARNIES WANTED

Join us at Mystic's Supernatural Carnival

www.DebraKristi.com

MOORIGAD

USA TODAY BESTSELLING AUTHOR

DEBRA KRISTI

For all the readers who love to get lost in an adventure. Here's your VIP ticket to Mystic's Carnival.

Mystic's Carnival. You may have heard of it—the name has been whispered in quiet conversation, mentioned in folktale. Many believe it does not exist. Let me assure you, it's as real as the air around you.

If you are lucky or so in need, you may be among the few who come to know the wonder of this mysterious destination. It's not your average carnival. No, not at all. The show of twirling lights, motor rides, and funny sideshows never moves, never sleeps, and can never, ever be found unless so wished by the carnival herself. Is she a living, breathing entity? I'll let you be the judge.

Follow now, if you will, into the story, and let our characters introduce you to the splendor of their world and the mystery that can only be found at Mystic's Carnival.

Safe travels, weary reader~

Zeke

PART ONE

THE DRAGON

THE MOORIGAD DRAGON

"Sing my precious little golden bird, sing! I have hung my golden slipper around your neck."

- The Nightingale

1

MYSTIC'S

Kyra

A grumble worthy of the grumpiest of dragons rumbled through Kyra's stomach. In a futile attempt to silence the beast, Kyra pressed the heel of her palm into her gut and peeked through the fall of her hair at the convenience store clerk. She stood at the first rack inside the door with nothing blocking her from the clerk's view. The last thing she needed was something as insignificantly stupid as a tummy growl to draw his attention. If he came over, well...

"Finding everything okay over there?" the clerk asked from his station.

She regarded the counter surrounding him. At least he had a protection barrier, even though he didn't know he needed one. "Yep," Kyra grunted, staring back to the selection of beef sticks and jerky on the top row of the rack. Within her pockets, her fingers searched, turning up nothing more than lint. The hunger tore at her stomach like werewolf claws, making human flesh all too appealing. Her eyes darted to the side, back to the clerk. A magazine was open on the counter, but he was no longer reading. The gum-smacking teen was now peering down the aisle at her.

Again, her stomach grumbled. Kyra bit her nails and returned her attention to the display. Terrible, nasty habit, nail biting. She'd have to stop. But not today. Not if it kept her from delighting in charbroiled teen for lunch.

Kyra had never slipped, never harmed a human in her life. Today was not going to be the first. But dang, hunger rolled through her like an ever-destructive tidal wave. *Food, must have food now.* From left to right, then left again, she shifted, awkwardly, in her moment of indecision. With the speed of a predator's strike, she grabbed two handfuls of jerky and ran for the door.

"Hey!" the clerk yelled.

A clamor followed her escape out of the store.

Using the doorframe as an anchor, Kyra swung her body swiftly to the left and bolted down the street, dropping bags of jerky in her wake. Mid-morning, the hustle and bustle of the commute hour had already subsided, allowing Kyra, for the most part, to easily weave through the sidewalk traffic. Her legs pumped in a labored effort weighted by exhaustion and malnutrition. If only the clerk knew what she was, what she could do, how hungry she had become, he wouldn't pursue. Only here, in this world full of naive humans, no one knew. That had been the point. It was the best place she could think of to hide from her family—among the humans. A place where all her kind would refrain from showing their true faces.

She ran and ran and ran, and still the clamor persisted behind her. Why was he chasing her over some stupid jerky? Who was watching the store? She chanced a glance back. No gum-smacking clerk chasing her down. Not anymore. Nope. She had a cop on her tail. *Smart kid.* She hadn't even noticed the cop.

On her right, a steady stream of moving cars. On her left, building after building, trapping her on a steady sidewalk track. The path took her through a barrage of people, all going about their daily lives. Some stepped out of the way, but a few grabbed at her, tried to stop her. Slow her down. Her eyes burned, and Kyra knew it was only a matter of time before her anger and frustration won, leading her to turn. *I need to get out of here.*

Spotting a turn, she increased her speed and jarred to the left. It was as if the universe had been listening to her, providing her an exit. Or maybe...just maybe...she had rubbed a genie's lamp and forgotten.

Her run faltered.

Dammit.

She was in an alley. A dead-end alley. No greater universal power or genie to the rescue. A trickster, the devil, her own idiocy would seal her fate.

Stupid. Stupid, stupid, stupid move.

Kyra spun around. The cop was at the alleyway entrance. Her tummy rumbled, an infinity of churns and boils. Clutching what few beef sticks and jerky remained to her chest, Kyra took slow and steady steps back.

The cop approached with caution. "You're going to have to come with me," he said.

Kyra threw out her hand to stop him. "Please, I don't want to hurt you."

"Was that a threat?" His eye twitched, and his hand tightened on his gun, ready to pull the weapon from its holster at the slightest sign of aggression.

Kyra's breaths were brisk and arduous, everything inside of her turning to an inferno. She had nowhere to go. The alley ended at a wall a few feet behind her. A strategic glance had informed her of all she needed to know—wall, no exit, and a whole lot of graffiti. Every kind of graffiti. There was a wildstyle, a couple of pieces, some stencils, throw-ups, and of course, stickers and tags. It was as if she were standing in a graffiti museum. But the work was beyond the average graffiti art. The pieces and styles came together to create a giant mural. A mural of a wild carnival. *Who paints carnivals on public walls?*

"Come on, girl. I don't want any trouble." The cop took several steps forward, and broken glass crunched beneath his shoes.

"Neither do I," Kyra said, backing up as far as she could. For a millisecond, the wall pressed against her back, and then she was falling, falling through the mural. A tiny yelp escaped her lips.

Everything was pulling, spinning, and the cop's astonished expression vanished in a blur, as if he were a drop on the water's surface. She was like putty in the universe's hands, being squashed and stretched and swiveled. She wanted to wretch. Hard dirt welcomed her with a thump, ending the experience as quickly as it had begun. All the loopty-loo rollercoaster feelings in her stomach ended, leaving Kyra with nothing more than a void in her gut.

"Ouch." She sat back on her knees and rubbed her elbow. Stared at the last bag of jerky laying in the dirt before her. After all that trouble, all she'd managed to secure was one lousy bag. That was hardly enough to satisfy her hunger.

"It's about time you showed up."

Kyra bolted upright and spun around. Before her, on a chair made from an old tree stump, sat an old man with a cane. A clearly blind old man, judging by his milky white eyes. His gray hair hinted to an age older than his dark skin cared to share, and he dressed like a grandpa. Or at least, how she thought a grandpa would dress. Kyra caught her breath. Behind him was the carnival, the one depicted by the mural. It sparkled and glittered and sang with glee.

"What in the name of supernatural magic?" Kyra's gaze wandered from left to right, taking in the endless sights.

The old man smiled, and, for an instant, Kyra worried his face might crack. "I understand it's all rather confusing. My name is Zeke."

He held out his hand. It was the hand of a working man. Worn, rough, and scarred. In general, Kyra had found working men to be more trustworthy than those in positions of power, but that was just her opinion, which didn't count for spit. She hesitated, staring at the man and the place, unsure if any of it was real. Maybe she'd hit her head in the alley and at this very minute the cop had her face-down on the ground and was cuffing her.

Zeke grunted, retracted his hand, and motioned to the carnival behind him. "This is Mystic's."

Her gaze averted to the colorful spectrum. Every possible wash of illumination jumped from the canvas behind him. Only, it wasn't a canvas. It was real, teeming with life.

It is, isn't it? Real?

Beyond the carnivals glittering gates rang the music of delight: game jingles, zooming rides, and laughter. At the front gate, a vendor handed out oversized balloons to giggling and squealing children who greedily clutched at the shiny floating bobbles. But the thing that most caught Kyra's attention, a funnel cake cart sat between her and the main entrance. It filled the air with the most delicious aroma. Still ravenous, Kyra pressed the heel of her palm into her stomach to stop the growling.

"What is this place? How did I get here?" She had heard rumors but had never... had she lost time? Slipped into another world? Another dimension? Fallen into a trap for the unexpecting?

"You have a lot of questions," Zeke said with a smile in his voice. "Quite understandable. But I assure you, you have nothing to fear." He leaned upon his cane handle. "Mystic's brought you here through the mural's portal. She's been watching you for a while now and decided you needed a place to call home...if only temporarily."

"Mystic's. The carnival brought me?" Kyra grimaced, making no attempt to hide her skepticism.

"Oh yes." Zeke's face beamed. "Mystic's is no ordinary carnival. She is a beautiful sentient being. Living and thinking. She cares what happens to you, Kyra."

"You know my name?" Kyra jolted back, her insides flaring to new temperatures. Her gaze darted across the crowd searching for signs of her kind. Any who might try to return her to her mother or father.

"She knows much," Zeke continued, ignoring Kyra's uneasiness. "She told me you would come, and I'm glad you did. I think you'll like it here. Like I said, this is no ordinary carnival. She caters to the supernatural."

Satisfied that no one was waiting to jump out of the crowd and haul her away, Kyra snatched the bag of jerky from the ground and turned her attention to Zeke. "Okay, but..."

"I think you should eat first." Zeke's glanced at the bag Kyra crinkled in her grasp. "I'll let one of our own fill you in on all the need-to-knows." He shifted in his seat as if looking for someone. "Sebastian!" he called across the carnival's entrance.

A guy in line at the funnel cake cart, clad in all dark attire—black pants, black shirt, black hoodie—responded with a scrutinizing stare. Something about the way he looked at her was like icicles across her skin, and Kyra thought she could feel his stare scrapping over her bones. He appeared hesitant to respond even as he abandoned his place in line and strolled in their direction. Her gut rolled, twisted into knots, and her muscles tensed. There was something different about him. Something alluring and dangerously different.

He crossed the open expanse with the sway of a guy who hadn't a care in the world and came to stand before Kyra. Like Zeke had done previously, the guy extended his hand. "Sebastian," he said. "I hear you're the new girl."

Kyra bit the inside of her lip and ogled him. He definitely agitated the coals in her fire. She didn't know if that was a good thing or not.

"Kyra." She placed her hand in his palm.

Sharp, arctic waves swelled over her skin, quelling her inner inferno. Kyra sucked back a deep breath and gazed into the eyes of the most incredible being she'd ever come across. Never had she met a being who could compete with her fire. She was baffled, confused, and intrigued. No longer did she burn, nor did he freeze. Their touch was a perfect body warmth.

Maybe the carnival was worth further investigation. She supposed she could hang around for a little while. Sebastian coughed, and Kyra blinked. He glanced to their clasped hands.

"Oh." Heat rushed to her head. She released her hold and let her arm fall to her side. *Was I staring? Oh, dear Rajūn, I was seriously staring. So embarrassing*. She shot a quick glance in Sebastian's direction before settling her gaze upon Zeke. "I guess I can stay for a bit."

"Wonderful." Zeke stomped his cane. "Sebastian, please see that this young lady gets something to eat."

"I'm on it." Sebastian turned and walked away.

Kyra's feet were planted firmly in place. Staring after him, she churned with anxiety, curiosity, confusion, and embarrassment. Her legs had become blocks of lead.

He glanced back. "Are you coming?"

And just like that, the lead turned to molten metal.

Kyra leapt and stumbled after Sebastian.

Mystic's

Eight Months Later...

2

NEW JOB

Sebastian

Sebastian made his way through Mystic's Magical Market. The walk was colorful and charismatic, and he never tired of the journey. His House of Tarot could be found midway down the pass, between Talia's Crystal Ball Gazing and the Palm Reader. Behind his establishment sat his tiny home of a trailer. And it was tiny, compared to the one Kyra had received many months ago, once she had decided to stay. Not that he minded. He didn't require much room. Simply a place to drop for the night.

Today's crowd was light, which suited Sebastian just fine. He wasn't in the mood for dealing with patrons who didn't much care for the truth in their fortunes. It's not as if he could control the cards. They told what they told. Stepping through his front walk, he ran his fingers through the multitude of hanging crystals and set a melody of fairy opera swimming through the air.

"Sebastian."

His cloud evaporated. Darkness, thick and suffocating, dropped over him. He grumbled and slowly turned back toward the market way.

Standing amongst the passing crowd was a man. A timeless, stoic man. A much-hated man. Hated by Sebastian, at least.

"How did you find me?"

"Don't be daft, boy." The gentleman brushed his fingers along the brim of his fedora. "You can't hide from me forever."

"It was worth a try." Sebastian stuffed his hands in his pockets.

"You have a job to do," the man said with a sparkle in his eye. It contrasted against the surrounding gloom he'd brought with him.

All Sebastian's self-confidence and pride melted away with the sag of his shoulders. "Not here." He turned into the House of Tarot and walked to the back, leaving the reading table as a barrier. The space was dimly lit. Sebastian would normally have called it mood lighting... for effect, of course. Today, it was a reflection of the situation pressing upon him. The outlining candles continued to flicker, yet appeared to put out less light than usual. Maybe it was Sebastian's imagination, or maybe, just maybe, this man sucked the light out of everything around him.

The gentleman entered. Impeccable gray suit, sharp tie, and a fedora. Sebastian had wondered on more than one occasion if he was a Frank Sinatra fan. "You have a job to do," he repeated.

Sebastian paced behind the table, restlessness pulsing through his legs. "I don't want another job. The last one you gave me was wretched, and it followed me here."

"If you had done the job correctly, there would have been nothing left to follow."

Sebastian rolled his eyes.

"Respect, boy. You show me respect." The man's expression reminded Sebastian of a shark. It wasn't too far off the mark. The man was, in Sebastian's opinion, a cold-blooded predator.

Sebastian sighed. "I don't want to do this."

"Doesn't matter if you want to or not. I've decided. It's been too long, and you are far overdue." The gentleman flicked his finger in Sebastian's direction.

Searing pain cut and curled across Sebastian's ribs, as if he'd been slapped with a branding iron. "Ouch!" He pressed against his side, breathed deep, and lifted his shirt. Scrolled up the side of his chest was the scribble of one word. "Why?"

"It's how I work," the gentleman said with a mild tilt of the head. "The mark will inform you of everything you need to know." With a smirk, he turned and strolled out of the tarot tent, not allowing Sebastian any further chances to rebut.

With a shaky hand, Sebastian raked his fingers through his hair. *Why did he have to find me? I don't want to do it. Any of it.* He looked down at the word again and studied it. *What the heck is a Balidhug anyway?*

He dropped into his worn, overstuffed chair in a slouch, the table at his side. So many times, he'd found comfort in the chair, but not today. Today there was no comfort to be found. Not in the chair. Not in his tarot tent. And not in his head. His fingers traced arcs over and over in the wood of the table, followed by an obsessive tap, tap, tap.

I could somehow infuse my tarot cards into the process. Maybe I'd hate it a little less then. His finger tapped the table again. It wasn't enough, and he knew it.

Tap, tap, tap.

There wasn't a single thing that could...

A tiny glimmer of hope sparked, and Kyra's name enveloped his developing plan. Her friendship had become the calm to his inner storm. Maybe, just maybe, her presence would make his required task bearable.

3
IN DEEP

Kyra

A flurry of heat particles swirled deep within Kyra's throat. They sparked and sizzled like a half-witted science experiment gone awry. Her nose twitched in response to the tickle.

For an endless moment, she admired the profile of the man standing beside her and held the fury within her at bay. She'd known Sebastian less than a year, yet it felt like a millennium. Only he had shown her patience and understanding where her family had shown none. He'd taken the time to work with her on balance and inner peace, helped calm her rage. It was because of him she was still sane, still walking the line of indecision.

Her skin shivered with heat, set in motion by his enticing form. A distraction from her practice she neither needed nor minded.

But I should mind, she reminded herself.

She released the fever from her lungs in one long, slow breath. It exploded from her lips in hellfire. Tongues of seething flame lashed out at the crisp air, the embers seeking new fuel, until a sharp widening of her lips killed the blaze. Kyra never tired of the art of fire-breathing. She could practice for hours.

Sebastian raised a brow in an oh-really kind of way, yet barely looked in her direction. He continued to flip through the deck of cards he held and made no attempt to hide the smile flirting at his lips. "I've seen you do better." He teased.

His words meant to challenge, not insult. Of that she was confident. There was nothing in all the worlds she was surer about than Sebastian. He was the best friend she'd ever had, possibly the only friend, and she trusted him with everything about herself. Well, most everything. Possibly a lot. Enough, anyway.

A silent, happy-to-play-along half chuckle rumbled through her chest. She lifted the whiskey bottle and took another swig, coating the inside of her mouth for further fire practice. She used the leather sleeve of her jacket as a napkin before turning to face him.

"Of course, I've done better." Kyra swung the whiskey bottle in a wide arc. "But we weren't sitting around *Normville* with our thumbs up our aft ends at the time, were we? So, it's not like I was trying that hard." She swirled the bottle of shimmery liquid and scanned the landscape for the umpteenth time. "Are we someplace in America? All human cities have begun to look the same to me. I prefer realms where we're free to be ourselves. Places of magic, like the carnival."

Today was the first time Sebastian had invited her on an errand outside of the carnival. She hadn't a clue to the true nature of the errand, but it was clear, whatever the task, it tormented him. He hadn't moved in the past thirty minutes. He stood in the same spot, leaning against the same stone pylon, playing nonstop with the same deck of tarot cards. His gaze would wander to the wide river several yards away, then back to the deck. She only hoped that her presence made whatever it was he had to do a tad easier. After all, she had assumed that was why he had invited her.

If he would just open up and share a tad bit more.

She'd told him more than anyone, little as it actually was. They were bonded through their unspoken genealogical pain, runaway status, and secret species prestige. He made life at Mystic's Carnival feel like some place she might want to stay long term. Like a real home. Something she'd never really had before.

Her parents never made her feel comfortable enough or welcome enough. Always pushing her to make the choice—the choice *they* wanted. And each of them wanted something different. Kyra remained unresolved on the decision that would soon have to be made. Had Anguis the Angry felt the same way? Maybe. Maybe that was why he was angry. He had become famous for refusing to choose a side. But he'd also gone mad. Angry and mad.

She'd been told so often to pick a side that it jumbled in her head like debris trapped in a spinning typhoon. She despised both her parents for it, and every member of their clans. It was their fault she was trapped having to make a choice, their fault she didn't belong. Running away was the best thing she'd ever done because it had led her to Sebastian.

The cards in Sebastian's hands stopped flipping. He turned, looked straight through her, a sense of vexation in his dark eyes. Kyra's chest squeezed, bruising her ego in one quick, stumble-fly reaction. It hurt. Physically hurt. Her hand clutched at the cement behind her, but the pain evaporated with the blink of his eye—that quick, that simple. As if it never were.

"I'm sorry," Sebastian mumbled, looking to his feet. "I didn't mean to hurt you. I guess I need to work more on my control. I haven't figured it all out yet."

Sebastian had been the source of her pain. Intriguing. Kyra leaned closer, the thirst for knowledge, a deeper understanding about him, nudging at her back. This was the first time she'd heard him even hint at his inherited gifts. She would never push, though. Not with Sebastian.

"I get it. I'll help if you want."

His face lifted, faking a smile, and he returned his gaze to hers, this time less intense, if only slightly. "That would be something."

She saw through his pretenses. Whatever he was wrestling with disturbed him more than he cared to voice. She didn't like seeing him so withdrawn, so cutoff, so distant. She wanted to reach over, take his hand, *force* him to open up. A blend of control and *just* enough compassion that would make her father frown. Only, that's how this friendship made her feel—compassionate.

Maybe the tough girl armor was the wrong one to wear in front of Sebastian. She knew little about his kind. So, little she had no idea exactly where to pinpoint his species. All she knew for certain was she and Sebastian were not the same. Not that she cared, particularly. She didn't want to push him away with her volatile personality. Behind his protective façade, she could see him trying. She could try harder, too.

The idea of someone in whom she could confide made her insides vibrate and her heart hammer, for she disliked harboring secrets. Secrets often came back to bite ugly chunks out of her tail.

Despite Sebastian's mood, the brooding look fit him. Even looked good on him. It was the way his dark hair fell over his forehead, or how his olive skin would darken, and his indigo eyes took on a look of great knowledge and vulnerability all at once. Kyra and Sebastian were far from similar, and yet, he could easily blend in among her mother's clan with his warm mocha skin and midnight hair, as long as the clan remained in human form.

She would never fit in. Fair skin and deep-set golden eyes were her traits, inherited from her father's side. She'd tried staying with her father and his clan, but the aspects inherited from her mother's line became intolerable for them. She was destined to be a nomad, a runaway, with no place to belong. Yet having a little of both parental lines sure came in hellfire handy on occasion.

A card dropped at her feet.

"Pick it up," Sebastian said. "You should like it. It's a good thing."

Kyra lifted the card and turned it around in her hand. *What does this mean?* She stared at the extensive art of the design. Kyra had a vague understanding of the tarot cards. She thought she had their various meanings memorized, but too often found herself confused.

"It's The Empress," he said, looking pleased. "She's telling you that big decision you've been struggling with is in your control." Sebastian threw her a sharp, meaningful look. "*Only* you decide what happens next."

The stone columns around them vibrated with an inconsistent hum of passing cars on the above bridge. Beneath Sebastian's stare, Kyra felt itchy and uncomfortable and naked. He knew her too well. Knew her secrets and weaknesses and fortitude. Knew the weight the decision laid upon her. She lacked the comfort of her guise. Having no witty response ready at the tip of her tongue, Kyra stashed the card in her back pocket with a silent acknowledgment, a customary torque of the lips.

The clatter of footsteps on the adjacent walking path drowned out to a shallow buzz at the back of her ear. Since they were well camouflaged within the shadows and foliage of the surrounding beech trees, she knew the activity overhead shouldn't give her any concern, and it didn't, not really. Sebastian was the cause of her internal nagging.

There was a reason he'd dragged her out here, far from their home at the carnival. And yet, all they had done was stand around and wait. If he was going to share the reason for the errand, she wished he would do it already.

Agitation had her swirling her glossy bottle of fuel faster and faster. It was only liquor, and she didn't need it, but for the purpose of her show, it worked well in creating the illusion. Practice made it convincing. "Why are we here? Why are we standing around doing nothing?"

His focus shifted to the grass at his feet, hiding his face from view. Still visible was the slight tic at the edge of his lip. "I'm waiting for something."

Obviously. Stop dragging your feet, Sebastian. "Great." Kyra leaned against the hard surface beside him, dropped her bottle of whiskey, heard it land with a solid thump, and reached for Sebastian's hand. She didn't care he wasn't clan. Didn't care if her father would disapprove, or her mother, for that matter. They weren't present. She only cared about the life she was building now. A life full of carnival misfits. And that included Sebastian.

She pictured her parents' faces if they could see the way she now lived. Ribbons of warmth raced through her blood at the thought. Her fingers glided across Sebastian's skin, gently weaved their hands together. "You can tell me anything. You know that, right? I'd take your secrets to the grave." She stared down at their hands, at their connection, a bristled knot settling in her chest.

Sebastian's fingers locked onto hers and squeezed. The hold was soft and warm and solid. A grip promising to never let go. And Sebastian's eyes filled with so much emotion Kyra didn't know how to interpret it. "That's why I brought you. I trust you unequivocally. Time I shared this part of me with you."

Trust. No one had ever trusted her before. The warmth welling within her heart expanded tenfold, and she imagined her bones bursting into cinder. Finally, *his* secret would be *their* secret. She tightened the squeeze on his hand, held fast as the world around them melted into wet paint. Nothing else mattered, only the steadfast love and loyalty of true friends. Within it, they found trust.

"I've never before known anyone with whom I felt safe sharing pieces of myself. Not until you." Sebastian stared at the deck of cards he held tight within his grip. The cards bowed, forming a loose letter C. "There's so much about who and what I am that I am ashamed of. Afraid to admit or to speak out loud." He glanced up at Kyra and held her gaze. "But I think...I think I'd feel safe sharing those parts of myself with you. I think you could help me better understand myself and come to terms with what I am." He blinked and dropped his gaze to his feet, once more.

Kyra bit her lip. Every molecule of her being had come to a complete stop, frozen in the moment.

Shouts broke out in the distance, destroying the moment. All signs of sensitivity washed from Sebastian's face. He looked toward the bridge above, toward the commotion, toward...what, exactly? Perking up, Sebastian stepped to the side, out from cover. Following his gaze, Kyra moved into the trees with him and turned toward the clamor.

On the long, stone structure that crossed the river, four men were fighting. It was three against one, more a beating than a fight.

Sebastian's lips curled into a sneer—a neither hostile nor jealous sneer, but the kind of sneer one plastered on his face when privy to disapproving bouts of behavior. "Look at those humans, beating on each other like dumb animals."

As if she'd jammed her fingers in a light socket, a jolt ran through Kyra. His words surprised her, yet she refused to believe they were his genuine feelings. The false stretch of his lips, strained look in his eyes, gave her reason to think he concealed something, and feigned prejudice to keep his true motives hidden.

"Don't be so judgmental," she said. "It's not like supernaturals are superior when it comes to stupid behavior. After all, why are you hiding at the carnival instead of at home with your family?" A shudder rolled over her, spurred by the thought that their stories could be similar. Was he also being forced into a marriage he wanted no part of? Why else had he remained so closed-lipped? Had he killed to get away? Or would he be killed if caught? Maybe his story wasn't anything so exciting. Maybe his story wasn't so different from hers. Full of speculation, she patiently awaited his answer.

He clenched the deck of cards, turning his knuckles white. Tension built between them. A new development to which she wasn't accustomed. She didn't understand it and didn't like it. His right eye quivered. "I have my reasons."

Anger churned inside her like liquid magma. Slipping and sliding around the bends in her bloodstream like a firewater jet slide. She'd swear the sun got fifteen degrees hotter. Heated with hatred for being shut out. One minute it was trust; the next an iron hatch slammed in her face. "I bet you do, Mister Tall, Dark, and I-Got-Supernatural-Secrets," Kyra mumbled, crossing her arms and letting a dismal scowl fall into place on her face.

Allowing herself to be controlled by petty emotions was unwise. She knew that. Especially when she wasn't exactly an open book, but her feelings rarely asked for permission before taking control of the helm. Her sentiments were the equivalent of a wild card in a poker deck. They could do just about anything.

Sebastian had never asked more than she was willing to give. She should show him the same courtesy. Not always so easy, though. She didn't have as much self-control as he did. Or appeared to have. Now something strange brewed between them. Over what? She couldn't define the emotions or the circumstances, which only made it worse.

"Damn be to Hades." Sebastian scuffed his foot along the ground. "I'm sorry, Kyra. I'm just stressed right now."

She pretended to assess him, even though there was no need. He wore his stress like a magician's cape. "It's kinda showing. Might want to tuck it back under your shirt."

Sebastian laughed. It was fake and lackluster, failing to light up his face the way his genuine laughter always did. Sebastian's body went ramrod straight. Smoke scorched Kyra's nostrils in her irritation. He ignored her—his stare transfixed at the far end of the bridge. "There! He's there." Sebastian took another step into the clearing, another step closer to the water, closer to the commotion of human civilization.

Someone stood at the far edge of the bridge, instantly recognizable as non-human. He moved with a sense of belonging toward the men fighting. Hard to describe, he was the type you didn't want to notice. You knew he was there when looking directly at him, yet you didn't want to see or acknowledge his presence. All Kyra could decently distinguish was a nondescript, dark gray suit and hat to match. Through all her travels over the years, she'd never seen anything or anyone like him. He was a mystery.

He was invisible to human perception. Alarms buzzed inside her like electrified wire. She wanted to be on the bridge, investigating the curious stranger.

Kyra tried to make her words roll out in a drawl, attempted to sound bored, unenthused. Instead, excitement—eagerness—escaped. "Great. Shall we go meet him?"

Sebastian's eyes widened and froze. "No!"

It wasn't that caught-you-naked-doing-something-you-shouldn't kind of look. No. It ran far deeper. She glanced between her friend and the new man. Something properly serious bothered Sebastian, and she didn't think it was her reaction. She wanted to bite right to the core of the *shituation*. "You know what's funny? I can't say with a hundred percent certainty, because he's so far away, but that guy smells a lot like you. Haven't come across that before. Is he related?"

That would clarify a few things. Kyra had been drawn to Sebastian's mysterious side. It was alluring, exciting. Whatever stood on the bridge was equally as mystifying. Of course, she'd been intrigued by the mystery back in the beginning. Now she was ready to be in on the secret.

Kyra had the strangest desire to look back at the man. One quick peek, she spied him already halfway across the bridge, past the four-man squabble, nearing their edge of the extension. He was so close now. The stranger tipped his hat in her direction, sending a horde of butterflies loose within her innards.

Sebastian blinked, sucked in his breath. The top tarot card of his deck flipped from his hands toward the water. The colors flickered across her sight, cutting through the air with more precision than a Lightning Bolt throwing knife. It sailed straight for the rough current.

Kyra reached out, missed the card. It was too far away. She looked back at her friend's drawn face, knowing the deck was his livelihood. "Don't worry. I got this." A too-cocky smile spread wide across her face. With a wave of her hand, she called upon the wind. It answered, like it usually did, churning her rust hair in its wake. The card swirled up in a loop and swooped back onto land, into her awaiting palm. Her cocky smile spread inward, warming and tingling and palpitating with success. She held the prize up to Sebastian. "See. I told you—"

A splash cannonaded behind her, the explosion blossoming a flutter of fealty throughout Kyra's hearty being. Surprise, confusion, they strangled her. Something yanked on her, called her toward the water. Shoving the card into the hands of a milky-faced Sebastian, she turned toward ripples rolling out from the one spot on the water's surface calling her—her target.

Three men ran away on the bridge above. One was missing. She looked to the water, then back to the bridge. The way the men ran reminded her of a snippet from a horrid, low-budget, human action flick. Her heart tripped over a beat, and she didn't understand why. All she knew was she had to go, had to follow the feeling, the pull. She half stumbled, half rushed forward, a trickle of sweat sneaking down her brow, quietly escaping her beastly anxiousness.

Sebastian grabbed her arm, dragged her to a stop. He was the barely-calm before the storm and ready to burst. "What are you doing?"

She looked down at his grip, her emotions pinging and ponging inside of her, torn between her loyalty to Sebastian and the inexplicable need now growing. "Someone fell in. I'm going to save him." Urgency coursed through her in a way she'd never experienced before.

"But...." He sputtered and paused and continued. "But...he's human." His voice hitched.

She flinched at his inferred bias, yet swore it was panic she detected in both his eyes and his tone. She'd never heard him utter anything so ugly, not ever. Not in all their hours playing poker in his trailer, or hanging in the back lot behind Big Eli with a bottle, making up stories about the people riding the magic circle of lights—the Ferris wheel. Not even on his darker days, when she would find him wandering by the wall of fog. Those days, they would walk for hours talking about nothing greater than nonsense. She knew he didn't truly feel that way. He had friendships that proved as much.

"So what?" She peeled his hand free.

"You'll risk exposing us." His voice hitched.

"It's a risk I'm willing to take."

She wasn't a hundred percent confident in her words but didn't want Sebastian to see her falter. Too strong was the pride pulsing through her veins. Besides, going after the man wasn't a choice she was free to make. She *had* to go. She didn't want to accept it, but knew it was true. Something pulled at her, and it was unyielding. Like she was on the end of a fishing line being reeled in. With an abrupt turn, she walked away, a piece of her breaking into bits with each stretched step put between them. She prayed their trust would survive whatever happened next.

Kyra stepped into the brisk, wild current. It welcomed her like a child returning home after a long absence. It had been too long since she'd allowed herself to swim, and the water was glorious to the touch. Overdue pleasure spread to the corners of her cheeks, and she dove into its depths. Cold, vicious liquid wrapped around every curve of her body as she began to change, shedding unnecessary human garments in trade for her true self. Her scales returned, covering her like a form-fitted bodysuit.

Like an untamed torpedo, she shot through the water, the greatest of water beasts. The turbulent river was no match for her strength. Her movements were second nature, a Sea Dragon's quick, artful angulation.

An abnormality, that's what she was. The blending of two dragon species, something they called Moorigad, something frowned upon. For good reason, too. The traits of both parents clashed within her, a constant storm, each fighting for control. A form of discord was the result. No longer beautiful water serpent or big, strong fire beast was she, but a malformed mixture of the two. And she hated it.

What should have been the long serpentine stretch to her spine was interrupted by a bloated belly. Her tail was too long for a Fire Dragon, too short for a Water Hydra, and ended in a hard clump of nothing. Had she been a proper Fire Dragon, her tail would feature a magnificent cluster of spikes. A great weapon at her disposal. But she wasn't. Hence, the clump. And the pathetic bones on her back supported a hide stretched too thin, riddled with an artistic display of holes. They were supposed to be wings. Instead, they were embarrassing.

She tucked her misshapen appendages in close and closed the distance to her target in a wing's bat.

Thick sediment made visibility onerous. Dirt and small pebbles caught in currents clouded her path, but hazy paths never deterred any respectable sea monster. Sound pulses sent out upon entering the water returned to her from multiple directions, pinpointing her needed location. Even through the filth she saw it, a large object falling to the river floor. She quickened her pace.

A muffled thump rippled through the water. Visible was a slight churn of dark chestnut hair and loose limbs flaring out like a discarded twill doll. He sported an ugly black eye and a scrape across the nose. Still, it was definitely the man she'd seen fighting on the bridge. A man now sinking to the bottom of the lake.

Fealty pulled at her again, pulled stronger. Pulled her to him. It played, danced, and fought with the competing emotions swirling in her chest—puzzlement and unease.

As a dragon, there were many things she could do beneath the water. Helping a drowning man breathe was not one of them.

She wrapped her talons tight around his limp form. Fear clenched, closed her throat. What if he regained consciousness, saw her monstrous self? How would he react? How would she react to his reaction? *Why should I care?* she reasoned. Problem was, a curious nagging itched at the back of her skull, solidifying her new truth. She did care.

Kyra sacrificed the advantages of her true full-being, yet maintained the majority of her strength and speed, by holding the scales to her body as she transformed back into something more human-like. She kept her long, webbed feet and arms, as well as her strong clump of a tail, to assist with thrust. The rest returned to the shape of a human female canvased in a brilliant, orange-scaled husk.

She bolted straight for the surface and provided air for the man's delicate lungs. A sputter that failed to summon consciousness was her unwelcome reward. His eyes fluttered; he choked on dirty water and failed to take a breath. Dragging him at her side, she made her way to the shore, to Sebastian.

He watched, restlessly waiting, a dark fog brewing over his demeanor.

Kyra shot Sebastian a look so hard it could leave a mark. She hauled the sodden man from the river. "Don't just stand there. Help me."

Her movements were stiff. The transformation of her legs and feet from long and webbed to normal proved difficult while walking. It was that—and her reluctance to address Sebastian's puzzling behavior. She'd done nothing wrong. In fact, she'd gone out of her way to do everything right. So why did she feel like a dragonet forced to pick sides in a game she'd never wanted to play? And why had Sebastian feigned prejudice against humans? She needed to understand.

Sebastian shoved his hands deep into his jeans' front pockets and shuffled his weight. His bangs hid his face in shadow. "This is a mistake. He was supposed to die."

Maybe so, except something inside her wouldn't let it be true. She was unquestionably drawn to the man, and she couldn't explain it. It was as if her free will had been stripped away, a feeling that caused fire to rage through her veins. Her heart squeezed, twisted into an ugly, fuzzy knot.

Kyra hoisted the man onto the grass, laid him out, and studied his face. "How do you know that?" she asked Sebastian. "How can anybody know who is meant or isn't meant to die? Maybe I was meant to save him."

Sebastian shifted. "I just know. Have a feeling, is all."

"Come on," Kyra said. "Don't be like that. I'll take responsibility for him. That gives him a good fighting chance." She bent down, pinched the man's nose, and pressed her lips to his.

The man coughed, then moaned, a stream of water spilling from his mouth shortly after. He rubbed the palm of his hand across his cheek with one long drag. His eyes flickered open, attempted to focus. A twinkle of mischief and a touch of tenderness greeted her. In the manner of a dopey drunk, a lopsided smile spread across his face and one hand looped up around her neck, pulling her closer.

Kyra let a nervous laugh escape and pushed away. She couldn't help but notice his wet clothing revealed a strong, sculpted physique. "Hold on there, stranger."

"You're so pretty. Must be a dream." His words slurred off his tongue, as if half the syllables were stuck to the surface, and his eyes glazed. He attempted to brush his hand along the side of her face. It skipped and bumped like a dragonling's firsts steps. "Like fire beneath the water." His fingers twisted through her red tendrils, pulled them straight. The weight of his eyelids proved too heavy, though, and they closed once again, returning him to a slumbering state.

She stifled a giggle and looked up to her friend, unsure of her next move.

Sebastian reached down, took Kyra by the arm, and helped her stand. "What the hell was that?" His voice was rough, thick, and his words pressed down on her.

"I made sure he was breathing. Breath of Life and all that. You've seen how it's done, haven't you?"

His shoulders relaxed. Face softened. "Oh, right. Looked like you were kissing him." Sebastian released her and turned away, his face reddening. "You are beautiful, you know. Right now, your skin still shimmers the iridescent orange your scales cast. It's magnificent."

"What?" Kyra looked down at her scaled bodysuit. It was fading, returning to bare flesh. Soon she'd be standing before him completely exposed. Naked. She flushed and crossed her arms. "Give me your shirt."

"If you wanted to get my clothes off, there are better ways to go about it." He glanced back and arched his brows, daring her.

A fireball of nerves dropped in her belly, and she pushed away the thought his words had planted in her mind. *He can't be serious. We're just friends. And he's definitely not a dragon,* she thought. *But what if... Maybe he wants something more. Could it be?*

She shook her head and put out her hand. "Stop. Fork it over."

Sebastian rolled his eyes, as if to say *Kyra's a fun-killer*. He pulled his shirt over his head and handed it to her. She hastily slipped it on. He wasn't a huge guy, and his clothing barely covered all the essential areas, maintaining her decency as her skin dried and her scales vanished.

Sebastian scratched the back of his bronzed neck and looked down at the almost-drowned man on the ground. "I still think you should toss him back in the water and forget about him. I mean, what are you going to do with him? You heard what he said. He saw you."

"Let me worry about that." She fixed a look on Sebastian's ribcage. She hadn't meant to, just couldn't help herself. Something new, something she hadn't seen before, trailed his side. Black ink. It was brilliant against his brown skin. She pointed. "What's that?"

He glanced down at the ink scrolled upon his side like a shopping list. He turned, moving it from her sight. "It's nothing. Just a...thing." The pothole in his words gave Kyra pause. She watched in silence as his hand worked through his hair with a mild shake, and he looked around the perimeter.

His actions more than his words told her the mark was supernatural. That meant it came from his family line, something Sebastian never talked about. Kyra knew she would need to tread lightly if she pressed further. “Is it from your mother’s or father’s side?”

Sebastian’s foot dug into the ground, indicating a truth he was yet unwilling to voice.

“Come on. You never share about yourself,” Kyra pressed.

“Not now. I’m gonna have to fade. I’m on the clock in a tick, and I have an image to keep.” He waved his hands, indicating his present state wouldn’t do.

Kyra needed no convincing. Sebastian seriously got into his role at the carnival. Only her gut hinted he was running away from her question.

“What about the reason you brought me here? Are we going to talk about that? Or maybe the man on the bridge?” Kyra took a step closer, practically willing him to stay.

Sebastian’s glance flickered back and forth between Kyra and the man at her feet, his palm scraping along his jawline. “Nah. We can do that later.”

Kyra rocked back a step, hovered protectively over the unconscious man. She wanted to pursue Sebastian, smooth things over, but she also wanted to stay. What was wrong with her? “Okay.”

“You gonna be all right if I leave you here on your own?” he asked.

Rubbing heavily at her damp skin with his black t-shirt, Kyra’s gaze darted from the bridge, now empty, to Sebastian. “I’m a big girl, don’t you worry.”

His lips twisted oddly to the side.

Straightening her spine, rolling the edge of his shirt tight within her fingers, Kyra snapped, “What? You don’t think I can?”

“Nah. It’s not that. It’s just...you’re not as mature and Merlin-esque as you think. You still make bad calls. Like this one.” With a lazy finger, Sebastian pointed to the river-drunk man lying at her feet. “I can’t help worrying about you.”

“Eighty-three is plenty old and wise. You needn’t worry about me. Go do your stuff. I’ll meet up with you later.” Proud by nature, born to be strong. She wanted to make sure he understood that about her. Kyra gently shoved him in the chest, nudged him in the direction of the portal.

He pushed back, reached over, and peeled a thin layer of hanging dragon-scaled skin from the side of her face. "If you're going to do stupid things, make sure you maintain the illusion afterwards." He gingerly rubbed the shimmery, orange strip of lizard-like skin between his fingers before letting it flutter to the ground. They stood impossibly close, and he lingered a moment longer than necessary, studying her face. With a sigh, he turned and headed for the small land pocket beneath the bridge, glancing back one last time.

It was a forever stare.

He stepped through the gateway between worlds.

Kyra yelled after him, "I'm sorry, Sebastian."

It was too late, his form already swirled and distorted. He was gone, returned to the carnival, their home away from home, the greatest destination for those who knew how to find it. He hadn't heard her apology, and she wanted him to know how sorry she was for messing up the afternoon. She had spoiled their time with too many personal questions and robbed herself of whatever task and disclosure he'd been ready to share.

She wanted to let things go, let them drift away with the wind, but she was like a dragonling with a bone. So unwilling to unclench her teeth. And something about the nondescript, suited man on the bridge screamed *father*. Sebastian's father, to be precise. Sebastian had done nothing to confirm nor to deny her suspicions of any relation, much less a parental one. Yet Kyra felt so dang sure. If it were true, why had Sebastian looked so forlorn?

She stared at the empty space where Sebastian had been mere seconds before, worried her actions had caused him not only concern, but something more. Her emotions swirled, the dark before a rain.

She sat beside the unconscious man and ran her fingers through his wet, tangled hair. His face was scruffy. He needed a shave, had suffered bruising across his cheek and nose, and probably harbored a battered ego. Despite all that, there were things about him she found attractive. Although not overly apparent, he hid strength beneath his flannel shirt, and she liked that about him. His angular jawline and muscular arms hinted to what he kept covered. His eyes had been tender when he'd looked upon her. And she thought it cute the way he now mumbled in his sleep. He muttered about magical lake princesses and heroic rescues.

She scratched the back of her neck and let out a breath. "All right, big fella. You're coming with me." She lifted him by the shoulder, and together they walked—he stumbled—toward the portal.

When they stepped into the circle, the world beyond shifted, slowly shimmered, and began to distort. A hand shot through the blur. Shot straight at them. Clamped down and clenched the man's soaked clothes in its grasp.

4
DESTINATIONS

Kyra

There it was again. That unexplainable fealty, an unspoken devotion, a sense of duty dragging on her like a forged steel shackle clamped around her flesh. Why did this stranger have such overwhelming power over her?

She hissed. Ripped the half-drowned man free of the grasp pushing through the portal, sending her and her wet cargo tumbling back, back, back.

The river-drunk crashed upon her, the moisture from his garments quickly spreading to hers. "What the fu—?"

Kyra cut him off, shoved him off.

He rolled over like a wet lump of beef and looked like yesterday's leftovers. Several days dead. He wasn't, though. She could hear, see, even sense him breathing.

They'd plummeted in at the carnival's front entrance. Whatever had tried to grab them had missed the opportunity. The portal had successfully spun them out of reach.

Everywhere she looked, people milled about. They stood in the ticket line, waited at the cotton candy vendor, gathered around the balloon peddler. None of them paid any attention to the new arrivals. For the carnival, that was the norm. Strange things were the norm. Anything, everything, all things were the norm.

Kyra pinched her forehead. She didn't want to deal. Not with anything so messy. She rolled her eyes, let them land on *him*. He wasn't going to pick himself up. Get himself out of the space of the portal. Get himself tucked away safe in her dragon's lair.

Nope. She'd have to do it.

She puckered her lips, allowing the pout for half a second. With a heavy sigh, she picked him up and hauled him through the carnival at break-wing speed.

Kyra nodded to a carnie or two, not taking time for much acknowledgment. Her cargo stirred, and she wanted him in the safety of her den—a 1970s Yellowstone Camper Trailer.

Down the midway, through the Fun Zone, across the valley of carnie campers to her own she charged. She kicked open the front door in a sliver-fold of time. Lucky, considering how the carnival worked. So unpredictable. Never the same map twice.

She deposited the man precariously on the edge of her bed and stood in awkward silence. Watched him cradle his head in his hands and felt utterly clueless. Clueless on what to do next. Like a pile of sodden books, his weight sunk into the mattress. Sunk into her list of woes. Now that they were safe, she questioned why she'd even brought him back to her trailer, or to the carnival. Not that she knew where else to take him. She only knew she felt some strange connection between them. Some strange need to protect him. Beyond that, she didn't know what any of it meant.

Scratching her head, Kyra looked away from the groggy man and wandered to the far end of the room, as if escape were possible in a trailer so tight. She glanced between the wall clock and her exposed legs. Her current attire was unacceptable in front of a total stranger, or for her performance soon to start. After pulling underwear, black pants, and boots from the closet and briskly fitting them to her form, she slipped a jacket on over Sebastian's shirt, shuffled a foot back, and turned to go.

She had just enough time to stop in and see Sebastian before her performance. She wanted—needed—to see where things stood between them.

The guy on the bed teetered and moaned. Kyra rolled her eyes and looked him over. "Why don't you rest? I'll be back to check on you later," she said, turning to leave.

"Wait. Don't go." His voice, choked by half the lake, fought to be heard.

She hesitated, hand balanced on the doorknob. Fierce dragon that she was, she had a funny fear of facing humans. This one, at least. She turned toward him. "Need something?"

"You saved my life." He started to stand, wavered, collapsed back on his butt. A wince etched into the lines on his face. "Not once, but twice. That was no easy task, and I don't even know your name."

She bit her lip, took a deep breath, and wondered what troubles she'd created by saving this guy. "It's Kyra. And it was nothing, really."

She meant it—mostly. The no-big-deal part. Saving him had been easy. At the time, she had worried more about being seen. Now it was something more. Saving him may have invited a giant pile of dragon dung into her life, if Sebastian's odd reaction was any indication. Or the creepy grab attack at the portal.

Still, she couldn't escape the feeling, the deep-rooted emotion that pulled her to him, made her protective of him. Nothing about this flew straight with her, and yet it did. Therein lay the problem. She was accepting of things she normally wouldn't be. It wasn't like her.

He extended his hand, and as he did, his eyes lit up the most brilliant shade of sapphire. That twinkle of mischief returned. Kyra's eyes widened at the sight of him. Embarrassing as it was, she couldn't stop herself. She tried to play it off. Yank her emotions inside, shove them down deep, and close the lid. She tried to pretend nothing was amiss. She tried all that and pushed forward to shake his hand. He kissed it instead. Her breath caught, clogged in her throat.

He rose from the bed, bringing his scrutinizing eyes closer. His heat closer. Everything closer. "Thank you, Kyra. I'm Marcus Blackall. I can never repay you, but I'd like to try."

Her heart raced like the quick beat of her feeble wings attempting flight. Then wrecking-ball-guilt slammed her. All the time she'd spent building a relationship with Sebastian, and in one day, she'd let a total stranger unnaturally affect her. On the day of Sebastian's admitted trust, no less. But she and Sebastian were friends, not lovers, so what did it matter? Only, it did matter. He'd acted so odd at the lake. She shook her head, dismissed the thought. Sebastian would never be interested in a volatile dragon. He had far too much patience and calm for her anger issues. She thrust away the guilt.

Marcus Blackall looked around with an appraising eye. "I take it we're at your place?" He paused, briefly, then snapped a sharp look upon her. "Why here?"

Kyra hesitated, feeling very much the moth caught in the flame at that moment. "After what happened, I thought it would be safer."

He nodded. Pulling at his wet shirt, Marcus looked uncomfortable. "You have a laundry facility around here somewhere?"

How absent-minded of her. Of course he would want dry clothes. "It takes forever to get things cleaned around here. Give me a second, and I'll bum a change off my neighbor." *Crap, crap, crap*. Now she not only felt guilt regarding Sebastian, but for overlooking Marcus's needs, as well.

"I'm not afraid of a long hike. Don't want to put anyone out."

Kyra paused, already halfway out the door, and returned her attention to Marcus. How could she tell him there weren't any electric dryers at the carnival, like he might expect? They only had laundry lines. Didn't matter. She turned back, and barbed knots formed in her throat, impeding further speech.

Marcus stood bare-chested, wet shirt in his hand. If that weren't enough to drop her chin, he wore a unique piece around his neck. It drew her eye like an impossibly strong magnet.

It was a tooth on a rope. And not the kind people bought in souvenir shops. Of that, she was most confident. It had once belonged to a dragon.

Maybe it was the tooth. The tooth pulled at her, not Marcus. She'd need to get a closer look, study it, if she wanted to know with any kind of certainty.

"I'll be right back," she mumbled, then ran out the door.

In fifty beats of a dragon's wings, she returned with dry clothes. Her neighbor, more than willing to help out and rack up I-owe-yous from Kyra, had provided her with clean threads. She tossed the garments into Marcus's arms and proceeded to move about the trailer showing him the important things, like how to latch the finicky bathroom door and where to find her chipped Fiestaware dishes, mismatched silverware, and odd assortment of snacks in the kitchen. After not-so-subtly hinting he rest, she flew out the door for her afternoon performance, eager to put space between them and get a chance to clear her head.

Kyra was the only fire-breather at the carnival. She preferred it that way. She danced, spinning wands of fire around herself in a spectacular display of beauty and danger. Their heat tantalized her skin with each pass. She never revealed her dragon nature, so the children's squeals of delight never surprised her when she swallowed the flames from the tips of her wands, before blowing the fire high into the sky. She'd seen humans do it, but they never compared to her ability. Her flames often reached fifteen, even thirty feet high.

Dragons were rarely seen in public. Water Dragons and young dragons even less so. Her build was not what people expected to see when they ran into one of the elder race in human form. Of course, she was a Moorigad, the rarest of all. Not that Moorigads were considered a race among her people. Regardless, she had yet to bump into another dragon at the carnival. And she'd never seen one performing any kind of show—anywhere.

The truth was, no one expected to see a dragon in a bustling public forum. The supernatural community considered dragons a dying breed. Practically extinct. In actuality, their numbers were vast. Removed and hidden. Falling into myth like Santa and his elves.

Dragons tended to be a private lot, but she enjoyed the life of an entertainer. Maybe Sebastian was right. Maybe she was young, headstrong even. Maybe she would change her mind about the carnival someday. That someday wasn't anytime soon. The carnival was the longest she'd ever stayed in one place. She didn't foresee herself leaving anytime in the near future.

The carnival was a supernatural misfit haven. Those who didn't fit in with their kind, fit in with carnies. No inquiries, no demands. That was Kyra—a misfit, a runaway. Not the typical dragon. Everywhere she looked, there were supernaturals. Every flavor, every shape. None of them a dragon, though.

With one finger in the air, she twisted and swirled her fire in a wide arc. It spun up like a tornado. She paused, allowing the crowd to take in the crackling splendor. When the applause reached a mighty crescendo, she smacked her hands together, spread them wide, and watched the flames evaporate.

Ribbons of lights strung high above the audience came to life, announcing the end of the show. Kyra took a bow, and the applause roared. There was no encore, nor a chance for the audience to settle down, Kyra immediately stepped off the stage and made her way through the crowd. The talker had done a great job building the hype; her tip no doubt would reflect. Plastering a semi-sincere smile on her face and shaking hands, she pushed past the people and worked her way through the mob.

A short, ragged man ran after her—the talker. "Kyra, what's your hurry? What about your cut?"

She tilted her head, barely glancing over her shoulder in a torn-between-two-actions way. She kept her gaze on the path between the rides and concessions, the ever-changing landscape of the midway before her. To keep her bearings. Keep her grounded. "Handle it. Will you, Higgins? I trust you." And she did. Whole-heartedly.

He wrapped his hand around her wrist, skin rough against hers.

The hand of a working man. "Kyra?" A mix of confusion and concern melded on his face.

She peeked down at him, at their connection. It felt strange. He felt strange. Why?

No chance to figure it out. A strong, familiar scent wafted up around her. "Crap. Can you smell it?" The scent was always so strong in the minutes right before the transformation. Like the carnival was building up, preparing. The stink of a chemical reaction. Everything was warming up to move, change the design. The constantly shifting layout would once again confuse patrons and carnies, alike.

A trickle of sweat ran down the side of Higgins' face, and he struggled to catch his breath. His eyes blinked, appeared blank. His cheek twitched, curved up ever so slightly. She looked away, hiding the smirk his struggle to keep up evoked. "Smell?" he said. "Oh, yes. Of course." He fell silent and watched her with an awkward discomfort about him.

Kyra bounced on her heels and glanced in the direction she wanted to be moving. "Would you mind handling my cut, please? I need to go." Urgency churned like bile in her belly. She needed to make sure Marcus was okay. The necessity, the urgency, did not belong to her, but she possessed it all the same. That was bound to get old fast. Maybe she should have let Marcus die. Maybe she should kill him now. Pulling free, she turned, left Higgins behind, guilt nibbling at her heels.

Metallic. There was always a fresh metallic scent in the air when things at the carnival changed or moved. Quick, sharp sound bursts, clicking and clacking and ticking like a chorus of finger snapping, invisible to the eye. Minuscule light flares flashed this way and that, as if hordes of fireflies fazed in and out of time. Swiftly as it began, it ceased. The magic complete. The carnival had shifted—melding from one scene into another. What had been her surrounding was gone to be replaced by another, new location. Sometimes the people within were moved, sometimes the fixtures, sometimes both. It was disorienting, frustrating, and yet, part of the carnival's charm.

A quick survey confirmed the relocation of the ring toss and cotton candy concessions. But the carousel stood fixed, as it should. The two-story marvel never moved. Like a fixed point. A beacon amidst unstable chaos.

She made her way to the colorful host of horses, calculated her journey beyond, past Big Eli—the Ferris wheel—on to her trailer. It was a guess, at best. Tonight, she hoped things would remain constant.

When the sun went down, the carnival sparkled. A magical array of illumination and merriment. Kyra relished it. Usually found it fun getting lost. It was a game, finding where she needed or wanted to be. Not tonight. Tonight, as much as she hated it, she felt obligated to get back to Marcus. Make sure he was all right.

Obligated? Maybe that was the wrong word.

She wandered forward, thoughts swirling around the mysterious man. Him standing half clothed in her sleeping quarters. The indescribable pull that drew her to him in the water. The dragon tooth hanging around his neck. Sebastian's heavy frown planting so beautifully on his face, clear disapproval as she'd pulled Marcus from the brink.

The carousel's song chimed to a stop, kicking her out of her daydream. Like a dragonet stubbornly clinging to foolish desires, she didn't want to wake. Not yet. She wanted more time to figure things out, but a fresh rush of delighted patrons poured around her, a mix of humans and supernaturals. Caught in a cluster of shimmering lights and jubilant laughter, Kyra found herself bumped, pushed, and knocked, disjointedly ricocheting here and there.

"Ouch!" She glared downward. A bulky, black boot peeled its tread from the top of her foot. No apology, its owner vanished into the crowd.

More metallic. More lights. More snapping. More shifting.

A gentle hand hooked around her fingers. "Kyra! So happy I found you. Have you seen Sebastian?"

Her gaze met Chelsea's bright, blue eyes. They glistened with excitement, sending a funny pang zapping through Kyra's chest. Chelsea was the human that always managed to somehow find her way to the supernatural carnival. The human that clung to Sebastian's every spoken word and followed his every step like a shadow. Kyra wanted to roll her eyes and moan, but she didn't. She smiled and looked the girl over. Chelsea was dolled up, and boys were gravitating closer. Fancy makeup and hair wouldn't help with Sebastian, though. Not if he was her goal, which Kyra knew he was.

Kyra pulled free and shoved her hands into her pockets, but allowed Chelsea to fall into step beside her. "What are you doing here? How do you keep finding your way? This place isn't safe for your kind traveling alone." She kept watch of the space in front of them and avoided looking at Chelsea.

Chelsea leaned in as if whispering a secret, her blonde hair falling around her face in a waterfall of forever-spiraling curls. "I love it here. I'm addicted. I want to keep coming back, and back, and back. I may ask for a job. And what do you mean, 'my kind'? Got a problem with humans?"

Kyra scoffed, ignored the question, and grounded to a flat halt. She watched the activity ahead, not really seeing anything. *Am I in danger of thinking like Sebastian? Am I becoming human intolerant?* Humans finding their way to the carnival without guidance was an anomaly. Or so Kyra had thought. The idea of one working at the carnival bothered her, but it shouldn't have. Maybe it was *Chelsea* working at the carnival that bothered her. Chelsea being close to Sebastian almost daily. The possibility Sebastian might like Chelsea back. *But it shouldn't,* she reasoned. *Not if I'm a good friend to him. The kind of friend he deserves.*

A quiver swam through Kyra's upper body. "You get a job here? That could be interesting."

Chelsea searched the crowd, acted like she hadn't noticed Kyra's scrutiny. Her watchful eyes feverishly darted to and fro.

"What are you doing?" Kyra asked.

"Oh, you know." Chelsea bit her lower lip and continued to glance from one person to the next.

Kyra resumed a strong, steady stride. Chelsea followed, and Kyra threw a resolved glance in her direction. "I haven't seen him since before—" She froze her tongue. Nearly let the gems of truth spill from the bag, forgetting, if only for a moment, Chelsea wasn't one of *them.* Kyra's face softened even as the curve of her mouth inverted. "Listen.

You're fighting fire with paper. He's never going to like you, because he won't even notice you. I'm sorry, Chelsea."

Chelsea twisted her hair in her hand and avoided eye contact. Her body language read awkward and embarrassed. "It's all right. I'm no longer jealous of you."

Kyra stumbled back a step, heat flushing her cheeks. "What do you mean, jealous?" She hated the audible crack in her voice.

A deep 'v' creased the center of Chelsea's brow. "Haven't you noticed the way he looks at you? I mean, who can blame him? With your eyes of gold and personality blazing brighter than the sun."

Kyra's heart somersaulted. "Sebastian isn't...he would never..." Truth was, Kyra didn't know. He kept so many secrets.

Chelsea played with the edge of her nightdress, a faraway look flittering in her eyes. "He doesn't mean to ignore me. It's just that he doesn't want to see. Not yet. He needs some time. Or maybe something. Someone to open his heart to the possibilities."

The words prattled from Chelsea's lips, and Kyra's fists clenched and unclenched, attempting to strangle the oxygen out of the air. Chelsea obviously wanted to be that *someone,* and for some inexplicable reason, that made Kyra nauseated. She felt fire rolling within her belly and imagined Chelsea as a tasty dragon treat. Kyra knew it was absurd even as the thought popped into her head. She had no romantic claim on Sebastian. Besides, Chelsea probably tasted like charred crud. "And you're willing to put in the time?"

Chelsea nodded, and her face brightened to match the confident resolve she wore.

"You're a better person than I am, Chelsea Briggs. I hope he comes around." If Kyra were honest with herself, she'd have to admit Sebastian was definitely worth the effort Chelsea was investing. But there were times when the truth was better left unsaid. This felt like a moment most worthy of a non-truth.

Chelsea's delight showed in a dazzling display of teeth and dimples. Guilt dropped like the Blarney Stone to the pit of Kyra's stomach. Thankfully, Chelsea couldn't detect the lies Kyra spouted. Part of her despised the omission and knew she should spill the truth, but she would die before giving Chelsea the satisfaction of knowing how much Sebastian meant to her.

What if Chelsea was exactly what Sebastian needed? What then? A good friend wouldn't stand in the way, regardless of her personal feelings. The girl had never given Kyra any real reason to dislike her. It was just one of those things. Sometimes people don't click, no matter what. Kyra glanced at Chelsea, assessed her. *I guess she's not* all *bad*, she thought.

Kyra took a deep breath and exhaled, rolling her eyes, she slid her arm around Chelsea. The action was stiff and unsettling, but she did it anyway. Maybe she'd earn a few points with the dragon gods. Fire, Water, either one would do. She was going to do Chelsea a favor. She hoped it'd be good for Sebastian, too. That whole thing about him being into Kyra had to be a gargoyle gag. She was a dragon, and he was not. What kind of future would they have? All odds were against them. Her parents would *never* allow it. They had already chosen her a suitor. Another reason she had run away. And a reason any relationship with Sebastian was over before it'd begun.

"Come on," Kyra said. "Maybe this time he'll notice you."

Together they pushed through the crowd, Kyra leading the way. All the while, she worried she would lose Sebastian to Chelsea. Her mind struggled with the notion, but she knew in her gut her friendship with Sebastian was stronger than some young girl's crush. No dalliance could destroy what they had, right?

Moments before, Chelsea's body language, her words, had lit up like a beacon, blinding Kyra to all other thoughts. She had missed the implication when spoken. "Wait!"

Chelsea snapped to a stop and watched her with the anticipation of a bored cat.

Kyra blinked hard. "What did you mean, 'he doesn't want to see'?"

"Sebastian doesn't know I remember."

"Remember what?"

Chelsea tipped her head, as if recalling. "The first time I saw him. Outside of the carnival."

Kyra dropped her hands on her hips. "Hold on. Where? Why would he think you don't remember?"

Chelsea threaded a spiral of hair around her finger. "I was a bit out of sorts. So sick I thought I was dying."

"You're doing a horrible job explaining things." Kyra's backbone wrinkled with torrid scales, but she continued to pretend nothing bothered her.

"I know. I'm sorry. I don't feel comfortable talking about it. Sebastian should tell you if he wants you to know," Chelsea said and tossed her arms loosely at her sides.

"He doesn't talk much about stuff. Rather private," Kyra said, the words spitting out between clenched teeth.

Chelsea studied the sawdust covering the ground. "I know."

"So, is that why you came here? After meeting him?"

"Partly. I guess. I don't know how it started happening, but I'm glad it did. One day, I was simply here, and now I never want it to stop."

Kyra studied Chelsea, considered her words. Her gut insisted the girl spoke the truth, only Kyra wanted more. More clues to Chelsea's condition, what led her to meet Sebastian, and her unique entrance into the carnival. More details. More information to fill in the gaps.

The carnival roared and yelped and howled.

A group of rowdy teenage werewolves, shoving at each other playfully, elbowed in between Kyra and Chelsea. Their conversation was cut off, and the girls got caught up in the excitement. Some boys danced; a few sang. A couple grabbed the girls and pulled them into a sway, boisterous laughter accompanying the move.

Chelsea struggled in the arms of a young, brown wolf. He roared even louder.

Kyra channeled her anger into the situation at hand. She embraced a dark gray youngster and ran her fingers through the fur below his ear, extracting a purr. She knew she shouldn't, but she needed to channel her frustration. Poor sap had the misfortune of being in the line of her fiery breath. "Hello, beastie," she said with an evil-as-sin grin. Fire raced around her irises. She felt empowered. Intimidating. Unrelenting.

The wolf stepped back, no longer a beast, but a boy. He hunched forward and hung his head low. "I'm sorry. I didn't know," he muttered and skittered away.

Yesterday's dinner dropped into Kyra's gut. It was a filthy, disheartening feeling. The poor wolf hadn't done a thing to upset Kyra, and yet she had given him a nasty blast of attitude. Why was she being so mean? A dark shadow eclipsed her, tinting her mood more than it already had.

Chelsea hooked her arm around Kyra's, a snicker escaping her throat. "That was crazy."

Kyra looked over Chelsea, scanned their path, and cleared her thoughts before answering. "Yeah," she mumbled, untangling their arms, "crazy."

The girls circumvented the remainder of the teenage fun. Despite her annoyance, Kyra couldn't help but giggle at Chelsea's apparent amusement. "How did you get away from your wolf?" she asked.

"Higgins. Can you believe that? Higgins was my knight in imperfect armor."

Together they glanced back through the mob. Short Higgins and his brown baseball cap bobbed up and down, putting distance between them. Cocking her head to the side, Kyra considered the man for a moment. Heroes came in all shapes and sizes. Even in an old carnie gent like Higgins.

Guilt. Again with the guilt. Guilt for the way she'd treated him only a few minutes before. Right then, she made a promise to be a better friend, a better supporter.

She sighed. Let the feeling release. Evaporate from her thoughts. Once again, she became obsessed with the anxiety Marcus created. Too long she'd been away, and it was taking longer than usual to find the trailer. Why was the carnival being such a bitch? Knocking her around like an inconsequential ball in a stupid carnie game?

The carnival crowd buzzed, busy for a weeknight. The sweet smell of corn dogs, funnel cakes, and popcorn permeated every square inch.

Families with children of all ages and all manner of species mingled. And there were couples. Multiple couples, so wrapped up in each other they'd become oblivious to the world around them. Kyra and Chelsea wandered by unseen.

As they rounded the carousel, Kyra expected to see her trailer. It sat among the many used as homes by the carnies, in what they called the Backyard. All stationed together, they created a mini community. It should have been visible beyond the Ferris wheel and a row of gaming booths.

A pop erupted at her ear. The sound bounced off her inner canal and volleyed through the eardrum like a bouncy ball. A pinprick of light exploded smack-dab in her line of sight. No. That wasn't right. Practically *in* her eye. Kyra was blinded by the intensity; everything went white. And the smell. The nasty metallic smell. It morphed into a sharp taste on the top of her tongue. She swallowed. Made it worse.

Through the brume of her flash-induced blindness, Kyra could make out Chelsea already on the move. Kyra's vision was returning in freckled spots.

Chelsea dashed forward, away from Kyra's hold. "Sebastian!"

He looked up, his dark hair dropping across his right eye. Sebastian sat next to the mysterious, ever-present Zeke on the bench by the lazy river. Zeke didn't work at the carnival. He was too old and too blind to be of any use in that department. Like Chelsea, he was a regular visitor. One could usually find him escaping the noise of the cattle rustlers and talkers, flashing games and screeching rides of the midway, in favor of the calm the bench by the water provided. He came for the company over anything else. Although, no one ever saw him come or go.

The fog surrounding the carnival, the fog that always surrounded the carnival, pressed exceptionally thick today, the tiniest bit of the river's water barely visible. The grass lay damp with dew and the air heavy like the hour before a rain.

Somehow Kyra's and Chelsea's last turn had dumped them at the front by the ticket booth, the same point where the portal to the carnival stood. Anyone coming or going did so from the front entrance. It was also the farthest point from where she'd planned to go. Glancing back toward the rides and games, Kyra could make out the flag at the top of the carousel. They were nowhere near it now.

Her chest heaved, irritation, resolution, depression setting in. With a sigh, she surrendered her trek to the trailer. Instead, she turned and approached Zeke and nodded to Sebastian. Chelsea huddled with Zeke, whispering, their hands wrapped in warm whimsy.

Sebastian stood and, with a quick flick of his thumb, wiped a dab of whipped cream from the edge of his lower lip. "My break is over. Need to get back." His gaze froze on the fog, his body growing infinitesimally rigid. Only a familiar eye would notice the change.

Chelsea scooted up behind him. "Going already? I just got here."

Heat whipped up Kyra's spine in a crooked zig. Where were all the ice lakes when she needed one? A cool down was necessary. She closed her eyes and reminded herself she was going to help Chelsea, as much as it pained her to do so. More importantly, she would help Sebastian.

Of course, that didn't mean she needed to start right that second. Procrastination was a good friend with whom she liked to flirt. This might be one of those times. Sebastian looked in need of a Kyra shakedown.

She crossed her arms and locked a spill-your-guts stare on him. He appeared deep in thought, running from his troubles. Or was it from her? Maybe it was from Chelsea.

"Are you okay?" Kyra asked.

He shook his head and, ignoring Chelsea, held up the remains of his funnel cake. "Want this? I'm not going to finish it."

Kyra pushed her lips into an irritated line, avoiding a scowl. Given the present company, she wouldn't push. She recognized avoidance, especially when delivered by Sebastian's blatant gestures.

The mound of sugar in his hand held zero interest for her. If it had been a ginormous turkey leg, that might have been different. Chelsea's devouring stare said something different, though. She clearly wanted that sweet eat. "Thanks," Kyra said, "but no thanks. Why don't you offer it to Chelsea?" This was as good a time as any. Throwing the girl a rib, Kyra motioned to his personal junkie club.

"Who?" Sebastian's brows pinched together. Confusion. Faked as it were, Kyra appreciated the gesture. It wasn't helping her efforts as matchmaker, though.

She frowned, knowing it was the proper response, although part of her was secretly delighted by his lack of interest. "Stop it, Sebastian. You know who I'm talking about."

He rolled his eyes in a yeah-yeah kind of way and began walking. "Later, Zeke," he called over his shoulder.

Kyra watched Sebastian stride off. He moved toward the lights and commotion of the carnival at a slow and steady pace. Chelsea, in tow, walked with a skip in her step. He handed her the funnel cake. Gravity pulled at Kyra, dragging her face into a sullen stare. Ten, fifteen, a hundred years could pass, and she would never understand Chelsea's sunny-side disposition.

Kyra's nostrils burned, a smidgen of smoke escaped. Anger struggled to control her emotions. Deep, dark, and disturbing. She rallied strength and courage and pinched her nose. She had done a nice thing. She should be content. But she was the furthest thing from content. She needed to pull it together, be a better friend.

Zeke patted the empty space on the old wooden bench. A spot where the paint chipped and peeled, exposing the aged wood hidden beneath, adding to its warmth and charm. "Will you sit a while?"

"Will you share your secrets?" Kyra collapsed onto the bench and pulled her knees into her chest. Her mind was now preoccupied with her tsunami emotions, but she would play his intellectual game. She smelled something on the blind, old man. Something she couldn't figure out. He was worth her time. That was certain. She stared at her knees. "I'm sorry, Zeke. That was really rude of me. I'm in a rotten mood. I won't make for good company tonight."

A hand gently patted at her back. A comforting absolution. Zeke stared straight ahead, joy playing at his lips. He leaned forward, his blind eyes not trained on anything in particular. "What secrets are you looking for?"

Kyra laughed. "You are one of the most mysterious men I know. I bet you have more secrets than you have years notched on your life belt. Sometimes I think you're as bad as Sebastian."

Zeke's apparent bliss slipped from his face like water down a drain. "Poor boy. You shouldn't be so quick to judge what you know so little about." His hand reached out, found her shoulder with perfect aim. There it tapped three times, before resting.

Silence overtook Kyra. She hadn't been quick—had she? She thought she knew Sebastian damn *dragolion* well. Outside of his secrets, that was. She knew where to find him when he was upset, knew he drank strong, dark coffee first thing in the morning, and knew his mood by the music he played. But she didn't know where he came from or what species he was.

She'd given Sebastian plenty of time to open up about who and what he was. She didn't expect all the gory details, but something beyond his dad was a dick and he unsuccessfully hid mommy abandonment issues would be nice. She'd shared all about her Moorigad status, and that wasn't something she did with ease. She stared into the surrounding fog, thinking of time, friendship, and trust. And Fog. Fog, fog, fog. Foggy emotions. Foggy definitions, foggy lines between them. Simply fog. *What caught Sebastian's eye in the fog?*

Zeke pulled out his leather tobacco pouch and bull's head pipe. Carved from mahogany, the pipe matched the color of Zeke's skin. The bull's eyes stared to the side-oblivion, and its horns reached for the stars. A fierce piece, it stood ready to attack or protect, whichever deemed necessary.

Zeke pushed and twisted, filled and packed the tobacco into the pipe. The most delicious scent of cherries accompanied the process. "How long have you been with the carnival, Kyra?"

Her gaze slowly lifted from Zeke's hands to his face. She wondered how he managed to get the tobacco into the pipe without spilling any. "Long enough."

"Long enough to know how things work," Zeke said with a smile in his tone.

Kyra sighed and dropped her head onto her knees, cheek to kneecap, to better watch Zeke.

"You know where this is going, don't you? You're here because *she* wants you here. The carnival wants us to talk. So, let's get to what matters, shall we?" Zeke folded the tamper and placed it back into the bag. He nodded ever so slightly. "When was the last time you saw your family?"

Not family. *Let's not talk about their sorry, scaled faces.* She cocooned her head in her hands, and a second later, Sebastian sleeked to the forefront of her mind. As far as she was concerned, he was her family. Plus, she'd seen some of his today.

"Is this about Sebastian?" Kyra fidgeted, twisting her fingers together. "Because I'm really sorry about what happened this morning, but I couldn't help it." Kyra's thoughts returned to the strange man on the bridge. The feeling chewed on her insides. She wanted to know, felt it important to know, practically *needed* to know if he was Sebastian's relative.

Zeke lit the pipe, took a puff. "And what *did* happen this morning?"

"You brought up family. I assumed you knew." Kyra dropped her legs and began tapping her feet on the ground. Black emotion swished around her. She didn't want to acknowledge it, but this detour was taking too long. She scratched her collarbone, shifted in her seat. How was Marcus doing? He'd been alone in her trailer for so long.

"Now, now. I don't mean to upset you. I only mean to look out for you. Young thing like yourself running off to the carnival. It doesn't seem right."

"What do you mean? I'm not that young. Besides, there are plenty of young people working here. Take Carlito over in the milk bottles concession." She motioned toward the gaming booths, toward the slender, young man smacking heavily on gum and flirting shamelessly with a couple of girls. Kyra watched him and scratched the back of her neck. Dang, her skin itched.

"Carlito is not my concern at the moment. You are. Don't you miss your parents?"

Kyra leaned back and threw her hands over the top of the bench. Closing her eyes, she listened to the water of the river, hoping it would sooth her, before answering. "Nah. My people aren't the type for attachments."

Attachments. The word lingered in her mind, pressed hard against her membrane. *What is this I'm feeling?* Her mind crept and curved around the itching, looking for the answer.

Zeke took a long drag on his pipe and let out a slow breath of smoke.

Utter, pure bliss, thought Kyra. That's what the smoke from Zeke's pipe was. Watching him smoke drove her desire deep to breathe fire and fume. And if it smelled like Zeke's cherry tobacco, that would be a pretty cool thing, too.

Zeke chuckled. "Your people."

"Yeah? My people. What of it?" Kyra craved her fire, could practically taste it. Found herself captivated by the smog emanating from the miniature bull in Zeke's hands. But it was not to last. The shackling feeling clobbered her, smacked her in the back of the head with the force of a frying pan—the feeling, the attachment. Fealty. Damn the irritating fealty. It pulled her yet again.

Not privy to her internal strife, Zeke sat back and crossed his legs. "It's not going to be easy."

Her feet tapped faster. Fingers weaved dragon scales tight. Thumbs wrestled in a game of vehement domination. Tension pulled fragmented and fragile across her shoulders. "What are you talking about?"

"Follow what's inside, be true to yourself, and you'll be fine." His hand reached out and squeezed hers. "I think that's your calling card."

"What?" Did he know what she was feeling? Was she supposed to follow the pull back to Marcus?

Something tickled the back of her hand. It was a burning ember. She blinked and looked up. Fire embers floated all around them, like fiery snowflakes.

"Oh," she mumbled. *Oh!* She jolted up and searched the horizon of tents, flags, and carnival rides. What she sought lay beyond. Fire raged in the living quarters, the wind carrying a message clear across to fetch her. "I'm sorry, Zeke. I have to go."

5
DEATH KNOCKING

Kyra

Using the scent as a guide, Kyra pushed through the crowd. The carnival could shift ten times or more; it wouldn't faze her. Nothing would stop her from getting to her destination this time. Not with the smell of fire to lead the way. Marcus waited in her trailer, and the trailers were burning.

People gawked, some pointed, at the rising smoke. Not everyone, though. Plenty went about their business as if everything were normal. Kyra considered the possibility the fire was like the shifting of the carnival, a personal experience unique to each individual.

Passing the carousel, she spotted Chelsea leaning against the railing, watching the horses. She grabbed the girl by the arm, turned her to face the smoke, and jabbed her finger toward the trailers. "Do you see that fire?"

"What fire?" Chelsea's voice hitched and fell, her face melting into shadowy lines.

Kyra pointed again, this time taking a softer approach and

watching Chelsea for her reaction. "That one, right there. You can't miss it."

Chelsea shook her head ever so slightly. "I'm sorry, Kyra. I don't see anything."

The girl was trying, the strain evident in her face. Tight lines around her eyes and lips, the pinch of her nose. Didn't matter. Wanting to see it, needing to see it. Who knew how the carnival worked? How it decided who saw what?

Kyra released Chelsea and ran, ran hard. Adrenaline pumping in a *ka-thump whoosh*, repeat. With each stride closer, more ash, more debris showered upon her. Something fluttered up against her. She grabbed it, its edges still glowing. It was a partially burnt card.

An instant light explosion—recognition. A tarot card.

She flipped it over.

No!

A dancing skeleton stared up at her. *Death.* So similar to the one she'd returned to Sebastian. Maybe the very same one. Sebastian had gone back to work. He should be safe. But then why was his card fluttering into her hand?

Bolting into the clearing, she cursed the drag pulling her to Marcus again. She *needed* to get to him. *Had* to protect him.

The trailers scattered out before her in no particular pattern. A few remained untouched by the flames, but the majority burned, each engulfed at varied degrees. Her friends, her family—so many in danger!

"Marcus!" The roar of Kyra's beast crept into her scream with a fever pitch. Called by the fire, her dragon clawed to the surface, edged into her features.

"Oh my! I see it now. Everything's burning."

Kyra snapped her head back. Found Chelsea behind her. The girl jerked back, waving her hands at Kyra, her face drawn wide with astonishment. And something else—a momentary wave of fear? In a whoosh, Chelsea's breath escaped, bringing with it unspoken apologies and understanding. Her eyes softened, body relaxed, and she lowered her hands to her side. "I'm sorry. I didn't mean to react so rudely. You caught me by surprise, is all. I had no idea you were so unique. Or that your eyes could be any more amazing. Golden fire." Chelsea waved her hand up to Kyra's orange, glowing skin and dragon-set eyes.

Smoke emanated from Kyra's nostrils. The change was kicking into full flight. "You should leave," she said with a curt edge. Now was not the time for handholding. It would only slow her down. Maybe even get Chelsea hurt.

Chelsea stepped forward, closer to Kyra. Head high, back straight, eyes focused. "No. I'm here to help." She looked around, urgency in her glance, and took off at a run toward the horses' water trough. Before Kyra could complain, Chelsea had grabbed a bucket from its side, filled it, and hurried over to the closest trailer. She threw the water on the fire and returned to repeat the action.

Water. Of course. In the presence of fire, Kyra had automatically responded with her Fire Dragon qualities. Her father's side. Just because she was out of the water didn't mean she couldn't call upon her mother's side—the Water Dragon. As a Moorigad she had access to both dragon traits; she'd use both if she must. She summoned the rain, a thankful smile gracing her face with the request.

Smoke filled the air. If she weren't a dragon, she would find it hard to breathe. No water fell from the sky, no rain, no precipitation responded to her call. Was it the unpredictability of her undeclared status? Neither water nor fire but moorigad, synonymous with confused? Baffled, she had no time for worry. Brilliant, orange scales were already spreading across her skin. They brought her strength, protection, and a touch of overconfidence. She was fully protected by the time she opened the door and stepped with ease into her trailer, having maintained her human shape.

The flames consuming the grass outside her cozy home, threatening to incinerate it in a moment's breath, had yet to touch the walls and spread inside. Everything still smelled like ash. Fabulous, fantastic ash. Unfortunately, it wasn't the time or the place to enjoy it. She needed to focus.

Hidden a step inside the door, behind cover of the side cabinet, she called out. “Marcus?” He groaned. Coughed. The sound came from the back of the trailer—the other side of the partition.

She vanquished her scales, commanded them to meld into her skin. They shifted, sank through the flesh until they were gone, dormant, unseen, and she appeared human again. She pushed the curtain aside, exposing the tight sleep space. Marcus held the side of his face, tried to rise, and coughed violently. She moved in to help, the weight of concern washing over her.

He slung his arm around her and bid a sorry attempt at a smile. It twitched at the edge of his lips, the sentiment never reaching his eyes. “Look at you. Three times my hero.” His lazy gaze skittered over her, his eyes struggling to stay open, to stay conscious.

Kyra nudged him lightly in the ribs. “Who knew I was signing up for such a needy guy?”

“Ha. Someone hit me. Crazy powerful punch, too. Tried to knock me out.” He struggled for breath. “I fought ‘em good, but guess they got the better of me. The place was full of smoke when I woke up.”

The pain pierced like a dragon’s spike to the chest, caused Kyra to wince. The people at the carnival were her friends. Why would anyone want to hurt Marcus? He was her guest. She wiped sweat and concern from her brow, supported some of his weight, and edged them both around the side of the bed. “Did you see who it was?”

“Nah. I couldn’t—”

Something rumbled, deep and loud, beyond the thin walls on their right. The trailer shook. Cupboards above the sink popped open. Dishes flew, catapulted at them as if by an unseen force. Kyra threw up her hands, deflecting the attack. The moment the assault slowed, she yanked Marcus by the collar, pulled him closer to the exit. A flash of light outside the small doorframe bled through the opening, pulling at Kyra’s attention. She looked closer, but saw nothing. The grass and neighboring trailers were no longer visible, the tiny doorway now a canvas of stirring embers.

Kyra found it beautiful and perplexing how thick smoke could resemble a wall. Only, it wasn’t smoke. Any dragon could tell the difference. Smoke, like fire, was a part of who dragons were—a part of their nature. What now surrounded her trailer was the same eerie fog surrounding the carnival perimeter. Primal, scary, and wrong. What was it doing inside? It never moved. Never wandered inward, within the carnival walls.

And yet...

Her eyes burned like molten lava when she attempted to pierce the haze shrouding her home. With every inch of visibility, the heat of her vision cleared, the fog pressed back, blocking it again.

Water suddenly sloshed through the mist, clearing a path in a way her vision would not. Thrown out in a spray, the water flew in Kyra's direction, carving through the haze like the sharpened claws of a Black Dragon through fresh meat. She inched forward.

Chelsea stood on the other side of the opening, an empty pail in her hands. Patterns of soot smudged her arms, hands, and knees, leaving her dingy and wet. "Kyra! You must hurry."

Muffled shouts and screams carried through the narrow path in the fog. It was chaos, and then it was silence.

Before Kyra could move, the door slammed shut in her face, sealing off her view of Chelsea and freedom beyond. Kyra stepped back and tripped on Marcus's foot. Beyond the close confines of their prison, Chelsea screamed, the sound pressing fear and urgency to course through Kyra's veins.

"What in the hell was that?" Marcus's voice pitched an octave, rang with worry. He steadied Kyra and stepped past her, his hand guiding her to the side. "This place is seriously screwed up. Where did you bring me?" He twisted the doorknob. It wouldn't budge. He threw his weight against it. Nothing.

Kyra scratched at the space behind her ear. Watching Marcus work so close to the fire made her skin itch. He wasn't impervious, not tough like her dragon-self. Her hand reached out and stopped short. She found herself captivated by the bead of sweat sliding down his cheek. She didn't sweat. Never needed to. The air escaped from her lungs in a low, steady rush.

He grabbed her hand and pushed her back a safe distance. "I'll get this. I just need a little more room."

She didn't want to take his masculinity; she only wanted to save him. Yet she knew how men could get. That part rarely changed from species to species.

Her lips tightened, a dammit-all resolve slipping into place, all while she studied the deep crease set in the center of his forehead. A frustrated warmth rushed through her at his need to play valiant hero. Of course, she could provide a quicker exit. Not that he needed to know that.

Marcus threw his body against the door a second time. His mass and the small frame collided with a crash. The tiny trailer rattled; still the door refused to open. It made no sense. Something strange was at work.

Heat continued to rise. The structure groaned. And Kyra's sixth sense stirred. It tingled down her spine, growing in intensity with each increased degree of severity.

With deliberate intention, she ran her hand down the side of his arm. It was slick with sweat. She edged up against him to make sure she'd be heard. "Something's not right."

He turned, looked down at her. "What do you mean?"

"Get away from the door!"

Kyra yanked him behind her as fast as she could. Fire exploded through every crack and gap in the front wall. It reached for them, expanding and spreading across the surface in both directions, lighting up the built-in dinette like a campfire. It glided across the ceiling, licked at their toes, slithered like a snake, and smelled of sulfur, delighting and frightening Kyra's senses. She was torn between wanting to embrace the flame and fearing its finality for Marcus. Without warning, and like a bubble, the fire blew up in their faces and pulled back, tight and light against the wall.

"Whoa!" Marcus tripped and fell. Faster than Kyra could glance back, he had picked himself up. His fingers raked and pulled at his hair.

Before them, flames hugged the wall, turning her home into a sizzling prison. At different points, the fire danced in flames of blue, yellow, and orange. *A magnificent masterpiece,* Kyra marveled.

"Stay behind me," Kyra said and tried to push Marcus deeper into the trailer. He wouldn't move. She had to act fast if she was going to keep him safe. Stay true to the pull, the fealty. Turning to face him, she found herself pressed up against him, his breath warm on her cheek. He held a frying pan. Odd. "You need to move back, away from the fire." She pressed her palms into his abs.

Marcus's hands grabbed her waist and his gaze pierced right through her. She shivered, feeling something between them she had yet to understand. His eyes darted to the window at their side, breaking the connection. "Can we go that way?"

Kyra grabbed the pan and slammed it against the window with all her might. It bounced back, leaving the window still sealed. "Would you fit?" She hit it again.

"Probably not."

She dropped the pan. "Back there." She pointed to the ceiling vent over the bed. Her redirect got Marcus moving to the back like she wanted.

He shoved his hands up against the vent. "Why is it boarded up?"

"A cat broke it. Fell through. I didn't want the thing coming and going whenever." Kyra glanced over her shoulder at the fire by the door, then back again.

His face hardened, the lines across his forehead cutting deeper into the mold of his skin. Beads of sweat trickled down his face, skipping over the grooves. The area around them turned pallidly still. The only sound, the sparks and crackles of the fire bellowing like a roar. Marcus grunted—it sounded like a rumble—and thumped at the barracked vent one more time. Kyra caught glimpse of a glisten. It was his eyes. She shook her head. Shook the vision away. She'd seen wrong. Seen a flick of the fire's light. If she had seen things correctly, Marcus's eyes were inhuman in the split of that second. And that couldn't be possible.

Marcus dropped his hands, took a step back. "I need leverage. This thing is on too damn tight."

Kyra blinked her suspicions away. Filed them for later. "This isn't working," she said and turned toward the front door, toward the fire.

Marcus's hand clamped down around her wrist, his skin warm and rough.

Before she could rush for the door, he whipped her back around again. "What are you? First you pull me from the bottom of the river. An amazing feat for a girl your size." He jabbed his pointer finger in her face. "Now you're implying you can walk through fire. And don't pretend I didn't see you, because I did. I saw you in all your *magnificence*." Marcus flailed his hands out to the side, emphasizing the words he threw at her.

Kyra grabbed hold of his shoulders, looked him in the eye. "That's a conversation for another time. Definitely not *now*." Her searching stare ping-ponged between Marcus and the hungry fire at their back. Urgency tugged at her. "Trust me?"

His chest heaved once before he spoke. "Yeah, I guess I do."

"Good." She gave his hand a quick squeeze before dropping it and turning toward the door. "Follow my lead."

Marcus seized her wrist again. "Why don't you change? Use your power to break us out."

Kyra's eyes widened when she looked back at him. It took her a moment to find her voice. "The space is too small. You could be crushed." She turned away, a chill running through her. She hated hearing him speak of her dragon side.

Facing the fire, she moved with haste. Her scales consumed her form in the first step, while allowing her to retain a human shape. Her arms sprang from her side, welcoming the warm caress of the blaze—a kindred destroyer. She'd gladly bathe in its heat all day if weren't for Marcus.

A crack and pop ricocheted through the trailer. Kyra tilted her ear toward the noise. It sounded like the leveling jacks, and that was bad. They kept the home steady and secure. A low groan, and the whole place shifted, then pitched. The sleeping quarters plummeted downward, knocking Kyra off balance. More cupboards burst open, tossing out pots and pans. They slammed into her, toppling her over backwards. She fell into Marcus's arms, both of them slamming into the edge of the bed behind them.

At the thought of him touching her scaly skin her heart pounded, accelerated with fear and excitement like an indie car at the start of a new race. She pushed away without looking, her back rigid. She didn't want to know. Didn't want to see the rejection in his face. Instead, she crawled toward the door and argued with herself about her feelings. She shouldn't care so much what he thought. Her life was good before Marcus came along.

Options were limited in the tiny space with Marcus present. Lethal and pointless was the use of fire against fire. She couldn't use her tail. That required her full form, and her full form would tear the place apart and crush Marcus. Again, lethal. Nails through the door was a possibility. But then her leverage would be pulling. Not ideal—wrong direction. It would suck more fire inward. And the call for rain still remained unanswered. She quietly called out yet again. No raindrops.

A crash shuddered through the quarters. She swung around to find the folding divider to the sleeping space closed.

"Kyra?" Marcus called from the other side. The panel shimmied.

Why not just open it? she wondered. One tug on the handle and she understood. The divider wouldn't budge. Instead it glowed a unique crimson aura. *Damn magic. Who is doing this?* "I'm going to get you out, Marcus. Don't worry," she yelled through the plastic divider.

"Whatever you're gonna do, better hurry it up!" His voice bounded back from the far end of the space behind the divider. Crashes and bangs accompanied his grovel yell.

A prickling sensation crawled over her skin, urging her protective side to the forefront. Enough concern for both of them nestled in her warm gut.

Looking back toward the main door, she fixated on her goal. Marcus's continued words became a buzz at the back of her ear, allowing her to concentrate. She took one step, then slid onto her butt, twisted toward the exit, planted her feet up against the hatch, and thrust. The door gave way to her power, and a hole opened. Breaking at the midpoint, the hatch hung precariously on twisted hinges. The piece bent and cracked, in danger of ripping in two.

Thick fog clung to the outside of the trailer like the hand lock of a stranglehold. Flames rushed to the newly created crater as if pulled by a vacuum. Sucked in through the hole, they fanned out like a wall. Kyra pushed off the floor and slipped through the gap feet first, singeing her jacket through the pass. Dropping into a roll, she moved away from the burning chassis and deeper into the heavy, moist gloom.

For all she could see, she may have rolled into a cloud. Everything was gone. Misty white. Nothing was where it should be. Not even her trailer.

6
UNEXPECTED

Kyra

She stood, disoriented, the trailer lost, obscured by the haze. Nothing but low-lying clouds pressing in around her, the soaked ground squashing beneath her feet. Panic churned like a cyclone within her chest. Spinning in the direction she believed her home to be, she called out, "Marcus? Can you hear me? Are you okay?"

A muffled laugh replied. It was close, in the fog with her. And for a split second, she saw it—saw him? A suit and hat. Distorted at best. And then the figure was gone, melting into the mist.

She shook what she hoped was a hallucination from her head. Problem was, she knew he was real. Breathing became increasingly difficult with each passing minute. Something in the fog was too thick, too gritty, even for her. She summoned fire up her throat. She would burn it clean.

Nothing came.

Chills ran up her spine, and she tried again, this time bringing the burn to her entire being.

Nothing.

A small cry escaped her lips, and she looked down at her clenched hands. They were no longer the strong hands of a human dragon. All signs of her scales had vanished. She was nothing more than a girl—an ordinary girl. Fear spread like hellfire through her entire nervous system.

What is happening to me? Staring at her hands, she flexed them open and closed and then open again, willing her tough, orange scales to return. The drumming of her heart pounded heavily against her chest, increasing to an unbearable rate. *Where has my dragon gone?* Kyra could feel her—her dragon Kalrapura deep within—but she was somehow suppressed, pushed down.

A twig snapped behind her, and she spun to the sound. "Chelsea?" Kyra's voice cracked, and she took a step toward the noise of the snap.

The sounds of footsteps on soggy earth coupled with heavy breath neared.

"No," she whispered. "I must get Marcus." She heard the panic in her voice and hated herself for it. She wasn't used to doing things without knowing she could fall back on her powerful dragon side. Yet no other options were at her disposal. Her dragon pushed at her interior walls, ready to burst free when she was in the trailer. Something about the fog had to be inhibiting her ability now. She turned back the direction she'd come from and found the trailer still obscured by the fog, practically impossible to locate.

Moisture collected in her eyes, the result of the mist in the fog. Not due to any weakness or frustration on her part. She stood strong on that point. Closing her eyes, she bowed her head and said a small prayer to Rajũn, the almighty dragon spirit. "Please, see me through this trial. This fog...and my abilities...I am trusting you to guide me."

Kyra reached through the opaque gloom, swatted it back, and took a step forward, toward where her gut whispered the trailer stood. Sucking back deep, she sputtered on the gritty air and blew with all her might. No change. No fire. She paid it no mind and ran the last few steps blindly until her hands found the trailer wall, fire burning along its sides.

Her breath hitched.

Fire. My trailer is on fire.

Emotions rattled her bones. She was afraid she'd been away too long. Afraid Marcus had already perished. Afraid that no amount of effort would make a difference. But she had to believe. She held firm to faith, to what she'd seen in his eyes, if only for a spilt second. Something substantial, something enduring, dwelled within Marcus. Something not human. Maybe it was a dragon, too.

Her fists slammed against the trailer's side with one quick blow. "Ouch!" She jumped back and looked down. No protection. She'd gotten burned. Her skin throbbed, ached in a fashion she was unfamiliar with.

"Kyra?" Coughs and sputters accompanied Marcus's voice from the other side of the wall.

Warmth swelled in her chest. Not too late. She could still save him. "I'm here. Are you all right?" She followed the sound of his voice, moving with haste. It led her to the back of the trailer, exactly where she'd left him.

Using the hitch as a step, she looked through the louvered slots of the window above the bed. Marcus had draped the bed sheets over himself for cover. He was already wrestling with the glass. Kyra joined in, attempting to pull a pane free. Her hand slipped, and the metal bit into her palm. "Crap." It hurt, but hardly. She was too focused on getting Marcus out.

Marcus's gaze shifted to take in her cut, but his hands continued to work. He pushed while Kyra pulled on the glass. The ceiling in the front dinette collapsed, and the divider fell from its mount. The heat intensified, and Kyra noticed the fire now nipped at Marcus's heels.

"The glass won't budge!" he bellowed.

Frantic, Kyra searched the area for anything she could use to break the glass. Except, the fog hid everything from sight.

Returning her attention to Marcus and the infuriating panels keeping him locked away, she continued to struggle, pushing and pulling, in an attempt to break one or more free. Kyra bit down, her teeth grinding, while she torqued the glass in her hands. She gave it all the strength she could manage. The glass popped. A quick crackle followed. It sounded like the breaking of ice.

The pane trapped between their hands gave, broke in two, and small shards blasted in all directions. Both Kyra and Marcus fell backwards.

Kyra's foot slipped on the hitch. As it slid forward, the rest of her body pitched the opposite direction. Her back broke the fall, smacking onto the muddy grass a fraction of a second before her head.

"Kyra!" Desperation and irritation scratched at Marcus's voice.

Her blood curdled at the sound. She scrambled to her feet, a sharp pain shooting through her spine. She ignored it and climbed back up to the window. The wall of the trailer was hotter than it had been a minute ago. She peered through the broken louvers, her gaze drawn past Marcus.

The trailer's front portion was completely engulfed. She was reminded of a bonfire, only extra intense and larger. Fire had spread to the edge of the bed, and Marcus beat it with the sheet. A red, satin sheet. Hardly impervious, and it too burned. They were out of time. The place would be gone in minutes.

Kyra screamed and reached through the space provided by the broken glass. A tight line stretched across Marcus's lips. It told Kyra everything he wasn't saying. He held in his pain and played the tough guy, but any fool could see the skin on his arms was scorched and marred. It must feel like he'd been flayed. He hid from Kyra's prying eye behind sputters and coughs, but she saw. She missed nothing. If the fire didn't kill him and she didn't get him out soon, would he die from smoke inhalation?

Blood trailed down her arm, running from the cuts slashed by the shards of glass pressed up against her. She pretended not to notice and focused on her want, her need, and pressed against the suppression and fought to release her dragon. Ice raced around her cranium, and her vision turned a blackened red. Pressure pushed out from her shoulder blades and in the space below. A rippling of points strained in two parallel lines, arching across her crown. Her fingers and nails stretched—grew into strong, long talons.

It took more concentration than normal, while not achieving near the beast she knew herself to be, but it was something. She'd beaten the asphyxiating soup working against her. Dragon talons bit into the side of the structure, tearing at its aluminum casing. The rips and tears created an echoing howl. Primitive snarls and growls responded.

Kyra jerked and slipped to the ground. She landed straddling the hitch. Since the noise had come from behind her, she turned to see what had startled her and caused her to drop. A portion of the fog had turned a hazy yellow and grown in mass. From its obscurity, a giant claw emerged and bore down on her. Her eyes widened, even as her body flattened itself against the trailer frame. The new manner of monster coming at her was strong as steel and made by man.

The backhoe loader's cab came into view. Within its tiny confines, Higgins waved his arms wildly. "Get out of the way, Kyra!"

Never looking away from Higgins and his tremendous machine, Kyra scampered to the side. She moved fast, and when the wall of the trailer unexpectedly ran out behind her she stumbled, and her butt met the grass.

Marcus yelled, his words obscured in the roar of the construction vehicle. The backhoe tore on a collision course, directly for the window.

Higgins jumped up and down in the small cab. "Out of the way! Out of the way!" His voice boomed.

No sooner did Marcus's face disappear than the giant yellow claw crashed down on the top corner of the trailer, pulling the structure apart like a box from the edge. Screams of tearing metal and splintering wood followed the claw's path as it tore down the length of the wall. The backhoe lurched, jumped back, pulled the grapnel with it. In its wake stood a doorway, a gaping hole where the wall and window used to be. Marcus jumped out over the remains of the torn mattress, the back of his shirt smoldering. He dropped and rolled, and Kyra ran to his aid. Smoke billowed from the huge hole, as if trying to follow him, and the flames collapsed what remained of Kyra's once-cozy trailer.

Kyra snuffed out the smolder, leaving a splotchy, plaid mess marking the remains of Marcus's shirt. He sat on the ground with his knees bent high in the air, showing off his blackened and marred jeans. He stretched his arms out across his legs giving Kyra a clear view of his heat soaked skin, glistening in soot and sweat. The air expelled from his lungs in one long exhale, and he set his tired, bloodshot eyes to look upon Kyra, who sat perched beside him.

"Too damn close." Craning his head, he took in everything around them. "Almost like something was out to get me." He continued to search the perimeter, his voice trailed off. A moment later, his gaze settled on Kyra once again. His body jerked with a small cough.

Unsure how to best comfort him, she reached out and gently patted his hand. The action was odd and awkward. Especially when she paused, her palm wavering against his skin. That's when she smelled it. Serpicose. She yanked back and stared at him. If Marcus was the source, that could only mean one thing. He was a dragon. Only dragons used Serpicose. For attracting mates, no less.

A sudden chill ran up her back. Her senses prickled, and her spine straightened. The fog moved, shifted and swirled. Kyra pulled her attention away from Marcus and looked to Higgins. A few feet away, he climbed out of the backhoe's cab. He took a step in their direction and froze. His head tilted to the side, lifting his ear to the sky. He was listening, and she wanted to know to what.

She opened her mouth, ready to call out, when his hand shot up, halting her. She looked up, her ears perked, tight at attention, desperate to hear what Higgins heard. Marcus did the same, his body still, attuned to the night. The darkness cried out. A deathly, frustrated howl spun through the air. As if in response, fog twisted around them, slow at first, then faster and faster until it reached an incredible rate of speed.

Kyra leaped to her feet, dragging Marcus off the ground at her side. She wanted the dizzying spin to stop. She stood ready to lash out at anything and everything tangible that might put a stop to the maddening spin. The twisting fog grew thicker by the moment. Higgins was lost to her, his image stolen by the storm. Kyra thought to lunge for him, meant to, even started to, but the fog squeezed tight like a noose. It pushed the air straight from her lungs. But as quick as the dense gloom moved in, it slipped up and away, vanishing into the night. As if it'd never existed.

Collapsing on her hands and knees, she gasped for breath, weary and confused. Sharp pains splintered through her chest with each gulp of air. Her hand shook as she wiped the sweat from her brow. Once again, her inner voice called to the rain. Despite her weak delivery, the element answered this time and a pleasant drizzle began to fall upon the smoky scene. Satisfaction spread across Kyra's face. She closed her eyes and wished, if only for a moment, that she could be a strong, powerful dragon like her mother. Then she could command thunderstorms instead of mere drizzle.

But Moorigads were never *that* strong. Never would she be as fast or as magical as her mother.

No thunder came.

With an unstable stance, she stood and took stock of her surroundings. Reaching over to Marcus, she clutched his hand, wanting confirmation she had succeeded in keeping him safe. His skin was warm and strangely comforting. That same feeling fluttered in her chest. New, yet becoming all too familiar. She didn't like it—the fealty. She ignored it. Or tried to. But it now mingled with new knowledge. Marcus might also be a dragon.

In any case, she'd managed to keep the man alive. That was something. Higgins was good, too. A little worse for wear, but still standing. His clothing crumpled and spotted with mud and sweat, she found it curious he looked so tired when Marcus had been the one fighting the fire. She wondered how he'd known they'd been in need of help at all.

Pulling a white hankie from his pants pocket, Higgins dabbed the sweat on his brow. "You two all right?"

"We'll survive, thanks to you." Kyra waved her finger at the construction truck. "Where did you and that big yellow beast come from? That's not standard equipment around here."

A funny look adorned Higgins' face, like he'd swallowed lemon juice. His cheeks and lips twisted, swished, and then he spat to the side. When he looked up he met her stare with a devilish grin. "Who you calling 'beast,' beastie?"

"Very funny." She looked down. Marcus still sat on the damp ground. He watched her from under the cover of a hand rubbing at his forehead. A battered hand with bloodied knuckles. She worried the fire's smoke had caused him yet unspoken health issues and knew his many cuts and mild burns should be treated as soon as possible.

She looked back toward Higgins, and for a moment, everything around her faded into a mesh of blurred sounds and lights, and she considered this man she'd pulled from the lake earlier that day. Had she done the right thing by bringing him to the carnival? How far was she willing to go for Marcus? Could it be her actions were not without consequence and his presence actually brought misfortune?

Higgins' cough pulled her back, made her take notice of him sauntering toward them. "One rule you should learn about this place. Nothing is ever gone or forgotten. Nothing is ever obsolete." He pointed to the yellow backhoe. "I pulled that old thing out of the vehicle graveyard. She's been sitting there since the day we finished the original setup. She came in real handy back in the day. Hasn't been much use for her since. Mighty glad she was sitting back there tonight."

Higgins' words sank in and Kyra's brows knit together. She pinched the bridge of her nose. "Are you saying you've been here since day one?"

Higgins rocked back on his heels, snapped his suspenders. "Yep. Of course, I was much younger then. You might have actually taken a shine to me. I was quite dapper, if you know what I mean."

"Higgins! You're just full of surprises tonight. How did you know I needed help?"

A light shone in his eyes, brightened his face. It didn't last long. It faltered when he turned toward the remainder of the small trailer community. With the lifting of the fog, everything stood in clear view. A small spattering of people moved amongst the rubble, some like lost and bewildered children, others with great purpose, urgently attending to those in need.

"Just had a feeling," Higgins said. "We should do what we can to help the others." His words were quiet and touched with an edge of sorrow.

"Of course." Kyra's tone lacked feeling. Elation, confusion, curiosity—an emotional tornado whirled inside her. Hating the lack of emotion she now expressed for others not Marcus, Kyra tugged at her singed jacket and tried to settle her personal storm. With a nod, she agreed and felt the obligation to her fellow carnies drop into place. Together, they stepped out to take on the aftermath, Kyra motioning Marcus to follow.

They'd taken only a few steps when an ear-shattering wail broke through the night's turmoil like the sharp crack of a whip. Drifts of smog wafted clear, and they caught sight of the source. An unfamiliar woman stood amidst the chaos, her arms clenched around her midsection and her nails clawing at the delicate fabric of her dress. Her expression, one of immense regret.

A heavy sigh of acceptance escaped Higgins' lips. Bewildered, Kyra watched as he stepped away from their little group and closed the gap between himself and the wailing woman.

He dragged his palm across his pant leg, wiped it dry, and then extended his hand in greeting. "We haven't had the pleasure. I go by the name Higgins." He leaned forward and lowered his voice, but Kyra still heard. "'Twasn't always the case."

Kyra wondered what he meant.

The woman lifted her palm, cupped the side of Higgins' face. Kyra thought her eyes were the saddest she had ever seen. "I am Kelian, and I've come for you," the woman said.

Marcus leaned into Kyra and lowered his voice. "What is that about?" He stared at the exchange between Higgins and Kelian a brief moment before tilting his face up to the large Ferris wheel in the distance. Kyra had no idea how to answer his question. Before she could open her mouth, he turned to her, his eyes wide with wonder. "Are we at some kind of carnival?"

Kyra had been eavesdropping on Higgins' newly developing situation, but Marcus's question forced her attention back to him. "Yeah." Nerves made her response sound less confident and more like a question. She twisted her thumbs through the front belt loops of her pants, stretched her arms, and pushed up on the balls of her feet.

An amused smirk from Marcus broke into a snort as he soaked in all the characters around them. He motioned to a few. "So, the people here are carnies?"

Silence fell over them when no one spoke in response.

Marcus nodded, and his lips twitched in a half smile. "Everything is now starting to make sense."

The knots in Kyra's chest began to loosen. She wondered if she would have felt this way had she ever brought someone home to meet her parents. Assuming she had stayed with her mother or father. Now the carnival was her home, and she wanted his approval. "So, you're..." She stopped herself. Why was she looking for his approval? Straightening her shoulders, she stood a tad taller. "You got a problem with any of this?"

He shrugged. "Nah, I guess not. I've never known any carnies before." Shoving his hands deep into his jeans pockets, he tipped his head toward two people beating a small blaze. "What now?"

Around them, smoke smoldered from fire-damaged trailers. The drizzle helped drench the burning remnants. People held hands or shirts to their faces, blocking the smoke, and went to the business of helping one another wherever needed—bandages for the injured, extraction for the wreckage-trapped, and flame dousing.

Kyra took a step backward and threw her arms out, attempting to encompass everyone in the vicinity. "We help, of course."

"Of course. What was I thinking?" Marcus's eyes sparked with a shy, I-should-have-known smile. He turned and headed directly for the two carnies he'd pointed out only moments before. Kyra wasn't sure if he expected her to follow, but she stepped in the opposite direction, thinking they could help twice as many if they split up.

She chose a destination, took a few steps, and then...

Someone called her name. She hesitated.

A veil of smoke drifted past, obscuring her view. When it cleared she saw Sebastian kneeling by the water trough, Chelsea curled by his side. Kyra's heart clenched and dropped into her stomach. *Good. This is good*, she reminded herself and slowly swallowed the lump forming in her throat. Sebastian stood quick, setting Chelsea to the side without a second glance. She shot a scowl in his direction when he hurried toward Kyra.

He stopped directly in front of Kyra, his eyes taking inventory of every inch. "You're hurt." He motioned to her bloody arm. "Were you in danger?"

Her gaze wandered past him to Chelsea and lingered briefly before locking on Sebastian's concerned stare. Kyra wanted to prove to herself and to Sebastian that she was fine. Fine if he and Chelsea became an item and fine if they didn't. Either way. She notched her hand on her hip. "I'm good. You know me, I can handle fire."

He didn't look convinced, his disbelief evident in the hunch of his shoulders and drop of his face. "Right." He shifted, looking uncomfortable, and for a minute, Kyra thought he wanted to touch her, maybe hug her, but he didn't.

Too much time went by without a word. What had it been? Four seconds? Six? Kyra realized she had been fixated on his eyes. There was something about the way he was looking at her. She glanced away, looked past him to Chelsea. The young girl was picking herself up off the ground.

Kyra motioned to Chelsea and lowered her voice. "Why do you insist on pushing her away with such venom?" She gulped, unsure she wanted to hear his answer.

Guilt clouded his eyes, and he spared Chelsea a peep over his shoulder. When he looked back, his features were darker, intensely hollow. "Can't you smell it?"

Smell? The mere mention of the word made her think of Marcus stinking up the air with Serpicose. Making himself sweet and alluring. She looked over to where she'd last seen him. He wasn't hard to find. It was as if she possessed an internal Marcus locator since she'd pulled him from the river.

He was with Ashlyn, the magical man manipulator. Kyra shouldn't have expected anything different. Only that logic wasn't completely true, and she recognized the lie the moment it slithered into her thoughts. The girl was rarely seen outside of the Magician's tent, putting Kyra's assumptions and criticism of Ashlyn to shame. Seeing her here took Kyra by surprise.

Her skin heated as she observed the two of them together. Ashlyn was young and beautiful, with silvery hair flowing like a stream across her perfect skin. Everything she did had a way of looking sensual. Marcus was only male, no doubt powerless against her supernatural ways. And no matter how much she didn't want to admit it, that irritated Kyra like a spike in her dragon's tail. And it irritated her that she cared at all, because honestly, why should she care what Marcus did? Again, she found herself scratching her head at this new lack of understanding or control over her emotions. And, it would seem, her actions too.

She wanted to walk over and punch him and then claw poor Ashlyn to pieces, even if it wasn't her fault. Ashlyn couldn't help what she was any more than Kyra could help being a Moorigad.

Lurking in the background, amongst the debris and filth like a hungry hyena, moved the Magician. Stiff and awkward were his steps, a glint betraying his curious eyes hidden in black shadow beneath the brim of his hat.

Kyra shivered, looked away. She knew what he wanted. Jealousy and irritation excreted from his body like a ruptured water main. It was undeniable, and thankfully, Kyra wasn't the object of his obsession. He made her skin crawl and the hairs on her arms rise. Would he hurt Marcus over a silly girl?

Kyra heard her name called from a distance. No, not a distance—right next to her. She turned back to Sebastian and pushed the thoughts of Marcus out of her head. So confusing, probably rude and selfish too, to be consumed with her own issues in the midst of discussing Sebastian and Chelsea. She must've spaced.

Now what had Sebastian said? *Can't you smell it?* Kyra sniffed the air. She was overcome with the acrid scent of ash, melted plastic, and just about every kind of burnt item one could think of. The grass was now dewy, and she smelled that, too. She didn't know what smell he meant, so she shook her head.

Sebastian leaned forward and whispered, "Cancer."

Kyra jerked back. "You can—?" She threw her hand over her mouth, stopped mid-sentence.

Chelsea joined them, stood awkwardly between them. "What did I miss?"

"Sorry. I had to make sure Kyra was okay." He spoke without moving his gaze from Kyra.

Chelsea dropped her head onto his shoulder. "I get it."

Kyra's lips twitched, giving Chelsea the best fake smile she could muster. Despite his words, Sebastian was finally giving the girl attention, even if he'd been quick to push her aside. At least Kyra understood why now. Or thought she did. It was possible Chelsea had figured out some time ago that he knew she was ill, and that was why she was being such a good sport about his treatment of her. *Does she know she's dying?*

Seeing Sebastian and Chelsea together made Kyra's heart clench with an indescribable ache, and she had trouble distinguishing the reason why. Was it because she was lonely? She massaged her shoulders and turned away. Maybe it was the visual of finality Chelsea represented, or the new addition in her life. Marcus's life was so fragile. Yet, he had promise of something great, something stronger.

Ashlyn was watching Kyra when she looked back, a deflated yet teasing smile settled on her face. Marcus was no longer at her side. The mad Magician had yanked Ashlyn away and wrapped her protectively within his cloak, like his most precious possession. Cold shivers ran across Kyra's inner scales. Not because it disturbed her in the darkest recesses of her core, although it did that, too, but because she recognized a piece of herself in the action, a bit of what she was becoming. And what she saw tasted bitter and ugly.

She ground her teeth and focused on Marcus. He made his way toward her, shirt in hand, dabbing at the sweat on his brow. Kyra wondered about Ashlyn's smile. She wondered about rumors that Ashlyn waited at the carnival for her one true love, the man who never came. And she wondered if the new pull she was experiencing was destined to turn her twisted and crazy like the Magician. Sudden panic took hold of her. What if Marcus was the man Ashlyn waited for? Would that explain the Magician's presence in front of her trailer earlier? Ferocious butterflies fluttered a mad choreograph around her insides, and fear gutted her. She fought the emotions the pull created, but they were stronger, or she was weaker. Her gaze shot to Marcus, and that's when she saw it.

Kyra's breath caught in her throat. Glowing in the moonlight across his broad chest was the dragon's crest. The symbol of royalty. Another trait, another clue, another piece to his puzzle. She'd seen his eyes; he had survived the smoke; he smelled of Serpicose, and now the crest. But there was no sign of his actual dragon. Where did his magnificent beast go? The men on the bridge shouldn't have gotten the better of him, and Marcus should have easily saved himself from the lake and her trailer. It didn't make sense. The man was a puzzle.

Marcus came to a stop in front of her and exhaled. "The rain seems to have put out the fire." He rubbed his eyes, looking two days spent.

He was right, the fire was nowhere to be seen. She breathed in the night air and looked up to the sky. Was it her imagination, or were the stars twinkling extra bright? She thanked the rain, releasing it from service. The smell of charred remains overwhelmed the underlying rich, dewy bouquet of peat moss and crabgrass, and was a secret welcome to her senses.

Another scent snaked in, mingled with the mix. Serpicose again. It smelled of smoldering moss and warm, wild berries. Kyra inhaled it. Savored it. Followed it. It led her straight to Marcus. Earlier today, she would have said the possibility of Marcus being anything but human was impossible. Now she no longer felt the same. She scrutinized him, and he stared back with an incredibly strong gaze. It stripped her to the bone, destroyed all her carefully constructed barriers.

Sebastian cleared his throat, commanding Marcus's attention. "I see you made it out in one piece." He made no attempt to hide the snark packed heavily into his words.

"Yeah. I have Kyra to thank for that." Marcus looked at Kyra with a gaze resembling an inside joke, something private between just the two of them, and she saw the mischievous twinkle in full force. "She's really something."

Something in Sebastian's eyes glinted. "Yes, she is." He turned and took Chelsea's hand. "Come on. Let's go."

Kyra watched them walk away, her chest constricting and stomach churning with acidic dragon's fire. She couldn't help thinking their exit was rather abrupt. Shifting her weight, she twisted to face Marcus. "What was that about?"

He brushed a stray hair from the side of her face, ran his thumb down her cheekbone. She startled, and he pulled back, looking apologetic. "Don't know exactly. Jealously, maybe?"

Kyra scoffed. That couldn't be right. Could it? Her heart flipped at the thought. Maybe she wanted Sebastian to be jealous. Her gaze wandered to Marcus's neckline and beyond to the unique markings on his chest. This time her fingers followed.

All kinds of emotions warred within her, and she didn't know what to make of them. Or what to do with them. On the one hand, she was pulled to Marcus, and on the other, it was clear she needed to figure out what she felt for Sebastian. Right now, though, her calling was clear. The darn, stupid pull.

Slowly, with deliberate lines, she traced the tooth he had tied around his neck, certain it was the tooth of an immensely old dragon. She couldn't say exactly how old, but it was definitely up there in years. Her fingers ran over it, feeling, sensing—nothing. No magic vibrated from the pendant that she could discern.

"This is a pretty interesting piece." Kyra twisted the tooth between her fingers.

Marcus laughed, one quick snort. "That old thing has been in the family for ages. It's become kind of a joke, actually. You'll laugh at the story that goes with it."

A wicked smile fought to take hold of Kyra's features. "Try me."

"Don't say I didn't warn you. The family has this story about descending from dragons. This thing," he removed the tooth hanging from his neck and held it out in front of him, "is supposedly the tooth of some great ancestor. Before tonight, I never considered it possible."

He fixed his gaze with hers, pressed his hand to hers with the tooth between them. "Laughable, isn't it?"

"Does it look like I'm laughing?" The fingers of her free hand traced the faint lines glowing across his chest. Lines only visible in the moonlight. They stretched out like the expanded wings of a large dragon. Marcus shivered, but didn't pull away. Instead, his hand grasped her hand, held it to his chest.

His eyes narrowed. "No, it doesn't. And in light of things I've seen recently, it doesn't sound so crazy anymore." He pressed the tooth into Kyra's palm and closed her hand around it. "Since you saved my life countless times, I owe you this and more. I want you to hold on to it."

Kyra looked down at the ancient piece she now held. "I can't..."

"I insist. Besides, I think you're more deserving than I."

"Kyra! Marcus! Get over here." Higgins' voice broke through sharp and urgent, invoking a gut-curdling urge to respond.

7
NECESSITIES

Kyra

Kyra's legs carried her with unnatural speed, leaving Marcus to struggle in an effort to keep up. The closer they got to Higgins' voice the more apparent the state of urgency. On the opposite side of the Backyard from Kyra's burnt home, screams for help emanated from a large pile of rubble. Only, it hadn't been rubble prior to the fire. It had been a trailer. A trailer that had imploded, or was being sucked into a massive hole, or something equally as horrific.

Chelsea studied the wreckage from a safe distance and Kyra and Marcus came to a slow stop at her side, taking a moment to survey the situation. Metal twisted and bent and rose in every direction. Sebastian was already hard at work with Higgins, trying to locate the source of the screaming. The sound blasted and bellowed and barked.

"Might as well payback some of the hospitality you've shown me," Marcus said and jogged over to the trailer rubble.

Kyra rolled her shoulders and started to follow, but Chelsea reached out and grabbed Kyra's arm, stopping her mid-step.

"Stay with me?" Chelsea asked, the hint of a plea in her gaze.

Kyra's brow pinched, and she studied the girl, trying to assess if she was going to faint or convulse or something else that would require humanly care.

"I just don't want to be alone." Chelsea crossed her arms and hugged herself.

Kyra chewed on her lip and shoved her hands into her pockets. "Yeah, sure." She shifted her weight in awkward discomfort.

Standing on the sideline, feeling discontent in her lack of action in the face of a crisis, Kyra gaze wandered back and forth between Marcus and Sebastian. The men wrestled with the twisted remains of a trailer, attempting to free a young girl and fellow carnie. Cries of the girl trapped within the rubble were audible all the way to where Kyra stood. The girl was an inexperienced vortex beast. She probably accidentally sucked all the destruction in upon herself. She could, conceivably, pull herself, Sebastian, Marcus, and Higgins into a forever blackhole or another dimension. A painful pang attacking Kyra's heart like a sour case of indigestion.

"Be careful, Sebastian," Chelsea yelled.

Chelsea's words threw fire upon Kyra's open sore. The human girl was a constant reminder Kyra had thought it a good idea to play Cupid. She tried not to think about Chelsea. Kyra had been dumb enough to push Sebastian toward Chelsea in the first place. Instead, Kyra busied her mind with other things.

The conversation with Marcus about dragons played in her mind. Clutching the tooth Marcus had trusted her with in her hand, she squeezed it before shoving it deep into her front jeans pocket. It said a lot he trusted her with his ancestor's canine.

"What's going on?" Talia, stepped up beside them. She held a red- and white-striped bag of popcorn and popped one piece after another into her mouth. Kyra didn't know Talia all that well, but she'd seen her often and had always waved to her. She was Sebastian's neighbor, the witch that ran the Crystal Ball Gazing and Palm Reader destination beside his Tarot Card tent.

Kyra's shoulders dropped, and she turned toward Talia with a roll of her head and a sigh. "It's Valentina, the new vortex girl. You know how inexperienced she is. Well, she must have gotten scared by the fire or something because she mutilated her trailer." Kyra motioned to the wreckage the guys were working on. "Pulled the whole thing in on herself. Now she's trapped. Marcus and Sebastian are trying to get her out."

"Yeah," Chelsea added with a head nod.

Talia's lips pulled tight, and she stared at the wreckage before them. "Well." She heaved a deep sigh. "I should probably help. We wouldn't want our boy to accidently end up in some destination unknown." She handed her bag of popcorn to Chelsea and walked over to the mutilated trailer.

Chelsea popped a popcorn kernel into her mouth.

Kyra watched Talia in hopes of seeing some grand magic that would fix the situation and get the guys out of danger. She watched and waited, but all Talia did was toss items around the demolished home and then chant.

Kyra sighed and rubbed the tooth hanging at her neck, the gift from Marcus.

What am I going to do about this guy?

"I need something from you," Kyra said to Chelsea, then turned to look at her.

Chelsea met Kyra's gaze. "Anything. Just name it."

Kyra had expected this response, suspected Chelsea would be eager to please Sebastian by helping his best friend. That's why Kyra had chosen her. To keep it quiet, for Sebastian's sake.

"Can you come with Marcus and me? I need someone trustworthy. Someone needs to keep an eye on Marcus and tend to his wounds while I take care of something." Kyra returned to watching her men. "I shouldn't be long, and you'll be at Marcus's place, so there shouldn't be any danger. Do you think you could do that?"

An awkward silence fell between them. Kyra sensed something wasn't right, causing an unpleasant sensation to stir in her gut. And though Chelsea spoke not a word, her face soured. She pressed in on her abdomen, and Kyra got the nagging suspicion Chelsea shared in the queasy stomach syndrome.

"Okay." Chelsea's voice was low and lacked her usual conviction.

Kyra knew she should question the matter, but she didn't. The fear it would throw her into relationship territory was too great. The last thing she wanted was to stand there with Chelsea discussing feelings regarding Sebastian, because honestly, she didn't know where hers lay anymore. Instead, she snatched Marcus away from Sebastian and vortex girl and made a beeline for the portal at the carnival's front entrance, Chelsea at their tail.

"Hey! Where ya going?" Sebastian's voice called from behind.

"Quick errand. Nothing more. I'll be back before you miss me." Kyra's words were sharp, had bite. She glanced over her shoulder to glimpse his face. Dark, glistening pools of onyx stared back at her. She snapped her head forward. Didn't want to see anymore. Didn't want to hurt him. His emotions were not her responsibility, she reasoned.

Dammit. Dammit. Dammit.

Sebastian hadn't flirted with Ashlyn, made her mad—that was Marcus. Part of her wanted to be mad at Marcus for falling under Ashlyn's spell, except the logical side of her brain knew he couldn't help it. It was Ashlyn, after all, and all men tended to be powerless in her presence. All men who weren't Sebastian, that was. No, Sebastian had done nothing more than be nice to Chelsea. Now Kyra was reacting like a soulless fire demon. She needed to pull herself together.

She pushed down the havoc-inducing swirl of emotions within her and pulled Marcus through the magical gateway. Promising herself with the first step away from the carnival she'd smooth things over with Sebastian soon. Or later. At least before late became too late and the festering turned to crusted rust.

Kyra, Marcus, and Chelsea soon stood on a quiet, tree-lined street in Philadelphia, where they began their trek toward Marcus's apartment.

IT WAS ELEGANT FOR A BACHELOR PAD. A WELL-CARED-FOR, BROWN LEATHER sofa set filled the center of the room, accompanied by smudge-free glass coffee and side tables. A few pictures decorated the walls, and accessories were sparse. It was a minimalist look. Beautifully impressive, especially for a man living alone. Not a single empty beer can or slice of cold pizza in sight.

Marcus Blackall tossed his keys on the rustic marble counter, told the ladies to make themselves comfortable, and disappeared into the bedroom. The sound of water soon came from the bathroom beyond.

The weight of inevitability dropping upon Kyra's shoulders, she notched her hands on her hips and turned on Chelsea. "What's going on? You've been quieter than usual." She crossed her arms and tilted her head to the side. The foul scent of irritated dragon smoke clogged her nostrils. "Please tell me this doesn't have to do with Sebastian."

Pllеееaaassseee!

Chelsea began to spin a hand in front of her face, as if willing words that wouldn't come. Kyra took her actions as a ridiculous bid for time. She didn't know if she should smile, laugh, or what?

"I'm sorry," Chelsea said, her face turning brighter than Kyra's hair. "I haven't been completely honest with you, and I'm afraid it will affect what you're trying to accomplish by having me keep an eye on Marcus."

Kyra raised an interested brow and remained silent, waiting for the girl to continue.

Chelsea bit her lip, reluctant, then continued. "The first time I came to the carnival, I thought it was a dream. One marvelous, impossible dream. But then I met you and Sebastian, and I kept coming back because I wanted the dream. Things felt, tasted, so real. I began to believe they were, miraculously as it may seem, truly real." Chelsea's big, remorseful eyes bored into Kyra. "But I only come to visit when I'm sleeping, you see? When I wake up, back home, I leave this place." Chelsea wrung her hands together. "What happens if I wake up?"

Kyra stared at Chelsea, her head buzzing with thoughts and possibilities never before considered. She remembered the cancer, wondered how it factored in. Kyra shivered. Tried to play it off, work it into a roll of the shoulders, not wanting Chelsea to see her reaction. Maybe the cancer was changing her. Maybe her carnival visits meant more than Chelsea realized. There were a lot of maybes.

Still, Kyra didn't smell anything other than human girl on Chelsea. But she did see the girl differently for the first time. "Are you telling me you're asleep right now?"

Chelsea nodded.

"Then whatever you do," Kyra said, "don't wake up."

Chelsea gulped, embarrassment slowly draining from her face, replaced by resolve.

Sebastian's words rang in Kyra's ear—cancer. Images swam through her head. Pictures of Chelsea in a hospital room hooked up to machines, with daily nurse visits and IV drips that kept her under, kept her at the carnival. Kyra cringed.

Marcus entered the room, and she snapped into the now. A light blue t-shirt hugged his chest and upper triceps and worked to compliment his perfectly-fitted jeans. He looked good, if you looked beyond his many bumps and bruises: cheekbone, nose, and arms. The colors in his outfit brought out the blue in his eyes. She fought the desire to smile a little too wide. "Very nice. Don't let that go to your head, though. I suspect you hear that a lot." The devilish grin she received in response was confirmation enough. "That's what I thought." She shook her head and rolled her eyes closed. Only for the count of a wing's flutter. "I have to go for a bit. You'll be good if I leave Chelsea here?"

Marcus closed the gap between them, placing himself dangerously close to Kyra. "We just got here." He looked puzzled and in need of a solid answer.

Kyra stole a glance in Chelsea's direction. "I know. Will you be good, though?" She rubbed her palms down the front of her black jeans and hoped he'd understand. She was uncomfortable with him getting so close. Especially in front of Chelsea. Her pulse increased, and she began to perspire. The tension was too tight across her shoulders. Oh, how her wings wanted to stretch. Her hands began to knead at the pain, and she took a minuscule step back.

He glanced back and forth between her and Chelsea. “Fine, but I don’t need a babysitter.” His eyes darkened, and an impenetrable veil pulled down over them. The lines across his forehead deepened, and his face flushed, if only slightly. He was trying to hide his irritation, ineffectively so.

She could play the lonely puppy-dog look on him, only it wasn’t her style. She was more of a breathe-fire-directly-at-the-target kind of dragon. “Humor me,” she said, her tone coming across flat, even though she didn’t mean it to.

Marcus stared at her, his eyes serious, giving no indication they would soften anytime soon. He huffed and looked away. “Are you coming back?”

Energy pulsed through her veins at a fierce rate. He may not possess his beast, but there was no doubt in Kyra’s mind he was a dragon. He exuded the pure force of a royal giant. “Promise,” she said.

“Swear it.” His voice was deep and strong without being overly demanding.

Kyra sucked back her breath. The dragon within him scratched at the surface, anything but dormant, and it thrilled her to the bone, though his demands irritated her beyond her dragon’s wing tip. “I said I would, didn’t I?” Snark bled in and around her words.

Pressed between the peddlers and marketgoers, Kyra found what she was looking for. The door stood open. A thick veil of purple velvet dropped down, obscuring the gap—mostly. Drapes, hanging crystals, bands of feathers, mystic doodads, all shrouded the fortuneteller’s wagon in mystery for the average visitor. They also made it impossible for anyone to poke their head through the door without rubbing against a group of dangling silver stars or glass teardrops. A clever early warning system sounding someone's approach. Sets of brass bells chimed when Kyra slid past into the show space.

Sebastian sat in an antique stuffed chair, the pattern worn without looking decrepit. It held a warm, comfortable appeal. His face was decorated in black and white paint, a skeleton pattern, the extensive art partially hidden by the shadows from the hood of his cloak. A lot of thought and effort had been put into the show—the illusion.

The old tarot deck he always carried lay fanned out on the antique cherry wood table between them, illuminated by the mellow flicker of candlelight. The candles, pillars of various sizes and shapes, hugged the edges of the small space. Melted wax dripped down the sides into messy piles on the floor, and the scents of musk and thyme filled the room, creating a full effect.

Sebastian looked up, his dark gaze locking in on Kyra's and warming upon their connection. "Wish you'd come at a better time. I'm working right now."

She dropped into the chair across from him and placed her money on the table. "I know. I'm your next customer." She bit her lip and studied his full ensemble. Not so much the cloak and skeleton paint, but the dark suit he wore beneath. If he ditched the tie made of rope, he'd look hot.

His brows bored down into his gaze, a sudden weight pressing upon them. "You're kidding. I'd do your reading for free, off the clock. You know that. Wait."

Money slid across the table, Kyra pushing it closer to Sebastian's hand. "No. Now is good."

His hand hovered over the bills, a rapid tap of his finger drumming on the hard wood surface. Kyra remained fixated. Black, chipped polish pulsated up and down, pounding thoughts of what she might have to do deeper into her psyche. She shook her head, looked up to meet his stare.

The lines on his face softened. "What's this about?"

She pressed the palms of her hands to her temples, ran them up and back, racking her fingers through her hair. "There's something going on around this guy I saved. Something dark. I need to figure out what it is before it destroys him."

"You should let him go. It's not your fight."

Heat ignited lashing fire around her irises, and she leaned into the table. Ash lingered on her tongue, a reminder her temper had momentarily gotten the better of her. She sometimes found it nearly impossible to control the anger bubbling inside her. Remaining still, she allowed the silence to grow between them. "Don't fight me on this. Just do my reading. Deal the cards."

His eyes narrowed, bored into her, but she knew he would follow through. His hand swept over the bill, hooking her fingers before she pulled away. There, he held her for a matter of seconds. It could have been five lifetimes for the way she felt. The worlds must have stilled, sucked the oxygen out of his trailer, because everything stopped in that tiny moment of time. Nothing else existed—mattered—but him, and them together. Walls fell, barriers broke, and truths were revealed all in a simple touch. She didn't want Chelsea to have Sebastian. She didn't want anyone but her to have him. Dragon heritage be damned.

The connection broke, but Kyra continued to stare at the same point on the table.

Sebastian crumpled the bill in his fist and stashed it away.

His hands moved quick and with the utmost skill shuffling and mixing the deck. "It's been awhile since we've had any time alone." He paused, hesitated, but didn't need to finish the sentence. Kyra knew what he was going to say. Since she'd saved Marcus.

She nodded, eyes fixed on the table. "I know."

"I still want to talk to you."

Kyra looked up, met his gaze. "We can talk about whatever you want."

They stared at each other, letting the silence expand, fill the room. The lines at the corner of Sebastian's right eye began to tighten. The right corner of his lip twitched. "Can we?"

"Of course." Kyra threw her hands wide open, and her backbone straightened, as if thrown by a mini shock blast.

"Then tell me, what are you doing with Chelsea?" Sebastian's hand grasped at the air, then dropped to the table. "Why are you trying to push me away? Push me off on another girl?"

Kyra's heart jumped, stumbled, and droplets of anxiety began to bead her brow. "What do you mean?"

His face darkened, and his eyes turned the color of a moonless night. "Stop trying to force a relationship out of me." A gentle smile slowly graced his face, bringing with it a warm, soft glow. "I don't need help in the girlfriend department. If I do, I'll let you know."

Kyra bit her lip and tried to hide her amusement. His warning was dragon song to her ears. She preferred to see Chelsea charred by fifty dragons than end up a couple with Sebastian. And the fact that he chose to talk about the girl instead of his supernatural heritage was intriguing. Was this a sign of jealously? Did he return her feelings? "No Chelsea, got it. What about the other thing you wanted to tell me?"

Sebastian shook his head. "We can discuss that later. Not in the shadow of Chelsea and yours."

"Mine?" Kyra raised her brow and cocked her head. "You mean Marcus?"

"Yeah. That." His eyes flickered up from the cards for the briefest of moments. "Let's do this. Okay?" He swirled the mess of cards together on the table and gathered them together for the third time. "Clear your mind," he instructed, then asked her to shuffle the deck and break it into four stacks. Kyra warmed within and did as he directed.

Through the years, Sebastian had established his own unique way of reading the cards involving pairs. Kyra watched in anticipation, an over sense of nerves wreaking havoc on her system. The back of her neck became clammy as he reached for the first pair—the pair representing her current situation. He flipped them over, and her heart sank.

At face value, one might think The Wheel of Fortune was a good thing, but she knew it wasn't always so. She stared at the card, realizing she'd have to accept any and all mistakes and decisions she'd made. And in this case, the Wheel of Fortune card was paired with The Tower card. The pairing had disaster scribbled all over it. Plus, The Tower card was inverted! She tried to remember what that meant.

Something about change and falling. Maybe that's why people were falling from the tower.

"Don't start freaking out. Most people misinterpret the cards."

Kyra looked up to find Sebastian watching her. She nodded and tapped the table. "Continue." She didn't want him to see the concern she nursed, or sense the knot nestled in her stomach. She glued her focus to the table and the cards spread upon it.

Sebastian pulled the top two cards from each pile in turn, moving from left to right, and placed them as pairs in a line. In her influencers spot were the inverted Lovers and The Hierophant. The Page of Cups and The Devil, upside-down, flaunted the things she should consider or ponder. And the final cards, an upended Queen of Wands and Death, were meant to help her decide a course of action. She hardly saw how. Her heart hammered, and the beast deep within her growled. She reached for The Death card.

"Wait!" Sebastian's hands clamped down on hers, and she froze. The beat of their hearts, the rush of their blood, drumming together in skin against skin, played like a Yinglong's heaven-bound song. She yanked her hand back. For a moment, Sebastian didn't speak, nor did he move. He sat perfectly still, a thoughtful look brewing in his eyes. He sighed and expelled the air from his lungs with the force of a ruptured volcano. He returned to the deck, moving over the cards, rapidly jumping from one to the next. "Not all is as it appears." He repeated the words again in a whisper. "Not all is as it appears."

"But death, The Devil, and a burning tower." Eyes heavy and shoulders slumped, Kyra fell back in her chair, seeping exhaustion. "Isn't it clear what's coming? Death by fire. Again."

Sebastian leaned into the table, closer to her. "Not at all. What I see is a big change in your future. Inevitable change. Set in motion by things you've already done." He pointed to The Wheel of Fortune, then moved his finger to the inverted Tower. "It may be painful, I'm not going to lie. Or it could simply be a slow process. See this?" He pointed to her influencers, the inverted Lovers and The Hierophant. "You're letting your ideals and beliefs sway your decisions. Could be good, could be bad. And it looks like a lover has more control in the situation than you do." He shook his head. "Really, Kyra? I would have thought differently of you." His gaze remained steady on her. It made her punchy, fidgety.

Scales bristled down her backbone. Heat burned along the rims of her ears. "Just read the cards, Sebastian."

At that moment, she hated him. Not because he was giving her a bad time, but because he was right, and she knew it. Marcus Blackall made her weak in the sense that her free will wasn't completely her own. It was the crazy need to be here for him and the pull to save him no matter what. She didn't understand it yet, and she sure as hell didn't like it, but Marcus was a dragon, like her. That had to be a good thing. She hadn't considered him a lover before he'd started stinking up her space with the Serpicose. Since, it'd made her wonder. Maybe they were a meant-to-be thing. What did that mean for Sebastian and whatever was happening to her feelings regarding him?

"What do they say?" she asked.

Sebastian's finger drew a small circle on The Lovers card. "Is it because you love him?"

Love? That's such a strong word to use.

His eyes remained low, watching her reaction.

She didn't care for the use of the word *love* in relation to Marcus. She pursed her lips.

Sebastian's gaze flickered up.

Her head shook, unsure how to answer. She couldn't love Marcus. She hardly knew him. So then why was she risking so much for him?

Sebastian's shoulders slumped, and he diverted his gaze. "Things to consider." His hand moved to The Devil. "Are you your own worst enemy? Stuck in old patterns and belief systems? Do your beliefs and routine prevent you from growing?" His mouth puckered, twisting his lips to the side as if daring her to admit her unruly dragon was making the decisions, but she was stubborn, and he knew it. They both knew it.

She wrinkled her nose and met his gaze.

His hand slid over to the Page of Cups card. "Moving forward, you must think before reacting. Don't be closed to alternatives, but keep an open mind." He tapped the Queen of Wands. "Seeing the card this way is a warning. Don't take risks with anything you're not willing to lose." He locked his gaze in a deep stare with hers. It spoke of things she couldn't quite place, but wanted to. So rich with meaning and emotion. It almost hurt to lose the connection, have him look away. Almost.

Sebastian exhaled and continued. "Death. It could mean your death or the death of someone near you. I suspect it means the end of something important, a cycle. But know this: death cannot be cheated. Where there is death, there is always death. Understand?"

She blinked, and her heart clenched. No, she really didn't understand. Or maybe she simply didn't want to understand. She wanted to cheat death, and as a dragon, she wasn't used to being told there were things she couldn't do.

With a sympathetic smile gracing his face, Sebastian took her hand in his own. It was warm, a cozy cocoon. "To take a mark away from Death, another must be paid in its place. Balance must always be maintained."

That she understood. She squeezed his hand. "We're talking about the man I saved, right? Death is coming for him, and it won't stop." She glanced down at the cards. What lay before her was a challenge, but not impossible.

Sebastian bowed his head, a sense of understanding filling the void between them.

Kyra released Sebastian's hand, and a frigid draft washed through her, chilling her to the tip of her tail. Every muscle tensed, shuddering with pain, and she wondered how Ice Dragons endured extreme polar conditions. She looked to Sebastian and blinked. He either didn't feel it, wasn't bothered by it, or was the cause of it. She shook off the chill like snow off a jacket and dropped her fists on the table. "Great. You know I'm not going to lie down and let that happen. How do I stop it?"

Sebastian's eyes widened, and he straightened in his seat. "You can't be serious. Were you paying attention to the cards? Did you hear the bit about sacrifice and cycles coming to an end? Do you want that for yourself? Tell me no!"

Kyra stood, pushing back the chair with a loud *screeeech* across the wood floor. "If you're not going to help me, I'll find someone who will." Her face dropped, and she looked away, turned to go. She hated it, hated walking out on Sebastian in this manner, but *it* gave her no choice. Stupid pull or Serpicose or both, stripping her of her free will. Clamping obligation and desire for Marcus to her like a set of iron shackles.

Sebastian was up and around the table before she could make it out the door. He blocked the exit. "Please tell me you aren't going to do something reckless." He took her hands in his own and held them tight. When she shifted restlessly, his thumbs began to warm small circles into them, slowly rotating across the backs of her hands. It reminded her of the infinite possibilities that waited for her. Encouraged her to show strength in the face of Marcus's magic. Made her feel—

Her hands pulled free and found the side of his face. Held him captive, eye to eye. "Reckless is what I do best."

He started to rebut. She didn't give him the chance. With all the fury and rage of her dragon she kissed him, hard and fast. She didn't know why she kissed him. She didn't know why she did half the things she did, but in that moment, it felt intoxicating and exhilarating and right. She would have happily curled up in that moment and never moved forward. Brief as it was, nothing else existed in the span of those few seconds. There was only him, his delicious lips on hers, and the perfect, salty flavor of Sebastian.

She thought he liked the kiss. More than liked it. Had returned it, even, but now... Was it a good sign or a bad one when a guy stood stone-stunned after a kiss?

Kyra stepped away and out of the wagon trailer before Sebastian could come to his senses.

Kyra melted into the chaotic melody of the mass moving along the midway. She thought she heard Sebastian calling her name, but didn't turn to look, only quickened her pace.

She'd kissed him!

And not a tiny peck or a sweet-nothings kind of kiss. The type one's not likely to forget, maybe ever. It was a game changer. A relationship changer. Or a friendship destroyer. What had she done?

Crap!

Crap. Crap. Crap.

Kyra's pulse increased, and she pushed her way through the crowd with more force than necessary. *Stay on task. Focus,* her inner voice repeated on a loop.

If Sebastian wasn't going to help her in the manner she desired, she knew someone who would. Someone who had been around a lot longer, with decades verses years of accumulated knowledge of who-knew-what at the carnival. She was placing her bet he'd point her in the right direction.

Unlike the majority of those who had set up camp at the magical destination, Higgins chose to live in the thick of it. His tiny abode was nestled behind the whining motor of the Roulette Wheel spinner. Clear electric bulbs were strung across his cozy porch, the circuit hum running across the line lost to the racket of the mechanical monster operating the ride.

An old metal patio table with folding lawn chairs pegged the owner as sociable, yet casual. The green and white plastic weave of the seats looked comfortable, and an elderly gent settled back deep in one, nursing his chipped coffee mug. Not who she expected to find. Harmonious clarinet sounds whispered from the faded vintage Shasta camper behind him, the music of a Benny Goodman quartet playing *Moonglow*.

"Good evening, Kyra. Won't you join me?" Zeke motioned to one of the empty chairs.

Her footing stalled for a fraction of a second while she considered how the blind man always knew who was around him. *Does it have to do with what I smell on him?* The scent was familiar, yet not. Her gaze probed the area for Higgins, finding nothing. The clarinet continued through a song change, bringing lyrics dripped in a woman's voice, a song of memories and a love gone by.

A crash bellowed from inside. The sounds of dishes clashing. Higgins tinkered in the trailer.

With collected courage in her heart and pursed lips, Kyra

approached and sat beside Zeke. "I never realized the two of you were such good friends."

Zeke set his mug on the table, gentle warmth spreading across his features. "We go way back. Higgins is a good man. The best you could possibly have in your corner."

Higgins appeared in the framed light of the doorway. He held up a silver coffee carafe. "Warm up, anyone?" Without waiting for a response, he meandered over, set a cup in front of Kyra, and poured. When it was full, he turned to Zeke and topped off his mug.

He pulled up a chair, putting his blind friend in the middle and giving Kyra a direct view of both men. He savored the steam from his mug of liquid warmth like he was lapping chocolate from the evening air. A contented smile crept across his face. The kind that comes from secrets and a unique sort of knowledge, and Kyra understood she was privy to some confidential boys' club. Except she had yet to learn their secrets.

Higgins pushed his coffee to the side and leaned forward on the table, arms crossed. "So, tell me, lass. What can we do for you?"

Kyra blinked, sank deeper into her seat. "Lass? Where did that come from?"

Chuckling, Higgins shook his head and covered his face with his palm. "I don't know. Days gone by, I guess. What a day it has been, hasn't it?"

Never had Kyra seen Zeke or Higgins so relaxed or delighted. She took a deep whiff of the coffee, curious if it was spiked. As she did, her gaze shifted to Zeke. He was nodding to Higgins in affirmation, but his eyes seemed to hide secrets. *What am I missing? Is this a reference to the fire?* Or was it something more?

Zeke ran a nail across the metal tabletop, extracting an awful screech. All eyes were suddenly alert and directed at him. "I believe the young lady wanted our help finding something or someone."

How does he know? Kyra cleared her throat. "Um, yeah. If you can." Kyra's words fumbled, tripped over her tongue in their attempt to get out. She was in the presence of men far more experienced than herself, and her confidence slipped. The last thing she wanted was to be judged. They may've looked old, but what were they? In their seventies? Just because she looked around twenty-two didn't make it so. They probably only had about ten years on her. That was her guess, anyway.

Zeke chuckled. Kyra pushed her lower lip out, the corners of her mouth curving down. She didn't see anything funny. He reached over and patted the top of her hand. "Please continue."

A gentle breeze moved through, kissing her skin as it passed. It was the sign she needed. The tiny hint of reassurance she walked the correct path. It was followed by one lone shadow flickering across the moon. Brief, but there nonetheless. And in that moment, she knew she shared company with giants. Centurions. Guardians of the gates, or carnival, or whatever the place truly was.

Her backbone straightened, every molecule racing through her body stood at attention. The dragon within her scratched at the surface, eager to play. It could be her imagination running wild, but she didn't think so. No. She had the tendency to trust her gut, and her gut was telling her these were no ordinary men. She had definitely come to the right place.

Confidence coursed through her blood like a vicious race to some unseen finish line. "I'm in need of magic of an extremely serious nature. Being that you've been here as long as you have, I thought you might know where I could find someone to help me in this endeavor."

Kyra couldn't read Higgins' face, but she thought Zeke looked thoughtful in response to her words.

"What kind of magic are you in need of, exactly?" he asked.

Her hands wrung tight around her fingers, a nervous habit she attempted to hide by placing them beneath the table. "I need a deflection spell. Something that will work with a soul. You know, confusing one soul for another."

Higgins coughed, sputtering coffee in an explosion from his lips. Zeke's mouth hinted at mild amusement, whether in regards to Higgins' reaction or to what she'd said, Kyra was unsure.

"I am only looking to confuse a process. Divert Death so he can't collect. I know there has to be a way." Her words spilled out in a rush. It was horrifyingly embarrassing. Leaning back, she bowed her head. Based on her tablemates' reactions, she was sure she'd blown it. They thought she was crazy. They weren't going to help.

Zeke cleared his throat. "I think you should attend to that." A finger flicked, and he gestured to Higgins.

The little man looked tired and troubled. His gaze traveled the trailer and porch, apparently finding nothing. "What are you talking about?"

A bang erupted from inside the camper. Higgins shot Zeke a dark scowl and hurried inside to see what was amiss.

Another blast broke from inside the cabin walls, followed by Higgins' howl.

It was curious how Zeke always mentioned things before they actually happened. Kyra knew that meant something big. And here he sat, listening to her problem without batting an eye—so to speak. Higgins, too. Yet her best friend, while begging her to trust him, had tried to talk her out of this course of action. He didn't understand and that spawned sorrow deep within her chest. Such emotion didn't belong sitting at the table with Zeke. Kyra scooped it up and tossed it over her shoulder, out of sight.

Zeke sat gazing forward. It placed him looking toward the Roulette Wheel. Kyra had no doubt he heard every creak and groan the mechanism made, along with each squeal and whimper the riders delighted in, even if he couldn't see the spin of the monstrous mechanism or the peoples' bright faces and wide, ecstatic grins. His skin shimmered with a thin layer of sweat, despite the comfortable weather. As the pops and clangs and cracks continued to emanate from Higgins' abode, Kyra wondered if Zeke gave himself a workout by somehow causing the chaos within.

Zeke reached over and squeezed Kyra's hand, capturing it perfectly in his first attempt. "Would you mind seeing to him, Kyra? I believe he could use some help."

She didn't like being toyed with, and that's how the situation felt. Like a game. One in which she was clueless, her least favorite emotion of all. With pursed lips and a traveling gaze, she looked for Zeke's hidden deception. Failing to find anything, she walked toward the trailer.

Kyra didn't know what she had expected to find when she stepped through the door. Maybe pots boiling over on the stovetop, spaghetti and pasta sauce exploding everywhere. Something to that nature. Instead, it was swirls, mystical beads of light twisting and twining around themselves. Spirals in various shades of color vined through the tiny kitchen. Each trail gave off its own distinct hum or sound frequency. Together they created a melody. One that called to her very core, made her want to walk straight into the center of the magical light show.

She took an anxious step forward. "What can I do?"

Higgins tossed his head to the side. "Have a seat." He motioned to a freestanding armchair pulled into the aisle way behind her. It blocked passage to the front of the trailer and barely fit in the camper. She started to protest, not wanting to rest, but filled with the urge to do something. "You came here for magic, didn't you? That's what you're going to get. Now sit."

The power of his voice disarmed her. Kyra backed into the chair, her gaze remaining on Higgins, wide with wonder. "Is Zeke doing this?"

Higgins huffed. "He wishes he were this groovy. But no, the task falls to me."

His hand moved over bowls and jars, mixing and conjuring things Kyra didn't understand. She leaned forward and peered out the door to Zeke, but he was no longer anywhere to be seen. In fact, the carnival was strangely silent. Lights beyond the Shasta Sleeper twinkled, dimmed, and dropped into darkness. With it, the sounds of people and rides vanished.

Kyra began to stand. "What happened to the carnival?"

"Stay seated, please." Higgins spoke without looking in her direction.

She paused, watched him intently, then sat back down. "I don't understand."

"It simply shut down for the night. Nothing to worry about."

"But the carnival never closes." Kyra's voice hitched. The display of magic had startled her more than she'd realized. Higgins was the last one she expected the magic to come from. She was only looking to be pointed in the right direction, not to actually find it. In him.

He turned to face her, his expression an unrevealing mask of emotions. "Tonight, it has. I thought we could use the quiet for what we are about to do."

The wood of the chair gave as her nails dug deep into the arm, her clutch tightening. "What have you done with everyone?"

His lip curved up a tad at the corners, causing a small grin to cut into his weathered mug. "Everyone is fine, Kyra. I doubt they even sense a change."

"What are you? All these years I thought you were a talker or a prat boy. Now I find out you're ..." She made a motion with her hand. "...you. Something full of power."

Higgins turned from his work, his eyes giving a sad tinge to the slanted grin on his face. "I'd prefer you see me as the friend I've always tried to be, rather than anything else. I've only ever wanted the best for you and anyone else who has ended up here." The smile won control, if only for a moment. It looked less like a smile and more like an effort to placate. "Each of you is like family to me. There isn't a thing I wouldn't do for any of you."

Kyra stood and wrapped her arms around him. "You're a good man, Higgins." His body, stiff at first with rigid arms at his side, relaxed and encircled her with a gentle pat to her back. She found his initial reaction baffling.

"Thank you," he said.

What was it she smelled rolling off him? She took a step back. "What's wrong?"

He shook his head like he was dismissing the question. "This is no small thing you're asking for here, Kyra. It goes against nature. Not only is it dangerous, but it could have long-lasting ramifications. Are you sure this man is worth it?"

Her vision blurred as thought took over and she fell back into the chair. She remembered the Queen of Wands and weighed risk against

Marcus's safety. "Yes." Even as the word slipped from her lips, she was unsure if it was spoken by free will.

With the look of a man half asleep, Higgins extended his hand. "Then I believe you have something I need."

Her forehead wrinkled, and her eyes dimmed. "Sorry?"

"I need something of his to bind the two of you together. Otherwise, this won't work."

Her eyes wandered off to the side window, stared out without really seeing. *Something of Marcus'?* She'd only just met him. How could she possibly have anything?

Kyra caught her breath and slowly looked down.

She pulled the tooth pendant from her pocket. It dangled in the air between them. Even now, she was stunned to have found Marcus the way she had. The tooth had to be magical. Must have called to her when Marcus fell from the bridge and hit the water. It was the only thing that made sense.

Higgins twisted the rope of the pendant around her arm in a simple infinity curl. "Are you ready?" he asked and tied her down to the arms of the chair using twine he produced from the magic show behind him. The twine glowed and shimmered in magic, tickling where it touched her skin. The pendant infinity curl swiveled, conforming to the ties, melding with the one on her right arm. She didn't have a chance to change her mind.

"Yes," she said. The word slipped from her lips as if in slow motion.

One blink and the trailer was gone. Trampled grass surrounded them. Her chair sat on a small patch within the well-lit, yet empty, carnival. Higgins stood at her side. Still sitting, she moved at the speed of light without physically moving at all. Zipping forward, she twisted and turned as if she sat at the controls of her own invisible aircraft. She was on a roller coaster, but not. She spun, fell through water, zipped through fire, unable to breathe. Water clogged her lungs. She choked on smoke and coughed up blood.

The wings of her dragon flapped at her side. They created a funny whooshing sound. *Am I in dragon form?* She didn't know. She was flustered, disoriented. Droplets of blood splayed out before her, expanding as they would in water. Everything whirled. Lightheadedness and nausea fought for control. She looked down. Blood seeped from her skin. It bled out everywhere. Made her weak and so very...human.

She spun in the midst of a bright light while her dragon struggled with another, larger beast. *Marcus's dragon?* Her dragon sparkled, exploded into dust, and swirled down into a bottle held in Higgins' hands.

"It is done," he said.

8

ALONE

Kyra

Kyra moaned. Her muscles strained, cried out in pain. What happened? She opened her eyes, found herself half sitting, half lying in the mini dining booth of Higgins' trailer. The metal window trim pressed into the skin above her ear. She sat up and rubbed her head. "I could use an aspirin."

No one responded.

Pushing gingerly away from the seat and sliding out from behind the table, Kyra surveyed the tiny space. Didn't take long. So tight was the space, she could take it all in within a blink. "Hello?" A few steps forward to the small sleeping area, she pulled the curtain back. She was alone. *That's strange*. Had they accomplished what they'd set out to do? Where had Higgins gone? Grabbing a bottle of aspirin from the many bottles cluttering the counter, she shook a few free and downed them. She didn't remember Higgins leaving. In fact, she didn't remember much after the wild magic show.

Kyra stood in the open doorway staring out at the carnival of lights and sounds, not really seeing them. She was thinking, reaching into the farthest recesses of her mind, grasping at the memories.

Remember.

She rested her head against the frame. *Remember, dammit.*

The cool night air whispered against her skin, but Kyra didn't hear it, didn't feel it. She was too distracted. Needing to remember. Remember everything. The events returned to her with the strength of a soft breeze. The spell, or whatever it was, had been completed. At least, that's what Higgins had suggested. He'd said, *It is done*. But what happened after that?

Ah, yes. She'd gotten dizzy, thrown up, and passed out. Kyra frowned. She had to be strong right now. Not fall victim to weakness. Sighing, she pushed away from the door and walked away from the trailer. Walked straight out of the park, directly for the portal, and a path back to Marcus'.

Sooner or later, she would discover if the magic had worked.

MARCUS ANSWERED THE DOOR AFTER KYRA'S THIRD KNOCK. NO LONGER comfortable casual, he'd swapped his blue jeans and t-shirt for black jeans and a silver-grey button up. And he smelled ...*um, wow*...of an overkill of Serpicose and cologne. "What's going on?" She pushed past him, swept the room in a quick gaze. "Where's Chelsea?" She turned around to face him. Pressed her fists into her hips. "And why are you all dressed up?"

"She had to go."

"What do you mean by that?" Kyra urged. Too much time had been wasted figuring everything out, and Kyra was gone most of the day. Daylight had checked out several hours before she managed to return to Philly and Marcus, only to find Chelsea gone. At least she'd managed to bind dress the wounds on his arms before disappearing.

Marcus shut the door and sauntered over to the sofa, took a seat. The dark leather settled beneath him with an *ehrr*. "You know. Disappear. Evaporate. Whatever it is you strange people do." He tossed his hand through the air nonchalantly.

Kyra balked. She'd seen a lot of things, but trusting Chelsea's story, that was a bit out of Kyra's realm of believability. Existing in a place only in one's dreams...*ridiculous*. With a deep breath, she filed that away to investigate later and motioned to Marcus. "Doesn't explain why you're all dressed up."

"You were gone a long time, Kyra." He stretched and laid his arms out across the back of the sofa. "I'm not much of the hang-around-the-house type. I decided to go out." He smiled. "You got here just in time. Now we can go together."

"I don't think..."

A knock came at the door.

"That would be them." Marcus got up.

"Them who?" Kyra asked, following him to the front door.

"The guys. We're headed to the club." He opened the door to reveal two large men standing at the threshold. "Give me a second, guys," he said to them and turned back to Kyra. "Do you need to clean up before we go?"

"Marcus." She pulled him away from the door. Away from the listening ears of others. "I don't think this is a good idea."

He smirked. "I'm gonna go. You can either go with me, or you can stay here. What's it going to be?"

Stubborn men were like a thorn in her claw. She wanted to burn him to ash and be done with him. Except she would never do that, and she didn't really feel that way. *Ugh...irritating*.

Fifteen minutes later, they were settled in the car and on their way to some club the guys had assured Kyra was filled with raw excitement. More excitement was the last thing she needed at the moment. The sky darkened, and a light drizzle began to sprinkle the windshield. Kyra stared out the side window. *Why do I have a bad feeling about this?*

Marcus rubbed her arm and kept talking with his boys. She was surrounded by people, yet very much alone.

9
COMPLICATIONS

Kyra

Kyra huffed, studied the club's swirling logo on the front of her glass, then took a swig of her tonic water. So many things were going awry, and the solutions evaded her. Sebastian, Marcus...where did she want to be? If she were honest with herself, the kiss she'd laid on Sebastian told all. She'd fallen for her best friend like a dragon falling from the sky, fast and hard. The new discovery played chaos with her resolve as protector to Marcus. Maybe the fact that Marcus was a dragon and Sebastian wasn't held little to no meaning for her now.

Therapeutically, her fingers caressed the dragon tooth now laced around her neck. As the liquid washed down her throat, she wished it were something stronger.

Inside the establishment behind her, life moved in a rhythm of dance beats. This favorite club of Marcus's broke all kinds of codes by continuing to serve past the legal hour. Kyra thought it absurd. Humans and their rules, she didn't understand them. It wasn't like the place was located in the heart of a residential area where the noise would disturb the sleeping. They were in the center of a big city, the sound of motoring cars only a block away.

After the night's rain, the lights of the city glistened off every surface. The morning's sun barely peeked its head over the horizon. Kyra set her drink on the table beside her, ran her hands along the railing, and gazed out at the changing colors of the sky. Her emotions had been in a constant state of flux since her time with Higgins. She wasn't sure if she was satisfied or extremely anxious with her decision. Spitballs of fire bounced around her innards like a dragonling's party game. Nothing Marcus had done had distracted her thoughts from Higgins and the unbreakable promise she'd made. Not meeting his friends. Not even this place. Had she made a mistake, bounding her dragon to protect Marcus?

Live music danced and swayed out onto the terrace through the open doors behind her. She smelled Marcus's approach moments before he leaned against the rail beside her. He dangled his beer bottle precariously over the sidewalk below. She didn't have to glance down to know there weren't many pedestrians at this hour of the morning, but she looked past his bandaged arms to the street anyway. In fact, there weren't many establishments open, or showing any signs of life anywhere. It was odd to her. She'd become used to the carnival never sleeping.

"How you doing?" His voice was low and husky.

"I'm all right," she lied and glanced back at him. His black eye was a reminder something wasn't right at the carnival. She averted her gaze. Three buttons of his silk shirt, a black-on-silver-grey, were unbuttoned, exposing the well-defined lines of his chest. Desire ignited with a spark. Vibrating low, it worked its way up her center core, moving slow, warming along the way. She recognized it for what it was. Serpicose swept around them, strong and sweet. As long as he had the power of the male dragon's mating incense, she didn't trust him.

"You're still upset." He inched closer. She shook her head. "Sure, you are. Don't try to lie to me. It's not the girl's fault, though. She did say it might happen. You keep interesting friends, Kyra."

"Chelsea was supposed to watch over you," Kyra mumbled and

clenched the railing tighter. When she'd asked the girl to come, she had considered her expendable, for the most part. It was one reason she'd asked. Now she worried for the girl's safety. Great. Another drop in the bucket of dragon dung that was her life. What if pushing Chelsea at Sebastian had forced them to bond on some level? What would he think of her if she were to cause the girl harm?

"It's fine. I'm fine. Besides, from what she said, it didn't sound like she could help it. What was it she said? Something about if she woke up, she would disappear. Sounded like nonsense, but it happened right before my eyes. She simply vanished. That's the kind of stuff that will drive a person bat crap crazy."

The warmth of Marcus's hand dropped over hers on the railing. Nerves raked through her, stiffening her shoulders. She took a deep breath and forced herself to relax. It was nothing, she told herself. Or maybe everything. He inched closer still. *This is it*, she thought, *he's going to kiss me.*

"Thanks for coming. The guys like you," he said and tilted his head. His face lit up and took on a sexy, eat-you-alive smirk.

As much as she tried not to return the gesture, she couldn't help herself. It spread a warm, tingly sensation to her cheeks. That's when she realized how much power he had over her. She would let him have this one, and for now, she would let Chelsea's disappearing act go.

Spending the last few hours with Marcus had been a notable change of pace. It was strange just hanging out, doing things like humans. She liked his friends. They were nice and played a mean game of pool. Upon their arrival at the club, they'd made her work to prove her ability. She sank the balls so fast they stopped giving her a hard time and started treating her like one of the guys. But hanging with them required her to hold back her authentic self. She wasn't sure how long she would be able to play the role or hold her dragon dormant.

Marcus notched his finger under her chin and lifted her face to meet his. "You've been quiet tonight. Why don't you tell me what's bothering you?"

That was just it. How was she supposed to tell him *he* was the thing bothering her? Before she could formulate her thoughts, something from the corner of her eye caught her attention.

It moved in a quick glide, swooping from high to low, and looked like a raven.

She leaned forward, studied it closer, more intently. Not only was the bird circling in the sky as if waiting for something below to die, but when it flew low, it flew to the arm of a man down on the sidewalk.

The same man she'd seen in the mist. The same man she'd seen on the bridge.

Kyra's heart accelerated and a trickle of sweat ran down her back. The decision to drink water instead of a martini suddenly seemed a profoundly wise choice.

The gentleman in the dark gray suit looked up at her, removed his hat, letting his midnight hair drop over his brow, and cracked a frightful grin. His face stretched so thin it looked as if it might shatter, break to bits. Kyra's chest squeezed so tight it felt like her ribs were collapsing. A shudder rippled through her soul. *This is it*, she thought. *Death.*

She spun around, took in every inch of the club visible from their vantage point. Marcus pressed up against her side, the warmth of his arm radiating straight through the bare skin of her tricep. Emotions ripped through her, but she knew what she needed to do. She wasn't going to take a chance with Marcus's life. She shimmied a step away, needing to keep a clear head and a clear lookout for whatever Death was sending at them next. Serpicose couldn't be allowed to muddle her thought process.

Marcus's shoulders hunched, and his eyes clouded over. The line of his lips followed with a downward tip. "What's wrong?"

The early morning exploded in a clash of thunder. It was the sound of breaking glass. Lots of it. The glass wall standing between the club and the terrace shattered and fell in a cascade of dangerous crystal shards.

All eyes turned toward the destruction as the body of a man came flying through. He landed on his face, where he remained, unmoving.

From the back, he looked like Marcus's best friend, Toby. Marcus lunged toward the fallen man, but Kyra held him steady.

A monster of a man climbed through the hole in the wall. His eyes glinted when he spotted Marcus.

"Been a long time, Balidhug." The man's voice reverberated deep and scratchy, like a growl.

Something dark—fear and knowing—spiked in Kyra.

Not human.

The thought had barely registered when the shot rang out. A bullet ripped through the air straight for Marcus's heart. Immeasurable pain rolled across Kyra's body like something was plucking the scales from her hide one by one, a hereditary instinct pushing her to protect. She tried to scream, but the sound lodged in her throat.

Pain. Excruciating pain. Rings of fire thrashed at her eyes, scales tore at her skin and plunged within, nails and wings dug and scratched, rammed deep into her skin. Twisted, torn, and crushed all at once.

Her entire being splintered, fractured in two.

The sliver of metal whizzed past her toward Marcus, and her dragon tore free from her human camouflage. Kyra wasn't even aware she could do that. Her dragon leapt forward and wrapped herself protectively around him, taking the bullet between the shoulders.

Kyra's human form convulsed, still tethered to her dragon, a fine bundle of invisible cords stretched between them. She caught the slightest reflection and distortion when they moved and twisted.

The blow of the bullet pushed her dragon, and Kyra stumbled forward, disoriented.

How is this happening?

Marcus remained wrapped safely within her dragon's beastly grip, cocooned and protected by her wings. Aimed high and at close range, the centrifugal force of the bullet slammed hard. Kyra's nails scratched and chipped as she clung to the brick and mortar in a state of desperation. Her odds grew insurmountable, with the bond pulling her human-self while her dragon form floundered, toppling Marcus and her beast over the railing.

Her entire body yanked in one quick moment. She was being pulled over the railing. Her heart raced around her ribcage faster than a bullet train.

No! I'm not ready.

The wind brushed past her, Marcus still sheltered within the folds of her wings, Kyra dragged over and down by the barely-seen cord.

Her falling thought, of Sebastian.

The ground came too quick, the landing far too hard.

EXCRUCIATING HEAT. HEAT SO SEVERE IT DRAINED YOUR SOUL. IT ASSAULTED Kyra in waves. Seared her flesh from the bones. Her eyes popped open to a vast landscape of treacherous peaks and endless canyons laced in moving fire. Rolling clouds of burnt orange and murky red rumbled in rebellious adulation over the molten terrain. She was unprotected. No scales. No shielded vision. No dragon. Her hands patted at her arms, her waist. It was all there, intact. At least her flesh remained unharmed—unseared, after all.

Did the spell work? Is Marcus all right? A sideways glance produced no hint of him or her dragon. A shudder rolled over her, the memory of her other-self separating and remaining tethered still so vivid. Higgins' spell was clever. Strange, but clever.

The rocky ground scratched her skin when she rolled over onto her knees and lifted herself up. She stood on a precipice, the drop on all sides sheer. On the other side of the dividing canyon, mountains rose to the left and to the right, towering far above. Flinching away from the flames and guarding herself with a hug, she looked for an escape. There was nothing.

Her fingers dragged through her hair, hard. *It will be fine*, she reassured herself. *Just another puzzle to solve.* She'd start with how she'd gotten here. Except she didn't remember. The last thing she remembered... What was the last thing she remembered?

Fire danced across the rocks and mountain peaks as far as she could see. In the void of valleys below, a storm of waterspouts churned.

Varied and not quite equal distance apart, they reminded her of a sloppy presentation of wardens. They rose from beneath as if yearning for something more. Spinning upward into nothingness, they lashed around like savage horses tied to a spike. The movement surpassed the angriest storm Kyra had ever seen.

Wanting to get a closer look, Kyra knelt, placed her hands on the edge, and gazed at the view below. Her hair whipped wildly in response to the howling tempest beneath her fingertips. A tempest that appeared to be getting closer. Was it rising to meet her? Or was her mountain sinking? Maybe the pit below was her personal Hell, and she was descending.

Never had she been so vulnerable, so weak. So *human*. She didn't care for it much. Didn't care for it at all. Her fist slammed into the dirt and rock, meeting its force and finding no give. The bones in her hand screamed, crushing and splintering with a wicked crunch.

Fire shot across her line of sight, kissing the skin of her upper arm. She fell back and rolled, letting the screams and words go as she cradled her wound. Cries turned to uncontrollable coughs. The acidic air burning her throat and nostrils. It tasted like charcoal and smelled of melted plastic. One unpleasant flip of her stomach and Kyra moved back to the edge of the precipice, fearing an involuntary reaction of the most human kind.

The wind lashed at her body, and she closed her eyes, allowed it to cool her clammy, sweat-beaded skin. It was a moment's reprieve from her nightmare. Chunks of her copper hair lay matted to her forehead.

Maybe she was ill. Lying sick in bed with fever somewhere, and this was nothing more than her over exuberant imagination. That would explain her thoughts constantly wandering to Sebastian. She wished he were with her now. He'd tell her to be strong, stand up, fight her way home. But how?

Gathering what courage she could muster, Kyra stood and faced the hell that surrounded her. *You don't believe in fate,* she reminded herself. Scooping a handful of rock and sediment from the ground, she tossed it forward, aiming for the space between the spiraling storms. "Show me the way out," she called to the wind.

The tiny stones shot straight into the closest waterspout, pulled in by its powerful grip. Some were devoured, others spun and scattered in every direction. She ducked, barely escaping the returning spray. She crouched on the ground, envisioning every space as a bed. She fought it, fought the will to sleep, but every muscle protested when she tried to rise again, her body overcome with exhaustion.

Sebastian kept her moving, kept her fighting. Envisioning him beside her was the encouragement she needed to push onward, not give in to the battle. Getting back to him was what mattered most.

Expanding spirals of water rose higher from the canyon floor and a rush of liquid broke over the top of her tiny stronghold—and over her. It fell with a mighty splash upon her, drenching her. Neither cool nor refreshing, it provided moisture—an uncomfortable wet and something extra unique to Hell.

Kyra dug her heels into the ground, crouched low, expecting to be knocked to the side, even thrown from her safe perch. It didn't happen. The water showered over her, a downpour of despair and depression. It washed away any desire to run or escape. It removed all hope and longing. As the spout jumped from the mountain and traveled onward, Kyra was left behind a hollow shell. The greatest emptiness stirring within her, scraping at her inner walls like a ravished dog licking clean its last meal. Gravity pulled her from her crouch flat to her knees, and she dropped without struggle.

Why am I fighting? I can't go back. Marcus is safe. He has to be. A soul for a soul, that's what Sebastian said. I maintained the balance. I was Death's collection.

She gave in, allowing her body to succumb and crumble to the ground. Her eyes fluttered, blurring the reds, oranges, and dark browns of the sky together in a mulch of color. Hell. That's where she was going. And she was making the journey alone. She didn't even have her dragon to keep her company.

Her hand flopped onto the rock in front of her. It drew her gaze to a large *something* flying against the horizon. Whatever it was danced with the fire, flirted with it.

Kyra might have been content to lie with her cheek kissing the dirt forever, had it not been for that beast caught in her gaze. A beast she'd grown so familiar with. She willed her arm to rise and reach out, but it was bonded to the ground by a thousand unseen threads. Or it might as well have been, for all the power it took to move. Kyra poured all her concentration and effort into lifting her arm, bound and determined to get the dragon's attention. Practically an impossible task. The weight and force required to hold the arm up threatened to drop it at any second.

Arm extended with fingers stretched out, Kyra called to her dragon. "Kalrapura!" Her voice was weak and carried little distance, but Kyra knew her dragon. Hearing wasn't one of her weaknesses.

Seconds. That was all she could manage. Her arm fell to the rock, her strength gone.

Crap.

She turned her head to the side and laid her cheek upon the pitted ground.

Brave Rajũn, give me strength.

"Kalrapura," she whispered, closing her eyes. She concentrated on the heavy breaths heaving at her chest.

This must be Hell. It's eternally slow and filled with endless torture.

The ground rumbled, and the skies roared, yet when Kyra opened her eyes, she saw nothing but the same. Except...her dragon was gone. She lifted her head and searched. No dragon anywhere. With slow, deliberate moves, she followed the reverberation and carefully pulled herself toward the edge. Spirals of water shot past her with a whoosh, climbing straight toward Heaven. Heaven, now there was a thought. She expected there was no reaching Heaven from this place. The spirals vanished into the churning, fiery plume above.

Mists of despair fell like droplets of oxygen. Discouragement took root, spurring her shoulders to slump. She didn't need to feel worse than she did already.

She'd never stopped to consider Heaven and Hell, but a big pit of depression, a constant carwash of despair, was not what she would have envisioned.

A mighty roar bellowed from below.

The mountainside shook, sending rocks and pebbles skittering down the hill. Kyra flattened herself to the surface, all while the pumping of her blood quickened and thunderous sounds rolled closer.

An odd rhythm echoed through the canyons, and thoughts of Kalrapura popped into her head. Kyra wanted to see her. Needed to see her. Needed to see where the bullet had hit her dragon between the shoulder blades, between Kalrapura's wings. She had to see what damage had been done.

And maybe, just maybe, if she got her dragon back, she could pull herself together again.

A crash resonated all around her. Wide-eyed, she held her ground. Another crash and an ear-shattering roar broke over the noise and turbulence. It dropped in her gut like a battle mace, just before the fire flared out over her head.

Dragon!

His talons dug into the edge of her little perch, and his chest pushed up and out with pride and power. He was a magnificent specimen, the most beautiful dragon she'd ever seen. But he was not her dragon.

Where was Kalrapura, her unique orange serpent?

The midnight beast towered over her, stretching out like a blackhole against the landscape of flames. Kyra tried to melt into the hard ground beneath her, but he was impossible to avoid. With the tiniest of moves, his armor hinted of red. Iridescent. His scales were a beautiful iridescent crimson. She'd only heard of, never seen, such extreme brilliance. Wings held high, he displayed multiple battle scars like a badge of honor. And the beautiful, barely-there, crest across his chest meant only one thing: he was either Marcus's dragon, or a member of his family.

Muscles locked and eyes widened, she stared, untrusting of the sight before her. She rubbed at her eyes; the monstrous beast was still there. *How?* It was the only cognitive thought she could form.

He stretched his neck and dropped his head down to Kyra's level.

Kyra sucked back a breath. *Glorious.* That was the second word that came to her mind. He was truly glorious.

His lips drew back, revealing two rows of dagger-sharp teeth. Weapons meant to kill—devour. One hundred percent pure. A real dragon. Not a mongrel hybrid like her, a Moorigad.

The dragon lunged, his jaws chomping down, trying to devour her. *Freaking, flying gargoyle! I'm dragon dinner!* Kyra skittered and rolled backwards. Surprisingly, the dragon instantly tumbled sideways, hit by an enormous flaming bird. The dragon roared, and the bird screeched as the two tangled in a dangerous choreography.

They flew across the scorched sky, slamming into mountain peaks and hillsides, tumbling rock and stone beneath their brute force. The dragon was bigger and stronger, but the bird—a phoenix—was faster and exceedingly agile.

There was something familiar about the phoenix. Kyra couldn't say what, though. Having never seen one before, she strained to think of what it could be.

Run, Kyra. A voice reverberated in her head. An old voice. A known voice.

She whipped around in search of the warned threat. Which way should she run? It had only been a few seconds since the beastly fight had disappeared from her sight. Thunder shuddered across the sky, moved from left to right, and with it shifted the land, knocking her off her feet. Her mountainside rumbled, and the dragon exploded into sight, having flown straight up the precipice.

Kyra's feet sought traction, desperately scrambling in the dirt. The dragon bore down upon her, looking ready, more than ready, to end her.

"Go!" the voice shouted again.

The dragon's claw slammed down, and Kyra jumped out of the way, using energy born of adrenaline. She barely escaped, felt the wind of his swipe brush across her side. He bared his teeth, let his foul breath wash over her, and lunged. The phoenix swooped in between them, and the dragon grabbed his wing instead of Kyra. She expected relief. Instead, a warm, wet tear ran down her cheek, and her heart lodged in her throat. Confusion tripped up her feet.

The dragon thrashed the phoenix to the ground even as Kyra stood directly in harm's way. The beasts were massive. Together they covered most of the small mountaintop. She dropped, rolled to the side, and heard the phoenix's cry pierce the hot air. She knew the dragon had laid into him. Her insides bled for him, but what could she do?

Dirt clung to her sweat-matted skin like an accessory, and she came out of the roll crying for the fiery bird. The dragon looked up and advanced. Kyra swore he wore a vicious dinnertime grin.

Kyra wanted to cry for the dragon, too, but found no tears. This place had diseased him, turned Marcus's dragon rotten and ugly to its cold, dark core. Was he beyond saving?

Fire was his resource, his to command, and he used it with utter confidence to cleanse the mountaintop, moving the flame with a gentle swing of his head. Kyra rushed from its touch, rolling out of its wake. Only, the mountaintop was small, and her roll was too fast and too long. The edge came quick, her body rolling and tipping over the side. Broken, bloodied nails scratched and clawed at the ground in her attempt to stay her fall. But momentum overpowered her, and she dropped into devil-may-know-what. Craggy cliff chunks bit into her limbs like piranha to the prey, and her body slammed and bounced off the wall, catching every jagged rock along the way. Each laceration was a lava lick at her skin. She bit her lip and held back the screams.

Her body smacked into a hard, crusted surface. Every limb tingled, and she was overcome with weightlessness, as if she floated on a cloud. It lasted half a second before her senses came crashing to the ground with the rest of her, her entire being weighting down like a ten-ton sack of sod. She knew she should keep moving, but somehow, she had managed a moment's reprieve from the beast, and she was exhausted. She closed her eyes and allowed another tear to fall. The sounds of the phoenix dying above slashed a hole through her heart.

"What are you doing here, Kyra?"

Kyra's eyes fluttered open and, fighting the sting that came with her vision, her gaze shot upward toward the familiar voice. Sebastian. Her heart danced at the sight of him.

He stood over her looking like a dark dream, if ever she'd seen one. He wore black jeans with dark military boots, a large leather band strapped to his right arm. His hair was shoved up in a mad mess, asking for someone to run their fingers through it, and the exposed skin across his chest glistened with sweat. At the sight of him, Kyra's eyes widened, and her heart expanded. A friendly face was the last thing she'd expected to find.

Finding Sebastian—he was her golden dragon egg, her treasure-filled cave. He was her everything.

This had to be the doing of the Great Rajũn. He'd taken pity on her and decided to show her mercy. "Thank you, Rajũn," she whispered.

"Your dragon god has nothing to do with this, Kyra." He took a step forward. "Now please answer the question. Why are you here?" He paused, looking deep into her eyes. "It wasn't supposed to be you. It wasn't ever supposed to be you. What did you do?" His voice, soft and soothing, caressed her like a warm, gentle hug.

She thought his eyes looked mournful, but...no, that was wrong. They looked frustrated. Furious. That's what she saw in him—irritation.

She pulled her knees in, squeezing them to her body. "What do you mean?"

Almost instinctively, she looked to the tattoos she'd first noticed under the bridge, running up the side of his ribcage. Before, she'd had no clue what they said or meant. They'd looked like gibberish to her. Now they were clear as the cuts on her skin. Maybe it was this place deciphering them for her. Or maybe she was in a new state of being, possibly one known as death, that gave her the ability. Whichever it was, she could see it was a list. And not a favorites or a bucket list. No. It was a list of names.

The top name was in a constant state of flux. It was her name, then it wasn't, then it was again.

Her thoughts returned to the man on the bridge, the same man beneath the terrace the night she fell—Sebastian's father. There was no doubt in her mind about that now. She didn't know how she knew, but she did. She looked to Sebastian. "Are you him? Are you Death?"

Sebastian's face brightened, boasting a laugh and an unconvincing smile. Thrusting out his hand, he helped Kyra stand. His arms folded in and around her, lifting her with ease. "Nothing so grand. I'm more like his errand boy. There are a lot of bodies between me and the top."

His touch sent a warmth and comfort through her she craved, desired. She never wanted him to let go. Why hadn't she figured it out so much earlier? She had let her pride stand in the way. "I'm sorry, Sebastian. Sorry I didn't listen. You were right; I shouldn't have gotten in the way. Now look what I've done. This was Marcus's fate, not mine. Sorry I didn't trust you."

"As they say, my friend, water under the bridge." He looked pleased with his pun. He brushed a few pebbles off her arm and stepped back. Cold dug into her chest and carved out a chunk, leaving a hole in its wake. She was petrified. Deeply, immensely petrified in this place, this unknown, without his strength guiding her. Of course, her pride still wouldn't allow the fear to show on the surface.

Instead, she pointed to his ribcage and watched as her name morphed into Marcus's. "But the names?" A line moved across the name below Marcus's, crossing it out while she looked on. Then the crossed-out name was no more. It disappeared from Sebastian's skin altogether. Kyra gasped. "What!" She pointed to the space where it had been. "What happened?"

He glanced down and shrugged. "Their need for me is done. They've moved on."

"Moved on? From where? From here?" Her voice hiked. "I thought this was death. Aren't I dead?"

Sebastian glanced to her, then out over the warring landscape. "I can see where you might think that, but this is more of a holding cell. Purgatory, if you will. Death puts up a darn good fight to suck you in. Wouldn't you agree? It's not easy making a comeback from this place, but it is possible."

A large boom, the sound of multiple cannon fire, blasted from the summit above, and there was a flash overhead, followed by spurts of flame bursting in all directions. Horrifying howls, enough to curdle one's blood, accompanied the display. It shot across the sky and died away. They stared up and watched the dragon take to the sky. Kyra suspected that could only mean one thing.

She swallowed the desire to burst into hysterical tears. "The phoenix, it's Higgins. Is it...?"

Sebastian grabbed her arm and held it tight. "He gave us time. He kept you safe."

She wanted to throw herself into his arms and hug him tight. Instead she kept her cool, showed her strength. "But I'm only here because I was keeping Marcus safe. No one else was supposed to die for that cause." She pulled her arm away from Sebastian and raked her fingers through the side of her hair, pulling it taut. Something squeezed all the air out of her. She couldn't breathe. Tears flowed down her cheeks freely. "I didn't know. I didn't know!" she screamed and fell to her knees, whispering. "Not Higgins, it's not fair."

It felt like eons she'd crouched crying, Sebastian hovering above her, but it had only been seconds. Sebastian kneeled and ever so gently, the palm of his hand ran along the curve of her back. "Life is rarely fair. But I need to know. Do you want to live?"

She glared at him. If Kalrapura still dwelled within her, her eyes would be circled in fire. "Of course, I do! I want nothing more, but Marcus..." And Higgins. She didn't deserve to live after what had happened. She looked to the scuffs in the dirt at their feet.

"Forget what I said." Sebastian's tone was sharp, causing Kyra to look up again. The dragon circled the skyscape above them and Sebastian pulled Kyra back against the wall, under cover of the cliff overhang. The sight of the dragon weighed Kyra's chest down with guilt.

She pointed to the dragon. "I need to figure out what to do about him." The dragon roared, his body a mere silhouette against the dark heavens above, twisting and turning in a mad search for prey.

Sebastian took a finger to her chin and moved her until their eyes met. "I don't care about Marcus or his dragon. That dragon can stay down here and burn for all eternity. It's a good fit. But I'll help you with him or Marcus if you so desire. All I care about is you. I want you to live. So did Higgins. As do you." He squeezed her hand in his own. "That's good enough for me. You fight, Kyra, and believe in yourself. Understand?"

His words rang in her ears, drowning out the sound of the crackling landscape, the sloshing water spirals, and the clamor of the dragon above. The weight of his speech and the beat of her heart had her soaring out of sight. She was flying, and she was grounded, Sebastian pulling her into his arms. She was everything and nothing at all. He was her center, her gravity and she wanted nothing more than to meld into him and make them one.

His lips descended upon hers, his kiss not rushed or rash like the one she had earlier pressed upon him, but soft, gentle, and perfect. Everything a first kiss should be, tender, beautiful, and devastating. Her wings flapped, her tail curled, and her fingers clutched, never wanting to let go.

He pulled away, smiled tenderly and, without a word, pushed her backwards with incredible strength. Her body shifted, lost traction, and flew up into the air, dragged by the pull of the twisting water spouts. She clawed at Sebastian's forearms while her legs dangled in the open air. He was her anchor, and she refused to let go. As she did, she saw the line start to form. It was faint, but it was there, wavering in and out across her name. She saw Higgins' name, too, inked below hers. And then it wasn't. She looked for an explanation in Sebastian's expression.

He was stone, gave nothing away. Until his hand betrayed him with one quick wipe of the eye. Confirmation that Higgins was gone.

"No!" she screamed.

A screech replied. The dragon descended, dived down on them from above. Her heart hiccupped, and her hands jolted. Sebastian's arm slipped through her grasp, and she flew into the water stream.

She yelled with all the might she had, hoping her friend would hear. Her words went out to Sebastian. "I trust you completely!"

Water everywhere, rushed around her and caressed her. *Sebastian. What will become of you?* She gulped a mouthful of water as she pitched and spun in the whirlpool. Despair overtook her and tossed her around like a rag doll. No! She wasn't going to give into it. Not after all Higgins had given up. She was making the decision to live.

Her arms moved against the force of the water, like treading through molasses. Still, she was determined, and so her limbs pushed forward. She pulled herself through the spiraling water like she was swimming upstream, directly up. Maneuvering herself to the center, she let the spin and the force of the water work to gently lift her.

Depression and despair continued to grope at her, nag her, but she focused on the light above. Maybe it wasn't Heaven. Maybe it was simply a way out, a way back to life.

One stroke. A hard push through the water.

I should have told him. Told him I love him, she thought.

She focused on Sebastian and how he made her feel. She focused on getting back to life at the carnival, and she focused on her dragon. Little distance was made. Still, it was something.

Another stroke and another, and she climbed a little bit higher in the tower of despair. It wanted to break her. It willed her to succumb to its power play of despair. She wouldn't have it.

She thought of Marcus. Would she check in on him when she got back? She wasn't sure.

She focused on Sebastian and the earthbound world. She could do this. She would get back to him and their life together.

A gulp of air for the edge and more treading. Her arms cut through the water six, seven more times, pulling impossibly hard up through the twisting current. She was strong even without her beast side, and she was determined. She continued to climb.

She focused on the scent of the morning after the rain.

She had to be close. She could sense it. Five more strokes.

Light flared out all around her, changing the blue water white, and the sound of the liquid moving at her ear morphed to a timed beep. She didn't know what it meant, but she hoped it was a sign she was close. Her pulse accelerated. Sebastian had been right. It was working.

Her body grew tired, and her arms ached from the work. She wasn't going to let that stop her. She threw her left arm up again, cutting through the current in a stroke, focusing on the carnival and the smell of popcorn. Oh, how she hated that buttery smell.

The sound of the beep increased until it was all she heard. The force of the water vanished and the glow of the blue all around her was gone. Oxygen. She inhaled deep.

Pain rippled through her like the Fireball ride from the Fun Zone—top speed, no pauses. She screamed, but heard only a moan. The darkness encompassing her caved and light exploded around her. It hurt to look. Hurt like Hades frozen over. Yet it was nothing but the overhead fluorescents of a room.

"Welcome back, sweetie." A nurse stood over her. Something warm squeezed her hand. The pain of sharp knives slashing ran along her muscles when she turned her head.

Her efforts didn't go unrewarded. Marcus sat at her bedside. Bandaged and bruised, but healthy. Alive.

The nurse checked a few things, then patted Kyra's shoulder. "I'll get the doctor." She stepped into the hall. "Room 206 is awake."

10

PHOENIX

Sebastian

Sebastian took the chiseled stone steps two at a time, rushing out of Purgatory as if the place were ready to implode. *Gotta make sure she's okay*. Wisps of fire and lava lashed up from the pits at his sides, lashed up around his path. He didn't allow them to slow his progress. If only he could snap his fingers, be where he wanted to be. Ah, but that would be too easy.

He ran up the stairs, leaped across the stones of the Madness Abyss, and plowed through the dimensional window of Unrealized Realities. Catching a stone with the tip of his toe, Sebastian stumbled and dropped into the murky ground of the immutable fog forest. Soft earth gave beneath his touch, and moist dirt and moss swathed his bare skin. With a mumble, he pushed himself back up, took stock of his location to gain his bearing. Trying to not get lost in the forest and fog was no easy task. Everywhere he looked it was the same—slender trees stretching up into oblivion and fog no thinner than cotton candy. So thick was the ground-sweeping cloud that it drowned out all exterior sounds, leaving him to wonder if he had only yards to cross to find the carnival, or miles.

Taking a silent minute, Sebastian closed his eyes, tuned into his gut, summoned his inner senses, and listened. A gentle breeze brushed against his skin, cooled his damp hairline. Frogs and crickets, bugs Sebastian didn't recognize, chatted across the vast woodland. None of it was what he sought. He probed further, deeper.

A whirl and a zip. Bings, bongs, and bangs. His head snapped to the sound, the carnival. His way out was there.

Slugging through the thicket in a weave around fence-tight trees, Sebastian pumped his legs with purpose, Kyra's name the only item on his urgency list. *Too long,* he thought, stumbling over grass tufts and roots. *It's taking too long.* Trees gave way to perpetual white mist, and it clung to him before letting him go, leaving him in the clearing behind the trailers of the Backyard.

"You need to go back, son."

Hell no. "Do you have any idea what I just went through?" Sebastian slouched over, leaned into his knees, and considered the old man and his possible motives. Zeke was perched in a folding lawn chair, facing the surrounding fog wall, as if he'd been waiting for Sebastian. Sebastian inhaled deep and let the breath go nice and slow. "Okay, I give up. Why do I need to go back?"

"Higgins cannot be left there."

Sebastian stood straight, scratched the back of his neck. "But Higgins died."

"Indeed." Zeke tilted his head upward. "But as his friends, we must help usher him into his next life."

Sebastian's stomach dropped with the power of the Zipper's downward swing. *Dammit all to Hell.* He owed Higgins this. Kyra would have to wait a little bit...but not too long, Hell help him. Body heavy and chest tight, Sebastian turned around and retraced his steps.

Back through the immutable fog forest, he raced. The window of Unrealized Realities shattered with his leap, sealing directly behind him. Sebastian practically flew over the Madness Abyss and down the eternal winding stairs into Purgatory. Again, fire and lava swept up around his path, but it didn't matter. This was the one place Sebastian found immunity from such torments. Likely, a sign of it being where he belonged. *No time to think about that now.*

The bird of fire lay precisely where Sebastian remembered, a most precarious spot. No matter. For Higgins, Sebastian would make it work.

In the molten orange sky above, the trapped dragon flew. The beast soared and flapped his wings in a mellow manner, making the dragon's flight reminiscent to a casual walk through the carnival. Never having been bothered by the beast on his previous visits, Sebastian suspected it was Kyra the dragon had wanted, not him, the Reaper.

Jumping off a short ledge, Sebastian crossed an almost invisible catwalk made of stone, being careful each step of the way. Narrow and worn smooth, the path was anything but safe. It led toward the mountain upon which he had found Kyra and the dragon, the trail disappearing into a labyrinth of tunnels within the mountain's core. But like the back of his hand, he knew them well and moved without falter.

Emerging on the opposite side of the mountain, Sebastian found little relief in the air. Strong, assaulting scents of sulfur sailed with the wind, which was torrid and dry. But at least his task was half accomplished. The phoenix, better known as Higgins, was a mere jog away. Sebastian made that jog in a matter of seconds.

Scratching his head, he stared at the massive wings, the length of the body, and wondered, "How am I..." He reached down and lightly brushed one orange feather upon the wing. In a fizzling shimmer the bird became a man, old and wrinkled, but small enough for Sebastian to carry. "There you are, my old friend," he whispered and squeezed Higgins' hand, allowing sorrow to worm its way through his veins.

Gently, and with respect, Sebastian hoisted Higgins into his arms and began the return trek, slowed by the weight pressed upon him. Upon Sebastian's side, where the mark that had born Higgins' name had burned, a funny tingle tickled the skin. The journey, slow but steady, delivered him yet again to the open space at the far back of the carnies' homestead area.

Sebastian stepped free from the wall of fog and paused. The grass squashed beneath his feet, as if recently heavily watered. This time, not only did Zeke await him, but several other carnies, as well. Carnies Sebastian recognized from the dark alley of Mystic's Carnival. Several of them—clowns. Now, there wasn't a smile to be found. An invisible melancholy tent had been pitched over their heads.

"Place him here, son." Zeke tapped a makeshift wooden table with his cane.

Sebastian narrowed his gaze on the timber pushed and piled beneath it. He raised a brow. "What's going on?"

"Just do it. Then step back."

His fellow performers and friends stood in a solemn circle around the table, waiting. Darkness intensified with each passing moment, making the sky appear as if it had been replaced by thick, dripping tar. Sebastian needed to find Kyra before all light was inked out. He moved forward and placed Higgins on the table. One of the clowns draped a sheet over the body and then nudged Sebastian to step back.

Flames burst to life—below the table, on the table, engulfing Higgins.

"From the ashes comes rebirth," said the crowd. Everyone stared at the flames as if waiting to find death is a lie. But death does not lie. Sebastian had learned that long ago. Slowly, one by one, the group dispersed, moving as if in a sleep walk, back toward the carnival.

"Thank you, Sebastian. You may go," Zeke said.

Sebastian peered into the fire. The flames licked and consumed all. He rubbed his forehead. He turned to face Zeke. "This rebirth thing, it's a funeral by fire. You expect it to guide him into the next life?"

"That's the idea."

"I felt..."

"What is it you felt?"

Sebastian looked to his chest, more precisely, his ribs, for the first time since feeling the sting. Higgins' name was there again, only this time it wasn't black. It burned in raw-flesh-pink, and it was fading. *What does that mean?* "Um."

"Oh. I'm sorry, son," Zeke said.

Sebastian's head snapped up. His heart racing. "What for?"

"He's sorry about me, boy."

Sebastian spun around, faced three gentlemen in gray suits and fedoras. It was the middle man with whom he was most familiar. This person from whom he'd run away over a year ago. His father. Sebastian stood perfectly still, not saying a word.

"It's time," the man said. "Time you come with us."

"No." Sebastian took a step back, bumped into a body. "I left." His voice pitched, but it was too late. Reaper hands clamped down on his arms and his father's men dragged him away.

Sebastian yanked and kicked. But three against one, he was outdone. "I have to be somewhere," he yelled.

They didn't listen. They hauled him back into the fog, back toward a reaping hell.

"But...Kyra!"

The fog swallowed them, and they were gone.

11

VISITING HOUR

Kyra

Two weeks had passed since Kyra had been discharged from the hospital. Two weeks since Marcus swept her up and brought her back to his place. Two weeks and he'd let her do little more than hole up, relax, watch television. Playing the overprotective Romeo, he wouldn't let her make a meal or wash a dish. He insisted she stay in, rest, and fully heal. He seemed more worried about her condition than she was.

She was bored.

Kyra rolled over, found the space beside her in the bed cold. She sighed and traced her fingers along the line where Marcus should be. He'd let her sleep in again. He'd been doing that a lot. She honestly did feel better. Mostly. Wished she could get him to believe her. All the sleeping filled the hours. What else was she to do?

A short stack of magazines sat haphazardly on the nightstand, right where she'd left them a day, maybe three days, ago. Picking one from the middle of the pile with a lazy hand, she pulled it free and dragged it across the bed closer to her. It was some variation of entertainment publication. She flipped through the pages, looking at the photographs and showing the articles no interest whatsoever. Everything and everyone pictured looked foreign to her. Nothing sparked the slightest memory.

Abandoning the exercise, she flopped onto her back and stared at the ceiling. Shouldn't she remember something by now? Anything? Her hand dug into the pillow behind her head. Anxiety and frustration boiled inside of her. She felt ready to pop.

Something was missing. Something big.

"Marcus?" she called and sat up to listen to the sounds in the other room.

The rustle of paper responded from the kitchen. "Yeah. What is it?" He sounded distracted.

Kyra leaned forward, extending her neck. "Do I have family?"

There was a pause. Kyra didn't know if she should contribute it to preoccupation or to him looking for the best possible answer.

"You never mentioned any."

She stared at the white sheets. Boring white sheets. Her gaze moved to the wall. Beige. Boring beige wall. The carpet was boring too. Everything about this place was boring. Somehow it didn't feel right. Didn't feel like her. Not that she knew who she was. But her gut told her she'd go wild with color and design.

Do I really belong here?

She dropped flat onto the bed, letting out a huge sigh. "I'm bored. Can we go out?"

"What did I tell you about that? It's in your best interest to stay home and rest."

Kyra rolled her eyes. Reluctantly she rolled out of bed and headed to the bathroom, grabbing Marcus's robe off the bed along the way. She wrapped herself securely in thick, white terry cloth, turned the water on in the shower, and wandered toward the mirror to fix her bedhead state.

If they weren't going to go out, she would pass the time using all his hot water.

Should it worry her she preferred the water at scalding temperatures? Sometimes it hurt, turned her skin a tender pink, but it reminded her she was alive. And being alive meant something when nothing else much did.

Tangles removed from her hair, she slipped under the water's spray. Beneath the cascade of water was the only place in the entire apartment that invoked any memory at all. If you could call it a memory. It was more like a feeling, really. A horrific feeling. She crouched on the floor, her body pulled into a ball and trembling. Hidden within the noise of the shower, she cried.

Why she cried, she did not know. She knew nothing about the origin of the emotion, only that it was hers, the only thing she knew to be honestly and truly hers. And so, she clung to the emotion like a lifeline.

On occasion, hidden within the sorrow and despair, warmth would spread through her chest, radiating from her heart. She yearned for those rare moments, longed for that feeling, even without understand its origin. If Marcus was the source, where had that intense spark gone in his presence?

She sat in the corner of the shower, the hot water doing little to warm her frozen soul, shifting through the emotions, searching for a tangible memory. She felt something just beyond her reach. Something on the brink of recall.

Three knocks came from the other room.

She sat up straight. She almost hadn't heard them, the knocks sounding like mere taps trapped within the pounding of the shower. If it hadn't been for her deep concentration she would have missed the sound all together.

Another knock.

And voices! Had company arrived?

Kyra hadn't moved so fast since, well, since she could recall. Water off, robe on, finger-combed hair, and she was moving through the bedroom, picking up bits and pieces of a conversation. Marcus was talking with someone, a male someone, about her. She didn't give a flying circus tent what Marcus had to say about her behavior, she was crashing that chat.

Kyra stepped out of the bedroom. Marcus was standing at the front door blocking her view of his conversation partner. Neither man had noticed her, yet. The visitor stood outside on the front porch. His foot was placed in the threshold, as if trying to keep Marcus from closing the door.

Why would he do that? she wondered. *What is going on?*

Kyra inched closer, moving forward until she could see their visitor. The stranger didn't look familiar, but he was rather cute. She bit her lip and looked him over. Definitely needed a few minor tweaks in the style department, but she could work with that.

She blinked. *What am I doing? I'm with Marcus.*

"You think so, huh?" the visitor was saying as he placed a firm hand on the doorframe.

"Yeah, I do," Marcus retorted.

A testosterone-driven pissing war. *Fantastic.* At least it was something different. Something not boring.

Kyra coughed into her fist and waited.

The conversation dropped and both men's attention snapped in her direction.

Uncomfortable in her skin wasn't something she was used to feeling, at least not the last few weeks. But now, now discomfort had her in its steely grasp. Maybe she should have slipped into something more modest. The visitor was a total stranger, and the way he looked at her...

Feeling naked beneath his gaze, she pulled the robe's neckline to a tighter close. She glanced down. The terry robe stopped mid-thigh. Too much leg for a total stranger. Far too much leg.

She took a deep breath and exhaled. *Too late now.*

One step for bravery, two steps for curiosity. Kyra moved deeper into the room. "Sorry to interrupt, but it sounded like you might be discussing me." She looked to Marcus and instantly knew by the look on his face she was correct. "You wouldn't be doing that without me, would you?"

"Sorry our conversation disturbed you." Marcus looked from the towel in Kyra's hand to her still dripping wet hair. "Why don't you finish what you were doing? I got this."

The visitor pushed his way into the apartment. “Kyra, you’re all right?”

Kyra’s gaze moved from Marcus to the mystery visitor. Her head spun with so many questions making it practically impossible to pick one out of the jumbled mess.

Marcus’s arm shot out and pulled her into his side before she could protest. It felt more like a show for the other guy’s benefit, than affection for her. Not that she would call him on it. The beast had a temper she preferred not to stir.

“I enjoy a break in the monotony,” she said to Marcus, then looked to *him*. Something deep within her soul wanted to know the stranger standing before her. “I’m good, thanks. Do I know you?”

He blinked and took a shaky step back. “You don’t remember?”

Something warm blossomed in her chest. It spread to her limbs and tingled at her hair follicles. He may have sounded concerned, alarmed, dejected even, but his presence did something to her. More than Marcus’s did. Was the supposed stranger sparking a memory?

“I told you she needed more time. She got a damn skull fracture. Lost a scary amount of blood. And it’s only been a few weeks. She needs more time to heal,” Marcus snapped.

Kyra patted his chest. “Don’t talk about me like I’m not here.” She looked to the visitor in the doorway. “I’m fine. Doc is amazed at my recovery.”

He stared at her, a glazed-over look taking up residency on his face. “I’m sure he is.” A smidgen of hope lit the corner of his eyes. “Do you remember anything? The carnival? Higgins? Zeke? What about dragons?”

The questions made her mind feel like a void. A vast hole of nothing. She shifted, crossed her arms, and scratched her elbow. “Dragons? As in that game people play, or collecting them?”

His eyes darkened, and a deep crease set in across his forehead. It made her wonder how far off she was. “Neither, actually.”

Marcus grunted under his breath. Kyra ignored it. She wasn’t fond of males getting piss-happy over anything they considered territory violations.

Curiosity had her shifting closer to the front door, inch-by-inch, allowing extra air between her and Marcus. There was something about the stranger she wanted to know more about. Or maybe it was what he knew about her. Whatever it was that was reeling her in, she wasn't about to fight it.

"I'm sorry, I never caught your name." She heard it as soon as the words left her mouth. She was flirting. Right in front of Marcus! What was wrong with her?

If she realized what she'd done, there wasn't a doubt in her mind Marcus would be on to it too. She didn't want to look, see his reaction. Her gaze remained glued forward.

The man's face brightened, his lips curling into a relieved smile. Laugh lines creased the edges of his eyes, eyes that sparkled in the most unusual indigo color. Unusual, yes, and yet it seemed the most natural color ever created within the spectrum. He thrust his hand forward in greeting. "Sebastian. Pleasure to make your re-acquaintance."

Sebastian.

She stared at his hand, waiting in the space between them. His name swirled around her, around the recesses of her mind like a story once read and put away. A childhood memory long since forgotten. But she didn't want things to be lost and forgotten. She wanted to remember.

Reaching out to meet his hand, she wondered what his touch would bring. A flood of returning memories? A flush of heat? Excitement, maybe? Her palm met his, but when she raised to shake, he lifted her hand to his lips and softly placed a kiss upon it.

Dragonflies took to chaotic flutters in her belly. In her head.

And then her hand was wrapped securely around herself, held warm and firm by Marcus. "Sebastian was just leaving. Weren't you?" Harsh tones raked through Marcus's voice.

"Actually..." Sebastian looked from Marcus to Kyra. He took a step into the condominium and stopped, a strange look washing over his face. "Marcus?" He narrowed his gaze on Marcus, a dark shadow falling over his fine features.

Marcus turned Kyra to face him and kissed her on the side of the forehead. He appeared distant. His neck and jaw muscles strained. "I really need you to go put more clothes on. I'll be there in a minute." He directed her toward the bedroom.

Her feet carried her a couple of steps before stumbling to a stop, the ground covered by the momentum of his nudge. Feeling bold and courageous, she planted her feet, crossed her arms, and firmed her jam. "No. I'd prefer to stay."

Marcus turned and walked toward her. "Kyra, what did we talk about?"

Her hand jumped to her neckline, searched and found what she was looking for. Like a metronome marking a beat, her hand ran up and down along the hefty cord around her neck, tugging at the ancient tooth held secure at center point. Every time she felt the slightest bit nervous, she turned to the cord and tooth. Even now she felt it working its magic to calm her.

"Kyra?" Marcus asked again, grabbed her wrist, and nudged her back toward the bedroom.

Her eyes fluttered, and she looked up at him. For a moment, her emotions had been so overwhelming, she'd gotten caught up in the storm and failed to respond. He now looked upon her with eyes softening, warming to deep pools of blue. They promised security and affection. Complete adoration.

She wanted to argue. Wanted to be reckless and unruly, but something held her back.

The ancient tooth hanging at her neck hummed ever so slightly beneath her touch. It sent tiny waves of calm through her chest and a flood of serenity throughout her entire body. She took a slow breath and allowed Marcus to move her back several more steps. She didn't fight him, even though she wanted to on some level.

"Why are you trying to get rid of me?" Her face reddened and the muscles along her jawline twitched, yet she continued to take step after step backwards.

"It's not like that," Marcus said, warming the sides of Kyra's arm.

"I'm looking out for you." His eyes burned with power and grit and determination.

Kyra could feel her eyes rolling. She was so sick of hearing those words. *I'm looking out for you.*

"Why don't you let her stay?" Sebastian said from the threshold. He held his hands up, as if pushing against an invisible wall. Lines creased his forehead as if the effort exerted from pressing the air was exhausting. He threw his shoulder against nothing and bounced back.

Marcus shot Sebastian a hostile glare. "Why don't you stay out of this conversation?"

Three more steps, nearly to the bedroom. She'd allowed him to nudge her right out of the room, right out of her free will. How had he done it? She didn't want to go, she wanted to stay. "Stop looking out for me," Kyra mumbled, staring at her feet, avoiding eye contact with Marcus.

At the bedroom doorway, she paused and looked at Sebastian. "I'm really sorry. If we were friends, I hope I remember someday soon." She meant every word and then some. She stepped into the bedroom and slammed the door.

The control that had moved her to the room snapped with the slam of the door. Relief washed over her. Sometimes Marcus could have the strangest effect on her. This was one of those times. She wasn't too keen on this aspect of their relationship. *How embarrassing*. She wanted to hate him, but couldn't. Why couldn't she?

She leaned against the door and slid to the floor. Their voices in the other room rose in anger. The sound hurt her ears. Not physically, but mentally and emotionally and psychologically. Everything about the situation was wrong. The knots in her gut knew it to be true.

She felt like a caged animal—a damn prisoner—unable to come and go as she pleased. If Sebastian knew her, why wasn't he taking her away from this place? Stupid pissing contest.

She paced the room. Left. Then right. Then left again.

Sebastian standing at their front door. Sebastian with his hands pressed against the air.

She caught her breath.

"What does it mean?"

Rage burned a warpath through her soul. So much commotion bombarded her. She was ready to implode.

She grabbed the first thing her hands managed to wrap around, tossed it across the room. Magazines flew in multiple directions, separate papers and pieces landing on the bed, the floor, the nightstands, anything. One flopped at her feet. A picture of large circus tents screamed, "Look at me!"

The ridiculous photo exercise finally had her attention. She lifted the picture with the utmost care. Sebastian had mentioned a carnival. That didn't set off any magic discovery chime in her head. Cheap concessions, fly-by-night rides, rigged-to-rape-you games. Nope. She had nothing. But this... She held the tiny, two-dimensional tent in her hand and wished she understood the significance.

The rage dissipated. Kyra sat at the edge of the bed and studied the picture. Something about it wasn't quite right, but it was close. Close enough that it stirred something in her. Was she feeling homesick?

Marcus stepped into the room. "Sorry about that." He heaved a heavy sigh and began to circle the bed toward Kyra.

Without a word, Kyra stashed the picture in the top drawer of her nightstand and shifted to look at him. "Why didn't you let me talk to him? He might have clues to my past that could be useful." Her hands squeezed the edge of the bed until her knuckles protested with pain.

Marcus dropped to his knees in front of her and clamped his hands firmly upon her upper arms. "I thought you trusted me."

Indecision wavered, shook her like a tree branch, and she could no longer see a clear path. "I do," she said, voice soft and lacking solid conviction. As the words left her lips they tasted bitter, laced with lies.

His hands slid up to her shoulders and began to rub. As he rubbed, he moved onto the bed beside her. "You're so tense."

She stared at the window blinds on the wall next to her. Slivers of light filtered through. "It's been a strange morning."

His hands worked magic, kneading her stiff joints and muscles. She closed her eyes and allowed her imagination to whisk her away. She no longer saw herself sitting in Marcus's boring condominium, but pictured herself on a bed made of a dozen soft pillows, all of them a rainbow of intense hue. In every direction, circus tents and spinning rides constantly morphed in color. Wherever she looked there were lights and twinkling stars and a forever deep midnight sky.

She lay among the pillows and marveled at her imagination. Was it a clue to who she used to be? Who she should be?

Marcus kissed the curve of her neck and with the skill of a true ladies' man, ran his hand along her collarbone. Kyra's mind raced. Her happy place, receding. Was she going to allow him this? After what had just...

Marcus's hand rolled over the ancient tooth Kyra wore around her neck. Heat flushed her system; a trickle of sweat dripped down the side of her brow. The stars twinkled above her head once again. A dozen misshapen pillows of different colors and sizes lay beneath her, and the vibrant backdrop of Fun Zones and circus life surrounded her. It was the night's soundtrack. Jubilant chatter, laughter, and screams of delight.

She wasn't fool enough to believe the mirage, the illusion, but she knew it was where she belonged. Wherever *it* was. She scorched the image to her memory.

Marcus rolled over, his hands exploring her cheek, her elbow, the side of her thigh. It was not Marcus she saw at her side, but the questioning stranger named Sebastian. She made no move, for fear of losing her connection to the magic. Until...Marcus broke the rule. His hand traveled out of bounds.

Kyra tensed, pulled back, and Marcus looked up.

Only, it was Sebastian Kyra saw. Yet she knew it couldn't be Sebastian. She knew that fact; logically, knew that fact. She was seeing Sebastian just like she was seeing the colors and lights and carnival rides.

Her body relaxed, melted, and accepted the illusion. She found it *euphoric* to lie with Sebastian beneath the stars.

Her mind might not remember Sebastian, but her heart clearly knew him.

Had quite possibly always known him.

Lost in her illusion, Kyra snuggled beside Sebastian, her body melded into his comforting embrace. The circus dissolved, turned to soft twinkling lights, twirling crystals, and warm, plush pillows.

I will find you, she imagined whispering the words in Sebastian's ear. *I swear it.*

12

DRAGON LIGHT

Marcus

Marcus rolled over on the bed and fluffed the pillow behind his head. Tonight, had been satisfying, even without sex. He turned and studied Kyra, let his finger glide along her collar bone. He liked that she smelled of him. "You alright?" he probed.

She gazed at the ceiling, a dreamy look on her face. "Mmm." It was all she had to say.

Her chilled skin warmed when his finger notched under her chin, turning her gaze to meet his and aligning their lips. His lips brushed against hers. She was inviting and vulnerable and he savored the moment.

Twisting to her side, her hands gliding like silk on butter along the outline of his arm, heading straight for his weakness, his more amiable, more forthcoming zone, the too-often-neglected patch beneath the ear.

Marcus's shoulders arced; he closed his eyes and sighed at her touch.

The phone rang. The sound came from the kitchen, where Marcus had left his cellphone sitting on the counter.

"Crap," he grumbled. He eased away from her, his attention already directed to the other room.

Kyra stared at him, a blank expression on her face. Marcus buttoned his shirt and leaned back over the bed. "You good?"

She simply nodded.

He kissed her forehead. "I promise it will only be a minute. You are my priority." He took a moment to gaze over her. "You're sure you're okay?"

Kyra nodded again, still silent.

Marcus breezed through the kitchen, picked up his phone, and continued moving toward the glass doors at the far end. He spared a glance at the number before stepping out onto the balcony and answering the call.

"Not the best time. I need to keep it short." He leaned over the railing and glanced at the other balconies to verify privacy.

"Is the girl still with you? The enchantment continuing to work?" the caller asked.

"Yeah, she's here. She doesn't remember anything."

A clucking of the tongue sounded on the other end of the line, and Marcus fell silent, waiting and listening.

"I told you to keep her isolated."

"I know. I have." Irritation began to claw at the back of his neck.

"Aw...but I heard you had a visitor. A visitor to whom she spoke." The caller's voice peaked.

"Yeah, so? I handled it. I can handle her." Red bled across Marcus' vision, and his temples throbbed. He hated the mention of Sebastian. Anything remotely involving the carnie boy gave Marcus a headache. He clenched his teeth.

"So you think, but tonight's visitor was no ordinary one. He is the single strongest link to the girl's memories. The most potent attachment she has made. If anything were to tip the scales and slip thoughts and images into her recall, it would be him."

Volcanic heat exploded through Marcus' veins, racing up his neck and across his face.

"It is most likely the thought of him that keeps her content in your presence...for now."

"The thought of him?" Marcus balked. "What kind of blasted charm did you put on that darn tooth anyway?"

"A simple complacency spell. If she is faced with something that causes her discomfort, her mind's eye will swap that for something that pleases her. So, if she looks at you and doesn't like what she sees, she will see the boy instead." The words ended with an almost inaudible chortle.

"No. No. No." His hand squeezed the phone with an anger infused ferocity. The phone's screen cracked with a soft *plink*. Marcus ignored it. "You get over here tonight, and fix it. Fix it now. Don't you realize how incredibly stupid that was? It could destroy everything! No wonder she was..." He fell silent. "Never mind."

Long, winded breaths whispered across the line, the caller awaiting a cue from Marcus. But Marcus was in no hurry to voice his composing thought. He'd been overcome with a wave of dominance. He was untouchable.

Moving to the corner, he dropped down, removed an old vent cover on the balcony's side wall, reached inside, and pulled out a large jar. Holding it before him, he stared at it with longing set deep in his soul. "What's important is I got what I wanted. All we need to do now is make it truly mine." Orange and gold sparks flickered in the jar, a swirl of blue.

"As we shall. In due time. We must first collect the remaining ingredients and decide upon a location."

Marcus laughed. "Right. Well, let's not waste time. Let's get it figured out." He hung up and set the phone down. Kalrapura snarled at him through the glass. Her long, serpent body twisted around and around, fully agitated in her tightly confined prison. Pointing his finger at the dragon, Marcus whispered, "You should play nice. We're going to get to know each other a whole lot better real soon."

The dragon hissed and filled the jar with fire. Marcus smirked and teased the dragon with a tap, tap, tapping of the glass before he placed Kalrapura back in her hiding place. He slipped back into the apartment quiet as a skilled hunter. Kyra waited for him in the bed, curled comfortably under the covers.

He slid into the empty space beside her, his hands slipping around her silky pajamas in one smooth motion. Until the magic of the pendant got fixed, that would be all he would allow. No way would she be seeing another man in his place should they get intimate. Sebastian was staying out of his bedroom. Kyra was his.

PART TWO
THE REAPER

REAP NOT THE DRAGON

"'Tis Death's Park, where he breeds life to feed him. Cries of pain are music for his banquet."

~ George Eliot

13
WRECKED

Sebastian

Death was always the same. Not the people or the place or the circumstance. That changed from one stop to the next. Each one unique in its own special way. But Sebastian had come to understand his calling in the past few weeks and now recognized the signs for what they were. Always present. Always pulling. And always overwhelming with the constant stench of death. His own personal calling card.

Sebastian had lost count of the number of souls he'd helped cross over since embracing his Reaper half. He'd fought his destiny. Feared being an icon of death. A messenger of doom. All to help Kyra escape Purgatory. For her, he'd do it again in a fluttered heartbeat. She was more than his best friend. He'd come to crave everything she brought to their relationship. Even the rage of her dragon.

Things were different now, though. He understood a Reaper's value.

And Kyra...well, she didn't remember him. At all. Of course, he would change that. Very soon. First, he had to get past Marcus's damn barrier spell. Sebastian clenched his fist and imagined it slamming into Marcus's jawline.

Damn Marcus for taking Kyra.

Damn him for keeping her from Sebastian.

And damn him for escaping the Reaper.

Sebastian stood beside his second stop of the day. If he had a choice, he'd be at Marcus's door right now, but the opportunity to get away from his father's prying eyes had yet to present itself. So, he tried to behave like any young trainee and assessed the scene. The asphalt spread before him, a dark and crumbled highway to the unknown—at least, unknown to most who found themselves in need of Sebastian's services. He knew exactly where it led.

An empty aluminum can lay at his feet. With slow and deliberate intention, he knelt down and retrieved the evidence. Beer. Sunlight reflected off its silver surface as he spun it with his fingers, then shoved it at the boy standing before him. Right into his hands. Hands covered with blood.

"Think that last drink was a good idea?" Sebastian cocked his head, indicating the mangled mass of metal sitting on the edge of the road. Steam poured out from under the crushed hood.

With an air of indifference, the boy peered from the crumpled can over at the crash site, before looking back at Sebastian. The boy's face resembled an emotionless wax dummy's. He shrugged. "Ehh. Sure, the car is a loss, but I have insurance, and look at me! Not a scratch. Pretty awesome. Right, dude?" He casually brushed the dirt from his shirt. "What the...?" He swatted harder, trying to remove the foreign object stuck to the front of him.

Sebastian knew it was wrong to feel the way he did, but he loved when this happened. A slow, deliberate grin spread across his lips. "That's my claim ticket, Lance." He soaked up pleasure in the taunting, the boy's name lingering on his tongue, dragging out slow and deliberate.

A tarot card clung to the fabric of the boy's shirt like a second skin—a dancing skeleton prancing across his chest. Sebastian watched blatant confusion and fear spread across the boy's face.

Deep valleys curved the flesh across Lance's forehead. "Hey man. Do I know you? How do you know my name?" His voice wavered.

"Think you made it out unscathed? You might want to take a closer look." Sebastian motioned to the wreckage across the road.

Lance flinched at Sebastian's words. He whirled around, faced the ruin, and darted forward. Sebastian knew he rushed for proof, proof of the Reaper's lies. There were always types like Lance. Never trusting. Always needing to see for themselves. There was no denying the moment Lance discovered the truth about his misguided assumption. The quickened pulse, the bulging eyes, the sudden intake of breath—something Lance hadn't yet discovered he no longer needed.

Crumpled behind the wheel in the driver's seat slumped an exact duplicate of the teenager standing near Sebastian. Only the one in the car looked like a broken doll, staring into a void. He was nothing but an empty shell, left vacant by the confused, departed soul.

"But—I—Sophie—" Lance stammered.

"Yes." The word dripped like castor oil from Sebastian's lips as he stepped behind the addled soul. He dropped his fingers upon the boy's shoulder in one quick tap before trailing them down his upper back.

Lance broke into a dance of shivers and shudders and twitches. A mask of dread slipped in, contorting his face and replacing his once-handsome features. A small cry escaped. He turned, glued his gaze on Sebastian, an overwhelming plea swimming in his eyes. "What did you—?"

But it was already too late.

He was sinking, melting down through the ground. Pulled by long, dark, shadowy arms, reaching and grabbing and dragging him under.

Sebastian watched until the boy was no more, knowing his destination was hot and horrific. Excruciatingly torturous. With Lance gone, Sebastian breathed deep, relief blooming in the knowledge the worst was done. He crossed the road, circled the battered car, and approached the passenger side. There she waited, as if in limbo, completely unaware. He placed his hand upon the open window with the tender touch of a grief counselor. The trigger. Her eyes popped open and her head snapped up.

The girl was still dressed in her high school cheerleading uniform and wore Lance's senior ring on a chain around her neck. "Where am I? What happened?" Her voice cracked, rough and dry, from a throat in need of water.

Sebastian opened the car door and laid his palm out before her, awaiting her hand, and offering to help her from the vehicle. "Come. Let me help you."

Her gaze danced over him, then over the car's interior again. "Where's Lance?"

Sebastian knelt, dropping down to the car's front seat level so they could meet eye to eye. "Don't worry about Lance. Let's take care of you. Will you allow me to help you, Sophie?"

Sophie sucked in a deep breath. Her frail body teetered backwards before slowly swaying upright. Slipping her hand into Sebastian's palm, she stood, stepped away from the car, and stared at her Reaper. Her eyes widened. "Your aura, it's so..."

Sebastian warmed her hand in his and looked away.

She tilted her head. "You don't want to know. Do you?"

Fact was, he didn't. He feared the knowing. Feared what his true aura would say about him. As long as he was ignorant of the truth, he could avoid admitting ugly truisms. "You can tell me if you want to," he said, "but it won't do me any good. I'm fated to what I am. I doubt the color of my aura will make a difference one way or the other." He looked past her, and his shoulders sagged. "Are you ready?"

Sophie followed his gaze, her own falling on the broken sight behind them. "Oh!" She turned back, allowed Sebastian to pull her away, away from the wreckage. "I didn't make it, did I?" Her voice was weak and tearful.

Sebastian understood. She didn't want to see the mangled remains in the car. In the last few weeks, he'd heard the request many times. They rarely wanted to know, usually preferred to remember themselves as they'd been before, not how they'd ended up. He agreed it was for the best.

"I'm sorry, Sophie." He glanced at her from beneath a fall of dark hair. "Do you need some time to let it sink in?"

Her eyes glazed over and she stared into the distance. "No." As if chilled, she crossed her arms and hugged herself. Sebastian supposed it was an attempt at self-comfort. "My parents," she whispered.

He brushed his hand back through his hair, shifted his weight. "It'll be hard, but they'll be all right. Trust me. If you'd like, I'll have someone check on them."

Sophie glanced up, her eyes bright with tears. "Would *you* do that?"

He jerked back. "Me?" He searched her face, looking for any doubt, but found none. "If that is what you really want, I will."

Sophie nodded. "It is. Thank you."

Sunlight bled through the trees lining the roadside, and Sophie's blonde hair reflected the light in ribbons of gold. *It's a shame she moved on so young, so senselessly*, thought Sebastian, but it was only his job to make the transition as painless as possible. He didn't get to choose who or where or when.

He pushed her hair away from her face and hooked it behind her ear. The action reminded him of Kyra. How many times he had wanted to brush back her wild red hair. Bravery had never backed him long enough to make that move, and now—

He shoved his personal baggage aside and focused on Sophie. "Are you ready?" he asked again.

She blinked and responded with a nod. It was a shaky nod. One that wasn't sure of its true answer, yet wanted to be.

Warmth spread across Sebastian's skin and the edges of his lips curled up into a smile. "Don't be afraid. It's a far better place you go. Makes this place look like detention."

Sophie's face glowed, garnished with a genuine smile and silent laughter. Sebastian smiled, too, outwardly if not committed inwardly. His heart warmed, taking pleasure in the small moments of his quotidian. Sebastian let his hand drop to her elbow. "In all seriousness, you've led a good life, Sophie. You have nothing to fear." He looked over her shoulder to a spot beyond human visibility.

The turn of his body, the pull of his arm, all signaled Sophie to follow his lead. Extraordinary light seeped through the opening, expanding in broad beams of intense emotion and illumination. It pushed forward and out, opening like no other door. Each time Sebastian lived the experience with someone, the crossing, their door, and what waited beyond was unique. Fingers of warmth, acceptance, and love slipped through the gateway, swirling and winding their way toward Sophie. Dazzling ambassadors to take her home.

Through the opening, Sebastian caught glimpses of the new world to which she was destined. One bathed in unimaginable beauty. So intense was the sight, he could barely look upon it. But it was not meant for him. It was never meant for him. This invitation was for Sophie and Sophie alone. Sebastian raised his hand to shield his eyes.

Verse swept through the gap, melodious words wrapping around Sophie, pulling on her like a magnet. Sebastian felt it. Felt the tenor in the music and felt her emotion. He felt it all. All part of his supernatural gift, the pros and cons of being a Reaper. He was only a Minor Reaper, but he was still bestowed with the gifts and abilities to guide his clients. His father preferred to refer to the clients as marks. Sebastian never thought of the individuals he helped that way. With some exceptions, such as Lance.

Sebastian felt the fervor flowing from the gate, urging Sophie onward. "You should go. You'll be fulfilled there."

When Sophie turned and looked back, she glowed the most brilliant color of rose. She threw her arms around him and hugged him tight. "My parents?" she asked, pulling back.

"Consider it done."

"Thank you. You're a good man." She turned to leave, but paused after two steps and looked over her shoulder. "I didn't get your name."

Sebastian fought a grin and looked down. He casually pointed to the bottom edge of her skirt. "It's Sebastian, and it's been a pleasure."

She glanced down and saw the tarot card plastered an inch above her hemline. "Is that your card? Will I find your number scribbled on it somewhere?"

Sebastian laughed. "You should be so lucky."

"You can't blame a girl for trying to get to know her savior."

His face drooped, body chilled to dry ice temperature. He'd dragged this one out too long. A savior? He was anything but. Sophie needed to go—leave—move on. With the sweep of an arm, he motioned for her to start. She sighed, but didn't argue. In slow, forever steps, she moved forward as Sebastian had suggested, on through the door and into the brilliance of the light beyond. Exceptional radiance, something he'd never know, flowed all around her, painting her the illusion of the perfect angel.

Three steps in, her footing faltered. She stopped and called back, "Maybe I'll see you again...in your next life?"

Sebastian's lips twisted into a smirk. "Nice thought. Highly unlikely. There's no place for my kind where you're going." He watched her face drop and knew it was time to terminate the conversation. "Goodbye, Sophie." He turned and walked away.

Circling the heap of twisted metal, Sebastian crossed the road. He walked directly to the man waiting where the asphalt met dirt. Waiting and watching. Tall and lean, the man stood supporting his weight against the side of a telephone pole. His hands were shoved deep into the pants pockets of his gray wool suit. Only one button was done on his jacket, and he wore his hat on a slight tilt. A slap-n-stick name tag clung to the breast pocket of his jacket. Bold red letters ran across the top saying *Hi! My name is*. Scribbled beneath that in black was the name *Mr. Smith*. Sebastian thought the tag and the man wearing it—his father, actually named Mortifier—were a grim joke. Nevertheless, the air vibrated around him, hinting to his importance.

He grinned at Sebastian. "Awfully sweet on that one. Spent far too much time."

Sebastian huffed. "You're entitled to your opinion. I see nothing wrong in treating them with a little kindness and respect." He glanced back at the gateway. Sophie was barely visible; the light practically enveloped her. *As it should*, he thought. That was her home now. The doorway flashed with unmeasurable luminosity, collapsing the window inward, closing off the passageway.

Sebastian turned back toward the man in the suit. Mortifier stood straighter, fixed his jacket as he regarded Sebastian. "I've been doing this a lot longer than you. You would be wise to heed me every now and then."

"I'll keep that under advisement...*Dad.*"

Mortifier laughed. "You do have a spark about you. Reminds me of someone." His hand flipped, exaggerating his meaning. It was unnecessary. Sebastian knew he'd meant himself.

His father punched a finger toward the middle of the street. The slightest of marks was now visible where the boy had descended. It left a scar upon the asphalt for all to see. Sebastian looked, but said not a word.

Mortifier circled around, placing himself between the site and Sebastian. "What did you do to him, before you sent him off? You added something to that unique cocktail of yours, didn't you?"

Sebastian's gaze slowly raised to meet the superior Grim Reaper's, his jaw tight. "I simply sent him where he was meant to go. You saw the kind of life he led."

Something gleamed in his father's eyes as he stared down at Sebastian. "Yes, that I know. But you did something else. Tell me."

Sebastian looked away, his face falling like a shadow slipping in at sundown. He didn't want his father to see his shame. Not now. Maybe not ever. He wouldn't understand. Mortifier felt fine sending souls to Hell. Ending life on the spot. Not Sebastian. And what he had done was worse. Not only had Sebastian tortured the man without reason, he'd crossed the line, violated the guy's privacy. Digging into people's secret thoughts and turning what he'd found against them was wrong. He hated himself for it.

"I gave the guy a nightmare," he said. "Plucked his most isolated fear and set it free to ravage his mind. I'm not proud, okay?"

Deep, dark, deranged laughter burst from Mortifier's lungs. It filled the air around them, and the sound of glass crackling responded from the wreck across the road.

"Enough! Stop it," Sebastian demanded.

His father, now quiet, took on a nefarious, loaded grin. "It's quite marvelous. Don't you see? You are exactly as I had hoped." He reached out to touch Sebastian, only to have Sebastian smack his hand away.

Sebastian notched his fists on his hips and narrowed his eyes, staring at his father. "All I can see is that you made me into a freak. A freak that was never meant to be." He raked his hand through his hair, took a deep breath. "I don't fit in anywhere. And I never will. Mom doesn't want me because of what I am. And you want me for all the wrong reasons." He turned in a slow circle and let his hand fall. It slapped across the front of his leg. "Don't think I'm here for some father-son bonding session. That couldn't be further from the truth." Sebastian stepped back onto the road. "Now if you'll excuse me, I have somewhere I need to be. Made a promise to a girl."

Mortifier took a step after him. "Best not be the dragon. You were supposed to take her. You know that, boy. She was your mark." His voice was stern, tinted with discontent.

Sebastian's back and shoulders tensed. He whipped back to face his father. "Her name is Kyra, and no one's reaping her, so back off." He pushed up his sleeves.

Sharp pain cut through Sebastian's calves and kneecaps, crippling him and dropping him to the ground. Every pebble pressing into his palms symbolized another minute, another day slipping between him and Kyra. Too much time had already been lost in finding the magic necessary to break Marcus's barrier.

Sebastian grated his teeth and, with great force, pushed himself up. Standing as if gravity willed him flat on his belly. "Why in Death's name did you do that?" He practically spat the words at his father.

Mortifier studied his nails. "Just a reminder of who the boss is around here. Stay out of dragon business, boy. And stay away from *her*. It's not time."

Sebastian brushed the dirt from his hands. "When will it be time? According to you, the time is never right." His father, this whole training process, was infuriating. Sebastian rubbed his forehead. "You said two hundred souls would satisfy my initiation requirement. That was the last one—two hundred exactly. I'm done. Free to go. You don't get to tell me what I can and can't do anymore."

Mortifier shook his finger. "Not so fast."

Sebastian's shoulders slumped, and his hands hooked low on his hips. "What now?"

"You will have more freedom now, but that doesn't mean you're not on probation. You're still a Reaper. You must still reap, or back under supervision you will go. Abuse your freedom, and back under supervision you will go. Mess where you don't belong..." His father assessed Sebastian. "Understand me?"

"I get it. I don't like it, but I get it." Sebastian turned, put his father behind him, and didn't look back. He'd made a promise, and he wasn't one to break a promise. Not even to a girl he'd never met before today.

He heaved a heavy breath. *How much trouble can a bunch of Reapers swing down on me if I follow my own path to Kyra?*

"You're not ready, boy," Mortifier called behind him.

Putting one foot in front of the other, Sebastian trudged down the empty road, the next town his destination—home to Sophie's parents and as it so happened, Marcus Blackall.

14

COFFEE

Sebastian

Sebastian walked into town with two thoughts on his mind: defying his father and finding Sophie's parents. He started with the simple one first—Sophie's parents. It was a relatively easy assignment for a Reaper. When you deal in death, you tend to get a built-in tracking system. Like a GPS for souls. The walk took longer than expected. Night had turned into morning. Cars now motored down the streets and people moved along the sidewalks, starting their day. Sebastian stood outside a five-story apartment building, looking up.

Just great, he thought and rubbed the back of his neck. People living in tight quarters. Too many bodies, too little space. Harder to pinpoint exact locations without walking the halls, getting close. Something he wasn't looking forward to doing. All the confined emotions would be insufferable. He hated his nobility, keeping a promise under such conditions. Through the double glass doors at the front, he could see a handful of mothers sitting around chatting while their children played in the lobby. *Double great.*

A giant yawn bound from his body and he stretched his arms wide. Sleep had evaded him lately, leaving him tired and cranky, hardly feeling up to the chore asked. An image of Kyra wrapped in nothing more than a robe standing beside Marcus flashed through his memory. It hit him fast. Dagger to the heart. He hated that day. The day she no longer remembered him, their friendship, or the kiss they had shared. The day she chose Marcus over their forgotten friendship.

He closed his eyes and rubbed his temples. This thing with Kyra—he wasn't going to let go, but couldn't let it consume him, either.

Stupid Reaper rules—damn them to hell. And Marcus, too. He could burn and take his infuriating magical barrier with him.

Taking a deep breath and exhaling slowly, Sebastian gazed down the block to the bustling coffeehouse. A cup of hot java to get the synapses firing, that's what he needed. Help focus his thoughts and get him back on his game. Could he suffer the coffee-seeking crowd in his less-than-ideal condition? He was willing to give it a try. Likely to be less people in the coffeehouse than in the building housing Sophie's parents.

He moved to the center of the sidewalk and headed down the street. When he hit the alleyway at the edge of the apartment building, he paused, looked down the path. Someone stepped out of a door several feet away. There must be another entrance into the building there—a quieter one. The side door off the alley could be used to get to Sophie's parents. It was unlikely mothers with little ones populated both entryways. He would try the side door later.

Content with the plan, his thoughts returned to caffeine, and his stride moved straight toward the small storefront with the elaborate Java Time sign hanging in the front. An odd familiarity floated over the place. The shop sign drew his gaze like a corpse in the middle of Sunday Mass. The sign showed time slipping down the front in the form of a melted clock face. Coffee poured from a tipped pot jetting out of the used brick wall. In a stream of neon lights, the liquid flowed over the clock and into a chipped cup braced above the entrance.

The sight birthed a déjà vu feeling. The kind bound to happen in his vocation. He'd been so many places, seen so many things, in order to help the departed move on. He was likely to run into some of the same situations and things occasionally. Then there were the memories. So many memories. Passing through the air, through the ether, through him, as his clients transitioned. Occasionally he would confuse which memories were his and which were not.

The door handle was warm to the touch, many hands having already used it this morning. He pulled open the door and stepped into the comfortable atmosphere the shop provided.

Within, people huddled in tight little groups. They sat at tables and sofa and chair groupings alike. Burning in a small hearth at the back corner was a fake crackling fire. The walls closed in with an exuberant collage of chipped and mismatched tea and coffee cups and saucers. Burnt yellow paint washed the walls, while thick weaved rugs softened bare spaces beneath rich wood furniture.

Sebastian was third in line, and although he didn't need to, he studied the menu. They didn't have what he needed, but he knew what he wanted. Straight black coffee. It would do. It had to. If only he could nab a vial of Talia's *Spiritual Peace* from the cupboard back in his trailer at the carnival. A splash of that in his coffee, and all these emotions and memories would cease to bother. He rubbed at his forehead, wished for silence—internal silence.

The feeling he'd seen this coffee shop before continued to nag at him. He glanced at the fireplace. Hmm, pretty damn sure he'd never been here before. Then the memory dawned. He'd looked through the front window on his way to find Kyra *that* morning, the morning she'd forgotten him. It had been a brief glimpse, but that was all he'd needed to imprint the image. He remembered.

He was minutes away from Marcus's condo. His chest heaved, inner conflict solidifying. The moment he'd walked into town, he should have recognized the tells. He'd known he was close, but had no idea how close. He'd been too focused on Sophie's parents. Now all he could think about was Kyra. He missed her, worried about her, and should have checked on her sooner. But he hadn't had the answers then. The answers that would get him past Marcus's doorway and the magical barrier the jerk had somehow erected. Now he'd lost an entire month to the search and his father's demands. Sebastian clutched at the side of his leg. The thought of Kyra with Marcus...

Imagery started to flicker through his mind. He tried to stop it short. Didn't want to go there. Didn't want to think about Marcus touching her, kissing her. His chest tightened and his heart *ker-thumped*. He needed to calm down. The tips of his fingers had begun to burn with anger. All the emotion welling inside had him wanting to reap, collect Marcus's soul. He should have. Should have collected it the first day he saw Marcus, when he'd been called to complete that very task. Had he done his job correctly, none of this would have happened.

"Dammit, Kyra." He ground his teeth and muttered the words under his breath. As much as he didn't want to blame her, part of him did. It was her heroics that had gotten them here. If only she hadn't saved Marcus that day.

If only.

So many if-onlys loomed in their past. He dragged his fingers through his hair, knocking the hood of his jacket back. He didn't care. Felt no need to hide here.

Soon he would put this behind them. He had what he needed now. Marcus could no longer keep him out. His hand slipped into his pocket, wrapped around the gift from Talia. The small charm in his pocket would get him through the doorway at Marcus's. Talia had guaranteed it.

Stepping to the front of the line, Sebastian placed his order and moved to the side to collect his coffee. Ready immediately, a young man handed him an open-topped cup and moved away, busy with other preparations. Sebastian reached around to grab a lid. After snapping it in place, he turned to leave, only to smack right into another body. "Oh, hell. I'm sorry." Sebastian wiped the coffee from his jacket and looked up. Involuntarily, he sucked in his breath. Kyra stood in front of him, an innocent twitch of a smile gracing her face.

He blinked hard. She still stood before him. Was it true? Marcus had let her out of the house?

She reached past him to the counter and grabbed a handful of napkins. "Don't be sorry. It was completely my fault." Separating one napkin from the pile, she dabbed at the coffee spill on his hand.

A warm tingle raced through Sebastian's body. He knew he had to say or do the right thing to hold the moment and make it count. Problem was, he had no idea what the right thing was. "I'm the one that turned in to you. Did I get you? With my coffee, I mean?"

Kyra batted her eyelashes and her gaze traveled across Sebastian's features. "I think I escaped unscathed. You're lucky." She laughed.

Sebastian raised a brow. "No doubt." He didn't know what to think of this version of Kyra. Without her memories, she'd been molded into a completely different person. Did Marcus have the power to make her into anyone he wanted? If he successfully rewrote her, what would happen to the girl Sebastian had known, and—? He couldn't finish the thought. His body began to burn again. Burn with desire to tear Marcus to pieces.

"I have a confession to make," Kyra said. Sebastian blinked and returned his focus to her. "I came over here because I saw you."

Sebastian's blood cooled, and his muscles eased. "You walked over to see me?"

Her face lit up, and it looked like she was trying to hide embarrassment. "Well, yeah. You're the guy who came to my home that day, aren't you? The one who knew me before?"

Sebastian's heart beat heavily in anticipation of where their conversation might lead. He could only imagine positive things. Still, he'd take it slow, be cautious. "Yes. I came looking for you. I was told, not so politely, to leave you alone."

White lips pressed firmly together, and Kyra released the breath she'd been holding, spewing a minute trail of dragon smoke from her nostrils, so small it was barely noticeable. Sebastian squinted at the curious sight. He watched Kyra cough, her hand reaching to cover her mouth, then reaching toward the counter to grab a napkin she used to blow her nose.

"Excuse me," she said, discarding the napkin in the trash. "I'm really sorry about that." She reached out, letting her fingertips graze the top of his hand, setting off a chain reaction. His blood vessels snapped and sizzled with pure adrenaline, shaken with excitement. "First, I caused your drink to splatter, then I coughed in your face." She blushed. "Would you have coffee with me? You aren't in a hurry, are you?"

Sebastian couldn't recall where he'd needed to be. Not with Kyra asking him to stay. Nothing was more important than solving the issue of his fervid dragon girl. Although, he suspected she wouldn't think of herself as anything needing to be fixed, figured, or solved. Not this new version she'd become. "Nowhere to be. I'm all yours."

"Great! I'm just going to get my coffee. Why don't you grab us a table?"

While Kyra wandered to the back of the line, Sebastian found a table near the wannabe fireplace. It crackled and popped, similar to the real thing, without giving off a lick of heat. Sebastian's instincts told him to sit facing the door. Always on guard, he watched his exits, covered his back at all times. Except this time. This time he sat facing the register and watched Kyra. In his world, it had been forever and a week since he'd seen her. In reality, it had only been a month, if that. All he wanted to do was absorb every angle, every fiber that was her. She didn't turn, didn't look back. Not until her order was complete. She was playing it cool. Or maybe she didn't care as much as he liked to think. He couldn't be sure. While she waited to the side for her coffee, she chanced a quick glance, and that was something, enough to build hope.

Sebastian liked to think the power of old Higgins' sacrifice was working to their benefit. Working to help bring Sebastian and Kyra back together after the ordeal in Purgatory. Sebastian owed him big time for all he'd done. They both did. Someday Kyra would remember, and when that day came, she would be gutted with guilt. She'd even missed the old bird's funeral.

He took a sip of his coffee and leaned back, stretching out his legs and crossing them at the ankles. Settling deeper into his seat, he took in the full view. Kyra looked good, healthier than she probably had in a while. At least Marcus was taking care of her physically. Sebastian jerked and shook the unwelcome imagery that had begun to play in his head.

"Do I have something on me?"

Sebastian looked up at Kyra. He could feel the tension creasing in his brow and at the corners of his eyes.

"You were staring at my outfit. Did I spill something on it?" Kyra looked down to her white pants in search of anything out of the ordinary.

"I was just taking in the change. That's all."

Kyra set down her coffee and a small plate of fruit and took a seat. She sighed, glanced over her attire, and casually slid the plate between them. "You're welcome to have some if you'd like. I didn't get a chance to eat yet." She slung her burgundy bag over the arm of the chair. As she did, the long curls she'd taken the time to twist into the locks of her red hair bounced with the swing and sway of her body. Sebastian found himself hypnotized.

He should have broken away from the Reapers, checked on her sooner. Should have found the witch, Talia, quicker, or pushed Marcus harder to see Kyra. Now she had been reprogrammed like some sort of minion. If he didn't know her better, he wouldn't even recognize her. This feminized corporate look was a long rock toss from the leather jacket rebel he was used to Kyra sporting. All this time, he had feared pushing her away in the process of saving her. That was nothing. Losing their friendship didn't matter, not when compared to losing Kyra as an individual.

He wanted to grab her by the arms, shake her, slap her across the face and tell her to snap out of it. If it didn't work, he surely would lose her after a move like that. He took another sip of his coffee and waited.

The silence between them grew. It didn't bother him. He enjoyed the simplicity of her company. That quiet—it was more than they'd had in a long while.

Kyra gazed at him, her lips tugging to the side. "I take it I didn't used to dress like this?" Sebastian didn't answer right away. He watched the muscles in her face, looking for any nervous tic. "You did know me before, didn't you? Before I lost my memory?"

Sebastian sat up and leaned forward. “I’ve never seen you dress like this. Jeans and cotton were more your thing.”

“Oh.” Kyra chewed on her pinkie nail, her gaze fluttering down to her cup. “I can’t remember her. The girl I was.” She shifted, stared out the side window, and her eyes shimmered. Thinking it the start of a tear, Sebastian began to reach across the table, but reconsidered and pulled back. She wiped her eye. “I work today. This is my work attire.”

“You have a job?” This interested him. Marcus had seemed so protective of her that night. Like a child unwilling to share his toy. Now he was letting her out of his sights long enough to work a day job.

“I work at the bank.” She motioned across the street. Sebastian balked. Kyra’s face fell into a frown. “Your expression says it all. Not the old me?”

“It’s fine. If that’s what you want to do with your time. Is it what you want?” Sebastian asked.

“That’s the problem. I don’t know what I want. When I woke up in the hospital that night and Marcus was there by my bedside, I thought he was the answer. Thought he was the answer to everything. Especially after the nurse told me he’d been there with me the whole time, waiting. They told me I was out for two days. Two days! He never left the hospital in all that time.” Kyra sighed, looked down at her hands. “Things are different now. I don’t remember my life, but I feel things. Does that make sense?” Kyra looked down, picked at the protective sleeve on her cup. “Sometimes I get glimpses of things, and I think—I feel they should mean something to me.”

Feelings were something Sebastian had more than his fair share of experience with. His own and those of every other soul who had passed through his Reaper half. He thought he understood but couldn’t be sure with a hundred percent certainty. But glimpses, that caught his curiosity. *Could she be experiencing fragments of memories?* “Mind expanding on that?”

She took a deep breath. “Marcus is fine. Marcus is...Marcus, you know?”

“Not really, but continue.” He was pretty sure they both had extremely different opinions regarding Marcus.

Kyra fidgeted, stirring her coffee. She spoke in a metered tone. "He's nice, and I enjoy his company, but I don't feel like he's letting me discover who I am more than trying to direct me. He got me a job at the bank where his buddy works so I'd stop complaining about being bored. I'm busy now, so I'm not bored, and his buddy Chet keeps a close eye on me, even though he tries to pass it off as just being friendly." She rolled her eyes. "We never talk about my past, and when I bring it up, he shuts down." She abandoned her spoon on the table and looked up, meeting Sebastian's return stare.

"What can I do to help?"

She fidgeted in her seat, looking uncomfortable. Nervous. "The funny thing is...I think you already are."

Sebastian laid his arm on the table across the front of him and leaned closer. "I'm sorry. I'm not following."

Kyra tilted her head back. The folds of her sage sweater flopped to the side, exposing the long gold necklace she wore. It slipped down over her white blouse. No hint of the tooth pendant Talia had told him to look for. Sebastian's jaw clenched, sending a tightened pain along the bone.

Kyra was frustrated, he could see that, but she didn't need to be. He was going to help her. When she looked at him again, her eyes sparked with what he took for determination. Her hand sprang forward, her fingers seeking his. Like a vine, her index finger twined around his, and her gaze melted into his return stare. "I don't know how to say this, so I'm just going to say it."

Sebastian glanced down at their hands, the way her pinkie wrapped around his, and a churn of warmth spread through his gut. Before seeing her, he'd begun to lose hope. Now pleasure, excitement, elation rushed him, tingled his senses, twitching and curving the edge of his lips to the heavens. Of course, he tried to play it off, mask it as an it's-all-cool grin. He looked back up to meet Kyra's gaze. "I'm good with that."

"I've been having dreams, and I think they're trying to tell me something. I think I'm trying to remember. In the dreams, it's always hot, and I'm always in distress, but every time you're there, and that gives me hope." Her fingers tightened on his. "Since that first day you showed up at my door, I've been determined to find you."

Sebastian knew exactly what memory she was describing. It made sense that if she remembered anything, she would remember that. It would have made a strong impression, a lasting memory. Purgatory was meant to dig deep into one's soul. The fact that she remembered him trying to save her... His chest was lighter than air. He could fly if he had to.

"Hey, Ky. I thought that looked like you."

Beside their table stood a medium-built guy. Dirty-blonde hair, brown eyes. Sebastian immediately disliked him. Maybe it was the way he placed his hand on Kyra's shoulder, or the way he shortened her name. He reminded Sebastian of Marcus. Kyra pulled her hand away from Sebastian and back into her lap.

"See you across the street in a few?" the guy asked.

Kyra twisted in her seat to take in the man standing at her side. "Good morning, Chet. It's nice to see you. Don't worry, I'll be there." She smiled, and it was the kind of smile you plastered on your face to show you had manners, when you really wanted nothing more than to be left alone. Sebastian was familiar with this look of hers. He held back a chuckle and watched her as the man continued to stand in silence at her side. With a sigh, she rolled her eyes at him. "I'll see you there, Chet." Her voice was short and decisive. No one could argue the message sent.

Chet lowered his head, making it impossible to see his expression. "Right. See you there. Watching the clock, Ky." He tapped his phone three times sharp, turned with an abrupt pivot, and walked away.

Sebastian sat back in his seat and stretched his legs out once again. "So...you go by Ky now?"

She shook her head. "It's just what Marcus and his friends call me." She looked at the time on her phone. Sebastian made note: she now carried a phone. No doubt so Marcus could get ahold of her whenever he wanted. "I have to get to work soon."

"Yeah, you have checking accounts to open and bills to count. Things like that?"

Kyra shot him a hurt scowl.

He felt the blow as if the car on the Kamikaze ride had slammed full force into his gut. “I’m sorry. That was a crap thing to say.”

“I get it. I’m not the person you remember.” She paused, glanced at her hands. “I want to remember who she was, I really do.” She looked up, straight into his soul. “Will you meet me here again? Say, tomorrow morning?” Her hand wrapped around his once more, this time with more strength than she’d shown previously. It felt like a plea.

Tension tightened Sebastian’s back and shoulders. It wasn’t the request that got to him. It was the sound of her voice, the anxious need. “Better yet, why don’t you ditch work? Come with me now. I can take you somewhere that might just be exactly what you need—” Without warning, Sebastian’s jaw locked up, his every muscle froze, and he couldn’t move. *What the freakin’ Hell is going on?* his inner voice yelled, and his eyes darted left and right.

“Sebastian?” Kyra inquired. “You were saying?”

He couldn’t respond. Couldn’t will his mouth to work or voice to answer. But his gaze narrowed in on the culprit, standing not-so-inconspicuously by the creamer station. Tall, gray suit with hat pulled down to shield his facial features and a cheesy nametag tacked to his chest, probably his father’s lame idea. All part of the everyone-get-to-know-Sebastian movement. Except, all the names were fake. So, what was the point? The Reaper across the room was no more named Mr. Johnson than his father was Mr. Smith.

Damn Reapers. Now Sebastian had a tail because his father didn’t trust him on his own. His gaze shifted to Kyra.

“Sebastian?” Kyra’s eyes bored into him, large and wide.

He knew the answer. Knew what it would take to escape the Reaper’s grasp. His chest heaved, eyes closed, and he gave up the desire to whisk Kyra away. At least, for the moment. His father could have this one, but Sebastian would win in the end, Hell be damned.

The lock on his body released, sending him stumbling back into the cushion of his chair. Quick to recover, his hand raked through the hair across the top of his crown. “Sorry,” he said. “Lost my thought.”

“Tomorrow?” Kyra reminded him. “Can you meet me here?”

If the Reapers weren't going to let him have this moment with her, maybe he could get tomorrow. He discarded the cool act and let her see the raw side of himself. All the muscles in his face loosened as earnestness took up camp in his gaze and posture. He sat up straight. "I can probably manage that."

"Only probably?"

He squeezed her hand back. "I'll be here, Kyra."

"Good." She stood to leave. Sebastian also stood. "Don't stand on my account."

"Don't be silly. I'll see you tomorrow." Unsure of what to do, he held out his hand. She stared down at it for a second before taking it in her own. The shake felt awkward and out of place.

She turned to leave, paused a moment, then spun around. Without warning, she threw herself forward, clasping her arms around his shoulders, pressing her soft body against his in a tight, warm hug. Even without her dragon, she burned like fire. Her heat embraced him, traveled through him, marrying them into one. All the time lost was forgotten. He didn't care about Marcus; she was with him now, in his arms where he'd always wanted her to be. He closed his eyes and buried his nose in her hair.

"You smell..." He paused, unsure of the word he wanted to use. "Different."

Kyra took a small step back. "I do?"

"Sunflowers," Sebastian said, tilting his head forward.

Understanding bloomed over her features. "You can smell them on me?"

"I can."

She bit her lip and her eyes sparkled, hinting to the wild gold they turned before she lost half herself. "I can't seem to get warm enough lately, so I've been filling the apartment with sunflowers to trick my mind. They are such a warm flower, don't you think?"

Sebastian nodded in agreement, but inwardly found her confession more than curious. Was she cold without her dragon to warm her?

Kyra scanned the tight confines of the café, then leaned into Sebastian once more. In his ear, she whispered, "Were we close?"

Her tone asked if they had been more than friends. He didn't know how to answer. He only knew how he had felt and no longer knew how she had felt. Not after the kiss. The kiss loomed out there like an enormous unanswered question now that she didn't have her memory to tell him what it'd meant. From what he'd seen, she'd chosen Marcus over him. "I knew you well, but I only knew what you chose to share. As for close...I think you can answer that yourself, can't you? You are with Marcus, are you not?"

She stepped back, slowly letting her hand fall away. "Yes. Marcus." Her gaze lingered on Sebastian's. It burned a desire in him he feared no amount of reaping or lust fulfillment would ever quench. He wanted to know what thoughts ran through her head. The want built with fierce intensity into untethered need.

"Tomorrow, then." She walked from him straight out the door. Once on the street, she spared him a glance through the large picture window. He watched each step of her trek across the street until she disappeared into the bank.

"Infraction 183. Failure to comply with a superior Grim." Mr. Johnson stood at Sebastian's side. Sebastian rolled his eyes.

Superior Grim, my blood scythe. My dad is far from superior. So what if he told me to stay away from Kyra. Thoughts and concerns for her eclipse my mind. I can't stay away. I'll do what I want.

"This is your first warning." Mr. Johnson continued. "You only get—"

"Yeah, yeah, I know." Sebastian sat with such force the chair scooted a few inches across the floor. He didn't care what Mr. Johnson had to say. Kyra, here. And now tomorrow. His mind buzzed with new thoughts and images. Possibilities. She had opened up new prospects. Prospects he was eager to explore.

He downed his coffee and smashed the cup flat on the table. Adrenaline pumped through his veins like the Four Horsemen racing into the Apocalypse. He stood and turned toward the nearest trashcan. Mr. Johnson was gone, his job done, the warning delivered. But something else at the front of the shop flashed, catching his attention. All too quickly it vanished.

What had he seen? He pushed at the tiny memory, hand pressed to the side of his skull. Someone had been watching him from the front window. Dropping his trash on the table, Sebastian bolted for the front of the shop. The street beyond was alive with the usual morning hustle. Cars zipped this way and that. People moved along the sidewalks with purpose, shops and businesses their likely destinations. Nothing looked out of the ordinary, yet his penetrating gaze searched all directions and came up empty. Maybe he was being paranoid. Maybe he had imagined the whole thing.

He pushed the suspicion from his mind and headed down the street toward Sophie's parents' place. Walked past shops and businesses to the narrow alleyway with a side door into their apartment building. Tall buildings on either side pressed in, trying to reclaim the ground, creating a dark and tight squeeze of a space. A single sound bounced off the stark brick walls confining the area. So narrow was the passage and so tall the sidewalls that little to no sunlight reached the asphalt. Not that it was dark enough to worry about losing one's way, only dark enough to hide distinguishing features.

An old, emerald Impala was now parked in the path, and the building's side door sat slightly ajar. There was no evidence of people nearby—no voices or conversations lingered in the air—yet Sebastian received a steady stream of memories. Thoughts and memories that made little to no sense to him. Were the owners all soon to be among the dead? If so, where were they? That was how Sebastian's gift usually worked. The dead and near-dead, whether they knew it or not, transmitted their thoughts and memories like a homing beacon for Reapers.

Sebastian stood at the entrance of the alley, perfectly still, alert, attuned to every click and scuff and echo bouncing off the cold, hard stone.

"Sebastian."

His name slithered along the cracks in the block walls, across the paved ground, unfurling like the tongue of a reptilian predator. Sebastian straightened and tilted his head to the sound, following the echo as it moved through the arena. Because that's what he saw this soon becoming—a field of combat. Three steps into the alley, the sound changed, morphed, became haunting. Hauntingly beautiful.

"I know you're here. Show yourself," Sebastian called out. He continued to move deeper into the tight space, closer to the apartment building's entrance. Muscles taut and jaw rigid, he prepared for what lay in wait. He considered himself ready for anything. The inner buzz from one of his mother's kind was unexpected. He'd not been in the presence of a Mara since his mother had abandoned him as a child. He'd been left alone to stumble through his learning and despised her for it. Despised his Mara half. Besides, Maras were not to be trusted. "Mother?" he whispered, taking another step into the shadows.

The car was hidden in the dark, a few feet up ahead. It rattled and creaked, bouncing twice on its hind springs. Expecting to find his mother working her sorcery on some willing schmuck in the backseat, Sebastian approached with caution. He peered through the Impala's side window. No one was inside. The car was empty. Any hint reminding him of his mother was gone. But something else caught his attention: movement around the front edge, near the headlight. A shuffle and scamper unlike the grace of any Mara. The muscle at the side of his eye twitched. Somebody was playing games, and he had never been one for games.

Mr. Johnson stood near the entrance of the alleyway, his silhouette highlighted by the light of day bright on the street beyond. He whipped out a notepad and started taking notes.

Hell's fire! Damn Reapers, thought Sebastian. *Is this a test?*

Metal groaned, and a green block popped up in his peripheral view. It was the Impala's trunk lid pointing to the sky. From the open space spilled a couple of quick, dark figures. Sebastian tensed, then threw his arms out defensively. Whatever they were, they had him flanked. He glanced at the building entrance. Could he make it without a fight? Did he even want to? Any kind of weapon would come in handy about now. Even one of those sickles he'd seen in so many silly images portraying Reapers.

He darted for the door. A blur shot straight at him, and pain splintered through his ribs. He felt the blow before he saw the crowbar. Fire spread through his side, sharp at the center and dulling as it spread outward. Ignoring instinct telling him to protect his ribs, Sebastian moved forward, pushing into the attackers.

Something caught him before he saw it, the weight knocking him to the ground. Metal netting had been dumped over the top of him. Everywhere the binding touched his skin stung, the links reeking of a bittersweet aroma. He scrunched his nose to block out the smell. It reminded him of caramel syrup, too sugary. He felt dizzy and the images before him swayed. It wasn't going to stop him, though. He shoved up off the asphalt, dragging the heavy curtain draped over him. Muscles ached in ways they never had before. Sebastian stumbled and fell into one of his attackers. A man blending in with the shadows.

A snort came from behind.

More hoots and chortles from the rear. Whoever they were, they had cast the net over him. Snuck up on him while he'd been engaged with the two who'd jumped out of the trunk— decoys.

"Can you believe this guy?" someone at his right said. "Look at him still fighting. Even wrapped in the Mara Web."

The what? No!

Sebastian tried to steady his breath, even as his heart attempted to hammer its way through his chest. He didn't believe it. Mara Webs didn't exist. They were a myth created to make humans feel better. Feel safe from the nightmare of monsters.

He struggled. With each move he made, the net tightened, hugged closer to his body. It wasn't a myth. He could feel the net working, turning his own power against him. It plucked his nightmares from his head and played them back, remaking his reality. Only he knew better. He knew he was still struggling in metal mesh, on the ground of a tight, dark alley. He knew the pictures he saw of himself, of Kyra, were only an illusion and nothing more.

And yet, they didn't keep him from struggling. He didn't want to see. Wasn't sure he could stomach his worst nightmares. And the more he struggled, the more he felt his life force drain from his body. Could he die? He'd never asked that question of his father. Right now, he really wanted to know.

Slowly, methodically, his hands reached out for the edge of the net. It took all his concentration, and it felt like an eternity to accomplish the task. Sweat trickled down his temple, and he was instantly on the boardwalk watching Chow Lien paint—the moment he had learned to harness his inner strength, use it as a shield. That was what he needed to do now. Needed to stay on point, to remember. His hands wrapped around the chain's edge and began to lift.

"You see that?" A voice on his left.

Sebastian felt a blunt hit to the shoulder blade, and he wavered. His eyes fluttered shut, open, shut, then open again.

He collapsed to a sitting position. Watched their feet gather around him. There were five of them. It was embarrassing, a Reaper taken down by five lesser beings. Be them demon or men, he did not know. Although he didn't really care much now.

Sebastian turned his face up to his captors. It was hard to discern between the truth and the images placed in his mind by the net, but what he thought he saw were demons disguised as men. They had to be Marcus's men. Demons and Marcus, seemed like a logical association. "I let her be. What more does Marcus want from me?" he bellowed, and felt his body burn with emotion he couldn't express.

One set of boots stepped closer. Close enough to see the scuff across the center of the right tip and the threads starting to show. "Think you got it all wrong, bud," the owner of the boots said and kicked Sebastian hard to the gut. It felt like a sledgehammer wielded by the carnival's strongman. Sebastian coughed, splattering blood across the cracked asphalt. "I." He kicked Sebastian again. "Honestly." And again. "Don't." And again. "Care." He leaned down, closer to Sebastian's eye level. "None of us care what you did or didn't do. Thing is, Boss wants you. That means I gotta bag ya."

Sebastian's glance darted to where Mr. Johnson had been. The Reaper was no longer there. In fact, he was nowhere. He was gone. This probably wasn't a test. It was too brutal.

The guy bent down, got right in Sebastian's face. His eyes were dark pools of ink. They matched the midnight matted hair that lay across his head and hinted to the beast hidden beneath the human mask. His teeth were sharp nails.

Sebastian studied him, tried to identify his species, but all he really wanted to do was sleep. His eyelids felt heavy. Letting his captors win actually seemed like a plausible choice.

"So, this boss of yours?" Sebastian prompted.

The guy poked him hard in the shoulder with his index finger. It knocked Sebastian off balance, toppling him all the way to the ground. All the bodies gathered around him laughed. Sebastian lifted himself partway up.

"She's going to take pleasure tearing you apart." His eyes sparked, and he rubbed his fingers together enthusiastically. "And I will take great pleasure in tenderizing you." His fist slammed into Sebastian's face.

Everything turned the most brilliant color of white. Sebastian imagined this must be what it looked like for his clients moving through the doorway onto the other side. So fantastical.

His head hit the ground.

He was drained and exhausted. Rest sounded like a good idea. Only for a few minutes. He'd soon have his strength back, and he'd bring down Hell's fury on these little brimstone shitters.

Closing his eyes, he forgot his cares and the real, unjust world. He let the Mara within him pick his future. Eyes closed, he drifted off to sleep.

He was only mildly aware when they shoved him in a trunk with the net still wrapped around him, and hauled him out sometime later.

15
EARLY

Marcus

The coffee needed to be stronger. Much stronger. What it really needed was a shot of the good stuff. Marcus opened the cabinet above the bar and grabbed a bottle of his private stock. Without a word to his houseguest, he poured a shot in the mug in front of him and took a sip. Better, but he wasn't there yet. He closed his eyes and rolled his head and shoulders. Way too much tension. His rotator cuff tendons popped.

"Tell me again," he said. "Why is he down at the club?"

Leila stood in the middle of the kitchen, still as a statue, her robes draping onto the floor like an old painter's cloth. "Because, old friend, I have use for the boy."

Marcus huffed. He wasn't pleased with the way things were going, but he wasn't ready to sever his relationship with Leila just yet. She was still useful. "Make sure you keep him out of my way. I don't want him meddling in any more of my plans."

Leila had her arms folded across the front of her, and the sleeves of her cloak covered every bit of her form, dripping down the front of her like melted wax. She opened her arms wide, breaking the impression, and feigned a small curtsy. Marcus knew it to be bullcrap. Stubborn as she was, she bowed to no one. "Of course, my lord. Your agenda is the priority above all."

"If that's the case, why not simply cut his throat? He's unnecessary baggage." Marcus took a slow sip of his coffee and watched Leila over the rim of his mug.

She lurched forward, slamming her hands on the counter. "He is mine! Understand? You don't harm him unless I say so." Her voice seethed with rivaling authority, and yet she spoke so softly Marcus found himself leaning closer.

There was no sweat or flinch on Marcus's end. His reaction was to laugh. Except, he knew laughter wouldn't serve his purpose. It would only upset the wild spirit standing in his kitchen, and he needed all his pawns in line.

"Very well, Leila. I'll play it your way—for now." He set his coffee on the counter. "But consider this a warning. If I find him, at any point, standing between me and what I want, I will not hesitate."

Leila's eyes glowed from beneath her hood. The effect diminished her pretty face. For the briefest of moments, Marcus tried to imagine what it would be like to be one of her conquests. Were the days so unbelievable, the sex so astonishing, that the nightmares were overlooked? The slow drain of life left unnoticed? He found it hard to believe.

The front door banged shut. Marcus spun around to see Kyra standing there with keys in hand, a stunned look etched on her face. Her burgundy handbag flopped from her shoulder to the crook of her arm. She didn't move. "I didn't expect..."

"Got home early." Marcus leaned against the counter dividing the small living area from the kitchen. As he did, he casually glanced back into the little room. Leila was gone, the sliding door to the balcony open. "You too, I see."

Kyra moved into the room. She set her purse and keys on the coffee table. "I was feeling a bit off. Decided to come home."

Marcus raked his eyes over her from head to toe. He could tell she was acting different, even if she tried to hide it. He suspected it had to do with her morning encounter. Even if she wouldn't readily divulge any information, he knew everything that went on in her life. He left nothing to chance. Negating the space between them, he wrapped her in his arms and kissed her tenderly on the forehead. "You all right? Need to rest?"

She turned away from him and laid the back of her head on his shoulder. The aversion didn't go unnoticed—the fact she made no immediate attempt to circle her arms around his waist. More often than not these days, her embrace was far too loose. He was losing her. He wanted to blame that damn carnie boy for showing up this morning, but he knew the truth. He'd been losing her for a while.

Didn't matter. Once he got his dragon back, she would fall in love with him. Women loved power. He would be the epitome of power. All beasts within the heavens, on earth, and in the underworld would bow to him. For he was, and would be again, the most feared dragon of them all. Fire raced through his veins, laced with the laughter of his oncoming victory. He would rule once again. Rule it all.

He looked down at Kyra. "I will take you for my queen."

She blinked, and the edges of her eyes crinkled as her face torqued. "What?"

Marcus didn't answer. Not with words. He turned her to face him and pressed his lips to hers, hard and furious. His hand dragged through the locks at the back of her head while the other pulled her in tighter and lifted her off the ground. She was his and no other's. He would mark her as so.

16

CAGED

Sebastian

Blood dribbled down Sebastian's chin, staining the front of his shirt. Liquid copper filled his mouth. He spat the blood clear, but its flavor lingered, seeping around his teeth and gums.

The Mara Web was gone, and he sat chained to a chair in the center of a large cage. The space was the size of a tiny bedroom, barely enough height for him to stand on his toes and stretch his arms above his head. As things stood, he wasn't moving from the spot. He'd given up struggling against the bonds hours ago.

The room containing his prison gave little clue to where he was. No sound from the outside world reached its way in. He took that to mean the walls were heavily insulated. The souls in the surrounding area hinted to a commercial setting. As did the memories of his captor. Memories—now they were an interesting reveal. Be it tomorrow or next month, the fact Sebastian could pick the memories from the air meant the monster in front of him had already been scheduled for demise. Sebastian had felt the same mortality in the alleyway, earlier. Although, there were more memories then, from more monsters.

Whack!

The hit was hard, solid, and Sebastian's head swung to the side with the force of the blow. The stocky guard grinned before hitting Sebastian in the jaw again.

Sebastian spat more blood onto the prison floor. "Is there a point to this? An interrogation, perhaps?"

The guard rocked back on his heels. "Nah. Just like it." He stood towering over Sebastian, filling all available space from the floor to the top of his cage.

"Excellent." Sebastian's word dripped with sarcasm.

The door at the far side of the room opened, the thick metal dragging across the cement ground with a *scraauch*. Light shifted and spilled in from the opening, and three people entered. *More toy soldiers*, Sebastian thought. Two took a seat at the table in the corner, ignoring Sebastian and his tormentor, but one made eye contact. He leaned against the edge of the bars, scrutinized the beating Sebastian received. Based on the guy's speckled gray hair, Sebastian guessed he was the oldest in the room. Then again, maybe not. It was only a mask, after all. All his captors had remained camouflaged in human form. For his benefit, he suspected.

"You've done enough, Dover." Stepping into the cage, the older guy dropped his hand on Dover's shoulder. "Leave some for me. Others like to have fun, too."

Dover's face morphed into a sure-thing sneer, as much as the monster-man could sneer, and in that moment, Sebastian saw the gray, wrinkled skin and horned nose. He narrowed his stare at his beast of a captor. "Absolutely, Boss," Dover grumbled, then spat at Sebastian and stepped aside, taking up residence in the far corner of the confined space. Sebastian ignored the gesture. Instead, he focused his attention on the new boss in the room taking point.

"If the purpose of all this is to annoy me, you're doing a damn good job," Sebastian said.

Boss laughed and dragged a chair into the space. Spinning the back to Sebastian, he sat straddling the seat and set his gaze on his captive. The seconds ticked by without a word. The sound of his steady breath imitated a metronome, not that Sebastian needed any relaxation triggers. He was fine. "You seem to be quite the prize. People want you something awful," Boss said.

Sebastian noted Boss was rather stout, most likely an aspect of his true being. Sebastian tilted his head, feigning sincere interest. "By people, you mean...?"

Boss pointed. "That's not going to work. You won't get any information out of me, nightmare creature. So, tell me—*thing*—what does it feel like to be the only boy in an all-girls club?"

Sebastian raised a brow. He picked up on the subtleties. Boss was talking about his Mara nature. There was no mention of Sebastian's other ability. He was beginning to think the Mara in him was all they cared about. Maybe it was all they knew about. He wondered how he could use that narrow knowledge to his advantage. He shifted in his tight position, tried to get comfortable and look laid-back, indifferent. He didn't want these guys to think he was intimidated. "It's kinda cool, actually. Who wouldn't want to be the only guy? The ladies adore me." Sebastian tossed his head back and gave what he thought might be a cocky grin.

Dover dashed across the cage and slammed him in the face, a head-butt—face to face. It was like getting smashed with a skull of iron.

Sebastian grimaced. Tried to pinch away the blinding light of fracturing pain. "Hey! Can you keep your dino off me?"

The room filled with low laughter. Boss looked to the group, assessed Dover, before returning his attention to Sebastian. "No, I don't think I will." He laid his arms across the back of the chair and leaned closer. "You see, that's not how things are going to work. You might be used to being something special," he used air quotes for emphasis, "worthy of VIP treatment, but you're not. On the contrary, you're a freak. You never should have been. Maras are like banshees, a role meant to be filled by women. So, tell me, why you?" He cradled his chin in his hand and waited for Sebastian's answer.

Sebastian spat more blood. He wanted to wipe his lip, but knew any effort to do so was a waste of time. A heavy sigh heaved through his chest. "I don't know. Why is anything the way it is?"

"You're an anomaly. A monstrosity. Her reason for wanting you is incomprehensible." Boss turned to his comrades in the room. "Right, guys?" They roared in concurrence.

"Who?" Sebastian questioned. "Was it the Mara I felt in the alley?"

Boss didn't answer. Instead, he stood, pushed the chair away, and began to pace within the cage's small confines. The keys clipped to his belt jingled at his hip, and his fingers clutched nervously at the side of his gun, never actually touching the metal. His other hand scratched at his hair. "What I don't get, and maybe you can explain this to me"—the gun came free of its holster, and he began to wave it in slow swirls—"is for a monster, Maras are too damn beautiful. I mean, demon-damn-dazzling. It ain't right. Look at you!"

Maybe he was about to die at Boss's pent-up anger and frustration. Didn't matter. Sebastian couldn't stop himself from grinning. Emotion such as Boss's was always personal. Considering what Boss was doing to him, Sebastian didn't feel too sorry for any misery some Mara had caused him or his family in the past.

"You got a name?" Sebastian asked.

Boss turned the gun on Sebastian and aimed it between his eyes. "What the demon Hell does my name have to do with anything?"

"Only trying to be civil. Don't want to share, that's fine. I'll call you Boss-boy. How does that sound?"

Boss-boy growl-grunted at Sebastian's insult of a name and pushed the gun up through his hair.

Sebastian remained steady, knowing any wrong move risked setting Boss-boy off in a terrible way. "Let me explain something I've come to understand about Maras." Sebastian watched Boss-boy as he moved across the back of the cage in the manner of a predator trying to decide what to do with its catch.

Boss-boy harnessed his gun and, watching Sebastian through squinted eyes, returned to the chair propped between them.

Sebastian took his cue. "A Mara's true face is anything but beautiful. You only see beauty because your brain cannot interpret the truth. It's easily fooled by the harmonics at which she resonates. It causes your brain to perceive her as magnificent when the reality is far different. Kind of like you folks." Sebastian turned his head and spat blood residue in the direction of their audience. "We all know you don't look like this in your true form, do you?"

Dover laughed. Not Boss-boy, though. He snarled, and his face shifted to a beast form, flesh pulled tight over his skull in long bands. Finally, a pure view. Sebastian immediately recognized him as a behemoth. The two at the table looked in their direction, and for a second, Sebastian could see their true faces, as well. Everyone in the room was a behemoth.

That couldn't be good. A room full of chaos monsters the size of hippos. Someone had it out for him.

"What purpose do you guys stand to gain holding me?" Sebastian asked.

"I don't like him." The call came from the table in the corner. Sebastian strained to see which of the two had spoken. It was unclear.

Dover's hand twisted on the bars of the cage, his gaze burning into Sebastian. Sebastian was confident that if it were up to that man, he'd already be dead. He wasn't sure what he'd done to deserve it, but pure hatred boiled in Dover's irises. The guy's festering emotions ate away at Sebastian's Reaper intake channels.

Boss-boy sat sideways on the chair. He rocked back and forth, carving a small hole in the seat with his knife. "Just keeping you out of the way. That's all we got to do. Keep you out of the way."

Things were clicking into place for Sebastian. He suddenly feared for Kyra more than ever. "What are you talking about?"

The behemoth snapped his head and stared at Sebastian. His eyes were stained with a multitude of blood-colored cracks. "Nothing."

Dover stepped forward. "Boss?" His head jerked back around. "His Majesty didn't say anything about keeping him alive. Only the Mara did. Since when do we take orders from her?"

"Damn straight!" Boss-boy said. The behemoths shook their heads. "But *he* is listening to her." Boss-boy stared into the space of the cell.

Sebastian glanced between them, soaking in their words and appraising their mental states. There was a Mara in the mix, working with Marcus, and for whatever reason, she wanted Sebastian. How could he use that information to his advantage? "Tell you what. Why don't you at least loosen these chains, so my limbs don't fall off? How 'bout we start there?" Sebastian spoke quietly. Every sound bounced off the room's walls, magnifying tenfold.

"Why don't you shut the freak up!" Dover yelled.

Sebastian went silent and watched him.

"What the hell you looking at? You think I'm funny-looking? A little too fat, too big? Can't hold a candle to a pretty Mara boy?" His hand twisted on the cage. The metal groaned and tore. He now held a long, jagged shaft like a weapon.

"Hey." Sebastian stumbled for words. "I think you need to calm down."

Boss-boy stood, moved the chair out of the way. "I probably should have told you. His dad was sucked dry by a Mara. He has a bit of a problem with your kind."

Sebastian's eyes grew wide as he watched Dover retreat and join the others at the table. Where was *his* father when he could actually use the bastard? *Damnation*. He didn't want to go out this way. Not before he saved Kyra from her plight.

Sebastian cleared his throat and addressed Dover. "Sorry about your father. You know I had nothing to do with that, right? I don't hunt like a Mara. You've got me all wrong." Dover's hand tightened on the metal rod and beads of sweat ran down the side of his face.

From the far end of the room, beyond the closed door, pops exploded. Shots were being fired. Confusion flashed across Dover's face. It turned to resignation and he moved back toward the cell with purpose. *Is someone finally coming to help me*? Sebastian wondered. Maybe. Or maybe it was something else entirely, and he was going to get caught in the crossfire.

Everyone in the room was on the move: Boss-boy on Dover's heels, the others running for the door. "They're coming. Secure the room," Boss yelled.

Sebastian looked around wildly. Scanned their faces and the door. "Who's coming?"

More shots rang out. Yells and screams echoed through the wall. A banging on the heavy metal of the secured door followed. Something was trying to break into his prison room.

"I'm here!" Sebastian called out.

"Shut up, you *freak*!" Dover shoved the steel rod through Sebastian's stomach.

Sebastian's mouth slumped open and he looked at the metal protruding from his body. Blood spilled out at an alarming rate. Dover stood before him with a wicked grin on his face. Sebastian wanted to knock the irritating look off, but his hands were still tied and his strength was draining fast. He whispered, strained and difficult, blood sputtering from his lips.

Dover leaned forward. Sebastian saw Boss-boy behind him, not disapproving of the turn in events. "What was that?" Dover teased.

Sebastian pulled deep from his core, looking for his voice. Dark, slithering power came up in a graveled gnarl, vibrating his ribs and vocal cords. The room resonated with rage and agony as the growl shifted into a scream. A pitch-black sound, through and through.

Dover stepped back, stumbling on air. "He's a Rea—" Blood streamed from his eyes and he fell to the ground.

Boss-boy grabbed his head, pressed into the sides, and screamed. Everyone withered. Howling, bleeding, dying. The room shifted. Moved in and out of shape. Sounds muffled. And Sebastian's breath labored. He lowered his head. Strength waned, and the chains still held him to the chair. His body slumped against them.

What have I done? Sebastian's mind stammered. *How?*

Footsteps. So many of them rushing into the room. A hand lifted his head and a face came right up to his. The small beam of a flashlight zipped back and forth across his eyes. "He's in bad shape, sir," the person said. He lowered Sebastian's head slowly.

Someone tugged at the steel bar in his stomach. Sebastian screamed. White-hot lights flashed through his body.

"Get him unshackled," someone said.

People began to tug and pull at him. Excruciating—he tried to yell. The pain was both dull and sharp at different points. A young girl dropped at his side. She pushed his hair back from his face. Drenched with sweat, it stuck to the side of his brow. "You'll be all right. I promise," she said.

Sebastian blinked.

She yanked the rod from his body.

Sebastian was instantly doused in Kyra's fire, plummeting into the screaming pits of Hell, and everything went black.

17
DRAGONS

Marcus

Sparks swirled like a hostile whirlwind within the glass jar. Marcus studied it a moment, before setting the jar in the passenger seat of his Mustang. His fingers drummed on the dashboard and he gazed out the front windshield at the vivid colors of the day. The cheerful birdsong in the trees, the bright sun illuminating everything in brilliance. None of it meant anything to him. All his concern was wrapped up in what the contents of the glass jar beside him represented. Was this the combination he wanted? He had to be sure. After a long pause, he picked up his phone and dialed the number he'd come to know so well. It rang only once.

"I'm ready," he said. "Let's do this thing." He listened to the voice on the other end, and a discontented frown began to form on his face. "Why not tonight?" He paused. "Yes, I want to do it right!" A streak of frustration flashed through him. "All right. We'll do it your way. You'd better be there."

He ended the call and glanced down at the jar. The dragon within clawed at the glass. They all did that. Never content in their temporary confinement. Just as well. Marcus didn't want complacent beasts. Not for this ritual.

Turning the key and roaring the engine to life, he shifted into gear and rolled back onto the street. He would take the newly acquired forest beast and add her to the others. Trees and bushes blurred past. The bridge. The same bridge where he had met Kyra. Now *there* was a special find. He'd lucked out finding her. If only he could pinpoint all the dragons in the same state as her—products of two different breeding lines, leaving her trapped in-between and young enough to still make a choice. He'd gotten two for the price of one with Kyra. Her dragon could morph either way. Such a treasure.

He glanced back down at the jar in the next seat. Not that beastie, though. Today's catch was an ordinary Forest Dragon. A relatively easy catch. Practically rolled over and begged him to take her. Oh, the things he'd done to her. His lips curled up and the tip of his tongue explored the edges of his teeth in a deliciously slow move.

At the corner stop sign, he moved out of the civic park and into the traffic of the city. His condo was fifteen minutes away, a little more if traffic got heavy. Glancing around at the cars pushing their way down the street, and then at the jar sitting on the seat beside him, an idea bloomed. He reached over into the back and grabbed the jacket he'd left there on a previous night, draped it over the dragon's prison, hiding it from view. He detected the tiniest of objections—a small roar—but knew the beast was securely trapped within the confined space. Safe from discovery. For now.

Twenty minutes later, Marcus pulled up in front of his condo. Carrying the magical dragon wrapped in his jacket, he locked the car and walked across the parking complex to the stairs. His condo was on the second level. He'd ascended halfway when his phone rang.

Pulling his phone from his pocket, he checked the screen before answering. His club. Tension was building in his jaw and neck before he pushed the button and put the phone to his ear, a bad feeling brewing in his gut. A voice on the other end immediately broke into bluster.

"What do you mean, he's gone?" Marcus listened, and his body tensed, filling with heat. "How are they dead?" He paused. "That doesn't make sense."

Marcus moved the phone from his face and yelled to the sky. He took a deep, steading breath before returning to the conversation.

"Don't touch anything in that room. I'll be there as soon as I can."

Hanging up and shoving the phone in the breast pocket of his suit jacket, he dashed up the remaining steps quick as he could.

Last thing he needed was the damn carnie on the loose. Kyra had left early to wait for the irritating carnie punk at the coffee shop that morning. She'd made up some lame excuse about work, but Marcus knew the truth. He had informants, and Chet was keeping a close eye on her. That's how he knew she'd held out until the last possible moment before abandoning the wait and checking into work. She'd also spent her break at the stupid shop. Marcus didn't want the boy to show up now, swoop in and act the big hero, mess up all his plans.

Marcus entered his condo and rushed from room to room to verify he was alone. Satisfied he was the only one present, he moved to his secret hiding place on the balcony. When he was sure no one was watching, he shoved the Forest Dragon into place with the others. The addition made a total of five liberated dragons. Five dragons he would make his own. Marcus smiled and slammed the front of the secret passage shut.

Now for Kyra. *She'd be so much more valuable at my side if she had her dragon*, he thought. *Plus, I'd be able to control her better*. Problem was, he wanted her dragon more than any other. Maybe he would get her a different dragon. A smaller, more docile beast. One more appropriate for his concubine.

He pushed off the wall and rushed back out toward his car. He had to get to her before the idiot carnie did. Who knew what he was up to? Blast that Sebastian.

Twenty-five minutes later, Marcus pulled into the bank parking lot to a cast of chaos. Red lights were spinning, cop cars blocked the entrance, and people wandered about in varied levels of excitement and fear.

His mind flew to the worst place first. Bank robbery. He was sure of it. How many banks were robbed in a day? He'd have to look up the statistics. He had foolishly let Kyra work at a financial institution. His jaw grew taut, and he shoved looky-loos and bank employees out of his path, making his way for the front door.

Chet grabbed his arm. "Hey man. A bank robbery. Can you believe it?" He took a long drag on his cigarette. "Caught the jackals, though." He pointed to a police car parked a few yards away, using his hand with the cigarette pinched between his fingers. Two people sat in the back. "They looked ordinary enough."

Marcus adjusted his sunglasses to better see the suspects. "What is that, a husband and wife team? They could be anyone. They don't look at all threatening."

"I think that was the point. Made it all the way to the counter. No one suspected. They looked so normal. It wasn't until Bethany panicked that we knew something was going down. If she had simply handed over the money, they probably would have walked out, and no one would have been the wiser. But she freaked and started crying. The gal next to her knew something was up. It just snowballed from there." Chet took another drag from his cigarette, shifted his feet, and shoved his free hand in his pocket. "The wifey perp, she pressed the demands on Bethany, and at that point, the husband whipped out the gun. It could have gotten real ugly, and it was pretty scary for a few minutes there, let me tell ya. But your gal—wow!"

Marcus's jaw clenched. "Kyra? What did she do?"

Chet clamped his hands on Marcus's upper arms. "She saved the day, man! She saved everyone."

Marcus knocked Chet's hands free and stormed toward the bank. He could feel the steam pouring off his skull. A policeman's arm shot out in front of him. "I'm sorry, sir. The bank is closed."

Marcus looked around the man, searching everything and everyone in sight. He spotted Kyra talking with another officer and pointed. "I'm here for her. She's my fiancée."

The officer looked over his shoulder at Kyra, made eye contact with the agent interviewing her, and then waved Marcus through. The doors to the bank were propped open. A patch of smeared blood at about waist height marked where someone had slammed into the exit far too hard. He recalled the male suspect holding an icepack on his head.

Kyra stood and moved across the room to meet him. "Bit of excitement today," she said with a tentative smile.

He walked around her, his gaze searching for anything amiss. "I can see that."

She turned, tried to follow him. "What are you doing?"

"Just making sure you're all right. I heard you were playing hero. That's dangerous, Kyra. When people do dangerous things, they tend to get hurt."

Kyra placed her hands on her hips and tilted her head to the side. Her red curls bounced with her stubborn poise. "I'm fine. You needn't worry about me."

He stopped and took a deep breath. His gaze fell on her cold, deep-set eyes. "This time, but what about the next? When are you going to stop playing hero?" Kyra jerked back. Marcus realized his mistake too late. She was smart, caught it immediately. That was one of the things he liked about her. It was also one of the things he found most infuriating. "How will I have you around forever if you choose to do foolhardy things like attack bank robbers?"

"Is that what you think? When have I played hero before? This, here." She gestured to the teller's window. "This was easy. I saw the whole thing in my head before I made a single move. I knew I could do it. If I hadn't known, I wouldn't have done it."

Marcus squinted. That made things worse. She was regaining her confidence. Soon he would lose her to the powerful being she was before, with or without her dragon. He moved in close until his cheek was against hers. Her breath warmed his skin, and he breathed in the scent of her with each and every inhale. Slowly he wrapped his arms around her. Her body trembled. It was excellent he could still make her tremble. He didn't care much if the tremble was out of excitement or fear. Either way, it granted him power.

His hand threaded through her hair, yanked her head back,

exposing her neck. As he skimmed the soft curve with his kiss, a gentle moan escaped her lips. Lips he would soon tease with his own.

She pushed him back. "Not here."

His grip tightened. "Never do such a foolish thing again. Understand?"

Kyra shuddered and shoved Marcus away. He grabbed her by the wrist and led her toward the car.

A police officer stepped in their path. "I'm sorry, ma'am. We aren't quite finished yet."

Kyra stopped and threw her hand to her chest. "Oh. So sorry. Of course." She turned to Marcus. "I shouldn't be much longer."

Marcus nodded and watched her return with the officer to the bank. He waited, stiff and stern, with his arms crossed. Chet came and stood at his side. Without looking at his friend, Marcus began to talk. "The blasted carnie boy escaped. I want him found, and I want Kyra watched even more closely until it is done."

"Got it," Chet said. He dropped his cigarette and ground it out with the bottom of his shoe. "I could take Kyra out tonight. Keep her occupied so she isn't looking for the kid. I'll take her to the circus she keeps asking about. She'd love that."

Marcus's ears started turning red, and he turned to look at Chet. "That is the most idiotic idea I've heard yet. The circus? Seriously, Chet? Get your damn act together, or I'll have to cut you loose!"

Chet gulped. "Sorry, boss. Wasn't thinking." He returned his gaze to the bank.

"That's for damn sure." Marcus stared at the bank and wondered what the next few days would bring. What the future with Kyra would bring. And what it would feel like to sink his teeth into Sebastian's skin, ripping him into dragon dinner scraps. The mere vision had him salivating at the chops.

18

ALICE

Sebastian

White light bled through the peace of the dark marsh behind Sebastian's closed eyes. He shifted, moved away from the annoyance. Hellfire exploded across his side and abdomen. He was being torn apart. Shish kebab wasn't something he ever wanted to experience again. He groaned, and his body moved, paused, and shifted some more, attempting to find a comfortable position. It wasn't happening.

His eyes fluttered, opened like slits. If the smell was any indication of what he would find, nothing good awaited. Wherever he was, it was rotten. He expected to find himself deep within the sewer system, among filth and waste. All he saw were dark, stark walls. He was lying stomach down on a mattress, though, and that had to count for something. Not the most comfortable mattress, nor the cleanest mattress he'd ever been on, but a bed all the same.

A cold, damp weight pressed against the back of his neck, and his body went rigid.

"Don't be alarmed. You're safe now. I'll see to it that you get all better."

The voice was female. He remembered a woman right before he'd blacked out. She'd been with the group who had stormed into his prison cell. She'd pulled the rod from his abdomen. In slow, methodical moves, he twisted, shifting to see her better. Every movement throbbed with torture. With clenched teeth, he held back the erupting madness. When he'd positioned himself away from the wall and faced her, he stopped, gently easing into place. His eyes closed to the burn flooding his system. Like lava rushing out around the wound. "Where am I?" he whispered.

She moved the compress to his forehead. "Somewhere safe. Do you have any idea what Balidhug's people wanted with you?"

Sebastian opened his eyes and gazed upon her for the first time with a steady eye. "By Balidhug, do you mean Marcus? He was the one behind it all, wasn't he?" Her lips twisted to the side. It was a look of unknowing. He reached out his hand and laid it upon hers. When he did so, he saw the crisscrossing bruises of the Mara Web pattern across the back of his hand. "It's all right if you don't know."

"I'm sorry. I only know what Davies tells me. Nothing more." She pulled her hand away and plucked at her bangs, straightening them over her forehead. Her dirty blonde hair was pulled back tight into a pony, and she had on little to no makeup. There was a vague familiarity about the girl, but Sebastian couldn't quite place the feeling. Maybe it was the loose, comfortable fatigues in which she was wrapped. Army beige. A wannabe soldier. The thought jumped into Sebastian's mind because she looked the part, but lacked the heart. That was the sense he picked up from her. Interesting that was all he picked up from her or the surrounding space, and due to simple observation. Not by means of any supernatural gifts. He searched inward. Had his injury dulled or nullified his abilities?

"Who's Davies?" he asked.

She didn't look him in the eye. She continued to wipe at his skin with the cloth. It tingled and sent an odd sensation through his body. About the time it began to feel rough against his skin, she would retrieve a bottle from the floor and douse it with more ointment. The only word on the label was *healer*. He would have preferred a bit more information. Some ingredients, perhaps. "Davies is our crew leader. He thinks since Balidhug's people wanted you, you could be useful in the fight against them."

Sebastian grinned, painfully so. He was a pawn, and both sides wanted to use him. But to what end? "What's your name?"

Her eyes flickered up' and her hand fumbled. She slipped a little too close to the bandaged hole in the side of Sebastian's abdomen. He winced, and his fingers clenched. Her hands flew to his chest, as if by touching him she could suck the pain away. "I'm sorry. So sorry."

"Forget it." Sebastian spoke between gritted teeth. "You didn't mean to. Name?"

She pulled back. "Sorry. I'm Alice."

"Well, Alice, I'm not sure what help I can be. I think I got grabbed mostly to be kept out of the way."

"Ah, but don't you see? If he wants you out of the way, that means you are a threat to him. So yes, you can be of help." She stood from her place on the side of the bed. "I should tell Davies you are awake now."

Sebastian slid his hand off the bed and reached to stop her. "Alice?" She paused at his side and looked down. He lifted the bottle from the floor. "What is this stuff?"

"Is it making you feel strange?"

"It does stir an odd sensation, and this label isn't very revealing."

Her lips lifted at the corners, and she reached down to take the bottle from him. She studied the worn typeset on the small white sticker before setting it back on the floor, this time at the head of the bed. A little farther out of Sebastian's reach. "It's identified that way on purpose. To protect the origin of the salve."

His interests were piqued. He tried to lift himself up onto his elbow, the move manageable, although stiff. "You can trust me."

She laughed. "Can I? I know no such thing. I don't know you at all. All I know is the behemoths took you prisoner. Clearly they beat you." Her hand waved over Sebastian and his makeshift hospital bed. "And something horrible happened to everyone in the room with you. Care to tell me about that?"

"Not particularly, no. Not my first choice."

"Then you can be content with not knowing more about the salves used to treat you." She smiled, tilted her head, and turned with a bob.

Sebastian grimaced, a poor attempt at a frown. He didn't feel the two situations stood on the same ground.

She took one step, paused, and looked back at Sebastian, an uncertain look on her face. The air in the room swirled, a mini cyclone appearing in the space before her. Her muscles tensed. Sebastian pushed himself to a sitting position. Every muscle, joint, tendon, bone, things he didn't even know existed, howled. *Holy Grim's Death.*

The swirl of air pulled in dust and dirt from every surface in the room. Darkening and calculating, a shape took form deep within the churning chaos. Alice's chest heaved, her breaths uneven and labored. The Grim Reaper, Death himself, stepped from the whirling mass.

Alice squawked, then slumped backwards.

Sebastian caught her and moved her gently to the bed. Dead weight. Her life force was gone. Sebastian glared at his father. "What did you do that for?"

Sebastian's father stood perfectly straight and proper. Suit, tie, and hat as usual. Shoes a scuff-free gloss black. "She held you captive. I'm here to liberate you. I show no mercy to your captors."

Sebastian held Alice's hand and stared into her eyes. "You got it all wrong. She was kind. She was healing me." He turned her hand back and forth in his own. He reached up and moved her head. "Where is she? Why isn't her soul coming to me?" His hand wrapped around the silver locket she wore, felt the warmth of her life force still trapped within.

"I already sent her away."

Sebastian bolted upright. The locket snapped from her neck and remained clasped in his grip. The room swayed, and his hand shot out to steady himself. It found the wall, slick with heavy gray paint, cold to the touch. *Don't let him see your pain,* Sebastian reminded himself. "Where were you when I actually did need you? I was beaten and held captive by ugly chaos monsters—behemoths." His gaze shifted from his father to Alice's body laid out on the dirty mattress. "Alice's people saved me."

His father looked around the stark room with an air of arrogance. "I didn't know. I only just received word."

Sebastian's eyes narrowed on his father. "Only just? Did Mr. Johnson take a slow stroll on his way to find you? Why didn't he do something rather than jot little notes and leave?"

"Johnson does things by the book. I told him to watch; he watched. Now come, let's go. I must get you somewhere safe." He swung his arm out, motioning Sebastian to come along.

Sebastian didn't move. He stared at his father, a storm of heated emotions clashing within him. Fury, frustration, hopelessness, sorrow, and shock, to name a few. "But Johnson, he—"

Sebastian's father jerked his head. It was a signal he wanted to go, not talk. "Yes, yes. Stopped you from foolishness with the dragon. That was the directive. Like I said, he's a by-the-book Reaper. Good man." Sebastian scoffed. "Now come along."

Sebastian still made no motion to leave. "What of Alice?" Sebastian adjusted the woman's arms, making them rest comfortably upon her quiet body. Carefully, he knelt and retrieved the bottle of ointment. Her locket still dangled in his palm. Unsure why he did it, Sebastian shoved the locket in his pocket. Maybe it was guilt. Maybe he would search out her family later, as he had yet to finish for Sophie.

"She is gone. There is nothing more to do." Mortifier grabbed Sebastian and pulled him away from Alice.

"You want me safe?" Sebastian laughed. "What do you care?"

"I care plenty. Someone or something is killing supernaturals. I don't want you to be next."

Sebastian froze, all of his muscles tightening. He pulled back on his father's grip. "What do you mean? Who has died?"

The Grim's eyes fluttered to a lazy close. "Does it matter?"

"It does to me!"

"So far, nothing more than a few dragons. But dragons are not easily conquered. The killer likely has the taste for it now. I've seen it happen many times through the years. More often with the humans, but it happens within the lines of a supernatural species, as well. He will move on, looking for more challenges. Some that will provide cunning and strong opponents. Do you see now? See why I must get you out of this place?" He took hold of Sebastian's arm and pulled him toward the vortex.

Sebastian struggled, but every bit of fight sent him another burning notch up the agony scale. "I really don't see it, Dad." Sebastian spat the title out with venom. "I just killed an entire room full of demons, and I didn't even mean to. Why would anyone, or thing, want to take on a Reaper?"

His father's eyes lit up. "You did? Congratulations, my boy." His hand came down in a solid pat on the back. Sebastian bolted his mouth shut, locking his jaw.

"Alice." The call rang out from the other room, the sound of footsteps approaching.

Sebastian's head snapped to the right and watched a dark-skinned man walk around the corner into the room. The official tag on his breast pocket read *B. Crane*. He hesitated at the sight of Sebastian and his father.

"Necessary?" Mortifier asked.

Sebastian clutched the bottle of medicine to his chest and returned the stare of the man in the doorway. "What?"

"As I thought," said the Reaper and flicked his finger. The man stumbled back into the hallway and crumbled to the floor. Sebastian didn't have to ask. The guy was dead.

"What is wrong with you?" Sebastian groaned. He wanted to yell, but lacked the necessary strength.

"You say that like it's a bad thing. This is a Reaper's way. Embrace it, Sebastian."

"A Reaper's way," Sebastian mocked. "Not *this* Reaper's way!" He hunched his shoulders. "At least, not the way I want to be," he mumbled.

"Stop us, then," his father said and pulled Sebastian by the arm into the vortex. With a swish, he removed them from the rebel's hideout. As Sebastian observed the white and gray swirls of dust and air spin around him, he watched the dank room where he'd been start to fade. More rebels rushed into the room, gathered around their fallen comrade.

One soldier looked up and pointed to Sebastian and Mortifier as they began to fade in the dissipating swirl of Grim transportation. That was it. That was the moment. All heads turned toward them, a couple pointing. He was now a suspect. It was clear they thought he killed the guy in the doorway. Probably Alice, too. Intimidating men rushed at the vortex. It was a moment of truth. Sebastian could stay and face the consequences, or leave with his father. He remained steadfast, and everything swirled into a churning mess of last-stop destination. Imminent collision with Alice's co-conspirators quickly passing.

Sebastian's gut twisted, a strongman's weight plummeting into his stomach. He threw off his father's hold and crashed straight through the churning chaos and whirling mist wall, directly out of the conveyor-cyclone into the darkening mass beyond.

19
UNFORESEEN

Sebastian

Alice had packed something white and gooey against Sebastian's wound, used a gauze bandage for binding. The salve wasn't working fast enough for his convenience. He wished for a quick heal or quick death. Either should erase the exploding pain in his side. At this point, he wasn't sure he cared which came for him.

Lights blurred in and out, and the rancid smell of piss and beer assaulted him. *What time is it?* he wondered. Maybe early dawn or the break of night? He leaned forward, reached out, hoping to find a firm hold, something to steady himself. He wasn't disappointed. Cold brick met his palm. He was standing at the corner of an alleyway.

The path from where he stood to where he wanted to go felt daunting, almost undoable. He wasn't sure why he'd come here. Maybe it was his need to tie up loose ends. Damn his nobility. He thought he had been concentrating on Alice. Sophie must have been lingering in his subconscious. When he'd broken free from his dad, jumped into the abyss, he could have gone anywhere. Should have gone to Kyra, but he hadn't.

He was standing beside the now-familiar apartment building filled with broken souls, and stuffed somewhere within were Sophie's parents. The building's side entrance blew open. Four people stammered out, two guys and two girls. One of the guys tossed a bottle to the side, the sound of breaking glass following. He laughed and wrapped his arm around the nearest girl, leaving the shattered bottle at the base of the door.

"Classy tenants," Sebastian mumbled, his expression drooping, memories of the green Impala and the alleyway beating racing across his mind.

Before the door closed and clasped shut, Sebastian staggered forward and caught the edge, stopping it with fingers sandwiched between door and jamb. Heavy as it was—metal, thick, and wide—it swung easily on its hinges, allowing Sebastian into the space of the building beyond.

He didn't harbor any expectation of what lay inside the door. If he had bothered to visualize the interior, what he found was a pretty good fit. Pattern-heavy carpet, old and worn, running up the wall three or four inches. Dingy and scraped beige walls, and several feet in from the entrance, down a not-too-wide hallway, one small elevator.

Sebastian rested his weight against the wall near the elevator and waited. Waited to push the button. Waited for his head to clear. Waited for an ounce of strength to return. Needing his faculties working well enough for him to get the job done.

Sadness, anger, desire, frustration—a whole flurry of emotion washed over him, and none of it was his. Each one came hand-in-hand with thoughts and memories from the tenants in the building. He was drowning in feelings, and he didn't understand if this severity of the curse was Reaper or Mara in nature. How could either species deal with this constant onslaught? His mind had been so quiet. Why had it all come back with such brutality?

He doubled over and vomited on the carpet.

"Oh man. The night's too young for you to be *that* wasted." A teenage boy bent down and looked Sebastian in the eye, his hair dropping across his face, obscuring one of his eyes. "What time you start the party?"

Sebastian shifted to better see him, noticed the dark bottle he held.

"Here, let me help you." The boy placed his hand on Sebastian's arm.

"I'm fine," Sebastian said under his breath and turned to fully meet his would-be helper. Wiping his mouth with the back of his hand, he stared past the teen to the doors of the elevator beyond. The machine groaned as it lumbered up several stories. The sound separated into an army of colorful bangs, clangs, and shrilling echoes. Sebastian wanted to throw his hands over his ears and scream at the world to stop, just stop!

The boy tugged on Sebastian's arm.

"I said I was fine!" Sebastian snapped and swung his arm, pushing the boy away.

The boy banged into the wall on the opposite side of the hall. His bottle dropped, its contents spilling onto the carpet. He glowered at Sebastian before taking off down the hall at a run. He crashed through the entrance, letting the door swing to a close with a hard bang.

Sebastian dropped to the floor and pulled his knees into his chest. He stared at the bottle left behind and thought of Talia's mind helper—*Spiritual Peace*. Before he realized what he was doing, he was reaching across the hall, grabbing the bottle, and sucking down the last few drops.

He closed his eyes and waited. Only liquor, not a magical elixir. A sigh the weight of his soul swept through him, and he pulled all the anger and frustration he felt inward, until it was the size of a pinprick. He had never been so out of control of his emotions. Not since before he'd run away to the carnival. Before he'd left his father.

He laughed, but there was no heart in the action. It was irony. He had let his father back into his life, and with him came the same landslide of excrement. Sitting there for a breath or two, as he did, Sebastian wondered how he could kill a Grim.

Heat settled around him, wavered in the air beside him like a gentle companion, and Sebastian realized he now heard nothing. The usual creak of a door or the squawk of a voice carrying down the hall still held fast, but the feelings and memories lingered no longer. "How?" he said to the vacant hall, tilting the empty bottle in his hand and giving it a scrutinizing glare. *Surely it wasn't—*

His back straightened and eyes widened. Anger. Anger was his key. Possibly even anger at his father, specifically. He wasn't sure, not yet. But he would find out.

The elevator door opened with a long scratch, and an old lady stepped out, small dog yanked by a leash at her back. She wrinkled her nose at Sebastian, hugged the far side of the hallway, and walked by quickly. The doors to the elevator started to rattle shut.

No. Sebastian pulled himself up and pushed away from the wall. *I need to be on that.* He threw his ragged body into the cold, tight space moments before the doors closed. Folding himself into the front corner, Sebastian crouched and listened to the silence. There was nothing—no rattle, no hum, no movement of any kind—but a pulse, slow and steady, up on the third floor. He reached over and hit the button for number three. The elevator jolted and began its ascent.

Thump, cha-boom. The elevator halted in a bang, the doors opening with a slow pause-and-go. Sebastian was on the third floor, what he sought—Sophie's family line—to the right. A sluggish beacon summoned him. Shoulder dragging along the wall, left foot schlepping in a tow-and-drop, he moved like a dead man walking. The wall as his crutch.

Outside the apartment, he paused, caught his breath, and took stock of himself. His torn and blood-covered shirt. His dirty, skinned knuckles. With hands shaking and moving deliberately slow, Sebastian zipped the front of his jacket closed and pulled the sleeves down to hide as much of his hands as possible.

He fought callously to keep his gift stifled, but holding on to anger was harder to do than he had imagined. The emotions and memories kept trying to slither back in to his psyche. Never before had he felt so overwhelmed, so tangled in the struggle for control. Maybe this was his father's intention all along. Kept from the carnival and the aid Talia provided long enough, Sebastian was forced to deal.

Sebastian fumed, the heat rising up his neck into his face. Mortifier didn't know what it was like. He couldn't. The Grim was all Reaper. He didn't have to deal with the Mara's gift—or curse, as Sebastian saw it. Sebastian wondered how the two supernatural gifts really affected him. He suspected he got something close to a double dose of overwhelming emotions and memories.

Either that, or the Reapers were highly effective in handling the onslaught. Sebastian had a long, cracked road ahead of him before he would learn to master the assault. It seemed impossible. Anger for his father boiled over. All the pain and heartache flashed before his eyes in big, ugly blotches.

And then there was silence. Serenity. He'd managed it again. Pure resentment of his father had sucked in all the unwanted emotions and memories. The hallway was quiet. Sebastian took a deep breath and stepped up to the door.

He knocked. Waited.

No answer came. But he heard sounds on the other side.

It sounded—Sebastian leaned into the doorframe—it sounded like a mad scurry. A rush of some sort. The noise moved toward him, and Sebastian stepped back, keeping a hand on the frame for balance. The door swung open, exposing a middle-aged woman with blonde, frizzy hair, pulled back tight, accentuating the lines at the corners of her eyes.

"Oh," she said and set down a recklessly folded box on the table beside the door. "I was expecting someone else. Can I help you?" She brushed at her clothing and tiny bits of paper fluttered to the floor. It looked as if she had been shredding documents. A lot of them, to create that kind of paper fluff. "Did Jon send you?" She turned and walked back into the apartment.

Sebastian shifted his weight, made no move to follow the woman into the space of her apartment. He didn't like the way she so carelessly turned her back on a stranger. Maybe if Sophie had witnessed better behaviors at home, from her family, she might not have ended up dead with Lance-the-loser.

"You're not a vampire, are you?" she called back to him. "Waiting for some kind of invite to come in?"

"I don't feel right." Sebastian leaned against the door. *Is she serious?* Sebastian found himself dialing back his anger, wanting to let his ability free so he could feel her emotions, understand what she did and didn't know.

"It's fine, honey. If Jon sent you, there's no worry." She fussed a few feet away with boxes, stuffing things in, closing them up.

"Jon didn't send me."

She stopped and turned to look at him. "Oh, my. How rude of me. I just assumed—"

Sebastian took one step through the door. "I'm here about your daughter. I do have the right place, don't I?" He glanced around the apartment. Items that gave a home a personal touch were conveniently absent. "You do have a daughter, right?"

"Oh, my," she said again. "Yes, I'm sorry." She stood, took two steps toward him. "Of course, it was she who sent you—"

Sebastian braved another step, closing the gap even more. "Sophie wanted, or rather, she requested—"

"Sophie?" A puzzled look replaced the focus the woman had worn as a formfitting mask. Her body froze, and shoulders slumped. "What of—?"

Sebastian's hand dropped over the curve of her left shoulder before she could say another word. "She has an important message for you." Before the last of his words even touched the air, a stream of impressions, feelings, and desires leaped from his fingertips and rushed through the woman's bloodstream, straight to her head, heart, and soul. Sophie's message of peace, love, and forgiveness swept through her mother's entire being like an unexpected flood. No corner of her conscience was left untouched. Her knees gave way to the weight of revelation and she collapsed, Sebastian catching her in his arms.

The flood continued, only now it was a cyclone of emotion coming from Sophie's mom—anguish and anger, understanding. She sighed and cried into his arms, accepting a truth she could not change. But there was something else—

Sebastian held her and attempted to comfort her. All the while, his eyes searched for that something, the something he'd picked out of her memories. The very something kicking his adrenaline into a top-speed spin.

He knew the moment he'd found it. On the wall, in a basic oak frame, hung a faded picture mounted on what probably used to be red construction paper. A very young Sophie stood beside a man, huge grins on their faces, a Christmas tree in the background. Across the top in kid-scribbled Crayola, it read *Santa brought me a daddy for Christmas. Jon B Davies.* On the other side of Jon Davies was another girl. A bit older than Sophie, she stood a tad taller and had her blonde hair pulled back in a pony.

Alice.

Sebastian's mind summersaulted. He took a step back, dragging Sophie's mom with him.

She pulled herself together and looked at him, confusion and knowing burning in her eyes. "What of Alice?" she said.

Shoot. Sebastian dropped his arms, took another step back. His hand reached into his pants pocket, felt for Alice's locket. Wrapped it securely in his grasp. He should give it to the woman, Alice's mother—he knew that—but for the first time since he'd started his Reaping gig, he was petrified. This woman had lost not one, but *two* daughters, and the blame for one could partially fall on his own head. He took another step back, another step toward the door.

"Where are you going?" she questioned. "You can't leave. You need to explain yourself. Explain this." She waved her hands between them, implying the memory and emotion exchange that had just taken place.

"I'm sorry. I'm so, so sorry. But I can't." Sebastian turned and scuttled out the door. His body protested, argued his decision to run, but he fought against it, pushed his physical limits and bolted down the hall. She yelled at his back, but he didn't turn to look, and he couldn't hear her over the labored beat of his heart. His hand slammed on the elevator button, flattening against the surrounding cold metal plate, depressing both the up and down options together.

The doors opened almost immediately. In his haste to escape,

Sebastian glanced at Sophie and Alice's mom coming down the hall after him and stepped through the opening, taking notice far too late the elevator wasn't sitting in wait.

Sebastian twisted and fell into the dark elevator shaft.

20

CRIMP

Marcus

By the light of day, Club Afterlife lacked that special something that made it popular with the crowds by nightfall. Marcus stood in the middle of the dance floor and stared past the pool tables to the large entertainment balcony beyond. He thought of the first night he'd brought Kyra here, how everything had gone so much better than he had anticipated. Losing her memory had been unforeseen, but so damn perfect. Now look at the mess Marcus had to deal with. He shook his head. What had Leila been thinking, bringing Sebastian here?

"Well, let's see it," Marcus said and turned to meet Rick's waiting, watchful eye.

Rick pivoted, did an about-face, and led the way to a private staircase. Bright and stark was the stairwell, its main purpose the flow of supplies. They descended several flights, passing various levels of the club along the way to the basement. Heavy, dark scuffs, trash, and blood littered the last several steps before they walked through the door into the open storage area. The large metal door to the area beyond remained open, and men worked in the dank space with high-powered hoses, spraying the walls and floors. Where Marcus and Rick stood, several bodies had been tossed in a pile to the side. Someone had scrubbed and cleaned up the rest of the wreckage already.

Rick stopped, and his gaze swept over the place, his lips twisting to the side.

"How many were there?" Marcus asked.

"According to the surveillance playback, about a dozen or so," Rick said with a mild nod of the head.

"A dozen," Marcus repeated, his tone dry, surly. "A dozen men and we only manage to take out three of them, while losing all our own?" His nostrils flared.

Rick took a step back. "Well..." He pointed to the busy cleanup in the next room. "Something we can't explain went down."

"What happened?" Marcus's eyes narrowed. He stared past Rick and walked through the door to the other room. The large cage stood at the far end. A guy whose name he hadn't bothered to learn was hosing the area down. Chunks of matter—flesh and blood—were pushed into piles by the water spray. "What in all dragons' domain happened here?"

"That's the thing. We're not sure. The surveillance turned to static right after the first shots rang out. There's no way of telling without getting ahold of an actual witness."

"Then get me a damn witness," Marcus snarled. "I want to know what killed my men." He stood rigid, felt the fury burning through his bloodstream. If the Mara bastard was responsible—

Marcus spun around and stormed back to the front room, to the pile of bodies waiting there. He kicked at the one on top, watched it topple over. Dark fatigues. No distinguishing markings on the clothing—but for one tiny little square of an emblem, a patch sewn to the lower left corner of the soldier's vest. Easily overlooked. Marcus growled.

"So. He found me." Marcus raked his hand through his hair and kicked the soldier again, for extra measure.

"It would seem so, sir," Rick said, stepping up beside him. "But they didn't seem as interested in where you were, as in what was behind this door." He pointed to the large metal brute hanging wide open. "May I ask what, or who, you had locked up?"

Marcus turned sharply, stared right down at Rick. "No, you may not." He pivoted and walked for the stairwell. "I want all this cleaned up before the club opens, and I want Davies and his silly army found and destroyed. Understood?"

"Of course. But shouldn't Chet be here? Isn't this his territory?"

"I have Chet working on another matter. Never mind about him." Marcus paused in the doorway, looked back over the mess. "And get me Leila on the phone. I want to have a chat with her."

"Sir?"

"Just do it." Marcus stomped up the stairs, his feet clomping on each step with a heavy clang. His mind was calculating, deciphering, planning. If Davies was on to him, then it was time to use Davies to his advantage. This was nothing more than a crimp in his otherwise perfect plan. The edges of Marcus's lips twitched and lifted, warm contempt spreading through his chest like a plague.

21

DOWNTIME

Sebastian

The black of the elevator shaft moved past Sebastian's falling body at incredible speed. Soon he'd be broken bits on the bottom floor.

The swirl of a Reaper's vortex rose around him, encircled him, pulled him in. Next thing he knew, he was lying on a foggy forest floor.

How had he done that? Sebastian wasn't sure, but he wanted to know. There were *so* many things he wanted to know. He stared at the branches of the trees above him for a breath or five before forcing himself to move. Everything within him protested when he pushed up on his elbows, stood, and took a step. He recognized where he was, though, and the prospects of a more comfortable resting place propelled him.

Red and blue and purple, a rainbow of colored lines aglow. They flashed and swirled, running in loops, dips, and high mountain climbs. Sebastian used them as a guide through the fog, stumbling on the first step into the clear. The puncture in his side screamed *mercy*. It slowed his pace beyond his liking. He thought of Kyra and an ache churned in his chest. He should be seeking her out, making sure she was safe, but he wouldn't be much help to her in his present condition. If anything, he'd probably bring her more trouble. And so, he found himself shuffling through the fog. The damn, irritating fog.

Still—Kyra was a dragon, and according to his father, dragons were dying!

He pinned his gaze upon the small funnel cake cart near the front of the carnival's entrance. Madame Rue didn't see him. Soon enough, she would. He would make sure she couldn't avoid him. He planned to hit the side of the thing and collapse. She would for sure see him and get help. Somebody was bound to make sure Sebastian got to his tarot card trailer and his bed. All he needed was a few hours of sleep. He'd awake in better shape. He felt sure of it.

Sebastian.

His name whispered through the lingering crowd. Unsure if he'd actually heard it or not, Sebastian looked to his left and to his right. Zeke sat in his usual spot on the bench by the quiet river. Or was it a lake? So hidden by the mist, no one was sure how far the water extended.

Entertaining the idea of joining the old blind man lasted a mere millisecond. Sebastian seriously wanted for his bed. Zeke waved, and Sebastian found himself waving back. He paused, his face wrinkling. It made no sense to wave at a blind man. His hand came down on the edge of the funnel cake cart. The delicious aroma of batter and strawberries mixed with a metallic smell. It was wrong, and it turned his stomach. He knew it meant a shift in the carnival. Things were about to move, like they often did. It was part of the allure of Mystic's Carnival—the magic. Things were always shifting and moving, pathways changing. One could never be certain of their direction. The carnival knew where people needed to go, and it led them there. Where you wound up wasn't always where you *wanted* to go, but you got where you needed to be.

Tiny sparks began to fizzle and pop in the atmosphere, and the support beneath Sebastian's hands vanished. He faltered, taking a step to catch himself. His shin connected with something hard, mid-bone.

"Gotcha."

A hand grabbed him. The pain sliced through him, the support pressing too close to his wound.

"Have a seat," Zeke said.

Sebastian plopped down on the bench beside the old codger. "Nothing personal, but I'd much rather be in bed right now than hanging with you."

Zeke folded his hands over his cane and looked out toward the funnel cake cart and the entrance portal beyond. Sebastian knew the old man wasn't seeing any of it, but it didn't matter. "Tired, are you?"

Sebastian slumped in his spot, unsure how long he'd be able to hold a conversation, or himself, up. "Very."

"Haven't seen much of you since Higgins' service. What have you been up to?"

Sebastian's thoughts ran through the memories of Higgins. His sacrifice for Kyra, his service, what Zeke had asked of Sebastian after Higgins' death, what Sebastian had ultimately done for them both. Sebastian had learned so much about Higgins and the phoenix that cold, rainy day. He looked toward the busy carnival and wondered what it was he had seen when he'd pulled Higgins' body out of Purgatory. What it had meant for the old man. "The usual. Keeping myself busy, that's all."

Sebastian rested his elbow on the arm of the bench and let himself fall against it, supporting himself by one hand pressed against his cheek.

Zeke cleared his throat. "See Madame Rue, there?" Sebastian turned his gaze back to the funnel cake cart. "She also misses Higgins and Kyra. She throws herself into her work as a means of coping. Is that what you are doing?"

Sebastian took a deep breath. He wanted to close his eyes and not open them again for an eternity of time. He fought the desire and instead, looked back at Zeke. "Do you think I'm avoiding dealing with things? Because if so, you're way off base. I'm going to get Kyra back. She is in need of help, and I'm going to bring her that help. I merely need to recoup first."

Zeke's head bobbed up and down slowly. "Good. Good. I have faith you will do right by her."

"I'm glad somebody does."

Zeke's hand squeezed Sebastian's, stirring him from a complacent state. "You must believe in yourself and trust your gut."

Sebastian stared at Zeke's hand. *How does he always know exactly where to reach?* "I'm just feeling a little defeated at the moment, and all I want to do right now is hole up and lick my blackhole of a wound."

Zeke's head turned in Sebastian's direction. "And how is that going to help Kyra?"

Sebastian's defenses raised a degree. "How can I help her when I'm mangled and torn to shreds? I can hardly walk without doubling over."

Zeke patted Sebastian's hand, his face and eyes loosening in an open and warm manner. "All right, my boy. All right," he said, his voice gentle.

Sebastian felt his insides turn to cinder. He despised himself, his damn inability to protect and save Kyra. He should have broken the rules that day in Purgatory, seen her safely back to the living. He was already breaking the rules by being there and helping her. She never should have landed in the hospital with no memory of who or what she was. And she certainly shouldn't be in a relationship with any man morally capable of what Marcus had done to Sebastian. Marcus was a complete dickhead.

If only he understood Marcus's motives.

"The answer is often right in front of you. You only need know where to look."

Zeke's words were spoken so quietly it was a wonder Sebastian heard them. Though he suspected Zeke knew he'd hear, regardless of the low volume. Despite his exhaustion, Sebastian's mind started running over everything he knew regarding Kyra's situation. There had to be something. Something he was missing.

"What are you fellas up to?"

Chelsea was walking their way. She wore a delicate smile and the usual white dressing gown, featuring a flared base along the bottom four or so inches of the skirt, puffy sleeves, and vintage medallion lace.

Today she also wore a light blue robe with a princess waist tie and slippers to match. She usually showed up in her night attire, like she'd crawled out her window after retiring to her room. Or out the hospital room window. Wherever it was she was staying these days. If only Sebastian had known the young cancer girl would become a permanent fixture in his life, he might have handled things differently the day he had given her a reprieve from death.

He hated getting to know her. Hated that she tried to make him care. It would make things more difficult, more painful later, when he was called to reap her soul. There would be no third chance for her. The cancer slowly chomped away at her anatomy. Her Grim bell would soon chime.

"We were only talking, child." Zeke reached back and patted Sebastian on the back. "I'm sure this young man would enjoy your company immensely."

Sebastian shot Zeke a what-the-hell look. Even if the old man wasn't aware of how Sebastian felt, the prompt was uncool. He wanted to crash, and *that* Zeke did know.

"Chelsea, hon." Zeke's hand reached in her direction and shook in the air. "Why don't you see Sebastian to his trailer?"

Zeke's dark skin vibrated in front of Sebastian; it was all he focused on. Everything else blurred at the edges. He didn't hear Chelsea's response. Her words blended with the hum and roar of the carnival crowd beyond the gates. He felt the desire to yak churning in his stomach.

Planting his hand firmly on the bench arm, Sebastian steadied himself and began to stand. "If you see Talia, can you ask her to swing by my place?" Sebastian didn't know the odds of Zeke running into Talia, but the forever-present carnival visitor sure had a way of knowing everyone and everything in the most magical way. Sebastian needed to talk to the young witch about Kyra and felt confident Zeke would make it happen.

He stood, his weight shifting, muscles straining, pain pulsing sharply through his core. White dots popped into his vision. They expanded quick and enveloped all the cosmos. Sebastian lurched forward, throwing a foot out to stop and correct his maneuver. It failed. He teetered to the side and succumbed to gravity.

A groan hissed from between his lips, the grass racing toward his face at a tilt.

"Oh!" Chelsea hurried to close the distance. Her hands came into view seconds later.

His vision dimmed. Turned to black. Everything was gone. All gone.

DANCING MIDNIGHT, LIKE BLACK SILK WAVING IN A BREEZE ATOP A SILVER MESH, floated above. The Mara Web. It was an impenetrable cloud cover, spanning as far as Sebastian could see. There was no escape, only net. Beneath him, soft ground mimicked his bed. It moved, molding itself to his form. His body trembled, unwilling to move, and a trickle of sweat ran down his temple. The only sky visible below the dangerous sky-high trap flowed in dark squiggles of purples and grays.

Sebastian stared at the shimmering crisscross pattern of the Mara snare, reason dictating in his ear, reminding him to be terrified. Of all the things he'd come across, the Mara Web made him the most vulnerable. But tonight, his logic switch had flipped to off, because Sebastian felt oddly at ease among the foreign terrain. No tension existed. He only wanted tranquility. Sleep.

As far as his average dream went, this one was seriously strange. But there was so much about Mara nature he had yet to understand. His mother hadn't exactly been the nurturing type, and when she'd left, he was a mere three years of age.

He closed his eyes. *Only for a short while*, he promised himself. He'd rest for a few minutes—fifteen or so—then he'd explore the new dream world. After his energy returned. He took a deep breath and released the tension he'd been holding. Warmth radiated across his body, generated from the pulsating pain in his abdomen.

What happens to the dreamer if he dreams within an already active dream? The curious notion had barely taken form in Sebastian's synapses when the memory of the mesh above faded into a crowded sky of flapping wings. Dragons. They covered the celestial sphere. Flying in swirling mists of burning embers. He couldn't blink, couldn't look away. It was mesmerizing. Extraordinary numbers for a supposed dying race.

Something pushed against his leg. Flushed and firm, it slithered up his body in one long, fluid motion. The something was a someone, and she was devastating and stunning and Mara. Her appeal went beyond exquisite. No doubt, Mara-magically conceived. The first Mara Sebastian had seen since his mother. The mother who hadn't wanted him.

Curvaceous bohemian dream: raven hair, cherry bruised lips, and eyes that even the devil would work to please. Sebastian pushed up on his elbows and his breath caught in his chest.

"Relax," her voice sang, washing over him like soothing bathwater.

He wanted to obey, and that made him feel weak. *I'm not merely Mara*, he reminded himself. *I am Reaper.* Somehow that had to make him stronger. Didn't it? He detested himself for succumbing, if only one inch or millisecond, to her Mara call. His head shook, fighting the effects, fighting to knock her hooks free. But look away, he would not. Miss the chance to witness or study or question a Mara? Wasn't gonna happen.

"Don't fight. Give in to the pleasure. Let us happen." She glided forward, her hands cutting the course and leading the way. She left nothing sacred, nothing to the imagination. "You are the only son of the nightmare, in a faction populated by daughters. I've wanted so terribly long to know you."

A violent cough burst from Sebastian's lungs. The craving for water helped him rein in his focus, fight the power of the Mara. Push her away or scramble out from beneath her was what he'd do if he were in full form. But he wasn't at his best, and there was no telling what would set her off. Sebastian straightened his back, pushing farther up onto his elbows. Before he could take a breath, she shoved him down and pinned him to the ground. Bullets ricocheted like wild shrapnel, bouncing through his shoulder blades and ribcage. He grimaced.

All that move revealed was Sebastian had a damn inconvenient, drawn-out healing process to complete. Nothing new was gained from his pain. A different method needed to be employed.

Delving deep within his soul, Sebastian explored the darker corners of his mind—the playgrounds reserved for dreams and nightmares. Pulling forth his Mara, he let the spectacular beast seep into everything—every move he made, every breath he took, every word he spoke. "I've been keeping a low profile. How did you find out about me?"

A deliciously crooked smile crept across her face. "Oh honey, something like you can't exist and there not be talk. People hear things. I hear everything." Her hand moved to his hip bone, caressed the curve millimeters above his belt. Sebastian froze, every muscle going rigid. "Imagine if I were to sit on you instead of some waste of a human." She straddled him with the speed of sudden, urgent desire and her body began to slow dance. "What would we create together?" She bent forward, bringing her lips close to his, rolling her breath across his cheek.

He closed his eyes and turned his head away. Reaper's Hell, the pictures she was bombarding him with. The things with which she wanted to tempt him. The things she imagined them doing. He'd never dreamed the Mara magic could be so intense or abusive. Sebastian started to pull away, drag himself out from beneath her weight.

A ripple ran over her figure. It morphed her dark hair to red. "I can look like anyone or anything you desire."

Sebastian was staring into Kyra's eyes. The Mara had taken her face. He wasn't fooled, and yet—part of him wanted to be. He could pretend, if only for the length of a dream, and he would have Kyra.

He shook his head and pushed her away. It wasn't Kyra. She wasn't Kyra, and she never would be. "Get off," he yelled. "You are not her. Don't pretend to be."

The Mara shed her Kyra disguise. The dark-haired beauty once again sat atop him, overpowering him. "You don't like it?"

"No, I don't. You are forbidden to take the form of another girl."

She smirked, her smile taking on a wicked curve. The kind Sebastian had become all too familiar with after his time spent working the carnival. She placated him with little to no conviction in her stature. "Very well. You can see how we are meant to be, can't you? Mara-*à*-Mara. It couldn't be more ideal."

Sebastian wasn't so sure. Although—he could learn a lot from spending time with someone of the same nature. That didn't mean he wanted to get personal with her. No way in Reaper's Hell.

He scratched the back of his neck and scrunched his brow. "I suspect a Mara is involved in a small matter I'm having trouble with currently. You wouldn't know anything about that, would you?"

She torqued her head to the side, batted her thick lashes, and brushed her lips along his jawline. "What answer will result in us working together?" Before he could blink, she was on top him again, pushing him down.

The blood rush was quick, the hardening unstoppable. *Not with her*, he thought. *Not with her*. He shoved her away and yelled, "No! I am stronger than you. I am a Reaper!"

He bolted awake.

CHELSEA SAT ACROSS THE ROOM IN HIS FAVORITE COMFY CHAIR. MOMENTARILY disoriented, Sebastian didn't say a thing, didn't move, simply searched the small trailer with a sweeping gaze. The dream came to him like a car slamming into a telephone pole. He pushed up onto his elbows. "How long have I been asleep?"

Chelsea bit her lip and delivered a timid smile. "A few hours."

Swinging his legs over the side of the bed, he sat up. His trailer was tiny. There were only a few feet between the top of his head and the ceiling.

Chelsea leaned forward in her seat. "What's wrong?"

Sebastian stretched his shoulders and released. He no longer felt pain from his wound. "A few hours are a few too many." He looked down and lifted his shirt. The bandage was new. He looked around the tiny space and stopped at the blood-soaked gauze wadded up and discarded with a small bundle of trash in his wastebasket.

Chelsea followed his gaze. “I hope you don’t mind. We took the liberty of cleaning you up and changing your bandage. It looked in need. The old one was in bad shape.”

“Who’s ‘we’?”

“Talia and myself. She came by earlier, said she’d come back.”

Sebastian nodded. That was good news. He needed to talk to Talia about Kyra’s pendant. Curious, he pulled back the bandage, then glanced at Chelsea.

“It’s all right,” she said. “It’s not anything I haven’t already seen.”

He suspected not. He had the strangest feeling where Chelsea was concerned. Tension built in his brow, and his eyes narrowed in at her, but he didn’t see anything screaming guilty, so he looked down at the wound. Only there was no wound. He was completely healed.

“How...?” Sebastian began, then cut off his own words.

“I think it was a combination of things. That stuff you slathered on did a miraculous job fixing you up quick. Zeke said it was the best medicine you could have found. Although, he didn’t look too happy about it.” Chelsea’s lips drew into a tight line. “Talia also came in with some wild mojo of her own while you were sleeping.” Her face lit up. “You should have seen it. There’s nothing like it in this world. It was magic!”

Sebastian shook with laughter. “That’s most likely what it was. Magic. Talia is a witch.”

The small room grew quiet and Chelsea absorbed her “oh-wow” moment. Sebastian could see it was a process for her. He was surprised that with as many visits as she’d made to the carnival, she hadn’t come to the realization already. Sebastian chewed on Chelsea’s comment. Why was Zeke bothered by the medicine used? Something didn’t feel right. Tension crept into his back and shoulders. “What was it, the medicine used on me? Did Zeke say?”

“I have no idea. He didn’t mention. I assumed you would know. Said all you needed was some downtime, and you’d be good as new.” Chelsea leaned forward in the chair. “You really don’t know what it was?”

“Nope. Alice wouldn’t—” Sebastian halted mid-sentence. Memories of what his father had done to Alice flooded his mind. Of Alice and Sophie—sisters, both now deceased. He should go to Purgatory and look for Alice. Except, if she went directly to one of the destinations beyond Purgatory—Heaven or Hell—he wasn't welcome there. His father had made it sound like she'd been sent straight to one of those places. If that's where Alice had gone, there was nothing left to do. No apology could ever be made.

The atmosphere in the trailer thickened, pressing him from every angle, pushing the oxygen straight from his lungs. Ties with his father must be severed. Sebastian needed to get out from under his control. Except, would that mean embracing his Mara half? He wasn't so sure that was the best thing. Sebastian frowned, considering the consequences of cutting his father out of his life. He couldn't do it. Not right this second, anyway.

Now, he needed to focus on the blonde in the dressing gown sitting across from him. "How long have you been sitting here watching me?"

"The whole time, of course." Her answer implied it had been a silly question, with which Sebastian did not agree.

"Why would you sit here that long?"

"Isn't it obvious?" When Sebastian didn't answer, Chelsea continued. "You looked like you were going to die. You had a hole punched through you. A hole! Somebody had to keep an eye on you. Make sure you were healing and not getting worse."

Sebastian shrugged. Her explanation actually made a lot of sense. So did his thought of keeping her outside of his friends circle. *Friends.* His heart panged at the thought. He yearned for Kyra's return.

Still, it was clear he and Chelsea were fated in at least one way, if not several. He watched her move about the trailer with caution. Black Death curled up cozy inside her. It would eventually call them together in an official capacity, and that's exactly why he hated that she'd wiggled her way into his life. He didn't want to feel something meaningful and painful when that day came. But there was something more to the girl. The puzzle of Chelsea had been bothering Sebastian for some time now. Yes, she was dying, but the *more* needed to be discovered. He didn't like not knowing. It left the door open for unwanted surprises. Only, dealing with her now would slow down his rescue of Kyra, and nothing was more important than Kyra. Not in his world.

Sebastian stood and stepped over to his tiny chest of drawers. "Chelsea, do you live at home?" He grabbed a clean shirt and switched out the tattered, bloodstained one he was wearing. Before closing the drawer, he grabbed a tiny bottle of Talia's *Spiritual Peace* tonic and shoved it in his pocket with Alice's locket. As a Grim reaps, no doubt he'd be needing a sip or two soon. He glanced at Chelsea. *Funny how I never pick anything up from her.*

"Where else would I live?" Chelsea asked. She sounded perplexed. Sebastian decided she was probably unaware of the severity of her condition. If she knew, she'd probably be in some kind of hospital where she could be treated, as he had envisioned her. It was most likely her unusual cancer that made her a void in a sea of memories and emotions of the dead and dying.

"Maybe you should..." He stopped and looked at her, letting his gaze take in all of her in silence. She deserved better than having her final days void of hope, trapped in an institute, hooked up to machines, slave to a regulated medicine routine. Sometimes ignorance was a blessing. He'd allow her that.

She stared at him expectantly.

He averted his eyes and instead grabbed his jacket off the edge of the bed. "Help me find Talia and my way back to Zeke."

"Looks like you're doing fine on your own." She rose from the chair and took a slow look around. He was doing fine, but he needed an excuse to pull her out of his trailer. Leaving her alone with all his personal belongings was not something he wanted to do. "I finally get to see the inside of your place, and it's so short-lived." She sighed.

He walked toward her. "Sorry." He paused for a moment. "Come on, let's go. I need to talk to Zeke." Sebastian opened the door and stepped into the brisk night, Chelsea instantly at his side providing support.

"Back from the dead, my boy?" Zeke waved Sebastian to the bench. "You had us all concerned. Glad to hear you up and about." Zeke spoke with a mere dash of emotion and stared at the front gate. He sat on the usual bench, leaning forward on his cane.

Talia burst from a cloud of smoke and jumped in front of Sebastian. She poked him and pushed him. Finger repeatedly jammed into his chest. She stopped with a snap and spun around. "Everyone's all like, dead, Sebastian's dead. I'm all, gah. No way. Watch this." She twisted her hands around each other with incredible speed. "Magic delivered." She bowed. Her brown hair sprung from her head in a wild mess, but she was always impeccably clean. Just fashionable Talia with a wild personality, wild hairstyles, and a wild wardrobe.

"Thanks for fixing me, Talia. I'm forever in your debt." Sebastian bowed his head. Working with her was always refreshing. Never the same thing twice.

Talia skipped backwards, toward Zeke on the bench. "You owe me for so many things, pretty boy, I'll be collecting until you collect me."

Right. Sebastian didn't care to think about collecting the souls of the people he knew. Why did Talia have to bring that up? "I need to talk to you."

"Yeah, yeah. Bring it on, hot stuff." She spun in a circle before plopping on an arm of the bench.

"The tooth pendant. The one you told me to look for. Kyra wasn't wearing it."

Talia flicked her fingers together so fast she could probably start fire with the proper friction. "You didn't look hard enough. She has it on her person somewhere. If she ain't wearing it around her neck, then it's someplace else." Talia's face began to twitch. Her eyebrow danced, and a wicked little grin snuck across her lips. "Strip her naked if you need to. You find it."

Sebastian laughed, felt his cheeks warm.

Chelsea coughed.

"Wait," Talia said and produced a ball of white smoke between her open palms. She studied it for several seconds before waving it away and facing Sebastian. "I had it wrong. Check even closer. It may be deeper than on her person."

"What does that mean?" Sebastian stared at her, confusion and disbelief flooding his system.

Talia slapped him on the back. "Think about it, pretty boy. I'm sure you'll figure it out. You're a smart guy." She danced a couple of steps back, a wicked grin gracing her delicate features.

"You done here? Sebastian and I need to talk." Zeke's tone was neither agitated nor annoyed, but Sebastian felt a psychic push telling him to hurry up.

Sebastian turned toward Chelsea. "Thanks for your help. I really appreciate it, but I've got it from here."

Chelsea looked stunned and disappointed but didn't argue. "I'm so glad you're going to be fine. I was worried." She kissed him on the cheek and ran from the scene.

Sebastian watched her go. She was a curious girl. Falling for her Reaper. Did her subconscious mind remember he'd let her live when she was supposed to die? Whatever bothered him about her, had he actually created it? His thumb and finger rubbed at his chin, attempting to coax the answer out. Only it wasn't there to be found. He moved toward the bench.

Talia hopped off the bench, pranced around the fringe, and eyed Sebastian. He stood with fists jammed in his pockets and feet planted shoulder width apart, prepared to go to war for the answers he sought. She leaned in with a small piece of folded paper between her fingers, shoved it at his chest. "Here's the deal. Old man there is going to gnaw your ear off, talk to you about...stuff. Listen to him, but add this to your to-do list. Don't forget the dagger." Sebastian's brow pinched, and Talia pointed to the paper. "It's all there. Read it."

"Time's short," Zeke reminded.

Talia jumped on one foot. "I know! This is important." Talia grabbed Sebastian's arm, yanking it free of the pocket. "You're going to thank me for this, too." She winked and began to rub and roll her hands over the bare skin of his forearm.

The friction warmed, sizzled, roasted his skin. Concentrated in a circle and splaying out along his artery, he melted. He tried to hold still, but damn, it wasn't easy. "Ouch."

"Sorry." She blew lightly across the burn. Something looking spookily like a tattoo now marked up his arm. "This will help you get wherever you need to be." She pointed to the design. "It will lead you to the nearest Gatekeeper, or whatever else you need."

"Gatekeeper?" Sebastian stared at the new art decorating his skin. White lines swung around, creating an elaborate compass of sorts, minus any polar markings.

"For when you need a shortcut."

Sebastian didn't look up, but continued to study the design. Watched the hand within the compass rotate. "I'm familiar with Gatekeepers." When Sebastian finally looked up, Talia was gone.

It was only the two of them now, Sebastian and Zeke. He turned to the old man sitting on the bench and leaning into his cane. May he be as wise as he appeared. Sebastian had questions. Something about dragons, and Kyra was at the cold heart of it. "Let's talk about Kyra."

Zeke smiled.

22

FORMALITY

Marcus

"Where have you been?" The muscles in Marcus's neck strained. One at the corner of his eye twitched. "You kept me waiting. Never keep me waiting." He paced the Great Hall, his footsteps echoing off the stone interior.

Leila laughed. "Do you think I fear you? It would be foolish to think so. I am the one with the plan. I make the rules." She swept into the room through the main double doors and strolled casually down the cascading staircase. "You must learn patience. Did you never learn its virtues?"

The former decadence of the Great Hall's décor lay in ruin, victim to decades of neglect and abandonment. Once the hottest spot in town, it was now buried beneath the cityscape, forgotten. Only the old and few remembered it, knew of its existence. Knew how to find it.

Five jars sat on the grand staircase. Within each, swirled magical storms, each of a different color and origin. The dragons, determined creatures that they were, thrashed at their glass cages with their magical essence and wild determination. They would never give up, never back down. That was one reason Marcus had chosen these particular dragons. Of course, many dragons fit that description. Not all, but many. Finding the right five had been nothing more than a formality. He'd never doubted he would get what he needed, that the convergence would provide for his own dragon's return. And more.

Leila sauntered across the wide, open floor toward him. "What of your young dragon?"

Marcus's back and shoulders stiffened. He didn't like it when Leila questioned his relationships, but he wouldn't let her know she got under his skin. He stood a smidge taller. "Chet is keeping Kyra entertained tonight. A work night at home. Or some such thing."

"You trust Chet?" A nasty hint of heartless ruination played in her words.

Marcus stood his ground, a stern burn in his stare. "My men would never defy me."

Leila laughed and closed the space between them. "You've been waiting all this time, and you don't have everything prepared? I would have thought you'd have the place prepped and ready to go."

Leila's walk reminded Marcus of a gait. She was too proud. He could fix that.

"Come." She grabbed a torch with one hand and two candles between her fingers with the other. "Let's get it set up."

Following her lead, they had the symbol created out of candles in a matter of minutes. Marcus walked the circle, lighting each wick in turn. Shadows reached away from the circle laid at their feet. The shadows danced, fading as they blew farther away.

"Put the dragons in the center, aligning them in an arc in front of you," she said, pointing out where she wanted Marcus to place the beasts.

He strode across the room. A smile warmed Marcus's heart as he continued to work, preparing for the ceremony. Setup was going to take some time, but in the end, he'd get what no other dragon before him ever had—the power of all species in one. He would be unstoppable.

SIMPLE. ZEKE HAD CALLED RETRIEVING THE DAGGER FROM THE DRAGON'S DEN an easy task. *Easy, my ass*, thought Sebastian, and he continued to run at a frantic pace along the country road. It was quiet, almost too still. No one around for as far as the eye could see. He couldn't believe he hadn't found a portal yet.

Actually, that was a lie.

The little white lines of the compass etched into his forearm burned, the arrow within continuously spinning around and around, never pausing long enough to indicate a direction in which he should tread. Just his luck—the new gate gizmo wasn't working. He'd been so sure there would be a Gatekeeper down this stretch of road. If only he could find a member. Any tired old member would do.

No. Scratch that.

The Gatekeeper needed to be young and inexperienced. The less experience, the more likely to bend, even break the rules, and that's what he was looking for tonight.

Sebastian shivered, recalled Zeke's words. Zeke wanted Sebastian to find Bolsvck, one of the most powerful dragons still alive. Yeah, that wasn't dangerous. Grim chance he would make time for a Reaper. Yet Bolsvck was the only one worthy of challenging Marcus, according to Zeke, so somehow Sebastian had to get to him. Had to enlist his help. And he was Kyra's father, so that had to count for something.

How much does Zeke really know? Sebastian wondered.

Sebastian had no time to waste, yet he was losing time looking for someone who didn't want to be found. Gatekeepers died, didn't they? He should be able to feel their souls, yet all he got was some kind of fuzzy resonance. It pinpointed a rather large area and gave him nothing more. Far too general. He had no clue what the distorted feeling meant, and Talia's gift—the compass—wasn't helping at all. To be privy to his father's vast knowledge would be a godsend, if only Sebastian knew a way to absorb it all in one sitting.

He laughed out loud. So much knowledge at once would likely

overwhelm him. Possibly turn his brain to pulverized roadkill. As this venture was likely to do. Dragons weren't known for their common courtesy, and there was a reason Kyra had run away to the carnival. Sebastian hoped Zeke knew what he was doing, sending Sebastian in search of Kyra's father. Something told him she wasn't going to like this when she got her memories back.

Sebastian stopped, braced his hands on his knees, and took a long breath. Running along the road wasn't working. There had to be something else. Something better. He had to think like a Gatekeeper. Look for them where they would most likely be. Of all the gates Sebastian knew of, none were on a main thoroughfare. Not ever. Gates were always hidden away, off to the side, in quiet places less likely to be traveled and observed.

Hordes of bats flooded his insides. The pressure of time was his enemy, stressing his mind, messing with his thought process, and making each minute feel direr.

He closed his eyes, cleared his mind, and said a silent prayer. More like a wish, but he hoped someone was listening enough to care. Unclear to him was whether the higher powers bothered with prayers from Reapers. Didn't stop him from trying.

If his gut was telling him which way to go, he wished it would scream. Subtle whispers weren't working for him. A gentle whisper seemed to be all he was getting, though. He couldn't even be sure it meant anything, but he followed. Turning to the left, he ran from the road, deep into the woods.

Each stride sank with a heavy foot upon the dirt path, and the farther along he moved, the more confident he felt. "Come on, Gatekeeper," he mumbled. "Show me where you are." The words had no sooner left his lips than the compass locked in on a location and pointed the way.

Ghastly Grim! Could it have been so simple all along? Why didn't he think to ask for the location out loud? He cursed himself, shook his head, and moved forward through the brush.

A natural path came in from the left and curved, merging with his direction of motion. He followed the pathway, and it remained steady with the compass reading. Wide enough for one at first, it narrowed to something small animals had likely made. Barely noticeable unless you were looking hard to see the route.

He pushed his way through, moving branches and sweeping around bushes. It was the longest, most drawn-out moment of his life. That he could recall, anyway. He'd probably been running for twenty minutes, but it felt like sixty. A small watering hole lay at the end of the path. *An ideal location for a portal*, thought Sebastian. Although, this location was rather far off the beaten path. More so than usual. Not that that meant anything. There were likely many portals in extreme remote locations he had yet to find.

Problem was he didn't actually *see* a portal. If there were any in the vicinity, he should pick up on their frequency or shimmer. He should get something. Anything. At least, that's how he thought they worked.

A quick scan of the perimeter revealed a small, oval-shaped pond with a brook dribbling in from above. The hillside stretched up and away at a gentle grade. Nothing marked an ideal portal location, nothing but—

A notion struck him. It was slightly crazy, but he had nothing to lose. Why not, he figured. Sebastian took a deep breath and jumped into the pond. *Hell, hope I'm right,* he thought. He prayed his feet wouldn't collide with muddy ground in seconds.

Sebastian slipped through the water, the chill slicing straight through his clothing and biting into his skin. He dumped onto the hard ground below, connecting with a jolt. Sharp pain splintered up his shins, but otherwise he was fine. The jump had landed him in a hidden room below the water's surface. The water moved above, at the ceiling, and the moonlight filtered through, bathing him and the rest of the space in a soft, cool glow. Clearly magical, it had to have been created by the Gatekeepers.

"Where did you come from?"

Sebastian spun around at the sound of the man's voice. Only feet away stood a tall, broad, dark-haired man. He looked like an official Gatekeeper, for all Sebastian knew—although he was young, and that had to be a good thing. Sebastian had only met one other before.

Sebastian stood and bowed his head. "Didn't mean to startle you. I need to use your portal. You haven't made this one an easy find."

The Gatekeeper's face hardened. "This one isn't active yet, so it isn't resonating."

Sebastian bit his tongue. He wanted to laugh at his mistake but knew it to be in bad form, so he chose to behave. "I came because I was looking for you. I need your help."

The Gatekeeper turned his back on Sebastian and pretended to go back to work.

Sebastian approached him with caution. "Did I offend you? I didn't mean to. You are only the second Gatekeeper I've met. I should have shown better manners. My apologies."

The Gatekeeper's gaze flickered over Sebastian. "It is forgiven. Think nothing more of it. Now go, as this portal is not ready for you yet."

Sebastian dragged his hand along the wall of water. It was wet, yet firm. Oddly warm against his fingertips. "What is this place? How did you hold the water back, create this air pocket invisible from above?"

The Gatekeeper stopped what he was doing, and a smug smile turned the corners of his lips. "Gatekeeper magic. It's not for you. It's only for my kind to know."

"Your kind. That's a lot of power for only one species to control, don't you think?"

"Look who's talking, Reaper."

"So, you know what I am. That saves a bit of time and formality." Sebastian squared his shoulders and placed his finger to his lips in a moment of thought. "Wouldn't it be nice to have a Reaper owe you a favor?"

The Gatekeeper's lips turned down into a frown. "How would that do me any good?"

Sebastian's eyes sparkled. "Are you kidding? Think about it."

The Gatekeeper nodded. "You may have a point. I can see there may be a benefit or two. What is it you want?"

Sebastian's insides buzzed, and he pushed down his anxiety over what he had to do next. "It should be rather easy. I need a couple of portals."

"I figured as much. Portals to where?"

"For starters, I need a quick one directly into Mobürn."

"There's a reason why there aren't any portals in or out of Mobürn. The dragons residing there want to be left alone. You are not dragon. They'll destroy you on sight."

"I'm very aware of the dangers. But this is a serious matter, and lives are hanging on a meat hook. Cut me some slack and help a Reaper out. What do you say? Will you or will you not help me?"

The Gatekeeper paced the small underwater room, his hand in constant motion, scratching through the back of his hair down to his neck. Tension emanated from him in thick, heavy waves, absorbing the oxygen, making the space almost unbearable.

Sebastian coughed into his hand, hoping to spur the conversation to a desired conclusion.

The Gatekeeper waved his finger like a nervous twitch. "If I do this for you, there will have to be a time limit. I can't leave the portal open indefinitely. Can you accomplish what you need to do within an hour's time?"

Sebastian's eyes widened. "One hour? To do everything? Find and talk to the individual I need and get back, or get stuck? Is that what you're saying?"

The Gatekeeper nodded.

"Looks like I don't have a choice. I agree to your terms." Sebastian put out his open hand.

The Gatekeeper sighed and narrowed his eyes on Sebastian. "There was more. What else did you want from me?"

"We can discuss that when and if I return from the first trip in one piece," Sebastian said. "Can we get started?"

"You mean now?"

"Is there any better time? I'd like to get going. Time is short, and I can't afford to waste any more."

The Gatekeeper shifted his weight and looked over Sebastian with an appraising eye. "I don't trust you."

"As you shouldn't."

"Why won't you tell me what else you seek?" He placed his hand on the tool harness at his side. The tool used to birth doorways to new realms and worlds.

Sebastian kicked his foot out, took a step. "Because, my new friend," his hand came down on the Gatekeeper's shoulder, "it may be a moot request, depending on how things play out in this first little adventure of mine."

The young Gatekeeper's eyes shifted over Sebastian and the surrounding room. He appeared to look at everything, yet see nothing. His eyes were completely glazed over. "Okay."

Sebastian puckered his lips and drew back his brows. Watched while the Gatekeeper pulled the tool from his belt and began to draw a circle on the ground. Completed, he stepped to the side and tossed something from his hand across the divided space. Next, he chanted a few words Sebastian didn't understand.

The outer lines of the circle began to glow a brilliant orange and red, beaming through the dirt. Like fire breaking through the earth. At one point, the light ignited in hot white. It took off like the wick on a stick of dynamite, moving over the line until the whole circle burned brighter, more brilliantly than before. The portal burst to life. A second later, it vanished. Sebastian knew the door was still there and had simply taken on its protective camouflage. He could feel the vibration, slight as it was, and knew exactly where to find the doorway.

The Gatekeeper turned to face Sebastian, no pride present in his demeanor. He looked concerned, rather than satisfied.

"Thank you..." Sebastian paused. "What do I call you?"

"I am Madoc."

"Thank you, Madoc. I owe you one." Sebastian shook the young Gatekeeper's hand, all the while his heart crammed up into his throat.

He stepped forward and dropped through the portal.

23
BOLSVCK

Sebastian

Sebastian slipped through the portal, his hands grasping for the edge. He dangled in the air, an uneven terrain of rock and slow-flowing magma beneath him.

"Reap me," Sebastian mumbled.

Is this madness or pure genius in the portal placement? he wondered. It would be difficult for a dragon to accidentally stumble through a door placed in the sky. Difficult for him to get back through, too.

Flinging his legs forward, Sebastian swung back and forth until constant momentum moved through his body. When his legs swung forward, he released his hold. He flipped forward and landed on a large slab of slate. Volcanic matter slushed past in cracked veins running around and through the rocks. Quick jumps and skips had him moving across the rocks, using them as giant stepping-stones.

From stories—and a few directions from Zeke—Sebastian knew where to go. The dragons would gather in the sanctuary. The dragon Bolsvck—the mighty dragon who had refused to rule, the most feared and revered of all dragons, and Kyra's father—should be found there.

Marking the time on his watch, Sebastian moved at top speed through the canyon. What he was looking for had to be at a higher elevation, so his gaze traveled the walls in search of a path.

In canyons settled with dragons, there was no need for roads or paths. At least, not for Fire Dragons. They could fly to their destination. Sebastian would need to make his own path, but first he needed to identify his target. As he rounded the first bend, he saw a large, oversized-brick wall marked what he'd been looking for. He silently thanked Madoc for getting him so close. A short climb, and he was slipping into the dragons' damp lair. Barely in and the rock began to break, fall away beneath his feet. He slid down the embankment.

Dark, sharp claws slammed down at his feet, stopping him short. Sebastian had been expecting a Fire Dragon. Perhaps a scout or centennial. He never dreamed he'd run into a Black Dragon on this little errand. But here he was, fuming breath and all. Sebastian's mind spun with a whirlwind of information. He tried to remember what he'd read about them in all his species research. Research he'd done after meeting Kyra the first time. Black Dragons were dangerous, terribly vile. Possibly the evilest of the species.

Sleek, thin skin stretched ghastly over his skeleton structure, and his wings looked like moldy Swiss cheese. Vapors of fungal green seeped from the sides of his mouth, and the strong accompanying scent of rotting corpses burned Sebastian's nose hairs. From deeply sunken sockets, he stared down at Sebastian with blood-red eyes and snarled.

The side of his lip quivered, lifting to show his all-too-sharp canines. "Your kind is not welcome here."

Sebastian's hands went up in peace and he bowed his head. "My apologies. I have come to beg an audience with Bolsvck."

Claws dragged immense scars through the earth. "Mighty Bolsvck does not lower to one such as you."

Sebastian glanced past the imposing dragon to the immense hole the cave opened up to. Muddy water ran through the center, dividing the cavern. On the far side sat a humongous red dragon with unique markings running the length of his body. His presence, majestic and commanding. The largest Fire Dragon Sebastian had ever imagined. He had to be Bolsvck. He wasn't alone, though. Dragons of all shapes, sizes, and colors moved throughout the sanctuary. The interior of the mountain was a bustling dragon community. Kyra hadn't lied when she'd said the stories of dragon extinction were greatly exaggerated.

Light poured in on the hollow from a break in the ceiling. It glimmered off Boslvck's hide, marking him for the treasure he was, a born leader of his kind. Near his front leg, up by the stretch of his neck, shining in the summer's light, was a Dragon King's marking. Sebastian watched him use his fire to warm the ground before cozying into a position on a high rock overlooking his flock—or dignity, as it were in this case.

Sebastian glanced between the Black Dragon and Kyra's father. "But I just need—" He took a step toward his goal, toward Bolsvck. A black arm swept down, claws extended. It hit Sebastian hard and fast. Knocked him off his feet and sent him flying backwards.

Sebastian crashed into the mountain's rock side. Splinters of pain shot out across his backside. A boil of hot, white pain ruptured his gut. Sebastian doubled over, threw his hands on his knees for support. *Air—need air.* He pounded a fist to his chest, and his windpipe opened with a massive gasp. "What the hell?" Sebastian stumbled forward. "I promise you, Bolsvck will want to hear what I have to say."

"Tell me. I'll be the judge." Smaller and brilliantly bright, a White Dragon stepped from around the corner. She pinned her sharp gaze directly on Sebastian. She might've resembled an ice carving, but Sebastian wouldn't be fooled. Supreme intelligence dwelled in the dragon's eyes. Sebastian would have to watch what he said and did, or he'd wind up dead—maybe.

The Black Dragon hissed, turned, and swept his tail wide. Sebastian jumped, the massive tail brushing past him far too close for comfort. He narrowly escaped the force of another hit or smack against the rocks. Earth shook, bringing small rocks crumbling from above, and the Black Dragon stormed away.

The White Dragon lowered her head and narrowed her gaze. "Do not keep me waiting, little creature. Out with it."

Sebastian cared for this dragon even less. She may be smaller, less intimidating in size and appearance, but there was a cunning about her that bordered on terrifying. Sebastian glanced at his watch. The portal would be closing soon. He had to hurry. "No chance of seeing Bolsvck?"

She straightened her neck, raising her head high. "None."

Sebastian let out a sigh. "You must make sure he gets this message. Dragons are being slaughtered upland, and his daughter Kyra may be in danger."

"His daughter is dead to us."

Sebastian blinked, his body jolting in response to her reaction. He refused to believe Bolsvck felt that way. "I fear the dragons being killed aren't random killings, but part of a bigger plan. I thought he should be aware."

The White Dragon opened one eye wider. White light shimmered around her and a woman suddenly stood before Sebastian. Her skin was pale, hairless, and covered in white scrolled markings. "And human forms of the dragons are being found?"

Sebastian nodded. "How did you know?"

She acted as if Sebastian hadn't spoken. "You were brave to come here and bring Bolsvck the news. I thank you on his behalf." She bowed her head, and Sebastian returned the gesture. With a gracious bow and back step, she pointed him toward the exit. To appease her, Sebastian pretended to leave.

The compass spun, showing him the way. The watch in his palm told him he had twenty-five minutes until the portal closed. Was it enough time? Probably not, but he had to try.

No dragons had followed him out. He slipped the folded piece of paper from Talia out of his pocket and read the instructions. *Get the dagger*, she'd said. No doubt an impossible task. He should have asked for a portal to the dagger's front door. Sebastian studied the diagram, and when he felt confident he knew it by heart, he slipped the paper back in his pocket and crept into the cave again.

There had to be a better approach. This time Sebastian would find it, use it. Reapers must have cool superpowers he wasn't aware of. Maybe he could go invisible. He thought on that. Didn't do any good if he didn't know how to make it work. All he knew how to do was reap, and he sure as Hell wasn't going to reap any dragons. Not if he wanted Kyra's father on his side. Question was, what was he doing associating with so many terrible and unstable monsters?

Keeping to the shadows, he crept as quick as he could, following the map now inked in his memory. He wasn't a hundred percent certain what the dagger was for, but if he understood the directions clearly, it would help retrieve Kyra's dragon, and that's all that mattered right now. He was getting the damn thing, at any cost.

Sebastian slipped around the corner and came face to face with the White Dragon. Orange eyes flickered, nostrils flared. Sebastian ventured a guess she wasn't happy with his change in direction.

"Didn't I show you the way out?" Her claws extended and began to tap.

Decision time. What was his defense move if he was avoiding the reap? "Well, yes," he said, vying for time. "But then I realized I forgot something." He reached down in his soul and pulled. Dug into hers, sifting, searching.

"And what was that?" She stepped forward, baring her teeth.

"This," Sebastian said with a snap of his fingers.

The White Dragon threw her head to the ceiling and roared. Sebastian hadn't known what to expect, never having dealt with a dragon in this way before. Wasn't even sure if dragons had nightmares, any fears, he could pluck. But there it was, prancing around at the front of her gray matter, waiting for Sebastian to swoop in and play. And play he did. He kicked opened doors, knocked down walls, and threw off unwieldy camouflage meant to hide and contain the dragon's deepest secrets. Her inadmissible horrors.

A massive White Dragon with a mean scar across his brow leaped through the rubble of a toppled memory wall. It was only a recollection, and he didn't see Sebastian, didn't engage. He roared at the tiny dragonling cowering in the far corner of the host dragon's mind. Anger rippled his hide, whipped his tail, and spewed smoke from his nostrils. The dragonling wailed, and the image evaporated, only to be replaced with another.

This one slammed into Sebastian, knocking him to his trance-state butt and shaking his Mara nightmare hold. The state of retrospection shuddered, leaving Sebastian struggling to maintain control. The source of the interference—a ginormous, iridescent red dragon. He spread his wings and flapped. His voice exploded in a blast of defending command. Legends crumbled and fell before him. Like a changeling, the beast's face fluctuated, beating back and forth like the thrum of his mighty tail, between the dragon and the man Sebastian recognized as Marcus. Only, Sebastian felt not a single drop of mercy in the man's soul. He hadn't detected such ugliness in Marcus's person. Sebastian hated him, plain and true.

Hellhounds and chaos monsters flanked Marcus's side, rushed, battered, and destroyed everything in their path. An army of zilants flew above, his to command. The winged, snake-like creatures hissed and wiggled, creating the impression of a slithering sky. Sebastian wondered how Marcus had managed to align all the lower demons. Or why he would want to.

Marcus yelled, a mighty bellow, and the zilants dove into the crowd of cowering dragons already under siege by hellhounds and chaos demons. Screams fractured the memory, knocked Sebastian clear. He'd only recently become aware of Marcus's dragon status. Now he'd learned of all the evil Marcus could control at the tip of his claw. Sebastian jerked, shook his head—and the thoughts—clear.

The White Dragon's nightmares had been enlightening, and Sebastian was now concerned beyond any Mara's nightmare illusion for Kyra. If Marcus had an army behind him this time, dragons could soon become Reaper business. Some really nasty dragons already feared Marcus. What did that mean for Kyra?

The dragon in front of him clawed at the ground, swung her body from side to side, and screeched at such a massive volume the sound bounced off the tunnel walls and set Sebastian's ears to ringing. He ran from the site as quick as he could. Ran before more dragons came to her aid and caught him in the process.

The thunder of their approach rattled the tunnels, the noise deafening as more dragons joined in the howling, rocks and sediment falling from walls all around him. Talia's map led him to a room not far from his run-in with the White Dragon. It wasn't much of a space. Round, no windows, only one entrance. What made it special, worth the trouble to visit, was the treasure it stored. Pure gold lined the walls in piles. Jewels, statues, goblets, and so much more. A dragon's hoard stored in the cavern, and on a pillar set high in the center was a shiny dagger, the handle simple, the blade set long with a curve. But he knew it was the one he needed, so he set toward it in a run.

Full speed in his stride, he hit the column and jumped. As soon as his hand wrapped around the dagger's hilt, he felt it. Incredible power. He knew why the dragons kept the weapon hidden away. It was dangerous to them, strong beasts as they were. He pulled the blade up against his chest and dove down against the column's base, back pressed to its cold surface.

"It's gone!" a voice cried out.

Sebastian crouched down and peeked around the side of the column. Thankfully he'd landed on the back side, not visible from the entrance. A small, youthful Fire Dragon stood in the doorway. He marched in, galloped around and sniffed the air, then marched out again. "Nothing. I got nothing. Must be gone."

Curious. Sebastian wondered why the young dragonet couldn't smell him. Not that there was time to worry about it. Dragons yelled and thumped in the tunnel outside. Sebastian glanced at his watch. Eleven minutes. He wasn't going to make it. He looked down at the dagger and thought of Kyra. Thought of Marcus and what he would do to Kyra. Sebastian zipped around the column, rushed for the tunnel and the portal waiting outside.

"Where did you come fro—?" The young Fire Dragon never got to finish his question. Sebastian had him flailing on the ground within seconds, squirming in fear of being pulverized by a gnarly Black Dragon.

Sebastian wiped the sweat from his brow. At the moment, he was thankful for his Mara talents, even if he didn't condone the use of them. He looked away from the young dragon pitching to the fever of his own nightmare.

Dragons now came at him so quickly it was like they were seeping out of the walls. He couldn't grab their fears and fling them back fast enough. Nor could he run fast enough. He dodged left, and then right, slid under the belly of one and realized that wasn't going to work. His plan was flawed.

He pulled out the dagger, ran with it in his grasp.

Smaller dragons backed away, slipped behind and followed from the rear. But the larger beasties were not so easily intimidated.

Darkness swam, swirled in Sebastian's belly. It ripped up his esophagus and exploded through the tunnels as he moved for the exit. Dragons fell away.

No!

Sebastian clamped his mouth shut. He hadn't meant to throw extinction at their souls. Never meant to cause them any pain, much less something worse. He glanced behind him. Dragons stammered, some collapsed, but none were dead. Thank the Reaper, none were dead. Sebastian put the wind at his back and ran faster. Ran with all that he was and all that he had. Ran because Kyra's life depended upon it.

They were roaring, screaming, howling behind him. He knew they came, but he dared not look back. Over the wall he went. Across the dust trail and slate rocks until he was leaping with as much spring as he could muster.

Sebastian swung through the portal not a minute too soon. It collapsed in on itself moments after he successfully pulled through to the other side.

"I didn't think you were going to make it," Madoc said. "Where to next?"

KNUCKLES SCRATCHED AND BRUISED, SEBASTIAN RAISED HIS HAND TO KNOCK ON the door. He should have worn fingerless gloves, hidden the damage so as not to alarm Kyra. Too late now. He knocked three times. The door swung open almost immediately. Kyra stood before him, binder in her arms. The binder toppled to the ground.

"Oh my God!" She grabbed him and pulled him into the apartment, closing the door behind them. "I thought you stood me up." Her hands wandered his face, traced a long line above his brow. It stung, and he flinched. How bad did he look? He hadn't thought to look in a mirror.

She pushed him deeper into the apartment and Sebastian hesitated, felt Marcus's barrier keeping him out, when Talia's charm suddenly worked brilliantly. Sebastian stepped beyond the boundary with only the slightest of resistance. Kyra led him to the sofa and pushed him down, then ran back to the bedroom.

"When she said…" Sebastian mumbled and looked from the dinette table to the counter and every other flat surface in the room, never finishing his thought. Sunflower arrangements adorned every logical space. He felt a smile tugging at his lip, but worry dropped it into a frown. She'd said she kept the flowers because of their suggestion of warmth. Why was she so cold? That's what he needed to figure out.

He studied the mess of work papers spread out on the coffee table. Noticed the highball glass, half full, sitting in a ring of condensation among the disorder. She was working from home—and drinking. He leaned forward, took a whiff. *Wowza!* Strong stuff. His body jerked up and away. Instinctively, his hand reached for the small vial of *Spiritual Peace* he was carrying with him. His skin itched. He wanted to take a sip now. He moved his hand away from the tiny bottle.

With a sigh, he relaxed back into the cushions of the sofa. Foot tapping, fingers drumming against his thigh, he was anxious to be moving. Dammit if he wasn't already messing things up in her presence. He should have grabbed her and left. She'd caught him off guard with her greeting, laying her hands on him the way she did. He liked it. Far more than he could put into words.

"Hell," he mumbled and dropped his head into his hands.

"What's that?"

Kyra was back. She threw herself down next to him on the sofa, flipping to face him. Their legs pressed firmly against one another.

Marcus would erupt like a volcano if he were to walk in. In her hand, she held a damp washcloth, and she began to dab at his forehead.

"Is it bad?" he asked.

"You haven't seen it?"

Sebastian shook his head.

"You should clean up okay. What happened?"

"Nothing you need to worry about." He watched her mouth while she applied ointment to his temple, followed by a bandage. She was stunning, so intoxicating; he didn't want to drag his gaze away. Yet it wasn't long before he found himself searching her neckline, looking for the dragon tooth Talia kept telling him to locate. Kyra used to wear the trinket on a string around her neck. Where was it now?

When she'd finished playing nurse, she leaned in and kissed her completed work. Sebastian closed his eyes and savored the moment.

"Oh, I'm sorry," Kyra said. "Did I go too far?"

Sebastian opened his eyes and looked at her. His brows felt heavy, weighted with concern for her comment. They pressed into his eyes. "What do you mean?"

"I thought we'd done that before. It felt right. Was I wrong?"

Sebastian continued to stare at her, his confusion still clouded.

"The kiss. Haven't we kissed before?"

His chest expanded, filling with air and understanding. Was she acting on feelings without actual knowledge? Or was she recalling the kiss she'd planted on him that night in his tarot card trailer? Either way, it gave him hope. Hope that she returned his feelings.

A small smile cracked his face. "We haven't kissed before. It doesn't mean I am opposed to it." He'd lied. But he wasn't going to count their one and only kiss to date. Not under these circumstances. And he wasn't going to take advantage. He would win her soul over in such a way that she'd love him for all eternity. Memory return or not. That was the hope, at least.

Kyra bit the inside of her lip and studied him. Pain, want, desire: it all moved through him as he looked back at her. Never had they been so close and yet felt so far. One mistake, and all possibilities for the future could shatter.

He sat back against the sofa. They should go—he knew they should go—but he didn't want to end whatever was happening between them. The edge of his thumb caressed the soft skin of her cheek. "Are you okay? Did he hurt you in any way?" His gaze wandered to her glass of liquid fire on the table.

Following his look, she shook her head and turned closer to him. They aligned, Kyra shifting until they were perfectly positioned, parallel to each other. Staring at her lips, he feared making a move and losing her forever. Then again, he feared not making a move and losing her forever.

She leaned in and pressed her lips to his. Soft, like silk gliding over smooth, bare skin. She was spring in the winter. Her lips curved to his, melted around them. The sweet, delicious taste of nectarines. It was unexpected and never more welcome.

Kyra slid back and gazed at Sebastian. "You're saying we've never done that before?"

His hands slipped from her face and glided down her arm, stopping above her elbow. "Not like that."

"Felt like a perfect fit."

Sebastian's gaze lowered. The kiss did feel perfect, yet he didn't feel right about it. As long as she didn't remember who she was, he would never feel right. His gut tied into a knot. She would be lost to him when she finally remembered. Remembered he took advantage. That dragon anger of hers would take over and she would hate him.

As gently as he knew how, he moved her to the side. "I'm sorry, Kyra. I never should have kissed you. Not while you're missing your memories."

"You didn't kiss me. I kissed you."

"But I shouldn't have allowed it. You may hate me later." Sebastian dragged his fingers through his hair, let his gaze wander toward the front door. "What of Marcus?"

Kyra slapped her hands in her lap. "Something's not right with Marcus."

Yes! Thank the dragon gods. She finally sees it.

A loud snore burst from the other room, the bedroom. Sebastian stared at Kyra, his eyes wide with questions.

Her lips tightened, held back a laugh. “Chet.” She giggled. “We’re supposed to be working. He can’t handle his liquor.” She pointed to an almost-empty glass on the bar separating the room from the kitchen. “I get so tired of being watched all the time.” She rolled her eyes.

Sebastian was proud of her, but didn’t want to hang around a second longer, tempting fate. As much as he loved sitting here with Kyra and had wanted the kiss to last for endless hours, there was someplace they needed to be. And Chet was a serious mood killer.

He clasped his hand around hers. “Listen. I’m going to ask something of you, and it may sound strange. Crazy, even. Will you trust me?”

Kyra’s eyes widened, looked excited. “What do I have to do?”

24
SACRIFICE

Marcus

Essence of Anodynse, incense extracted from the spinal fluid of dragons, wrapped around Marcus. It created a thick magical cloud, crisscrossing his body. Marcus knelt before the flames built upon sacred stones from the temple of Rajũn, the first dragon and great water deity.

With slow, deliberate movements, Marcus directed the vapors toward himself. He inhaled and sniffed them. Absorbed them through his naked skin. He came before the bearer of dragons a clean slate. Sweat glistened over the curves of his physique, droplets falling from his body in trickles. Leila moved around the perimeter, fanning the outlying flames, and temperatures rose.

Tossing and thrashing in their jars of effervescing energy, the dragons of sacrifice sat arranged on the floor of the Great Hall in a diamond around Marcus. Kyra's dragon represented water and fire. She had been placed center, directly before him. To the left, in a mesh of mossy glimmer, was a forest giant—a Green Dragon. To the right, trapped in a brilliant display of illumination, the shrewd ice beast.

Behind him, a slightly too docile mountain dweller, and at front point, ears frilled, horn scraping at the glass, a vain Blue Dragon hissed and chomped.

Marcus warmed with confidence. Nothing could stop him now. Soon he'd absorb every one of those dragons within his soul and be more powerful than any dragon to ever exist. Never again would the dragon council be able to banish him.

His skin tightened across his chest. He laughed out loud as fire and fumes consumed him, his own dragon sliding in, returning from Purgatory. His beast reeked of death and decay. Didn't bother Marcus one bit. His heart was dark, and he liked it that way.

"Keep chanting!" Leila scolded. "Your beast is not secure until the chant is complete."

Marcus shot her a stern look but followed her demands. His chest burned. Possibly with anger. He wasn't used to people telling him what to do. She was the first in a great while to even try.

Leila came to the fire with a knife bearing the markings of his family crest. She tilted it at an angle so he could verify its authenticity.

He laid out his arms palms up, hands curled into fists, and gritted his teeth in preparation for what came next. Leila cut matching marks into each arm using the tip of the blade. When completed, the cuts looked like eyes with a line running through them. Blood ran from the newly cut slashes and small brass bowls on the floor below caught the runoff.

With the matching eyes of Rajũn cut into his arms, Marcus opened his arms wide to receive. Leila moved to his bare chest and pressed the point of the knife to the place just above his heart. His heart stopped, his chant paused, and his eyes flickered down to her. She stood so close. Nothing could stop her from plunging the blade deep into his soul. She tilted her head up to meet his gaze and smiled gingerly, as if she'd heard his thoughts.

His insides burned. A fury of hatred for her whirled out of control, the control she exhibited over him the accelerant. Yet, he feared her. For that reason, she would have to die. Not yet, though. After he got what he wanted.

She smiled at him, and he didn't trust it, didn't trust her. The smile was too knowledgeable, too deceitful. The knife tip stung. Sliced through his skin with the burn of a wild flame. He didn't look down. Instead, he kept his gaze steady on her and savored the singe.

Every sense heightened, making him acutely aware of each breath, every change taking place around him, within the room. He closed his eyes and concentrated. Leila's body heat changed, and she shuffled away from him. Marcus picked up on her subtle vibrations moving through the old tile floor. She was walking backwards, toward the first of the dragons. Why was she trying to be so quiet? Was she double-crossing him? Trying to inhibit his ability to follow through?

If so, he would finish it. He would finish her. He'd been born for finalities.

Leila uncapped the first jar. The lid sprang free and the monstrous Forest Dragon jumped out onto the jar's edge, both beast and her majestic power bursting free like a sandstorm bursting through a once-closed door. She released a resounding war cry as the magical energy, disguised as a euphoric light show, swirled up out of its prison and across the room toward Marcus. Like dust pulled to the vacuum, the dragon's magic drew straight into Marcus's body through the cut on his arm.

Marcus reeled backwards, the force slamming into him like a full-grown gargoyle. Power surged through his arms, lightning quick into his bloodstream, the desire to tear a giant hole in a mountain's side a new and exciting prospect.

The sound of another jar opening, the cap hitting the hard ground, froze Marcus's arteries, and ice crusted his bones. The power of the Ice Dragon had entered his system through the symbol cut in his other arm. The floor came up to meet him, his hands slamming flat onto the filthy tile. His upper torso was weighted down, thrown out of balance with the rest of him.

His muscles strained, his jaw locked, and he pushed himself up. He refused to show weakness. Weakness was for the inferior. Leila might as well have put a torch to his ears, for the way they felt. They could have been turning to ash by the moment, they burned with such intensity. He tilted them to the ceiling.

A minor shift in the environment had occurred. One not likely detectible by any creature, human or otherwise. Yet he felt it, if barely. A second later, he saw it—a portal.

"Hurry," he growled.

Leila glanced behind her at the shimmering air a moment before it snapped straight and disappeared. She ripped the top of the third jar open and dashed around the diamond to the fourth, releasing both giants almost simultaneously. The dragon essences came at him from opposite directions, colliding into the marks cut deep in his chest. Magic misted around Marcus and the stones with the forceful fumes of a dragon-induced bonfire.

His goal was almost actualized. One more to go. Absorb the magical life force of each dragon. Power and rage coursed through his blood, his bones, his everything.

Sebastian and Kyra slipped out of the portal and collapsed onto the floor of the Great Hall.

Marcus's gaze narrowed in on Kyra. His heart remained steady and his mind started calculating. The little carnie had messed everything up, bringing her here. She was supposed to be his. He had the perfect little Bronze Dragon picked out to tame her.

Leila ripped open the final glass prison, releasing Kyra's dragon, Kalrapura. Orange flecks of light floated up into the air, up between Marcus and Kyra, and Marcus envisioned Kyra as the dragon who had pulled him from the water the day he'd first found her. That dragon, that Moorigad, would now be his.

"Marcus!" Kyra screamed. "What are you doing?"

Leila moved a step closer to him. "Don't get distracted. Keep the ritual flowing."

Sebastian lurched forward and pointed at Leila. "You! You're helping him?"

Kyra and Sebastian had their hands linked together. Kyra now grabbed his arm and pulled close to his ear. "You know her?"

"Only from a dream," Sebastian said. Kyra started to pull away from him, but Sebastian clutched onto her and held tight. "It's nothing, Kyra. I'll explain later."

Marcus's skin was scorching. The more he watched Kyra with the idiot carnie, the more it throbbed. He'd have to obliterate the boy. He was too much of a liability. Always getting in the way.

Or...he could consume Sebastian, like he had so many demons in the past. Yes. Consume him and take within him the power of a Mara. A wayward grin twitched at the edge of Marcus's lips. Satisfaction, anticipation, and excitement warming his skin.

Then unmatched power slammed Marcus in the chest, knocking him off his feet. He laughed and laid his head on the ground. Every part of him tingled, dancing to life on a new level of awareness. Never had he felt so incredible, and he had Kyra to thank for it. Wicked delight curled at the edges of his lips, and he was only halfway through the ritual. It was only going to get better.

Five dragons, and all their magic and power, were his. Now miniature versions of what the beasts once were flew in complete disarray above him. They were nothing more than vessels for the dragons' spirits: their vitality, their hearts, their liveliness. Soon, even those would belong to Marcus.

Sebastian scrambled to the side. Marcus saw him coming, knew what he was up to. Sebastian lurched for Kyra's dragon and Marcus roared. The walls vibrated. Marcus flexed and morphed in a fraction of a second. It felt like someone had shoved a steel-toed boot far up his aft end and pulled his intestinal tract out. Excruciating, but he got a tail out of the process, and he swept it across the room, sending Sebastian airborne. He creamed into the far wall. Fell in a heap on the floor.

Kyra screamed.

Leila laughed.

And the sacrificial dragons, now void of their magical core, took flight, screeching objections that echoed throughout the hall.

Sebastian pushed himself into a sitting position. "You captured each of the dragons' essences?"

Marcus sneered, didn't answer. He was beginning to bulge and bubble all over his body. His intestines were boiling. The process was cooking him from the inside. *Bloody dung*, he silently cursed.

Discomfort washed away, and peace found him. He was dragon—sort of. A deformed mutation of a dragon. Not for long, though. He would fix that.

He stretched his long neck high in the air. Then—*snap!* He chomped down on the Ice Dragon. Caught her mid-flight. Devoured her slowly. Allowed himself the satisfaction of enjoying every tingle and twinge gained from the beast's life force. He was drunk on her power, so drunk he could sleep for days. Of course, he wouldn't. There were four more dragons on the menu.

The remaining dragons flew in a defensive form of chaos, their cries bouncing off the walls of the old party hall. Spotting two dragons clinging close together, Marcus lumbered toward them. They separated. He pitched to the side, caught the Green Dragon by the wing. Flipping her around, he tossed her up and caught her as she pitched back down.

As before, his power surged and his desire to nap increased.

Three more to go.

And it continued. The mountain dweller, the horned Blue Dragon. Marcus devoured them both.

Kyra crouched in the corner, screaming, spewing words of hate and loathing. He didn't care. He'd fix her later. Sebastian stood, brushed the dirt off, and looked a lot like a thorn in Marcus's claw. Damn boy didn't know when to give up. Silly, he even had himself a toy dagger. As if that would help. Marcus roared with laughter.

Kid couldn't do anything. Marcus had one dragon left to go. Kyra's dragon, the prized Moorigad. He'd saved the best for last.

Sebastian grabbed Kyra, pulling her from Marcus's reach. "Do you trust me?" he yelled.

"You know the answer to that," Kyra answered.

"There's no room for doubt."

Marcus roared. He hated talk of trust between Kyra and Sebastian. He hated Sebastian.

Kyra's eyes grew wide, and she stared at Marcus, then nodded to Sebastian.

Sebastian grabbed something from the back of his jacket. Marcus lumbered closer and watched Sebastian press what looked like the dagger against Kyra's skin. Red spread from the spot as Sebastian sliced a line into Kyra's forearm.

"Ouch!" she yelled and grabbed her arm.

Kyra's dragon shrieked, turned, and looked toward the carnie pair. Kalrapura suddenly moved at an alarming speed in their direction. Marcus chomped down where she had been, but she was gone.

A tiny sound escaped Kyra's lips and she began to shuffle backwards, her stare glued on the dragon diving directly at her. She tripped and fell into Sebastian's arms. The dagger clamored against the tile floor.

They were not allowed to ruin this for him. Marcus pinned his sights on Sebastian and hurled into him with all his rage at the helm. He wanted blood, and the Mara bastard's suited him perfectly fine. The blow knocked Kyra sideways, hurtling her into a heap on the floor. Sebastian yelled for her and whipped the dagger out from his side, where it had fallen moments ago.

Too frantic? Panicked? The Mara boy accidentally cut himself on the leg, pulling the dagger free. Blood dripped down Sebastian's calf. A victorious grin was already spreading across Marcus's face. Careless mistakes would make him an easy kill.

Behind Marcus, Leila danced in a circle. A circle of insanity. He would crush her sooner rather than later, Marcus decided.

Sebastian swung the dagger at Marcus. The blade barely grazed him, yet he burned with the fires of a thousand Hells. Marcus let out a roar of a Dragon King magnified to the power of twenty. The walls shook, crumbling dirt from its old stucco. Bits of the ceiling cracked, broke free, and plummeted.

Kyra collapsed on her knees and hugged herself, favoring her head. She was like a wounded animal, and Marcus savored the vision. She scrambled across the littered floor and pulled at Sebastian's wound.

Sebastian grabbed Kyra's wrist and pulled her to her feet. She wavered. Marcus's upper lip pulled back, exposed his sharp canines. He was ready to devour, and devour he would.

Sebastian rapidly scanned the hall, his gaze coming to rest upon Kyra. Marcus knew what the boy was doing. Stupid boy was looking for Kyra's dragon. He still thought he could save her. Marcus roared with laughter, and he saw Kyra's eyes glaze over. Marcus roared again, and this time, the air trembled. Orange specks shimmered, floated around Kyra and Sebastian, and Marcus's howl only grew louder and more intense.

A shock wave exploded around them, and Sebastian and Kyra, even the ginormous dragon that was Marcus, were knocked off their feet. Marcus lay in a heap as tingles of energy seeped out from every place a cut had been on his body. Orange, gold, and slight flecks of blue oozed from his dragon husk in a surge of magical, churning dust. In a whirling dash, it moved across the hall and disappeared in the explosive shock wave around Sebastian and Kyra.

Marcus's claws dug chunks out of the ground. He growled and rushed at Sebastian, his eyes ablaze with plans for his ingestion. He was getting Kyra's dragon one way or another. If he had to eat both of them to get it, so be it!

Whoosh. The portal oscillated.

A rush of air flew into the hall, slammed into Marcus, threw him to the ground. Marcus couldn't believe his eyes. He was staring up at Bolsvck, eyes burning with fury, nostrils flared and ready to burn. What would possibly bring Bolsvck here now? Unless the Dragon Elders had finally recognized Marcus's potential.

Marcus's chest puffed, and his shoulders squared. With a whoosh, Bolsvck's wrecking ball tail slammed Marcus in the breast sending him tumbling backwards. He scrambled, lunged back, missed his mark, and chomped on air. A wing the size of a small building knocked Marcus sideways. Didn't matter. He would still win this. He was confident. After all, Bolsvck was a dragon of legend, which meant he was old. Marcus still had strength and youth on his side.

Still, Bolsvck was big! And he blocked Marcus's clear line of attack at Sebastian, or capture of Kyra. Bolsvck spread his wings wide in clear protection of his daughter beyond.

Marcus thrashed at the ground and roared. The punk Sebastian was taking his girl back through the portal. There was nothing he could do to stop him. Not with Bolsvck standing in the way. Marcus bellowed. He would kill them for this. Kill them all. Fired with anger and frustration, Marcus swung his powerful tail, slammed it into the sidewall. Drywall and concrete cracked and shattered, and debris splattered across the room. He lunged at Bolsvck, jaws chomping.

Muscles bound with fire and fury, the two dragons twisted and spun in a heated battle of strength and cunning. Marcus's confidence led the fight, but Bolsvck was a hardier opponent than he had anticipated. Plus, tingles and sparks continued to nip at his body, along the incisions meant to pull in and trap the power of additional magical beings. Marcus clobbered Bolsvck once in the side but staggered from the weight of his own blow. Had he lost something? Had one of the sacrificial dragons somehow escaped?

His head swooned, and he struck out, forcing Bolsvck to keep his distance. Marcus's breath came in long, labored efforts.

"Give it up, Balidhug. You cannot best me," Bolsvck sneered. "You made a mistake trying to take power again. You should have stayed wherever you were. Remained quiet. We would have left you alone."

"What do you know?" Marcus yelled. "You are stuck in your old ways. You won't even lead, but the people, the dragons, need a leader. I will be that leader."

Bolsvck huffed, lumbered in a slow circle around Marcus. Marcus searched the area, every dark corner, for Leila. He saw no sign of her. *Damn that Mara bitch for bolting when I could use her most,* Marcus hissed internally.

"You cannot rule by way of destruction," Bolsvck said.

Marcus let the words slide in one ear and straight out the other. There wasn't a thing Bolsvck could say Marcus wanted to hear.

"You only live because I allowed it, nephew. You'd be wise to heed me now."

Except maybe that.

Marcus's head snapped forward, his nostrils flared, eyes blazed wide. "I am not your kin!"

"Are you not? Are you so certain of your truth?"

Marcus shook his head back and forth and back and forth. He would not believe. He was no descendant of the wretched royal family. Claws flared, razor-sharp, he lashed out, pulling flesh from Bolsvck's face.

Everything around them erupted in chaos and noise. The thunder of Bolsvck's uproar. Bolsvck's fire consuming all oxygen. The walls crumbling and falling. And the hulk of a talon slapping Marcus across the Great Hall. The last thing Marcus saw, before his heavy eyelids succumbed, was Leila peering down at him.

25
ERRONEOUS

Sebastian

Sebastian and Kyra rushed from the portal, their shoes slipping on the damp grass. Arcs of silver tinsel glistened in the moonlight, remnants from the sprinklers having run only moments earlier. Kyra caught a mud patch and slid. Sebastian's arm shot out and steadied her.

The surrounding city assaulted him, attacked with thoughts and memories Sebastian was too weak to combat. He pulled the tiny vial of Talia's *Spiritual Peace* from his pocket, took a swig. It was like a warm rinse gliding over his brain. The nagging, the internal chatter stopped.

They had arrived in the city park, the final location Madoc had set up a portal for Sebastian. He owed the Gatekeeper big for all that he had done. The passage behind them quivered and snapped shut, just as he had been told it would. No one could follow them now.

Sebastian released a deep breath in relief. The night air around them chilled his sweat-coated skin. Things may have turned out all right, but it didn't stop him from stressing in the process. He looked over at Kyra. She was watching him.

"What the Hell was all that?" Kyra burst both in words and body language, her arms flailing and swinging around, attempting to pinpoint the portal.

Sebastian shifted his weight and studied her. There was a change in her. He wondered... "That was your boyfriend, up to no good. You saw that, right?"

"He was trying to eat my dragon!"

Sebastian jolted. Inside, he was a mass of exploding fireworks. "You remember your dragon? What else do you remember?"

She shook her head and gazed at the grass off to the side. "I don't know. It's all kind of hazy." She looked back at Sebastian. "Was that my dad?"

"Yeah, I think it was." Sebastian's lips curled into a crooked grin.

"Don't move!"

Sebastian and Kyra snapped their heads to the side. They were surrounded by what looked like soldiers. Sebastian recognized the way they were dressed. They looked a lot like the group who had rescued him previously. His chest fluttered, and confusion flooded his brain. "What—?"

"Quiet! You weren't given permission to speak."

Someone whacked him in the back of the head with the butt of their rifle. The waves of pain rolled through his skull like an earthquake. He spun around and reached for the gun. Tense pain punched through his chest. He slipped and sank to the ground, landing on the wet grass. His whole body exploded with electric pain. He fought against it, wanted to stand up and fight, but couldn't find the strength. Wires carrying the powerful current clung to the front of him. They lit him up like the carnival Fun Zone, and it hurt like a son-of-a-monster.

Somewhere Kyra was yelling, but he couldn't see her. There was a barrage of shouts and yells. Too many shots being fired.

A man lowered his face to Sebastian's. His eyes were dull and lacked the spark of life, but Sebastian recalled him immediately, having seen his mug earlier in the day—in a family portrait. He was Jon Davies, father to Sophie and Alice. This was bad. Extremely bad.

Alice's father narrowed his gaze directly in on Sebastian. It was commanding, hard. "You are wanted for the murder of Officer Alice Sullivan and Lieutenant Byran Crane."

Sebastian balked. "You've got it all wrong." He tried to respond. Tried to lift his arm, felt his hands sear with flame.

"No," Jon Davies said. "You got it wrong when you decided to visit my home." He leaned into Sebastian's space, and Sebastian tried to melt into the ground beneath him. "You made an even bigger mistake when you kept Alice's locket as a kill souvenir."

Sebastian didn't even have to reach into his pocket. At the mere mention of the locket, he could feel the weight of it. It pulled at him, wanted to drown him in a forever sea of guilt and sorrow. Damn Reapers. Damn Maras, too. He hated them all. Hated himself for being either, and for being both. "Tell your wife I'm sorry."

Davies narrowed his stare at Sebastian. The walkie clipped to his belt squawked. Static and hum came to life and announced a flurry of activity at Club Afterlife. Balidhug's men were on the move. Davies grunted. "He can't hide from us. Moves again, we'll find him. Now we have you." He pushed a foot against Sebastian's shoulder and rocked him. "You working with the beast, boy?"

"Me? Work with Marcus?" Sebastian stifled a scoff.

Yells and screams erupted on their right. A deafening roar quaked through the park trees. Men and women flew past them overhead. His accuser looked up, his face widening, eyes bulging. His brow narrowed, his gaze flooding in confusion. Poor guy couldn't grasp what was happening. Not yet. Sebastian knew. He knew exactly what was going on.

In a flash, Davies was gone, knocked away by a large orange tail. Kyra the dragon appeared before him in full water form. She scooped Sebastian up and took off into the night.

Funny how things could end up. It had started with Kyra, the girl who held his heart, rescuing another in a similar manner—sort of. Now it was him she held, and they ran from the people who wanted to destroy the man she'd previously rescued, and who now wanted him dead as well. His life was completely messed up, but at least he had Kyra. For now, anyway.

Or did he?

He bobbed up and down on the shoulder of the big orange beast, feeling woozy. Damn electrocution, damn organized movement, and damn two Kyras.

Wait. Sebastian rubbed his head. Why were there two Kyras? He narrowed his eyes, stared at the girl running behind them. "Kyra?"

"Slow down, Mom. You're moving too fast."

Mom! What? He'd gone to see her father and failed. How had her mother gotten here? Sebastian tried to turn, get a better look at the dragon holding him. He slipped. Everything went black.

Sebastian's eyes sprang open, his body already bounding off the bed. "Kyra?"

Chelsea's hand pressed against his chest and pushed him back to the bed. "She's fine. She's outside arguing with her mother." Chelsea rolled her eyes. "You, sir," she shoved her pointer finger at him, "shouldn't move so fast. You've had a tough time of it recently."

Sebastian shook the fatigue off. He felt fine. Taking a mental inventory of his faculties, he really did feel good. Interesting, considering what he'd recently been through. "I'm fine, Chelsea." He grabbed her hand and paused. Stared at her, searching her eyes.

She pulled away, looked away. "Something wrong?"

"No." He said the word hesitantly. "For a minute, you didn't feel like..." He decided not to finish the thought. He didn't want to concern her. Not until he understood what was going on with the girl.

"What, Sebastian? Feel like what?"

"Nothing." He sat up, felt inside his pocket and found the locket still there. He pulled it out and stared at the scrolling *A* on the front. Round and gold and a bit dinged-up. The only thing special about it was its sentimentality. Sebastian opened it, sought the pictures Alice kept close to her heart.

Sebastian stared at the open locket exposed in his palm. Stared at the miniature tracking device expertly placed within.

Shoot.

He dropped the locket on the bedside table.

Shoot. Shoot. Shoot.

That was how Davies and his men had found Sebastian and Kyra in the park. Were they tracking them even now? Tracking them all the way to the carnival? Could Jon Davies and his group of soldiers find a portal to lead the way?

Sebastian lifted his table lamp and slammed it down on the locket with a mighty force, smashing the tracker to bits. He looked up at Chelsea's stunned face. "You said Kyra was outside?" He stood and walked right past Chelsea, out the door of his trailer into the night beyond.

Kyra leaned against the wall of the trailer, watching the lights of the carnival. She looked cozy wrapped in her sweater, hands cocooned within the sleeves. At the same time, she looked heartbreakingly distant, lost in thought.

"So, you found your way back to the carnival," he said, hopeful of what this meant for her memory.

Kyra jumped at the sound of his voice. She turned to face him, her face bright with surprise. "You had me worried."

"No worries. See? I'm fine." Sebastian spread his hands to the side to emphasize how fine he was. And he was fine. Never felt better.

Kyra blinked, but said nothing.

Sebastian took a step closer. Familiar with her many faces, he could tell something bothered her. He wanted to know what gnawed at her now. "Your mom's here?"

"Apparently my dad told her where to find me." She chewed on her lower lip before continuing. "You wouldn't know anything about that, would you?" Sebastian shrugged, but said nothing. Kyra rolled her head. "This whole thing with Marcus has her agitated. She says it's time. Time for me to make a decision. Do you remember anything about that?" Kyra gnawed on her fingernails.

Sebastian's brow tightened, weighed down, narrowing his sight. "You don't?"

"Not really. Vaguely. I remember very little."

"But you remembered the carnival. You got us back here safely." He glanced around, feeling a fog of confusion. He noticed Chelsea walking away from the trailer, a bit of huff to her step. Knew there was something about her, something he should be following up on, but he was with Kyra now.

"I didn't remember the carnival," Kyra said. "I was running after my mom. She had you, and I didn't want to lose either one of you. Next thing I knew, we were falling through another one of those things you took me through earlier. A portal, you called it. We ended up here. My mom was not happy, but some old guy—I think his name was Zeke? —he said the carnival brought us here because this was where we were supposed to be." Kyra looked after Chelsea and pointed. "That blonde girl showed us to your place, and we got you situated." Kyra moved in closer, so close their noses were mere inches apart. "She has a thing for you."

"I wouldn't go that far," Sebastian said and tilted his head, exploring the side of Kyra, memorizing her. "And your dragon? You have water and fire. What will you do?"

Kyra inched closer still. He could feel her breath on his skin. "That's the thing. I can't feel my dragon. I don't know if I can do anything."

Sebastian felt the tension yank up his spine like a coaster car making the ride's first climb. "Are you still cold?"

Kyra nodded and pulled her long sweater closed tight around her.

He shook his head. "That doesn't make sense. I saw Kalrapura. We saw Kalrapura. Didn't you feel the blast of her return?"

Kyra shrugged. "I admit I felt something. But to be honest, all I've been able to think about since the day you showed up at my door is you."

Sebastian turned away. "None of this makes any sense. I cut you to draw Kalrapura back to you."

Kyra tugged at his arm, pulled him back. "How was that supposed to work, exactly?"

He raked his hand through his hair. Dammit. Why hadn't it worked? What had he done wrong? He looked up and met her gaze.

"The blood, of course. It's your blood she should be drawn to first. Above all others."

Kyra bit her lip and nodded.

"Yeah, I. Just don't—" He stammered, recall taking hold. "The tooth pendant. Are you still wearing it? Maybe it's working to suppress her, somehow?"

"What tooth pendant?"

"The one Marcus gave you. You used to wear it before..." Sebastian hesitated.

"Before I lost my memory?" Kyra finished.

He nodded, one quick tilt of the head.

"I haven't seen anything like what you speak of."

Sebastian's brow furrowed, and he rubbed at his forehead with his thumb and forefingers. He'd thought it all out so carefully. Where was Kalrapura?

Kyra placed her hand along his cheek and looked deep into his eyes. Her touch was one of warmth and sincerity. "It's all right. We'll figure this thing out together. I have faith in you. In us."

Sebastian cracked half a smile. He wanted to really smile, but in the last hour things had gone from bad to oh-crap. Now he had some serious Mara hunters on his ass, and for the first time, he realized something. "I need my dad."

"What?" Kyra startled.

Sebastian had surprised even himself. "I need to better understand myself if I'm going to protect us from this new threat in our lives. In order to do that, I'll need my dad."

"Ah, all right." Kyra wrapped her arms around him. Sebastian straightened and gazed into her eyes. "I thought," she paused and sighed, "or hoped, you didn't want anything to do with him?"

"I don't, but I'm gonna have to look past that for now."

"You're doing that for us?"

Sebastian bowed his head slightly.

"I don't know how things were between us before I lost my memory, but I know how I want them to be now." Kyra's fingers brushed along the edge of his lips.

"How is that?" Sebastian's hand skimmed along the curve of her neck, slipping up along her jawline, the delicate edge of her ear.

No further words were spoken. Words were unnecessary to express their feelings regarding each other. Their bodies melded into one, her light enveloping his darkness. His night complementing her day. They were yin and yang, opposites fitting together in perfect concord and tranquility.

Her dragon raced through him, burned him, and he knew they would solve the puzzle. Kalrapura was there. He could sense her, feel her. Together they would bring her to the surface.

Their kiss was all he had hoped for in a true first kiss and what he never dreamed they would have. Every part of him—his body, his soul—longed for her. His limbs burned for her. The fire shot through his system like a hellhound on a vengeance mission. He wanted to scream. He only kissed her harder, deeper.

He never knew desire could hurt this way. It prickled across his back and spine, pushing out, wanting more. More Kyra. More everything. He was consumed by her, burned for her.

"Sebastian!"

He heard the scream. Once. Twice. He opened his eyes.

Kyra was on top of him. He was laid out on the ground. His hands were scorched, and flames burned from his fingertips. She beat him with a rag. Massive wings, riddled with holes, wrapped out around him.

"She's in you. The dragon is inside you!" Kyra yelled and continued to beat at the fire.

No. Sebastian stared up at the night. Somehow, somewhere, something had gone terribly wrong. Could he fix the mistake? Or would he forever be a Reaper and a Mara—and a dragon?

PART THREE
THE LOVERS

PLIGHT of The DRAGON

"In all chaos there is a cosmos, in all disorder a secret order."
~ Carl Jung

26

ROYALS

Sebastian

Sebastian flailed on the damp ground, thrashing his arms into the mud, the flames licking at his skin. *Excruciating,* his mind screamed. In reality, it merely tickled, but his brain could not comprehend the meaning—not yet, anyway.

The luminescence and sparkle provided by the trailers, signs, and wizardry wonders found in Mystic's Magical Market, his little home and pocket of fortunetellers and wannabes within the supernatural destination known as Mystic's Carnival, was lost to him now. There was only the chaos, and fire.

Kyra batted and slapped and hit him with her hands. It didn't hurt. Her touch comforted, reassured Sebastian he still mattered in her world. The image of her danced before him like a moth losing survival's fight to the fire: exquisite flickers of orange and red, death courting life's essence. His vision impaired, bleaching a rainbow of colors from his sight, he stared through a filter of senseless heat and anger. And everything around him, absolutely everything, smelled of burning and ash.

The word *dragon* slithered around the bends and folds of his grey matter. In the earlier struggle, he and Kyra had retrieved Kyra's dragon half, Kalrapura. They'd saved her from Marcus. From being devoured or absorbed for his malicious scheme. But in returning her to Kyra, they had failed. How in Hell's Gates had the dragon ended up inside Sebastian?

Kyra's words crashed back into his thoughts. *She's in you. The dragon is inside you!*

His skin charred from his fingertips toward the bend of his elbow. His back shook with spasms, exploded in torment, slicing from his shoulders down the sides of his spine, ripping the fabric of his shirt. Massive wings, salmon-colored and torn, swung from behind him and around Kyra. They curled up and flapped out of sight, before reappearing at her side again.

Sebastian tried to focus, not on the wings, but on Kyra. It was difficult. His mind swirled with emotion, and she remained unclear, washed in tones of crimson quivering with gold. What if scales started to replace his skin? Or the man he was ceased to be?

"Calm yourself." Her steady gaze eased his physical madness, and her voice swam through his head straight to his heart, releasing the iron lock around his internal peace. She was the medicine he needed, and he would let her guide him. He knew nothing about the condition he now faced.

Pushing his arms to the side and abandoning the burn of his hands, Kyra straddled him and lowered her face close to his own. The distance between them was mere inches, and even after all they had been through, the scent of sunflowers still lingered on her skin. He remembered the sunflowers in Marcus's apartment, the smell wafting around her at the coffee shop. She'd said she was cold, that the flowers gave her the illusion of warmth. Her physiology was probably built to balance the strength and heat a dragon radiated. Without the dragon's fire, she was chilled. He, on the other hand, not meant to harbor such a beast, was burning to cinders.

Her palms cupped his cheeks, and they exchanged endless dialogue through their gaze, no word spoken aloud. Kyra's stare bore straight to

Sebastian's soul. His breath froze, and his heart skittered...and he felt the dragon coil.

"Control can only be found in the calm of one's own mind." She touched her forehead to his. "Search and find yours."

Her words washed over him like the healing waters of serenity. The warmth of her skin, the gentle caress of her hands along the curve of his jawline—instant tranquility.

The wild flapping of wings subsided. The throbbing in his back dulled. And the flickering heat of fire burning inside him abated. Sebastian was almost himself again...or at least looked the part. He no longer displayed any uniquely dragon features. He took a deep breath. So deep it reached into his gut, tried to claw at the core of his being. He wished he could will the dragon back to her. Will it through their touch. But nothing was ever that simple.

In the span of a few days, his life had been shredded and taped back together in a special kind of horror.

They might have saved Kyra's dragon, but they hadn't stopped the ceremony. Marcus now had the strength and power of multiple dragons running through his veins, had a small army at his beck and call, and wanted Sebastian dead. On top of that, some kind of rebel military force had targeted Sebastian as enemy number one for the deaths of two fallen comrades, two deaths Sebastian had not caused. He had his father Mortifier to thank for that one. There was also an insane Mara after him for her personal breeding stock. If that weren't just ghastly gross. *Not gonna happen.*

But now...now he had a dragon trapped inside of him. An all-powerful, beastly, hybrid dragon, inside of him, a Reaper! What did that make him? A reaping dragon?

Sebastian sighed and closed his eyes. At least Kyra had returned to him.

He opened his eyes and gazed up at her. He could see forever and back. She was his now, his tomorrow, his for all days until the end. The end of time, or the end of him. Kyra was, and would always be, his everything.

Two arms hooked under Kyra's armpits, lifted her up and away.

And just like that, she was gone.

"Kyra?" Sebastian croaked and started to sit.

Two men grabbed him, hauled him to his feet. Both men were slender and tall, a deceiving build for the strength they displayed. Maybe they were a new show here at the carnival, one Sebastian had not yet seen. After all, they were dressed in vibrant orange and red. Sebastian glanced down at his all-black attire, the shirt smattered, torn, and singed.

Before them, a third man held Kyra by the arm. She wrestled, but in a manner meant to show her discontent, nothing more. A vexed scowl carved firmly into the lines of her face, and her gaze cut from Sebastian to her far left, where a woman approached. A stride behind the woman walked another man, as if subordinate. A grand total of four men, all in matching neon pajamas—what was the occasion?

Kyra's shoulders dropped. *No.* Her body language couldn't be a sign of concession. Sebastian shoved free of his watchful hold and surveyed the situation. Kyra appeared to know one or more of the people present, so...probably *not* a new carnival act. Whoever the woman was, still walking their way, she had quite the entourage. And she presented Sebastian with a distinctly unique welcome-home party. A lump logged in his throat. He'd spent far too much time away from Mystic's Carnival, mostly because of his ludicrous Reaper training. Something he suspected his father had manufactured for his own selfish reasons.

The woman drifted toward them with the grace of a soaring eagle—magnificent, beautiful, lethal. She was a perfect china doll brought to life, if that china doll came from a secret assassin's line, with her nose tilted to the sky and her fragile frame wrapped in rich garments of intricate designs. Whether she was important or only thought she was, she clearly believed herself to be above everything and everyone in her perimeter.

Sebastian rolled his eyes. *I've dealt with her kind before. As has every irritating Grim Reaper. In death, we are all equal.*

She stopped a few feet in front of them, her lips pursed, one brow arched. Striking, she reminded Sebastian of...of...

"Kyra." The name wisped from his lips like the morning fog

through the trees. His gaze shot to Kyra, and he took a step in her direction. Hands clamped onto his arms once again, stopping him in his tracks.

Kyra didn't spare him a glance. Her eyes were mere slits and focused on the woman. She showed no fear. No confusion. Only anger stirred in the one he loved.

He studied the woman and understood. Same bone structure as Kyra, only her skin and hair were darker. He stood in the presence of Queen Shui, leader of the Water Dragon Clan. Kyra's mother. Not only that, she had brought her men-servant dragons with her. He was surrounded by dragon shifters.

"Well, crap," he mumbled.

"Careful with Kyra, Ryhuu. She is not her full self at the moment," Queen Shui spoke to the man with a firm hold on Kyra's arm. He nodded, a silent and respectful bow. Queen Shui then turned her weary attention to Sebastian. "You think," she began, slow and metered, pretending to fiddle with the way her sleeve hung, "you are worthy of my daughter?" She tilted her head and delivered an intense stare Sebastian had no doubt was meant to intimidate.

Sincerity and devotion tore through Sebastian's spine, straightening his back and squaring his shoulders. He fought against the ache of the dragon at battle within him, shoved the men at his side away, and locked his gaze on Queen Shui. "Your interpretation of the situation is a bit off. I'm not at Kyra's side because I feel worthy of her. On the contrary, I may spend the rest of my life trying to be—"

"Stop it!" Kyra jerked toward her mother. "I'm sick of your judgmental opinions and overbearing conditions. Why must you always push people around like pieces on a game board to be controlled?" Kyra yanked her arm free from Ryhuu's hold and tossed him a don't-even-try glare when his hand reached for her again. He pulled back, clasped his hands before him, and put his head down. Kyra approached her mom.

"You have feelings for this..." Queen Shui glanced from Kyra to Sebastian, her gaze appraising him from head to toe, her hand fluttering in his direction. "Thing."

Kyra's chin dropped, and her nose wrinkled. "He is not a thing. He is my friend and just as important as you or me." She pointed at her mother and proceeded to pound her chest with a clenched fist.

"May I—" Sebastian started.

But Shui's hand shot up, stopping him mid-sentence, her attention never veering from Kyra. "It is because of your misguided emotions that this one is not already dead." She closed the distance between herself and her daughter and caressed Kyra's cheek. "You need time to come to your senses. You've not been well."

Kyra shoved her away. "There you go again. Deciding what I need, when I am quite capable of making those decisions for myself." She let out a heavy sigh. "I agree, things have been a little messed up lately—"

"Understatement."

Kyra ignored her mother's interruption. "—but I'm starting to see through the haze. It may take some time to get all my memories back, but I *feel* things I know to be true. I feel them deep in my core." Kyra pressed at her belly. "I know Sebastian is my friend. And..." Her gaze flittered to Sebastian. "I think I love him."

Sebastian sucked in his breath. He'd waited so long to hear her profess her emotions, and now she'd done it here, in front of a bunch of stiff and irritating dragons. "Kyra?"

"Don't be silly, child." Queen Shui stepped between them, blocking his view of Kyra. "You are too strong and too important to lower yourself to a lesser being." The queen sniffed the air. "Once you are returned to your true self, you will understand." She turned to the men flanked at Sebastian's sides. "He shall be taken to the forked cells within the caverns of the Devil's Eye." Her hand waved dismissively. Iron-tight grips locked upon Sebastian and began to drag him away.

"No!" Sebastian yelled and dug his heels into the ground, wrenched his arms at his sides. His captors did not let go. They slowly dragged him backwards, away from Kyra and her mother.

Kyra's hand latched onto her mother's sleeve, her gaze steady on Sebastian. "You can't do this, Mother. He can't breathe beneath the water. Not like you and the others."

Fire exploded across Sebastian's skin. The dragon within him no longer slumbering, flames covered his arms, shoulders, and chest. The men holding him jumped back and stumbled to a safe distance. Sebastian lifted his palms to the side of his head and roared to the heavens. "Make this stop!"

"Interesting," Queen Shui said, taking a step closer. She studied Sebastian more intently than she had before. "You smell of so many things, demon. You hid the dragon well within you."

"Calm yourself, Sebastian," Kyra yelled and moved to her mother's side, grabbing her by the shoulders. "You see? You can't harm him. He has my dragon-side inside him. He has fire...*and* he has water." Kyra's face lit up as if she knew she'd backed her mother into an impossible situation. A stalemate. The queen would have to back down or lose her daughter's chance at becoming a true Water Dragon. "We need to keep him safe."

Sebastian crossed his arms and batted at the fire. He barely noticed Queen Shui turning to face Kyra, leaving a mere sliver of her profile in his view. Be it his efforts or his state of mind, the fire consuming his limbs subsided. He took a deep, labored breath and crouched to the ground in an attempt to steady his mind. When he raised his head, he peered directly at Shui and Kyra.

The queen's dark hair curled and twisted in an intricate exchange similar to a basket weave, although he could easily envision slithering serpents. Nevertheless, no strand was out of place. He suspected much of her life was the same—neat and orderly. But not her daughter. Kyra was the queen's draw of the Fool from the tarot deck, infinite possibilities lay out before her in the form of one unpredictable daughter. And with Kyra's fiery personality, events were bound to upset Shui's perfect order. Sebastian's lips curved into a delicious smirk. The kind of smirk a guy gets when he's about to knowingly and freely sign up for a no-good deed.

"No harm will come to your dragon, Kyra," Queen Shui said. "Whatever it takes, we will discover how to extract your other half from that beast." Her body nudged ever so slightly in Sebastian's direction.

Laughter burst from his lungs. Of course, she would see him that way. Beneath her daughter and beneath all other dragons.

She turned to face him, her eyes glinting a ferocious gold. He stood and met her stare. "You find humor in this situation, do you?" she said. "I trust all humor will snake away should you discover the dragon you harbor will devour you from within."

Sebastian grinned. He wasn't afraid. Death was in ally. They played for the same team—sort of. A fact Queen Shui had no knowledge of.

Kyra stood behind her mother, lines of utter horror and panic settling into her features. Sebastian didn't feel the fear or the panic. He was thrown back to the question he'd had when he'd been captured, beaten, and tortured at the hands of the behemoth working for Marcus. Was death even a possibility for him, for his species? He didn't want to find the answer by way of trial. He scrutinized Queen Shui, wondered if this was her best poker face.

The ground rumbled, and the surrounding trailers shook, crackled, and moaned. Black shadows eclipsed the lights of the spinning and twirling carnival rides around them, and the sky broke into a frightful thunder. The heavens darkened, but the moon was still visible. Something colossal filled the space above. Dark, crimson wings soared in, swooped down, collapsed into a man on the ground. Another dragon shifter, but clearly not from the Water Clan. The new man stood tall, muscular, and completely naked. Sebastian averted his eyes.

"Showing off again, Bolsvck?" Queen Shui said.

So, this was Kyra's father in his human form, the man Sebastian had stolen the dagger from to restore Kalrapura. Sebastian moaned internally. On his list of worst days ever, this had to be near the top. He was, without a doubt, *not* making a good first impression with either of Kyra's parents. He would end up dragon kibble when this dark fairy tale came to a conclusion.

Bolsvck scoffed and walked past the queen to Kyra, pulling her into a hug. "It is good to see you well." When he released her, he turned to Sebastian and pointed. "This one took something from me. I shall have it retuned. *Now*."

27
MEMORIES

Kyra

"Stop it!" Kyra said and needled her father in the back. "You're going to stand here, naked, and accuse Sebastian of thievery?" She pushed past him, making sure to slam into his arm. "What kind of man does that?"

"I have nothing to be ashamed of," Bolsvck declared, standing tall. "And the item the boy took is of great importance. It shouldn't be in the hands of one so unworthy and untrained. Especially now."

"Now?" Kyra raised a brow. "You mean since Marcus tried to kill me?"

Bolsvck made a funny sound. It came from deep in his throat and reminded her of a chuff, much like the carnival lions or tigers made. Was that normal for dragons? Did she do that?

She chanced a glance in Sebastian's direction. He was feeling the back of his jacket, probably searching for the dagger. *He doesn't know I moved it while he was sleeping.* Although he was attempting to be inconspicuous, she'd picked up on his actions quickly. The others might catch on, as well.

She gawked at her father, raised her hand to shield her eyes, and blindly pointed to his southern region. "Mind covering that, at least?"

Some of the men accompanying Queen Shui leaked a laugh but were silenced with one sharp glower from their sovereign. The stoic woman watched Kyra's every move like a dragon ogling a soon-to-be-procured treasure. That was how she felt, too. Like a prize Queen Shui intended on winning.

"Honestly, child. Your modesty bewilders me," Bolsvck said and tore the banner off the front of the Palm Reader's trailer beside him. It was clear by his lack of inhibition and the way he wrapped the fabric around his middle, tying it with one strong knot, that he was a simple and no-bull kind of man. Task completed, Bolsvck's grin questioned if there was anything else he needed to do to please her.

"Er...thanks." Kyra rocked back on her heels and rested her balled fists on her hips. Trying to figure out what to do next, how to diffuse whatever the situation was between her dad and Sebastian, her mind spun like the carnival rides in the distance. She didn't really remember her parents that well. Didn't remember much of them at all. Only enough to know they were her parents, not enough to feel familiar or at ease around them. Then again, maybe she never had felt easy around them; her gut was trying to lead her to that conclusion now. She only had to listen better. But not knowing her parents, not remembering them or herself or her history with them, she hadn't a clue how to proceed.

As for Sebastian, she only knew what her gut was telling her. And right now, it was telling her to protect him.

She exhaled, let her gaze wander beyond the small dragon circle. It made her feel trapped, forced to remember things she couldn't. Around them, the crowd was busy having a splendid time. People wandered past on all sides. Some held hands. Some traveled in large groups, talking or joking amongst themselves. Others snacked on carnival treats—kettle corn, cotton candy, enormous hot dogs. She found herself wondering what it would be like to live one of their lives, rather than her own. She didn't see a sad face among the populace as they decided between visiting the crystal ball reader or rune caster or astrologist or...or...or *wow*.

She ogled beyond the crowd, beyond the Mystic's alley where they now stood, and for the first time since arriving, took in the full view of where she was. There was so much to this supernatural carnival. So much more than just a carnival...or a circus. As far as she could see, there were extraordinary things to behold.

Impressive purple- and white-striped Big Tops, enchanting red and black show tents. Marvelous games so whimsically bright their lights bled from one to another. And rides...twirling, turning, twisting, whirling. Reaching to the moon and back. Music mixed with screams of horror and screams of glee and screams of devilish ecstasy. Mystic's was an orgy of color sprinkled with stardust in the most spellbinding way. How could she forget such a place?

For a moment, she was admiring the massive exposition and seeing it as it currently appeared, and then she wasn't. The carnival was the same, for the most part, only less crowded. Rides appeared to move with more ease and less urgency. Sides of the tents rustled in the evening breeze, and the majority of the screams came for the area of the Ferris wheel, which appeared to be in the center or far back of the carnival compared to where she now stood. Was she somehow remembering a different day at Mystic's Carnival? Kyra blinked, and the current chaos resumed.

Maybe it was her imagination, but a few of the people wandering their direction down the lane appeared to be heading straight for them and staring right at her. A red-haired man caught her attention, and her insides tightened. She realized her mouth was agape and snapped it shut.

She wanted to grab Sebastian's hand and flee the area, but already knew she wouldn't, couldn't. Whatever instinct fluttered inside of her telling her to run, an equally, more powerful one punched at the flutter and yelled at her to stay, face the fear. Even if she had no idea what it was she feared. Others in the crowd must have sensed it, too, as they moved to the sides, allowing the approaching strangers a large berth.

"We are taking the boy to forked cells at the Devil's Eye now."

Kyra snapped to and turned on her mother. "Not if I have anything to say in the matter."

"Kyra." Ryhuu brushed her arm, only this time, there was a gentleness in the gesture.

She jerked away, crinkling her brow at him. "Who are you to insinuate yourself into these matters?" Her gaze slowly moved over Sebastian's tired and beaten presence to her mother's slight shoulder shrug. There was a dynamic at play here she didn't understand. *What am I missing?*

"Don't you remember me?" He reached for her hand. Again, she brushed him away.

"The boy will be going with us," Bolsvck said. "He shall be held in Mobürn until we are satisfied that he has given us all the information we desire and deem him no longer necessary."

"I don't agree," Queen Shui was saying when Kyra stepped between them and addressed her father.

"What does that mean?"

"What do you think it means?" He spoke as if talking to a child in some sort of classroom exercise.

Kyra's hand twitched. She wanted to punch him. She knew exactly what going to Mobürn meant; she only wanted to hear him say the words, clearly and decisively, to her face. He was going to torture Sebastian. Torture and then kill him. It was as if Bolsvck had poured a bucket of ice water on her. No, she was immensely colder than plain ice water. Her body temperature was absolutely frigid. And the stupid smirk on his face screamed *challenge me*. Maybe that was exactly what he wanted. Was he trying to provoke her?

"Sir?" Bolsvck broke their gaze and turned, met an athletically built female with coppery-red hair. At her side, another sentry.

Kyra pulled at a strand of her own hair. Hers was longer. The other girl's was short, but long enough to have the sides pulled into a pony at the back, where it poked out like a pumpkin stub from her skull. The girl sneered at Kyra and handed Bolsvck a garment made of what looked to be a combination of faux leather and steel, but likely wasn't. Kyra moved her gaze from the girl to the new item and studied it intently. Bolsvck replaced the Palm Reader's banner, wrapping the new garment around his middle like a kilt.

"Kyra?"

Kyra jumped and met the gaze of a red-haired man, the other sentry. Her insides fluttered and back-stepped, and she back-stepped too. She had been staring at her father, and probably in a most inappropriate way. But she wanted to know what the kilt was made from. Dragon scales?

"Kyra?"

This time it was Sebastian who had spoken. She glanced over her shoulder, the reflection in his indigo eyes melted the frost plaguing her body. When she turned back, the red-haired man was standing right in front of her. Her breath got stuck in her throat.

In an instant, Ryhuu was right beside her, standing impossibly straight and proper. "She is not interested, Drakhögg. You should step away."

A diabolical smirk took over the redhead, Drakhögg, and he shoved Ryhuu in the chest. "She doesn't want you, wet-meat. Drag your dragon tail back to your sinkhole ocean home, and stay there."

The darker man glared at Drakhögg and didn't budge. He stood firm, a rather unreadable appearance upon his face.

Drakhögg shoved Ryhuu in the chest a second time. "You'll lose."

"Water will win," Ryhuu said. "In the end, water always puts out the fire."

Drakhögg's face lit up like an invigorated wrestler on steroids, and he leaned forward and exhaled in the other guy's face. "You forget, Ryhuu. We are more than simple fire. We evaporate water. Kyra will make the right choice."

"Will you both stop talking about me like I'm not even here?" Kyra said, her voice rising in both pitch and tone. "Who are you to decide what I will or won't do?" Turning away from them, she glanced back at Sebastian and silently mouthed, *what are they talking about?* Sebastian yanked at the men holding him hostage and nodded for her to join him.

"Ryhuu is your intended," Queen Shui said.

Kyra snapped back around. "I'm supposed to marry that guy? Since when?"

"Don't listen to her." Bolsvck brushed Queen Shui's words aside with a wave of his hand. "It is Drakhögg with whom you shall be wed." He slapped the redhead on the back and beamed with what appeared to be a mixture of pride and satisfaction.

"Both of you have arranged marriages for me?" Kyra backed away from them, backed up until Sebastian's arms clamped around her own. "No wonder I can't remember any of you. I've chosen to block it all out."

Both her parents spoke in protest at once.

"I suggest you give the girl some time to absorb this new information."

All heads turned to the side, where an old man stood smoking his bull-headed pipe.

"What do you know, old man?" Drakhögg asked, an angry bite in his voice.

Both Bolsvck and Queen Shui rose a hand to hush the overly bold Fire Dragon. "Show Zeke the utmost of respect," Bolsvck said to Drakhögg. Drakhögg shook his head, rolled his eyes. Kyra stared at the new arrival, with his dark skin, white eyes, cane, tweed jacket, and little cap. There was something oddly familiar about him. If only she could... She searched her memory. Searched and searched and searched, but she came up blank. She let out a sigh.

"I know more than you would think," Zeke said. "Would you mind?" He motioned toward Kyra and Sebastian. Both Bolsvck and Queen Shui stepped to the side, allowing Zeke an uncluttered pathway. A girl stepped to his side, and together they walked toward Kyra, the girl gently guiding Zeke's way. When he stood before Kyra, he softly patted her cheek. "My dear, you have been through so much." He tilted his head toward Sebastian. "Might I suggest a ride on the carousel?"

Bolsvck stepped forward, his chest pushed out. Queen Shui stood behind him, stern and concerned tells crackling her face. "Are you suggesting the two of them go enjoy the carnival...together?" Bolsvck asked. "I will not have my daughter tramping around with *that.*" He tossed a hand in their direction.

Zeke laughed, a mild and reassuring sound.

"Are you mocking me, sir?" Bolsvck stepped closer.

"I assure you, I am not." Zeke turned to face the leader of the Fire Dragons. "I fully understand and respect your customs and beliefs." He rubbed his chin with his thumb. "I only wonder if it might benefit all parties if Kyra retrieved her memories."

The group fell silent, and Kyra's gaze wandered from her mother to her father, then over to Ryhuu and Drakhögg.

It was Sebastian who cut through the wordless moment. "You know how to restore Kyra's memory?"

"I may." Zeke swiveled slowly with his cane planted firmly in the dirt. "I may not. Like I said, fancy a ride on the carousel?"

Kyra spun around and grabbed Sebastian's arms, clasping at the elbows. Her eyes widened, and her breath was deep. "Do I want to remember? Because I think I do...if it means remembering you."

Sebastian leaned his forehead against hers and spoke in hushed tones, as if to keep their words private. Kyra wondered if privacy were possible in their present company. "Good or bad, our memories make us who we are. I love the person you have become because of your vast experiences. I wouldn't change a thing about you, Kyra. You're an amazing dragon and an even more amazing woman. You put the glow of the sun to shame."

Kyra's skin tingled, and warmth blossomed in the core of her chest. In that moment, for him, she could fly. Her fingers sought his, weaving together until she couldn't tell where she ended and he began.

"How?" Kyra asked Zeke.

"Follow Talia here." Zeke's hand wavered in the air to the young girl at his side. "She'll show you what needs to be done."

"We can trust her," Sebastian whispered at Kyra's ear.

Kyra bit her lip and studied this new female in her life. Her stomach clenched.

"I still don't understand the need for *him* to be present," Queen Shui said, squaring her shoulders.

"Exactly," Bolsvck seconded.

"Sebastian was, and as you can see, still is a big part of the life Kyra has chosen. If you wish for her to remember, it is best to have a tether, someone who understands her and won't judge her." Zeke nodded at Sebastian. "He is best for that role."

"Then I will go." Drakhögg stepped forward.

"As will I." Not to be outdone, Ryhuu also stepped forward.

Kyra rolled her eyes and rubbed her temple. This testosterone match made her head hurt.

Ignoring the dragon men, Zeke placed an arm around Kyra and moved her in the direction of the rides. He motioned for Sebastian to follow. Talia walked steadily at Zeke's side.

"Sebastian currently safeguards a large part of Kyra." He tossed a meaningful glance in the direction of the dragon ring. "Understand now?" Bolsvck, Queen Shui, and all their people stood in place and said nothing. "Good. I only require the two. Any more, and it will muddle the process. Please refrain from following." Zeke glanced at Kyra and winked. They walked the path at a mild to slow rate. "When it is done, Kyra will return to you."

"And the boy," Bolsvck yelled.

Zeke did not respond.

"I shall go. Make sure everything goes all right. Make sure they both return," Ryhuu said.

Kyra glanced back, saw Queen Shui stop Ryhuu with a touch to the shoulder. At the back of the dragon crowd, Drakhögg's head snapped up. He'd been in tight, a little too tight, with that other girl dragon. The one that made Kyra self-conscious.

"Send no one. We will return," Zeke called over his shoulder and kept walking.

When the dragons were out of view, Zeke stepped to the side and took a seat on an old bench pushed out of the crowd's way. "This is it for me, for now. Talia will take excellent care of you. She's a good girl."

"Thank you, Zeke, for everything." Sebastian took the old man's hand in his and squeezed. He knelt close to Zeke and whispered something Kyra couldn't hear. The not knowing made her eyes burn.

When Sebastian stepped back, dragonflies swarmed a chaotic ring inside Kyra's gut. She should say something to this man who had somehow stricken respect and compliance in her parents. But that alone kept her feet from taking a step closer. "Thank you for your help," she said from where she stood. Zeke smiled, and his blind eyes glistened. Kyra's brow narrowed, and she studied him hard. She almost stepped closer. *Is he really blind?*

"Let's go," Talia said and started toward the array of spinning lights and magical music.

The air was thick with the scent of hot dogs, turkey legs, caramelized bacon, and something else. Something metallic. Something...burning? Kyra regarded the scenes on her left and right. From what she could see, nothing was burning, but that didn't rule out an electrical fire. A flash snapped near her right ear, and she turned to see what it was. Another flash to the left. Tiny flashes everywhere, like lightning bugs exploding. She jerked her head and jumped.

Sebastian tightened his hold on her hand. "Don't worry. You've been through this many times. It's Mystic's—the carnival. She's getting ready to change."

Kyra paused and stared at him, a wrinkle in her forehead. "What do you mean, change?"

"You're about to find out." He pulled her closer, wrapping his arm around her waist. Studied her with concern brewing in his dark, sultry eyes. "How are you dealing with the knowledge that you're a dragon shifter?"

"I don't know. I feel like it should bother me, and yet..." She paused, peered down at her hand and flexed it. She could almost see it morphing into something scaly with wicked-long nails. Damn, she had a wild imagination. She squinted back toward the flashing lights of the rides. "It's almost like that's what's wrong here. I'm supposed to be a dragon, but I'm not." She glanced at him. "Does that make sense?"

"In your amusing Kyra-speak, it sorta does." He rubbed her arm. "I don't want to alarm you, but this place is full of things of a supernatural nature. Like dragons, but not like dragons at all. Does that make sense?"

Kyra's lips twisted to the side, and she thought about what he'd said for a moment. "I guess it does. Like you?" she asked. "You're not a dragon."

"No, I'm not. Your parents made that abundantly clear."

The metallic smell grew stronger, and the flashing increased.

"She's working slow today. Must be giving you a chance to acclimate."

"Who?" Kyra asked.

"The carnival," Sebastian said. "Like your people are dragons, and I am not, the carnival is an entity all her own. A rather interesting being, at that." He admired their surroundings, giving pause to his commentary. "She will move us visitors around the landscape of her domain as she deems necessary. You used to tell me it was a fun challenge, making your way from one place to another when Mystic's wanted you to go someplace else." He laughed.

"I bet," Kyra said, and suddenly everything around them spun in a whirlwind of flashing lights. Kyra stumbled. Sebastian caught her. When the world was once again calm, they were standing in front of the carousel.

"And here we are. Exactly where we need to be. Guess she's feeling helpful." Following Talia, Sebastian led Kyra to the ride's entrance. The metal railing around the carousel was cool to the touch. Kyra wrapped her palms around its smooth surface, wondering how many hands had run along its veneer through the years while they waited their turn at the adventure, wearing the railing down to such a fine, feather-touch feel.

A musical voice rang overhead. "Mystic's Jubilee commences in fifteen. Party favors are still available lakeside and at the front gate."

Sebastian turned to Talia. "Today is the Jubilee?"

"Yeah. Great timing you two have, huh?" She jumped over the gate and motioned them to wait. After whispering something to the ride attendant, she pushed a button on the control panel and talked into the mic. "Sorry folks. This ride will be shut down until after the fireworks show." Her announcement was greeted with a cluster of complaints and protests. "Phil here," she pointed to the ride attendant, "will be handing each of you a ticket that will not only give you access to the priority line upon your return, but a free show at the Magical Bibelots tent." Thrilled oohs and ahhs resounded, and people dwindled away after Phil handed out the tickets. Soon there was only Talia, Sebastian, and Kyra. Even Phil left.

Kyra stared at the double-decker merry-go-round with all its masterfully carved whimsical creatures; unicorns, gryphons, lions, bats, sea creatures, swans, even a dragon. It was exquisite, but how in all things supernatural was a ride supposed to help her retrieve lost memories?

The gate opened.

"Riders, pick your steed," someone yelled. Kyra saw no source for the voice, only Talia directing them to the second level. Kyra's steps were slow and deliberate, her hand clenching the railing till the blood drained from her fingers. The warmth of Sebastian's hand at the small of her back pressed her onward against the tide of trepidation, until she stood toe-to-toe with the glowing amber light carved into the landing at the top.

28

CONFRONTATION

Marcus

Naked and covered in grime and gore, Marcus sat on the bottom step leading to the once-grand entrance of the Great Hall. Before him, in the formerly opulent and popular space, now neglected by time, lay a ruin of crumbled walls and collapsed ceiling. Nothing but rubble. A few hours before, the dome ceiling of the club stood three stories high, and now the damage was so severe, a hole worthy of his condo's square footage now exposed the dark, twinkling night.

Rage and frustration raced the threads of his blood veins, burned like dragon fire through his muscles and across his skin. The deed should be done. Bolsvck should be dead. *But he's not.* Marcus ground his teeth and growled, sending the tiny pebbles at his feet into a slow scatter. To hell with Leila for abandoning the fight. Curse the building for collapsing. And damn it all for giving Bolsvck a chance to escape. Marcus would make sure he didn't get a second chance.

Blood and sweat trickled from Marcus's brow, and the taste of copper lingered on his tongue. He wiped the blood from the cut on his lower lip. A glass of whiskey was what he needed right now. He'd even settle for a beer. The long-forgotten Great Hall offered none. Not even a water source. All utilities had been shut down ages ago. It had been decades since the place had seen life—until now. His ritual.

A wickedly satisfying grin melted into place, his lips curling like a jackal discovering dinner after days of starvation. A sputtering gurgle rumbled in his throat, a sinister laugh even for one such as himself. He didn't care; he was focused on what had gone right. The night hadn't been a total disaster. He had success on his side. With the help of the Mara, Leila, he'd triumphantly absorbed four upperclan dragons, making him the most powerful dragon across all the clans. Surely no one could defeat him now. Again, he laughed, this time out loud. The sound echoed through the chamber and, in response, bits of plaster fell from the wall.

He was no longer just a stupendous Fire Dragon of bygone and cast-out royalty. He was a powerful Ice Dragon, a mighty Bronze Dragon, a monstrous Forest Dragon, and an ostentatious Blue Dragon. A combination the supernatural community had yet to behold. When they did, they'd have no choice but to bow to him. Fighting would be in vain.

With a grunt, Marcus stood. His feet carried him across the debris-covered steps in search of the neatly folded pile of clothing he'd set aside prior to the ceremony. If the fight with Sebastian, and later Bolsvck, hadn't disrupted the pile, his phone should be sitting on top.

Red flashed across his vision. The color accompanied a shearing pain at the back of his eyes. "Sebastian." The name slithered between gritted teeth.

Damn the carnie kid for ruining everything. If it weren't for him, Marcus would possess the power of the Moorigad Dragon, as well. *I'm going to kill him.*

Marcus found his clothing, rumpled at the far end of the bottom step, covered in a layer of busted cement and stone. The black t-shirt appeared greyer than midnight, and his jeans had a mild tint of beige. The apparel may as well have been pulled from a gravel pit. His shoulders slumped, and he let out a long breath.

“Bolsvck,” he grumbled. Snorted.

His gaze narrowed, forehead pinched. He didn’t see his phone with the unkempt pile of dusty clothing.

“Where’s my phone?” he snarled. Sharp dragon scales pushed through and prickled his skin. Smoke curled and rose from his nose. He snapped at nothing, nothing at all.

Damn carnie. He was to blame for everything.

Marcus riffled through the clothing, picking up each piece and shaking them to remove as much grime as possible. It did little good. He was going to resemble a disaster victim when he left this place. He glanced down at his hands, arms, and feet. Such a mess. He detested messes.

A shrill pitch rang out, bouncing off the hard walls and echoing against the dome ceiling—what was left of the ceiling, anyway. He turned, his gaze quickly scanning the floor. Another shrill ring, and this time, Marcus caught sight of a light amidst the cluttered steps. With his clothing clutched in one hand, he sprinted across the space and snatched up his phone, answering on the third ring.

“Rick,” he said and paused, listening. “Yes, but there were complications. Gather the crew. I’ll be there shortly to explain everything.” Listening again, Marcus notched the phone between his cheek and shoulder as he slipped into his jeans. “No more games. This time we prepare for the big one. We’re taking the fight directly to Bolsvck.” Marcus laughed at Rick’s reply. “He’s a has-been. Dragon jerky. He won’t even see us coming.” Marcus hung up, slid the phone into his back pocket.

“I know where you can find Bolsvck.”

Marcus turned, glared at the top of the stairs, and charged. Taking the steps two at a time, he finished the climb within seconds. His hand wrapped around Leila’s neck and squeezed, his momentum continuing, moving him forward, pushing her backward until he had her slight body pressed into the ungiving wall. Her hand clasped over his, her breath sputtered and choked, but she didn’t fight. She merely held his gaze with her bottomless-pit eyes.

The muscles in his hand relented. Marcus paused, his course of action momentarily forgotten. The fires of Purgatory burned all around him. Their heat licking at his skin, the vapors filling his nostrils, the sweat drenching his garments. He blinked, blinked hard, shook his head, and saw the Great Hall once more. "Get out of my head, Leila," he said, baring his teeth. "Use your Mara tricks on me again, and I'll end you."

She closed her eyes, and he allowed her a moment of muted misery. A moment to come to terms with her fate. Maybe he'd kill her right here. Did he really need her now that he had the dragons? Probably not. Still, there was Kyra. He didn't have the Moorigad yet, and he wanted that one so bad it made his tail twitch. He pulled his hand away, and Leila dropped to the ground.

"You left." Marcus stared down at her, his muscles tensing into tight knots. There wasn't much she could have done had she stayed, still, he hadn't given her permission to leave, and the betrayal was like ice skewers to his spine.

"I did." She peered up, her face wrapped in the hood of her cloak. To the Mara-uneducated, she had the appearance of a beautiful woman-child in need of rescuing. Marcus wanted to reach down and swoop her up in his arms. He resisted, knowing the feeling to be false. She was false. Everything about that tiny moment was false.

A deep grumble bellowed down in his chest. It burst forth in a mixture of roar and words. "What did I tell you?"

"I'm sorry, my lord. So sorry." Leila hid her face from view. "It can't always be helped. It is our nature. To defy our nature would be—"

"Shut it." He didn't have time for her family history. Time was his leverage, and they were wasting it. "You're either with me or against me. Which is it, Leila?"

Her hands rose at her side, a sign of submission. "With you, of course, my lord. It is for you that I left. I had to follow the dragon child to protect your interests." She glanced up, her eyes barely visible beneath the fall of her hood and dark hair.

A mild hint of deceit wafted around her, and Marcus narrowed his eyes. That was a new sense: truth tracing. No doubt, it would come in handy. He studied every line and hidden quiver along Leila's body.

Savored and deconstructed every distasteful odor rising from her body. She may have followed Kyra, but she probably still had a hidden purpose for that damn carnie boy. The Mara worked a dual agenda. An agenda he'd be wise to never forget. With a clawed hand, he reached down and yanked Leila to her feet. She met his glare, a doubtful smile twitching at the corners of her lips.

"I didn't leave before making sure you would be triumphant, sire." A gleam came to life in her previously lifeless, black eyes.

"And how did you do that, exactly? Because from where I'm standing," Marcus gestured to himself and to the demolished surroundings, "I don't see glorious success."

Leila's hands twisted together in a tangled, twining agitation, a maddening bubble of laughter leaking between her lips. "Not as planned, my lord. Not as planned. But you're alive." Her eyes widened, glistened.

Is she going mad? Marcus leaned back, straightening his back. He held her shoulders firmly in his grasp. If down the loon well was where she was headed, he had no more use for her except to wreak havoc upon his enemies.

"Alive you are." She cocked her head to the side and paused, as if waiting for approval. Marcus had none. Leila continued, her hands flailing at the fallen ceiling. "It was meant to destroy him. It failed."

Acid dashed along his tendons, flexing his muscles, jolting Marcus back a step. "You dropped the building on me?" His voice hitched between each word.

"Not on you." Her voice rose, and her body appeared to drop. She was suddenly much smaller, a lost child staring up at him. "It was meant to devastate Bolsvck."

"You failed." Marcus took another step back and crossed his arms.

"Indeed. Their magic is so unpredictable," she said, shaking her head.

"Magic?" He turned and studied the damage yet again. "You did this with magic?" He turned back and narrowed his gaze on her. "Mara magic?"

Leila chuckled. "Maras don't possess that kind of ability. This was helped by human mechanical magic."

"What do you mean?"

"You know." She wiggled her hand in the air between them, as if she could miraculously transport into her palm whatever she had used to manifest the destruction. "Those little mechanical devices with things attached."

"Explosives?" Marcus's brows arched. "You used explosives? Where in all the dominion of Rajũn did you get explosives?" He raked his hand through his hair to the back of his neck and rubbed. Turning away, he began to pace the landing.

"From Chet," she said.

Marcus spun around and studied her. He detected no lie. This new advantage one of the dragons had granted him was unexpected but handy. Which was the sneaky dragon lot that kept their lie-detecting ability a tightly kept secret?

"You said you trusted Chet," she said, dropping all defenses.

He had. And he did. Maybe he shouldn't, smelling the hint of stagnant water swimming around Leila's responses. The scent wasn't strong enough to suggest complete disloyalty, but her personal intentions had never been clearer. Damn carnie boy. What was the allure?

"I assured him it was to help you. To further our cause." She was talking faster now, nervous. That was good. He liked to incite fear. She was usually a conceited and arrogant woman. She needed to learn her place in his organization.

Marcus tilted his head and glanced toward the door. Leila had left it partially open. He grabbed her arm and swung her in the direction of the exit. "Come on, we're leaving."

A car horn sounded somewhere above them.

"But." She stammered. Marcus smiled. He was delighted to have finally knocked the bitch off balance. "I saw no one when I returned."

"Because no one was there." He wrenched open the door. "Rick dispatched the driver after our conversation, since my Mustang has been temporarily disabled." Marcus pointed to the hole in the ceiling and the car teetering at the top. Leila said nothing. She ducked through the door and led the way up the narrow and curvy flight of stairs to the surface. Marcus marched behind her.

A dense carpet of ancient trees hid them from view when they emerged. The door previously hidden from sight now lay flush on the ground, cloaked with the flora. Several yards away, a sleek, black sedan awaited them at the edge of a small paved turnabout. Marcus's Mustang had been parked at the far end of that same turnabout and now threatened to drop into the Great Hall hidden beneath the lush landscape.

Marcus jabbed Leila in the back, propelling her forward. She hissed but moved toward the car at an acceptable speed for her short stature. He held her firmly by the arm, eliminating any possibility of her slipping away.

"The carnival," she said without a glimpse at Marcus.

"What about it?"

"That's where you'll find Bolsvck, my lord." Marcus's jaw clenched, and Leila continued. "He arrived moments before I left to come find you."

When they reached the car, Marcus opened the door and shoved Leila into the backseat. "To the Den," he said to the driver and forcefully nudged Leila again, making room for himself.

"You do not treat me that way." She raised a finger to his face. He batted it away and elbowed her into the far door. "I have cooperated, my lord."

"You have tried to deceive me, and you have failed." He pulled the door shut, motioned the driver to go, and turned away from Leila, staring out the window at his side.

Something moved in the tree line. Several somethings.

29

RIDERS

Kyra

Kyra's gaze was fixed on the glow at her feet. She couldn't remember ever riding a carousel, but what she was now admiring didn't appear normal. Lines swirled outward from one center point, swinging around and curling back in on themselves. A pulsing green and orange light traveled the design, working its way from one end to the other and back again.

Talia made a funny sound behind them, one of those move-along coughs. Sebastian dropped his hand from Kyra's back, turned to Talia, and pointed at the marking on the carousel floor. "This your doing?"

"It is." She stepped past them and stood on the other side of the mark, appraising her work. "The lines represent all that was, all that is, and all that will be." She glanced up and studied Kyra. "For you, of course." Talia tossed Sebastian a quick lift of the brow before pointing to the moving colors. "The amber and emerald running through your lines should heal and clarify your personal memories through your mind, body, and soul."

She looked up and locked her stare on Kyra once again. "Your heart plays a big factor in the success of what we are about to do. You need to be true to your heart. Let it feel what it wants to feel, and don't fight it." She took Kyra's hand in her own. "Don't fight anything that comes to you, understand? Bad times, sad times, let them in."

Kyra nodded and glanced back down at the moving glow at her feet. Muscles in her chest and shoulders tightened. Breathing had become a labored endeavor. She was a dragon. A giant, mythological dragon! What memories awaited her? *Am I ready for this?*

Sebastian's fingers brushed along her hand, fitting hers within the curve of his palm, as if his hand was molded for a perfect fit. When his fingers laced between her own, she stared up into his indigo eyes and found her strength.

"All right. Let's do this." Pulling Sebastian behind, Kyra began to walk the circle of the carousel, heading straight for the dramatically painted dragon.

"Not the dragon," Talia called from behind them.

Kyra paused, and both she and Sebastian peered back at Talia. "I thought..." Kyra didn't finish her statement, but rather stood with puzzlement on her face. Her thoughts swam around the carousel dragon. She was supposed to be a dragon, and Sebastian had a dragon inside of him. The dragon seemed the logical choice.

"It has to be the elephant." Talia pointed past them.

Kyra glanced over her shoulder. "I don't see an elephant."

"Keep going. He's around the curve."

"Why the elephant?" Sebastian asked.

"Memory," Talia said with a shrug.

Appearing satisfied, Sebastian took the lead, taking the curve in long, strong strides. Kyra and Talia followed. The elephant was there, waiting for them as soon as they cleared the bend. The animal stood taller and wider than the others, taking up the space of one and a half horses.

"I'm supposed to get on top of that big thing?" Kyra pointed and wrinkled her nose.

"Not just you," Talia said to Kyra. "Both of you." She turned her attention to Sebastian. "For this to work, we need to have both elements of Kyra's life on the elephant."

Sebastian exhaled and extended his hand to Kyra. She scanned from his hand to the elephant and back to his hand. "All right."

Once again, a musical voice sang over their heads and throughout the park. "Commencement time is almost upon us. Be sure to grab your party supplies!"

Kyra took Sebastian's hand and stepped up to the elephant. "What's going to happen at commencement time?"

"The celebration will begin with a grand fireworks show." His lips pressed firmly together.

"Something's bothering you," Kyra said. "What is it?"

"Probably nothing."

Kyra narrowed her gaze.

"I'm uncomfortable having a bunch of unpredictable dragons on site when the park is overfilled for the celebration. That's all."

Kyra smiled. "Well then...let's get this over with, so they have no reason to linger." She turned, placed her foot in the stirrup, and hoisted herself up to the top of the giant, shiny, wooden elephant.

After making sure she was secure, Sebastian turned to Talia. "What happens now?"

"You two will take a ride on the carousel. The magic will do the rest."

Sebastian scratched the back of his neck. "How will we know it's working?"

"You'll know."

The ride jolted, and merry-time music started to play. In slow, rhythmic motion, the animals began to move up and down and up and down.

"Time to join her." Talia pointed to Kyra at the top of the elephant, then turned and left.

"What happens now?" Kyra bent down, lowering her hand to him.

"No idea. Guess we're going to find out." He climbed up and swung onto the elephant behind her.

His warmth surrounded her, and if she were honest with herself, she liked it, desired it, even. Talia had said she had to be true to her heart for the magic to work. Did that include what she was feeling toward Sebastian? "You smell like soot," she said.

"Sorry. I'm afraid I don't have much control over this new arrangement."

She studied him with tenderness and affection pressing to expand her heart a thousand-fold, and yet that word *arrangement* nagged at her. She smiled as if nothing worrisome touched their lives, allowing the sun to sparkle in her eyes. "I don't mind." She leaned into him, tilting her head to better see him. She spoke at a whisper and hoped he couldn't hear the erratic dance her heart was performing. "Did you know about my arranged marriages?"

His gaze was soft, understanding. With the slightest touch, he swept a hair from the edge of her face. "I did not. But it doesn't surprise me."

"Why's that?" Kyra relaxed into him and watched the colors move dreamily past. The carousel was building momentum.

"You told me they were forcing you to make a choice between the Water and Fire Clans. They probably thought pairing you with a suitable companion would make your decision easier." He wrapped his arms around her waist.

She continued to hold onto the pole, even though part of her wanted to take hold of him, instead. "Why do I have to choose?"

"I don't pretend to understand the ways of dragons, Kyra, but you are a Moorigad. It means both traits of your parents run through your blood." He rested his chin on her shoulder. "You once told me about a legend of the first Moorigad, Anguis the Angry, you called him. He refused to choose. Like you, he was a hybrid of water and fire. And as you know, it can be an explosive combination. The war that raged within him not only drove him mad and destroyed him, but through his madness, caused unmeasurable devastation and death in the process. Since then, every Moorigad has chosen a clan. Given one side of themselves up, so that the other side might survive."

Kyra straightened, a chill running through her faster than lightning. In a split second, she was a tangle of arms and legs, turning around in her seat to face Sebastian.

His hands went up in a defensive blockade against her not-so-graceful turn. "Woowa! You trying to knock me off the back of this thing?" He leaned back, avoiding her leg swinging across the front of him.

"Sorry." Kyra flashed a sheepish smile up at him and settled into place with her back against the pole and her legs crossed over his. "It's just..." She paused and stared down at her fiddling hands. They rubbed up and down her legs, warming her thighs. "When is this thing, whatever it is, when they make me choose, supposed to happen?"

"I don't know."

"Will I be the same afterwards?" She tilted her head and gazed deep into his eyes. "Will I feel like the me from before?"

"I don't know."

The carousel was spinning at top speed, but Kyra no longer concentrated on retrieving her memory. All her concern huddled around the thought she might lose herself over some dragon ritual she didn't want any part of. Her insides fluttered and tightened. "Will I remember you? Still care for you?"

"I don't know, Kyra. I'm not privy to the ways of dragons."

"What do you know?" Her voice pitched and jumped an octave. Sebastian arched an eyebrow, watched her with quiet concern moving across his features. With a flop in her belly and a tightening of her throat, Kyra bit her lip and grimaced. "I'm sorry. I didn't mean that." She sighed and gazed up into his dark, caring eyes. Love and sincerity gazed back at her. It washed over her like a storm at sea. And in that moment, she remembered the power of the Water Dragon rushing through her veins, pumping in her blood, invigorating her soul.

The world exploded in a hundred and one colors and sounds, fireworks filling the sky, a jubilee of music and merriment rising all around them. It was magically intoxicating. She stared at Sebastian, her gaze dropping to his lips. The kiss she had bestowed upon him at Marcus's place lingered at the forefront of her mind. What if her returning memories came in the form of feelings and desires? She grabbed Sebastian and pressed her lips to his. A thrill shivered up her spin.

Sebastian kissed her back, opening up to her like the night unfolding to the dawn. It was shadow and light, the moon and the sun, night and day, the earth's molten core melting the arctic ice. Polar opposites coming together as one, and within that magical moment, the most perfect moment, Kyra remembered.

Her fingers laced through Sebastian's hair, and she kissed him harder, giving every inch of herself and never wanting to let him go. All the while, who and what she was flooded back to her, memories exploding into existence out of nothing, like popcorn from a hot oiled tin. She remembered the Water Dragon, Ryhuu, trying to push her into a submissive role. Her mother thrusting the Water Clan life upon her, denying Kyra her fire side, and their many fights as a result. Kyra had fled. Her father hadn't acted much better, verbally assaulting the Water Dragons with every conversation. And then there was the irritating match with vain Drakhögg, a man too full of himself to appreciate anyone else.

Why were male dragons such dragonic dicks?

Dragonic dicks like Marcus, trying to control her by blocking her memories, her own free will, and individual thought. Her cold abated a smidgen at the thought of him. At her hatred for him. Yet it was herself she despised more, for falling into his trap and allowing herself to befall a damn-foolish weakened state. Be ripped in two.

Her heart squeezed. Chelsea. What had happened to the cancer-riddled girl she had dragged away from the carnival to help the lying-sleaze Marcus? Emotion rushed Kyra, crushed her, and tears began to stream down her cheeks. It was because of her Higgins had died. She remembered everything. And it was for her Sebastian had fought fire and fate in Purgatory and had come to knocking on Marcus's door. She pulled back, caressed Sebastian's cheek with her palm.

"Are you okay?" His thumbs brushed tenderly at the sides of her face.

She shook her head, peered down. "I remember. I hurt you atrociously, and the memories claw at my core."

Using his index finger, Sebastian lifted her face till their eyes met. "Kyra, dragon-darling." Ever so gently, he kissed her forehead and whispered, "You never have to apologize for what was. Besides, you weren't yourself." His thumbs erased the tear tracks from beneath her eyes. His lips lifted in a reassuring smile, but it was sadness she saw staring back at her.

The ride was crawling to a stop, the melody fading into the rush and roar of the crowd. Kyra's innards dropped like magma, and her throat squeezed shut. She never wanted this moment to end. Never wanted to get off this carousel with Sebastian. Didn't want to know what came next—something told her she wasn't going to like it. Parents and suitors waiting, wanting to do who-knows-what to Sebastian. Marcus coming for them both. And in his own family realm, something was definitely knocking Sebastian's foundation off kilter. So much sadness in his eyes.

"Ready?" he said.

She wasn't. Her fingers clutched at him as if he were her last breath in a life worth living. Her body pressed to his, trying with all desperation to drag him closer. There was no close that was close enough. Their lips connected with a heated passion that would turn normal men to ash.

And then it was over. Sebastian pulled away and dropped off the wooden elephant. He extended his hand to Kyra. "Come on. Time to go."

A cold breeze swept through her. She blinked and stared down at Sebastian and his outreached hand, but he looked away. Her heart fluttered and sped up. She felt like a dragonling awaiting her mother's punishment.

She took his hand and slipped off the animal. They walked around the circle toward the carousel stairs. "Sebastian?"

"Everything's going to be fine. I'll make sure of it." He glanced over his shoulder, and the edge of his lips twitched as if he wanted to smile but couldn't quite make it happen. He returned his attention to the path, blocking his face from Kyra and filling her soul with black, ugly dread. The This-is-Your-Life carousel was supposed to fix things, and yet it seemed to be pushing Sebastian away. Why was he acting so withdrawn?

They descended the steps as if they walked toward Death's door, slow and with hints of trepidation. When they'd ridden the elephant, Kyra had seen her life in a flash. Her time with Sebastian. Her time with her family. Was it possible he'd seen too and didn't approve? Or was his icy change the result of something more sinister? Something the ride had shared with only him? She watched Sebastian from the corner of her eye. Overhead, the sky continued to pop and sizzle, illuminating in every vibrant color imaginable in an unprecedented fireworks display.

Talia sat on the gate. "Those dragon dudes are waiting for you." She spoke to both of them, but her gaze narrowed in on Sebastian. "I think you should find yourself scarce."

"Done." He glanced at Kyra and let out a long breath, then turned to Talia, "Can you make sure Kyra gets back to her family?"

Talia nodded acknowledgement, and Kyra yanked Sebastian's arm, forcing him to pay attention to her. "I can find my way around the carnival just fine. I don't need a babysitter. But that's beside the point. I want to go with *you*."

Sebastian grimaced. "Yeah?" She hit him, and he flinched. "You're gonna have to deal with your parents sooner or later. Might as well do it now. You can't keep running forever."

"Listen to who's talking." She crossed her arms and squared her jaw.

He shook his head, scratched his fingers through his tufts of hair. "My situation is different."

"Is it really? At the core, it all boils down to standing up for what you believe in and making sure your dad hears you." She was talking about Sebastian now, not herself, but the words had just as much meaning in her own life.

"Right here, right now, your folks might be able to put you back together. And you need that." He took her hand and squeezed it. "You can't go on feeling cold because you're missing your dragon half."

She pulled at their hold, dragging him closer. "But you have my dragon, so it stands to reason I should stay with you. I'm complete when I'm with you."

It was as if all the lights went out at the carnival and Sebastian stood at the nucleus. He became a void of emotion, a void of life. A complete and utter black hole. His eyes were blacker than the blackest of nights and his aura a storm cloud of forsaking. He turned away. "There's no fixing this, Kyra. I don't belong in your world." He pulled his hand away, and his face hardened, cracked with wrinkled lines of disgust. "You're an irritating dragon. Who's got time for that?" He turned and walked through the gate.

Talia stared after him, a blank expression on her face.

Kyra's mouth fell open as she watched Sebastian walk away. Every cell in her body felt completely absent of life. He was her best friend, the only one she'd ever loved, and he was walking away. *What did I miss?*

"I love you, Sebastian," she called out to him.

He didn't look back.

30
REVELATION

Marcus

Marcus shifted against the fine leather of the backseat. The air smelled of coconut air freshener, as well as Mara and zilant, the two others in the car with him. But that wasn't what bothered Marcus. There was something else, something not within the confines of the vehicle, but close enough to ruffle his shackles. That something kept him glancing over his shoulder and out the back window.

His finger tapped on the door panel, finally pressing down on the widow lever, lowering it a crack. An abundance of scents rushed past, all from the surrounding area and the area ahead. A mingling of nature and human that, in his mind, never should've come to be. It was human fear he smelled now. Human fear, rust, and bad petrol. And the sweat—the fear—was intensifying, as if the source were somehow aware of Marcus's suspicions. Or maybe it was simply getting closer. Were they in visual range?

"Slow down, Darren."

The driver glanced toward the backseat. "Think someone's following us?"

Leila stretched like a cat waking from a nap. The lack of interest she demonstrated set Marcus's ears to smoking. He wasn't sure how long he'd be able to put up with her, if she would even last until the plan came to fruition. *She may have to meet her demise early.* And if so, let the Mara, maker of bad dreams, meet her own nightmare. It was his purpose after all, to bring the lesser beings to their knees, and she was by all means a lesser being. Marcus squinted, watched her from the corner of his eye.

"If we are being followed, will we lead them away from the Den? Or just stop here and kill them?" Leila asked and fell back into the seat. She didn't sound exceptionally interested either way.

Kill them, yes. Marcus's tongue ran longingly along his teeth, and he sniffed the air once again. Fear. Plenty of fear. Human fear. "Pull over."

"Sir?" Darren tilted his head toward the back. The road ahead was barren. Mostly trees, with the occasional house buried deep within the thicket.

"Pull the damn car over, now." Marcus was already opening the side door. The tires hit the side gravel, sending a shower of pebbles hammering like a hailstorm at the car's underside. The car hadn't come to a complete stop when Marcus stepped from the backseat. The door slammed closed, barely missing his arm, and the sedan swerved to a hard stop several feet beyond.

Light shimmered dimly through the trees, the sun barely beginning to peek its waking head over the horizon. Marcus caught sight of a small, battered pickup truck headed in their direction. Headlights flickered with each exaggerated bump in the road. It could be nothing, but if the fear emanating from the rusty wheel bucket meant anything, he was betting the little beater was someone tasked to follow him. And that someone had a pretty good idea of what they were following. He, or she, was scared out of their skin.

Marcus stepped into the shadows. The black sedan purred quietly, waiting in plain sight. Even though the distance between the two vehicles closed with each breath, the rate of closure was decreasing. The truck was slowing. But stopping, no. It ambled up to Marcus, its engine pinging and tinging. A great getaway car, it would never make. Marcus hunched his shoulders, planted his feet, and narrowed his stare on the truck's little cab as it drove passed. Two men sat side by side. They probably planned to move by like nothing was amiss. Just a couple of guys running their daily errands. And it might have worked, had it not been for the stink of fear and the one man failing to hide his gaunt reflection of terror when he glanced out the side window.

His eyes said it all. He knew what Marcus was, of that there was no doubt.

A roar reeled up Marcus's throat. His leg swung back, throwing his body into a back twist-roll. A dark dance of the ages, limbs and shapes shifting, expanding. Garments ripping to shreds. Where once there was a man, now there was a gargantuan dragon. Dark and gnarly with innumerable sharp edges. A massive claw smashed down on the tailgate of the rambling truck, slamming it to a stop and smacking it into the road. Yelling erupted from the cab's interior. An explosion of pops. Marcus was being assaulted with gunfire. The passenger hung out the side window, weapon in hand.

Marcus's dragon howled, and smoke poured from his nostrils. Sucking back the vapors and filling them with his internal rage, he let loose hellfire. The truck's paint scorched, bubbled, and peeled. The man squealed and ducked back into the cab. Marcus stormed forward, picked up the vehicle, shook it, and tossed it to the side of the road. Ginormous dragon wings flapped as he turned, hitting and spinning the truck farther into the tree line.

"We're under attack!" The words came from the wreckage, followed by an unrecognizable static reply. Damn two-way radios. Marcus spun back and rushed the heap of metal. A man pulled himself from the vehicle, now sitting on its side, and stood on top of the wreckage. In his hand, he now held an automatic weapon. Marcus laughed, baring his teeth.

"You think that will stop me? Tiny human, you can't stop me." He lowered his head and snorted, covering the man in dragon smoke.

"Maybe I..." The man glanced through the window at his feet.

"We won't stop you today, but you can be sure Jon Davies will find a way."

The Black Dragon Marcus, now a mix of many dragons and their mighty gifts, straightened, stretching his neck high above the man. A dark cold swirled in Marcus's heart. It grew, swirling faster and faster at the mention of Davies's name. Marcus stood deathly still, like a statue, and then his tail twitched. It swung so fast the man only got off one shot before being smacked in the side by something the size of a fallen redwood. Automatic fire rang up through the trees and into the sky, only to be eclipsed by silent. The man's body slamming into a nearby tree and slumping to the ground.

"Hurry to the Den. Yeah, now." The voice was a mere whisper from deep within the cab.

Marcus's lips peeled back, exposing ready-to-kill teeth. All his attention was now focused on the remaining man. The mousy human inside the truck sending men to *his* Den. He'd heard too much. Was giving away too much information. Marcus turned and swung. The dragon's tail flattened the cab. All went silent.

He chuffed, blew dark thickets of angry smoke, and thumped his tail upon the hard asphalt road. The little truck hadn't been much to behold before, but now Marcus couldn't pull his gaze from the mangled heap.

Someone cleared their throat behind him. He swung around, wings extended, teeth exposed. Darren, the driver, stood next to the dark sedan, a small phone clutched firmly in his grip. "The men are assembled, sir," he said, a mild tremor in his voice.

With a swing of his tail that countered the shake of his head, Marcus advanced on the car. Darren stumbled back into the safety of the driver's seat and closed the door. By the time Marcus reached the car he was once again a man, having shed his dragon shape for the time being. Still burning with adrenaline, he didn't feel the rough asphalt against his bare feet.

Marcus slipped into the backseat and stretched his back, combing both hands through his hair. "Darren, get ahold of Rick. Tell him there has been a change. We're moving to plan B now."

"Yes, sir." The car engine came to life with a gentle purr, and within a minute, they were in motion.

"Feel better?" Leila handed Marcus a flask. He took it without hesitation but paused before bringing it to his lips. He stared at the item in his hand and narrowed his gaze. Leila groaned, snatched it back, and took a swig of the liquid. "Satisfied?"

Marcus smirked. "A man in my position can never be too careful."

"If I wanted you dead, I would be much more original in the execution. Poison is so ordinary." She twirled a lock of her hair around her index finger and allowed her gaze to wander along the length of his naked body. "A species of your fine stature has far too much energy worth harvesting. It would be a waste to snuff it out in such a mundane manner."

Marcus's face hardened. He knew what she was inferring, and he would not fall victim to any Mara. She would never suck his life force. Death would befall her long before she got the chance to even try. Maybe he'd kill her with some of her own medicine because, damn, she oozed of sex and longing, and the fires of passion raged through his blood after his little confrontation. She might be the perfect outlet for his current state of vexation. He dropped the flask on the floor.

"Eyes front, Darren," Marcus said and grabbed Leila by the throat, throwing her down against the seat.

"My lord." Her voice was breathless.

"Do your Mara thing. Make yourself resemble Kyra."

"As you wish." Leila's dark hair faded to red and her bone structure shifted.

"Good." Marcus slapped her across the cheekbone. "Exceptional." He hit her again and then thread his fingers through her hair, yanked her head back and to the side. His lips grazed along the curve of her neck, pausing at the base of her ear. "This means nothing." He kissed her, not out of passion but out of frustration and rage. He meant to control her. Destroy her.

Leila gasped.

Marcus's phone rang.

He grunted, pushed Leila aside and grabbed the flask from the floor, washing away any lingering desire with a long swig of fire water. Ignored, the phone continued to ring.

Leila lazily sprawled out across the far corner of the backseat. "I know your secret."

Marcus snuffed a laugh. "What secret is that?" He handed her the flask and picked up his phone, checked the missed call. "Damn," he muttered, narrowing his gaze on Rick's name on the screen and hitting redial. Leila's fingers brushed his when she took the flask from him. The touch pulled Marcus's attention away from the screen, if only temporarily, and he glanced sideways at her. "Consider it a peace offering." He glanced between her and the flask.

Her eyes sparked, and her face lit up with a wickedly know-all grin. "Do you fear your followers would think less of you if they knew the truth?"

"What are you talking about?" Marcus's voice was gruff and filled with agitation. He hated games. Hated them almost as much as he hated Bolsvck.

"When you were..."

The phone in Marcus's hand stopped ringing. Rick's voice came across the line, and Marcus threw up his hand, signaling Leila to pause their conversation. Cupping the phone to his ear and tilting his head toward the window, seeking what little privacy he could in the car's interior, Marcus talked low and quick. "What do you mean—how is that possible?" He listened, his face hardening by the second. "We don't have time for this. Cut our losses and move forward with the new plan... Yes, plan C." He rubbed the back of his neck. "We'll be there in..." Marcus leaned forward and tapped Darren in the front seat. "How long till we get to the Wilkes Barre Market Street Bridge?"

Darren tilted his head toward the back without taking his eyes off the road. "We're a ways out, sir. I'd say we still have an hour twenty before we get there."

"We'll be there in an hour," Marcus said to Rick. "Right, see you then." He ended the call. "Speed it up, Darren. We're taking casualties, and an hour to get there is just too long."

The momentum of the sedan increased, speeding down the tree-encroached road as if escaping, as if the trees might swallow them any moment. Marcus bent down and picked up a parcel from the floor. He had ignored it up until now. Hadn't felt a sense urgency. Now...now he wanted to be ready to move at the swing of a dragon's tail. He tore open the box and pulled his grey suit free. Rick always knew exactly what Marcus needed. A cocky smile found his lips, and warmth blossomed in his chest. He'd be one damn sharp gentleman when next he saw Kyra.

Leila rustled in the seat beside him.

"Sorry," he said. "Continue with what you were saying before." Marcus shook out his clothes and began dressing.

Leila studied him, her index finger running back and forth along her lower lip. "I only wondered if it concerned you."

Marcus raised a brow and waited for her to continue.

"When you were tossed into Purgatory, you were done so without provocation. You had done no wrong." Marcus's gaze narrowed. Leila's eyes widened, and she began to talk faster. "Everyone knows your father was guilty of horrible things. Nasty, vicious, atrocious things."

"Enough about him."

"But you were clueless. A young boy too full of himself to notice what was going on in his own family."

Marcus growled.

"Do you think your men would think less of you if they knew the truth?"

Marcus grabbed Leila around the neck, tossing her flat against the seat. "What's your point?"

Leila wheezed, and her voice came out strained. "I know you hold Bolsvck responsible. Davies, too. But Bolsvck, like you, was just another pawn in a larger game. I know the name of the man who actually tossed you into that Hell. The man who helped Davies orchestrate the undermining plot."

Marcus released his grip, sat back, and regarded her. "How do you know this man?"

"My mother told me." She smiled, and it reached into her witchly dark eyes.

"Your mother knows a Grim?" He folded his arms across his chest.

"She does, indeed. Or, she did. He came to her once, took pity upon her and granted her more time." Leila nibbled on her little finger. "Some might say he took a special kind of liking to her. He told her things. Your story was among the things he told her."

"Tell me who this man is." Marcus leaned forward, his voice fully demanding.

"I'll do better. I'll take you to him." Her eyes fluttered to the car floor and back. "But tell me first, how did you get out of Purgatory?"

Marcus groaned, leaned into the door, and dropped his head. "That was a low point in my life. The year in Purgatory was equal to a thousand Hells beat into my soul. On the 367th day, I stumbled across the devil. I made a deal." He flashed a look that was bitter and blithe and bleak, all in one. "You know how that turned out. Traded my dragon half."

Leila pursed her lips. "You met the devil?"

"Not the actual devil. Don't be so gullible."

She shrugged. "It could happen. You were in Hell's waiting room."

Marcus huffed, rolled his eyes. "I don't believe Bolsvck was a pawn. He's too smart for that."

"And too selfish? You think he purposely stole the crown from you?" She smirked, and Marcus frowned. "It was your family who took the rule from his a generation ago. He is the rightful king. And yet, he still refuses to officially claim the crown. Don't you find that odd?"

Marcus's jaw seized, and lava surged up his esophagus. Clenching his hands into fists, he fought the urge to strike down right there in the car. And yet, he needed to hear and to know. "It doesn't stop him from leading them!"

She grinned and her dark eyes gleamed. "It's a popularity thing, my lord. The dragons refuse to listen to anyone else. Except for the fraction, of course." She licked her lips.

"The fraction?"

"The rebels." She tapped a finger on the window's edge. "Davies was the one. He led the rebellion against your father. It's because of him your parents are dead, and he played a huge role in sending you to

Purgatory." Leila shifted in her seat, moved her back against the far door. She blinked and flashed a bedroom-eyes gaze at him. "Would your men think less of you if they knew?"

"Knew what?" Marcus's fingers dug into the leather seat.

"How clueless you really are." The side of her cheek lifted in a deadly grin. "In all your years of planning to take back the throne, did you ever wonder why Bolsvck never claimed his birthright? And yet, all the clans follow him willingly. Or..." She paused, thoughtful. "Did you ever stop to wonder how Davies was disgraced enough to land him where he is now? No longer a dragon, but neither a man?"

Marcus's spine shot tent-pole straight. He stared at Leila with blood-boiling intensity.

"I see I've hit a sore subject." Her hands pressed against the door, pushing her up to appear taller. "Things are going to get interesting." Her face darkened, contorting into something else. Something monstrously magnificent.

The door behind her flew open, and Marcus lunged to stop her. He was too late. She was already vanishing from the car in a shadowy, black fog.

31

SUITORS

Kyra

"Why?" Kyra stared after Sebastian, her thoughts and emotions an obliterated devastation zone. The cracks and pops of the fireworks overhead were like bullet fire to her heart. "Why is he walking away, after all we've been through?" Her voice was weak, feeble, and she hated it.

Talia stared at the crowd, her face drained of color. "We should get going."

Kyra grabbed her by the arm. "What aren't you telling me?"

"Nothing," Talia said, her eyes growing wide.

"Don't lie to me. I can see it all over you." Kyra released her. "You're as pale and as stiff as a corpse. Something's going on."

"Kyra, everyone here is trying to help you—"

"Don't try to placate me. Spit it out, before I'm forced to torture it out of you." Kyra planted her feet, jammed her fists onto her hips, and seared Talia with her stare.

Talia opened her mouth and said...nothing. She glanced to the spot in the crowd where Sebastian had disappeared. She blinked and looked back at Kyra. Her indecision couldn't have been more evident.

"There you are!"

Kyra turned to see Drakhögg and Ryhuu striding toward her. Great. More dragon dung to deal with. This day couldn't possibly get any worse. "What are you doing here?" she asked them. "You were supposed to wait."

"We got tired of waiting for you to return and grace us with your beauty, so we decided to sniff you out," Ryhuu said, with what Kyra assumed was meant to be a charming smile. Really not.

She rolled her eyes. "Sniff? Seriously? Gross."

"Sniffing was necessary," Drakhögg said. "We were beginning to think this crazy carnival didn't want us to find you. It kept changing, setting us on a different course. Insane place, this Mystic's Carnival. But hey, we're finally here because of this." He pointed to his nose. "You used your sniffer all the time...when you were complete," he added with a hint of arrogance. "Do you remember now?"

"I remember why I don't like you, so you can stop trying." She threw her hip out to the side.

"I do love when you play hard to get," Drakhögg said, placing his arm around her waist.

She shoved him away. "Try impossible. It's never going to happen, Drakhögg, so give it up." She started walking away. Talia didn't follow. Kyra wanted to say something to her, but not here, not in front of these morons. With her memories back in place, her disgust for Drakhögg had soared out of sight. The scum-sucker would do anything to get into her father's good graces and a place of power—including her half sister, Keahi, the sneering redhead who'd walked into the carnival at Drakhögg's side earlier.

Ryhuu snagged her hand, stopping her attempt to escape. "You made the right choice. Your mother will be proud."

"Think again, Ryhuu," she said. "I haven't chosen you." She peeled his hand away. "I'm choosing *me*. You both lose." She pointed to both guys, then spun around and walked away.

For the way she felt, her heart had to be withered and dead, sucked of life by her exquisite Reaper. *He left me.* How could she go through life feeling this way? The answer was, she couldn't. She would never be happy with Drakhögg or Ryhuu. Never be happy making a choice between the Water Clan and the Fire Clan. The only right choice for her was Sebastian. She would find out what was going on between them. And if he wouldn't have her, then maybe remaining a Moorigad would destroy her and put an end to her misery.

She thought about what Drakhögg had said about the carnival morphing and sending them on different paths when they were trying to find her. Maybe Mystic's agreed with her. Maybe the carnival didn't think she belonged with either dragon clan. Her walk turned into a march, a purpose and destination finally pulling at her.

"Where are you going?" Ryhuu called from behind.

"To set the record straight."

She heard the shuffle of feet and knew the morons had fallen in behind her. That was fine. They needed to hear what she had to say, too. All the dragons did, so they would leave her the damn dragolion alone.

"The people seem to truly enjoy the fireworks show," Drakhögg said. Kyra tossed him a sideways shut-up glance. "How do you think they would react if a bunch of dragons took to the sky, adding their fire and ice?"

Ryhuu made an odd sound, making it clear he did not approve of the idea.

Kyra's stride faltered; her jaw clenched, and her fingers twitched. She turned on Drakhögg, feeling a sense of rage and fury burning around her like Hell's fire. "Are you a complete moron?" His brows raised, and he glowered at her. Kyra marched up to him and swung her arm in an arc, pointing to all the people in the crowd, and spoke softly. "Most of these people believe dragons are a myth. You've done such a fine job at keeping to your own and staying out of sight that people have forgotten history and rewritten it as folklore. Would you mess that up now over something so foolhardy?"

Drakhögg stood tall and shook his head. "Of course not."

"You sure?" She prodded him in the chest. "Because your very presence here threatens the lie you've all created."

He twisted his lips tightly together and said nothing.

Her heart warmed at seeing him put in his place. Now that her memories had returned she couldn't help but see Drakhögg as a young Marcus in the making. It took considerable willpower not to go all dragon-attack on him. "Now shut it. I prefer to walk in silence." She eyed Ryhuu to make sure he understood that also meant him. Satisfied and with a triumphant smile firmly in place, she began her advance on the enemy—her parents.

A five-minute walk along the midway meant five minutes to think about the many things Marcus had done to her. Five minutes to count the number of pieces she would tear from his body for each and every wrong. At the end of those five minutes Kyra stood before her parents, Ryhuu and Drakhögg flanking her sides. Mystic's had provided her with a clear path to her desired destination. No side ventures or detours this time. She must be doing the right thing. The celebration had ended in a big bang, a cannonball to the heart, leaving the sounds of celebration to be swallowed by the murmurs of dragons.

Each of her parents had managed to amass a miniature army in her absence, their numbers having grown from four or five each to something around forty or fifty total. Kyra couldn't be sure, but there were enough dragons to further chill her body temperature. Rubbing her arms, she wished for a coat made of hot coals.

Hot coals. Right.

Her extremely human body probably couldn't handle such abuse.

Mystic's Magical Market, usually rife with laughter and whimsical fun, was now oppressed with clan tensions. Sebastian's concerns flew to the front of her mind. He'd been right; this was no place for dragons. Not with Mystic's Jubilee in full swing and the strain of Kyra and her Moorigad status pulling and pushing the two sides. She had to make them leave.

Kyra stared at her mother, a silent game of superiority playing between them. Bolsvck pushed through the crowd, making his way to the front, to his daughter. At a quick glance, Kyra guessed his clan had grown to include far more than just Fire Dragons. She saw representatives of all types gathered around him. Much must have happened since she'd left her father's clan. Last she knew, only the Bronze and the Black consorted with the Fire. *Curious.*

Bolsvck broke through the mass of supporters around him, his face beaming. He clasped his hands together. "You have your confidence back. Magnificent. You remember, then?"

Kyra's stare shifted from Queen Shui to her father. "I do. And you can all go now. I know why I left and why I'm here. I haven't changed my mind."

"You can't dismiss us that easily, dear," Queen Shui said.

"Quite right," Bolsvck said. "You've risked yourself for far too long, little dragon."

"There is nothing little about me!" Kyra leaned in, raising her voice.

"The point is," Queen Shui continued for Bolsvck, "you are in danger of losing yourself to the Moorigad curse."

"Moorigad curse," Kyra mumbled and rolled her eyes. "When's the last time you heard of a dragon falling to the curse?"

"None are so careless as to let it happen," her mother said. "They choose. They protect themselves."

"You must let us help you, Kyra." Bolsvck stepped forward with his hand outstretched.

Kyra shook her head. "The idea of a dragon going mad, dying because of an internal battle of traits is ridiculous. I don't believe it. Anguis the Angry was probably an isolated incident, not a curse. You've just never given any other dragons a chance to prove otherwise. And if the curse is true," she shrugged, "it doesn't matter. I've made my decision." Kyra turned and shoved Ryhuu and Drakhögg away. "Take these ridiculous suitors out of my sight, and all of you, leave the carnival before someone gets hurt."

"Kyra! You come back here right this instant!" her mother called.

"Kalrapura."

Kyra paused at the sound of her dragon's name called out by her father. She turned and focused on him. "What about her?"

"You are incomplete." Bolsvck pierced her with his cold, hard stare.

"You are missing your dragon soul."

Kyra's heart started uncontrollably flipping and flopping. "She's fine. I have her."

"Don't lie to me, child." Bolsvck advanced another step.

Beads of sweat trickled along Kyra's hairline. She had the sudden urge to wipe her palms on her thighs. But she didn't. She didn't want to give away the lie she was hiding. As if not wiping her palms would keep her father from knowing the truth. He'd probably smelled the truth the moment he'd said Kalrapura's name.

"We're not leaving until you are fully restored." Bolsvck's face softened. "At least give us that."

"You don't need to do that. Sebastian has her safe, and we'll get it all fixed soon enough. You don't need to worry." Kyra's heart was racing and her head spinning, searching for a good excuse to make them leave.

"Do you have a place you stay? Someplace we can rest?" Queen Shui asked.

Kyra's eyes widened, and her chin dropped. "For all of you? No. There are way too many. You need to leave." Kyra started to pace, agitation getting the better of her. "Besides, my trailer burned down."

"Trailer?" her mother repeated. "You were living in a trailer?"

"Now where are you staying?" Bolsvck asked.

Kyra stopped moving, turned introspective. She'd thought she would be staying with Sebastian, but now...now, she had no idea. Her trailer, her perfectly comfortable trailer was burnt and broken, and her best friend...She looked to the Ferris wheel spinning high above the carnival's horizon, remembered the many times she and Sebastian hung out beneath its platform.

Beneath the Ferris wheel, they'd sit with his tarot cards and her bottle of whiskey, make up stories of the people in the swinging passenger cars passing above their heads. On the rare occasion, they'd bear witness to a carnie marriage, fellow carnies riding once around the wheel together. Once, she even allowed herself to imagine she and Sebastian tied that knot.

How she wished for those days again. Life had been good, before she'd let Marcus in. One dumb, simple act brought her life tumbling down like a juggler's dropped balls.

Itty-bitty flashes of light burst here, there, everywhere. The air smelled metallic.

Queen Shui swatted at the light. "What is that?"

"The carnival is about to move people and things around. Maybe she'll boot your dragon tails out the door," Kyra said, then mentally added, *One can only hope.*

New to the carnival, some of the dragons had yet to experience a shift. This move by Mystic's was accompanied by many a dragon moan or cry or roar. Kyra could hear their sounds through the shifting swirl, but only momentarily. They were all swooped to new, different locations. Ones that were not hers.

A sigh of relief escaped her lungs when the carnival world came to a stop, and Kyra found herself standing in front of her restored trailer home. "Thank you, Mystic's," she whispered. Replacing her destroyed den was the second best welcome home gift Kyra could imagine. The magic of the carnival never ceased to amaze her. She wanted to hug the dingy little trailer. Kiss the cold, hard metal siding.

"This is where you live?"

Kyra jumped, turned around to see her parents. Her heart dropped into her gut, and her pilot light blew out. Cold, so excruciatingly cold.

"Our presence disappoints. So sorry, little dragon." Bolsvck stepped onto her front patio, if you could call it a patio. It was an imaginary line in the grass where she had set up two chairs and a rusty table. Sometimes she and Sebastian would hang out there to watch the midnight fireworks show.

"It's just..." Kyra hugged herself. "I can't..." Rubbed her arms, up and down and up again. "Can't do this..." The grass came up to meet her far too fast. It too was cold and damp. Her parents rushed to her, had their hands all over her, their voices flickering in and out.

Queen Shui placed her hand on Kyra's forehead. "She's so cold."

"She's a Fire Dragon without her fire." Bolsvck turned Kyra to face him. "She's slowly freezing to death."

Kyra eyes drifted close, and she whispered his name. "Sebastian."

32
ECLIPSE

Sebastian

Sebastian had let Kyra's fingers slip from his grasp and had seen his world eclipse into darkness. Arctic waters crashed over him, collapsing him into an unfathomably raw end. Frozen, he stepped into a sea of bodies, not seeing a single one of them.

The fire within him had turned to ice even as Kyra's voice rang behind him of love, his only possible salvation. Eyes glossy and with a chest pummeled with stone, he pushed forward. He didn't look back. He couldn't look back.

How could Zeke or Talia not warn him? Up until the carousel ride, he'd believed he'd find a work around. That his Reaper side would somehow allow him a win, or at least a cheat. But the carousel had shown him the truth. It showed him what needed to be done and how it should be done. He couldn't drag Kyra through more misery. To save her, he'd have to make her hate him. It was the only way.

All around him, the world danced and sang with celebration. He couldn't feel their joy, not even one ounce. The winter-wind fire had consumed his heart and left a void. One step at a time, his legs dragged him toward the lake, toward the bench where he knew he'd find the old man waiting.

Embers flickered across his chest and neckline. A rippling sensation rolled up his back. Reflexively, his hands stretched, opening wide and then closing into a fist. He repeated the motion over and over and paused at the sight of claws protruding where his nails should be. Did no one in the celebratory crowd around him see what was happening? Like an army of dragons swooping in on the attack, he was swarmed with thoughts and emotions of Kyra. Kyra and him. Him without Kyra. Could he still attempt a cheat? Keep the dragon and keep Kyra? His shoulders dropped. No. Kyra was dying without her dragon, and she couldn't be less aware.

He dropped to his knees, screamed to the heavens. It was not the scream of a man, but the sound of internal torment, morphing and changing from the pitch of a human into the roar of a dragon. Overhead, the fireworks exploded in a grand finale. Cinder sparked the sky like falling stars dragging down a blanket of black and following the big show, everything above melted into midnight.

The sound of the crowd was nothing but a hushed drum now. His weight collapsed in on itself, leaving Sebastian sitting on the ground, head down. All there was now was a shell of the misfit Reaper. He still harbored the lost dragon, and return her to Kyra, he would. But his longing for them, for a relationship, had turned to dust, like a vampire caught in the sun.

"For Kyra," he whispered and stared at his clenched fists in his lap. His breaths were deep, measured, but he'd never been hollower. *If only it didn't hurt so much. If only I could feel numb.*

For Kyra, he could do this. For Kyra, he would be strong. For Kyra... he would let her go.

Concentration spread from his soul like the endless strings of lights threading their web across the carnival. The process was not for the impatient by nature. He had to relax and let it happen as it must, like a ride on the Ferris wheel. The Ferris wheel would never challenge nor try to become the roller coaster. So would the process of putting the dragon back in the box never be as easy as slamming the lid shut.

Hands now flared out on his thighs, Sebastian sighed and let his body go limp. His fight gone. And with his fight gone, so did the claws slowly creep back to the sleeping dragon, receding into nothing. If things weren't so bleak, he might have smiled at the small victory.

He glanced up and grimaced. *When did I sprout wings?* Large, orange dragon wings wrapped around him like a protective cocoon. He may have managed to put away the claws, but the dragon back in the box, not quite yet.

Sebastian stood. The wings swung around and folded against his back. He took a step and froze.

"That's a new look for you," Mortifier said.

"What are you doing here?" Sebastian shoved past his father. "Shouldn't you be out reaping or something?"

"Is that any way to speak to your father?" Mortifier fell in step beside Sebastian, straightened his lapels.

Sebastian rolled his shoulders, wiggled his upper body, and managed to collapse the wings into nothingness. He was once again just himself—sorta. "It is, when the father is you."

The crowd was thick, people swinging party favors of every possible design, cheering with delight, and throwing confetti into the sky. A few people pointed and gawked at him, but the majority moved about their business as if Sebastian's transformation was an everyday occurrence at the carnival. Maybe it was. Maybe he didn't look like a real dragon, not in his current state anyway. Or maybe, like so many things at the carnival, he was accepted as another act, another form of entertaining magic. A stray firework exploded overhead, pulling any remaining attention away from Sebastian. The fireworks were over, but the party was still going strong. Sebastian pushed through the fray, hopeful his father would get lost and be unable to follow.

"Will you stop for a minute and talk to me?" Mortifier grabbed his arm. Sebastian paused, glanced down at his father's hold, took in a deep breath, and let it out slowly. "Thought I taught you to dress better." Mortifier lifted his finger, indicating Sebastian's thrashed shirt.

"I have somewhere to be. It's really not a good time, *Dad*." Sebastian stressed the word, making clear how little the man meant in his life. They were not friends. They weren't even happy co-workers. There was almost zero respect between them, and in Sebastian's book, that was grounds for zero relationship.

Although already standing straight and tall, Mortifier stood taller after his son's comment. As if his entire body stretched toward the moon, so that he could peer down on his son even further. "Very well, I shall walk with you," he said with a tip of his head. "And you can tell me what has happened here. What is going on with you?" He fanned his hand in a flamboyant gesture toward Sebastian.

Sebastian yanked his arm free. He was getting tired of people jerking and tugging him around. "It's nothing you need to worry about." He brushed at his arm where his father had held him. "Could you just go away please?" Sebastian said, throwing his hand up in a stop-don't-follow-me signal, and started walking again.

Mortifier stayed in step. "I told you to stay away from the dragon girl. Why," Mortifier's hand clenched into a fist, and he shook it at his temple, "do you refuse to listen? Look at you. You have her dragon curled up inside you, squeezed in around your heart." He talked with sharp, decisive moves, slicing and beating the air with his hand.

Sebastian closed his eyes and took a deep breath, searching for the calm Kyra had helped him find when the dragon first emerged from inside him. "Haven't you ever felt for anyone besides yourself?" he asked. "Felt so strongly for someone that they became entrenched in your core being? In your soul? Became a part of who and what you are? Or have you always been this soulless creature?" With all the theatrics of a carnie, Sebastian gestured to his father.

The elegant and superior Grim Reaper stood in silence for a breath, his dark eyes revealing nothing, but Sebastian thought he detected something in the movement of a brow, the bat of a lash. "You may love her, I'll give you that, but such love will be the end of you." Mortifier moved ahead of Sebastian, forcing him to a stop, and seized both of his shoulders firmly in his grasp. "You must snuff that dragon out before it destroys you, burning you from the inside out."

"I'm not going to do that." Sebastian locked stares with his father.

"If that's the only reason you're here, you may go now. Your message has been delivered and rejected."

Mortifier released Sebastian, let his arms drop at his side, and began to laugh. "You are a stubborn one. I have to admit, I'm rather proud." The laughing stopped, and his face fell deadly serious. "But the dragon does have to go."

"I said *no*!" Sebastian's response ran long like the tail of a circus tent flag, his gaze locked on someone else in the crowd. "What is he doing here?" Sebastian asked, pointing at Mr. Johnson.

"That's a pretty interesting story, actually." Mortifier placed a hand in his pants pocket and cocked his head to the side.

Sebastian stared at the Reaper with the ridiculous Mr. Johnson name tag. He imagined walking up to the man and punching him in the face. He had left Sebastian in that alley to be beaten by behemoths, and nothing good had come from that situation. Everything that followed ran through his mind in fast forward. Alice's death, Alice being the sister of Sophie, the girl he'd reaped only days earlier. Both girls being daughters of some big military leader named Davies who didn't like him much. Sebastian's hand slipped into his pocket and found Alice's pendant still there. What did that mean? Why was he holding on to the jewelry?

The exuberant mass around them began to somber. Sebastian glanced between his father and Mr. Johnson, wondering if what he was seeing was a physiological reaction to multiple Reapers being in one place. He never noticed it around himself, but now there were three—no, wait. His gaze was pulled a few feet to the left and right of Mr. Johnson. Five Reapers.

A glance wasn't enough, Sebastian was suddenly turning in a circle to check the entire scene. To the left of Mr. Johnson stood Mr. Brown, then Mr. Elder, and Mr. Cane. On the right, Mr. Lee and Mr. Vargas. That made eight Reapers, if he counted himself, and he had to count himself. He was a Reaper by nature. He had no idea if he was putting out vibes the Mystic's party was picking up subconsciously.

Sebastian's insides churned, acid and dragon tail. His fingers dug into the back of his neck and pulled at his hair. "Why so many Reapers,

Mortifier? What's going on?" His eyes widened, and he pinned his father with his stare.

"Told you it was an interesting story," Mortifier said, a lazy and untrustworthy smile widening across his chieftain face. The six Reapers standing in a circle around them took a step forward.

Flashes reminiscent of mini firecrackers burst to life, the air within the circle and beyond crackling and sizzling with dots of fire. The waft of metallic air weighed heavily upon Sebastian, as did something else... the carnival herself, pressing into him? It was as if he were being pushed to the ground and spun around, the desire to hurl overwhelming.

Then all was still.

The carnival had moved them, and fast. To where, yet unclear. In a dizzy haze, Sebastian toppled onto his side and knocked into something ungiving, painful, and cold.

Next to him sat the red, weather-worn, wooden bench by the lake. The one in which Zeke could usually be found. The soft lapping of the water eased Sebastian's quickened heart, and the smell of Zeke's cherry tobacco gave him a sense of hope. He hoped Zeke would have a better answer than what the carousel had presented.

With a sigh, Sebastian rolled off his side and checked the perimeter. No Reapers nearby. *Thank you, Mystic's.* His muscles relaxed, but his heart still ached a thousand dragon jabs to its core.

"You gonna come up here and talk to me, or sit on the grass all day?" Zeke said, nudging Sebastian with the end of his cane.

After Sebastian's run-in with his father, Zeke was a welcome relief. Sebastian let out a soft laugh, a touch of madness evident in the refrain, and stood. "I'm getting there, old man. Don't have a blowdown." Acting confident and assured on the surface, Sebastian took a seat beside Zeke, but inside, it was as if Sebastian's tents had been blown down, and he had no clue how to repair the damage, or if it was even repairable.

A snort. A cough. Zeke elbowed Sebastian. "You don't need to pretend with me. I know your heart, and it doesn't match the show you're puttin' on."

Crossing his arms across his chest, Sebastian pressed into his chest with the heel of his palm. Pressed hard where his heart should be, only it had been clawed out by Kalrapura, or possibly gnawed up and devoured.

Not to be deterred by the silence, Zeke dropped his hand upon Sebastian's leg and delivered a firm pat. "You're hurting, son. Shall we talk about why?" He tilted his ear to better hear Sebastian's answer.

Sebastian presumed that was why the carnival had brought him here, to talk to Zeke. He was searching for a magical resolution, and he prayed Zeke would be the key. The one to deliver a miracle. But now that he was here, with the ravaged mess laid out before him, he had no words. His throat squeezed tight. Sebastian shook his head and scratched his neck. "I don't even know where to start."

With a nod and a comforting grin, Zeke sat back and placed both hands on the handle of his cane. "When one is overwhelmed or confused, sometimes starting at the beginning is the best."

Sebastian peered down and nodded, and then began, spilling forth every detail of his adventure since Zeke had charged him with the deed of finding Bolsvck and the dagger. Plus a few earlier events he'd neglected to mention before, but now thought may be of significance.

He told Zeke about the deal he'd made with the Gatekeeper and the horrid things Marcus had done. He talked about Davies's company of soldiers and the death of the man's daughters. He even mentioned the visit he'd had from the Mara. He talked until his throat was dry and body, numb. So much information poured forth, he could have talked for days, but in actuality it was probably more in the minutes range.

Sebastian sighed and leaned over his knees. "And now I have Kyra's dragon inside of me, and I need to figure out how to get her back to Kyra." He stared at his clasped hands, played a thumb war.

"But you already know the how, don't you?" Zeke said and stared with his blind eyes out at the carnival entrance.

Sebastian cradled his face in his hands. If he could have sunk any lower, he just might have. "If I am to believe what the carousel showed me, yes," he said, his tone morose and full of bitterness.

"No reason exists for the carousel to show you lies. You should believe," Zeke said.

Fury and frustration coursed through Sebastian, straightening his spine. "I don't understand. The ride, the magical..." He waved his hand in the air before him, searching for the right word. "...process was about getting her memories back. It shouldn't have had anything to do with me."

Zeke patted Sebastian's leg once more. "That's where you are wrong, my dear boy. The whole ordeal was about who Kyra is today, yesterday, and tomorrow, and a hundred or more tomorrows beyond that. That's where you come in." Zeke pointed his finger at Sebastian, a mild tremor in the motion. "You hold the key to her future. It is for that reason the carousel showed you what it did."

All of Sebastian's hope and energy deflated. "There's no other way?"

"None known," Zeke said solemnly.

"So...in order to return Kalrapura to Kyra, I have to die? Literally shish kabob myself with that strange looking dagger-thing?"

"I'm sorry, son." Zeke wrapped his arm around Sebastian and hugged him to his side. "I only have this to give you." With his free hand, Zeke placed a folded piece of paper in Sebastian's palm and closed his hand around it. "In your darkest moment, find the answer to the question you did not know you were asking."

A frown formed in the space between Sebastian's eyes. A riddle was not what he needed nor wanted right now. He unfolded the paper and stared at the ink scribbled upon it. Zeke wanted him to find the tent of Magical Bibelots. One item in particular. Thankfully he had Zeke's expert scribble drawing to help him find it. The tent was tucked away deep within the carnival, never easy to find. Mystic's liked to play hide-n-seek with that particular destination. But he could find the place; it was the item he questioned. With all its spikes and claws, it didn't appear extremely friendly.

It was astonishing how cold he could feel with a Fire Dragon renting space in his soul. His chill plummeted past Death's touch. He hadn't thought he could feel any worse about the situation. He'd been wrong. Remove all hope, and he could feel far worse.

And Kalrapura...she twisted and spiraled inside his core, roaring for all the kingdoms and realms to hear. Or maybe it was just for his benefit, Sebastian wasn't sure. But in that instant, he knew. Knew what the dragon was saying.

He stood with the abruptness of a killer's surprise attack. He turned, barely, to face Zeke. Every muscle, tendon, and neuron snapped with needed excitement. "Kyra's in trouble."

33
CHILLED

Kyra

"So cold." Kyra's words escaped through chattering teeth. She imagined ice on her lashes and her breath morphing into puffs of smoke. As cold as she was, she wouldn't have been surprised if she mirrored a frost giant, minus the size. A flurry of activity kept her from slipping into a place of peace.

"Look at me, girl," her father demanded. A soft moan was her response. "Don't sleep." His strong hands pressed against her skin, grabbed her arms, rattled her whole body with vigorous shakes.

"Stop it," she said, letting her head loll from side to side. She couldn't remember where she was, or how long she'd been there. Someone, not her father, tried to wrap a blanket around her. Her eyes fluttered open. Queen Shui kneeled close, pressing the cover to Kyra's skin, rubbing. The blanket was her own, taken from her bed. Behind her mother, stretched out like a theater backdrop, was her trailer. She was home. "Did you go into my trailer?" her voice hitched, if only slightly.

"Sweet child," her mother began.

Kyra's hand flailed weakly at her mother. "Don't, Mom." She tried to push away from her father, but he kept a strong hold on her. "It may not be much—" Her voice cracked. "But what's here is mine." Her hand grasped at her mom. "Understand? Mine."

"We're not trying to take anything from you, child," Bolsvck said. He cupped her hand in his and blew fire-rich warmth upon her. Kyra closed her eyes. "Shui, start a fire to raise her temperature."

Her mother's footsteps moved away, and her father lifted her in his arms, began carrying her. Shivers and shudders rocked through her body, and she curled into his chest. It was like snuggling against a furnace.

Incomprehensible voices reverberated through her head. She pressed into her skull, wishing the pain to stop. "Get him out of here," Bolsvck boomed, his chest undulating the tones to sharp stabs in her brain.

Kyra sank deeper into Bolsvck's chest, yet turned to see what the fuss was about. She couldn't imagine her father being upset by Drakhögg's presence. Ryhuu, maybe, but not the man her father so heavy-handedly pushed her to marry. Neither stood before them, and she was thankful not to have to face them.

Instead, it was Sebastian. He and Queen Shui stood several yards away, heads together and arguing.

He came back. Her heart leaped, and she clutched her father's arm, her eyes silently pleading with him to let her stand on her own two feet. He ignored her plea and held her tight.

"Bolsvck," Queen Shui said, turning from her heated discussion with Sebastian.

Bolsvck didn't respond. His silence rumbled through his chest like a fury barely contained. With a pinched brow, he listened.

"As much as I hate to admit it," she said, "this boy does make some sense."

A disgruntled roar rolled deep within Bolsvck's body. With it, more heat seeped from his skin, enveloping Kyra. "I don't think—"

"Don't think. For once, just do as I suggest." Queen Shui straightened her spine.

Sebastian's gaze met Kyra's, and as thrilled and happy as she was to see him, he appeared quite the opposite. The cold intensified, turning her insides to ice. If it were possible for her to drop to a deeper low, she didn't see how. In that moment, she was every bit a dragonling clinging to her father for protection. Protection against heartache. With each advancing step Sebastian made, her heart clenched tighter.

Bolsvck took a step back, away from Sebastian.

"Bolsvck, please. For our daughter," Queen Shui said.

"What does he want?" Kyra whispered to her father. Sebastian stood before her now, so close she could almost reach out and touch him. Part of her wanted to do exactly that. At the same time, fear held her back. Irritating fear. She didn't remember ever being intimidated when it came to relationships. She was strong. She was dragon.

With outstretched arms, Sebastian motioned Bolsvck to transfer Kyra to his hold. "Please, sir." Sebastian spared Kyra a glance. "I can feel Kalrapura inside me, and she wants to be with Kyra, to help warm her." He slapped his arm. "See this? This is what she needs."

Kyra stared at the marking he pointed to. She didn't recall ever seeing it before. Like a tattoo, but etched in white rather than black, and it resembled a watch or compass. "What is that?" Bolsvck said, speaking Kyra's thought.

"It's a bit of magic I recently received. It guides me to things I desperately seek." He glanced at his hand. "In this case, it's what Kyra needs right now. As you can see, the arrow is pointing back at me." He twisted his arm, and the little hand swung and spun until settling back in place, pointing directly at Sebastian. He grimaced at Bolsvck. "The compass isn't pointing at me. It's pointing at Kalrapura." Sebastian's arms jolted. "Honestly."

Bolsvck grumbled and released Kyra to Sebastian, a deathly serious warning in his eyes. "This is my daughter, and you are not one of us. You watch yourself, boy."

"Of course, sir." Sebastian bundled Kyra in his arms and held her tight. She'd considered her father a comfortable warm fire when she'd nestled into him. Sebastian put out far more heat, and she couldn't get close enough or warm enough. She wanted more, so much more. She buried her face in his chest. “It will be okay, Kyra. I’ve got you now. I’m going to fix you,” he whispered at her ear.

She didn’t like to think of herself as broken, but if anyone were to tend to her less-than-perfect nature, she wanted it to be Sebastian. Besides, if she were honest with herself, she *was* broken and in desperate need of fixing. She was one of two pieces torn apart, and in order for the world to be right again, those pieces needed to be glued back together. “All right,” she said into his chest.

Sebastian’s grip tightened, and he pulled her closer. “I need to employ a little help from our resident witch. Will you allow it?” he asked of her parents.

Queen Shui’s hand fluttered up. “I don’t care much for witches.”

“The fewer involved in the matter, the better,” Bolsvck said.

“Maybe so, but you have this particular witch to thank for Kyra’s returned memories. I believe she will be able to help with the return of Kalrapura, and in raising Kyra’s temperature until that happens.” Sebastian shifted to better view both parents, who stood at far ends of Kyra’s non-existent front patio.

“Is this witch a female?” Bolsvck narrowed his glare on Sebastian.

“She is. At present, we have no warlocks working at Mystic’s.”

“I will allow it,” Queen Shui interjected.

“Shui.” Bolsvck’s voice boomed, and his eyes sparked when he turned his glare upon her.

“Shut it, Bolsvck. This is for Kyra. Curb your overprotective nature for now.” Queen Shui jammed her finger at him in an accusatory manner. Peace ceased to exist after that. The quarrelsome pair attacked each other with every hurtful word they could dig from their internal dictionaries.

Kyra and Sebastian appeared to be temporarily forgotten, and so Sebastian slinked away unnoticed, Kyra still in his arms. Kyra spied over Sebastian’s shoulder as they left the Backyard. Watched her parents fade into the scenery.

Sebastian moved quickly through the carnival, and Kyra watched familiar faces and places move by. From the Backyard, where she and so many other carnies lived, through the Fun Zone and gaming area, toward Mystic's Magical Market he pushed. Talia's trailer sat among the many mystics and readers setting up shop at the carnival.

"Do you really think she can help me?" Kyra studied his face. He appeared tired, stressed, and bothered. And he didn't look at her but kept his attention on their path.

"I hope so."

Kyra bit her lip and stared out at the glare and sparkle created by the lights from all the rides. In the distance, a small peek at the carousel. The very place the two of them had shared a magical moment she'd thought was the beginning of something precious. Perfect and predestined. Until he'd shattered the magic, and their everything.

Beyond, ribbons of lights changing color in a mesmerizing manner, the overseeing Ferris wheel spun. Silly as it was, the magical, mechanical beast bloomed hope in her heart. If only they could ride it together to the top, maybe he'd drop the stubborn act and they could get back to what they used to be, get beyond whatever was influencing Sebastian. There was nothing like the magic of a good old-fashioned carnie marriage, or so she'd been told.

But the Ferris wheel was receding, becoming a mere bleep in the distance, and Sebastian was rushing down Mystic's Magical Market lane. Fortunetellers of every type lined the sides. She knew the place well, having come here many times to visit Sebastian at his little trailer of tarot cards.

"Talia," Sebastian called out when he was nearing the witch's den of crystal ball gazing. "Are you there, Talia? We need your help." He shifted Kyra in his arms.

"I can walk," she said in a small voice.

"Maybe so, but you don't have to." Sebastian glanced at her and smiled. The smile didn't reach his eyes, nor light up his face, as she knew his heartfelt smiles could. A dark fog misted through her chest, and her chilled bones iced. She tightened her clasp around his neck to fight the dread overtaking her soul.

Garnished with countless strings of colorful buttons, charms, and trinkets, the entrance to Talia's tent was both eccentric and mysterious. The design encouraged further exploration. When they were only steps away, the drapery pulled back, exposing a portal into a delightfully unexpected space. Not that it was truly a portal, as in a magical door, but what lay beyond the entrance was enchantingly otherworldly. Talia, the young witch, stood at the edge of the entrance, holding the fabric out of the way. Sebastian slipped into the tent and turned around.

Kyra had passed by Talia's tent on several occasions, but had never bothered to go inside. A miraculous and surreal world of magic lived inside the tent walls. Once they walked through the door, the ceiling seemed to evaporate, leaving only the night sky, complete with twinkling stars, above their heads.

The sidewalls were no different, appearing as a forest one could wander into and get lost. At the far corner of the tent, rocketing fireworks lit up the sky. They were subdued, yet completely perfect in the meager, wonderlit arena. Kyra assumed the celebration display was designed to coordinate with the Mystic's Jubilee, but she couldn't be certain. Maybe it was always like this.

In the center of the space, which resembled a small grass clearing in the middle of the whimsical tent forest, sat a small collection of wooden chairs gathered unevenly around a purple velvet-covered table with a large crystal ball in the middle. Kyra knew everything around her, aside from the table and chairs, was an illusion. Logic reminded her they weren't in the middle of any forest but were actually standing somewhere in the middle of Mystic's Carnival. For such a small and young witch, the magic was supreme.

"What's going on?" Talia asked, letting the colorful bangles at the door drop back into place.

"Kyra is freezing. We need to reunite her with her dragon as soon as possible." Sebastian paused and glanced to the chairs by the table. Using his foot, he scooted one away from the table.

"Not there," Talia interrupted and pointed toward the back of the tent. "Through there."

Sebastian walked into the tree line, and for the briefest of moments, they were standing in the forest, mammoth redwoods stretching as far as the eye could see—and then they weren't. They had entered a backroom. A room hidden from Talia's clientele.

Against one striped tent wall was an unremarkable bed and a rack filled with clothing and costumes. On the other side of the room, behind a shimmering, sheer curtain, were bottles and boxes of various colors and sizes. Some were stacked on a table or stool, others hung from the ceiling in a cluster of designs: spirals, pyramids, and extended drops of baskets.

"Over there." Talia pointed to the bed. Sebastian promptly set Kyra on the mattress, pulling the blanket up around her. It resembled a story blanket, likely Talia's story. Square after square of stitched pictures depicting things Kyra only half recognized.

"Thank you," Kyra said, hugging the blanket snuggly around her body. Sebastian sat on the bed beside her and attempted to rub warmth back into her.

In quick movements, Talia threw back the shimmery curtain and began grabbing at bottles. "You want me to mix something up that will help keep her warm, right?"

"If you can, yes." Sebastian stood and took a step in Talia's direction.

"It's okay. Stay with her," Talia said, and Sebastian returned to the bed. "I think I can whip something up for you." Between pouring ingredients in a beaker and snagging boxes and bottles from her assortment, Talia glanced back at them. "Do you know how you're going to return her dragon?"

Sebastian gazed off to the side. "I think so. Zeke helped me in that area."

Talia nodded and turned back to her work. A whirlwind of thoughts and emotions buried Kyra. Her insides burned from the cold, and her heart dropped into her gut. Was it her imagination or were both Sebastian and Talia avoiding eye contact with her?

She clutched at Sebastian's arm. "How will it be done?"

He leaned in close and spoke softly. "Right now, you just focus on finding your heat and let the rest of us worry about dragon details."

Kyra's brow wrinkled. "Kalrapura is part of me. I need to be involved in those details." She chanced a glance at Talia, saw her quickly look away.

Sebastian frowned and regarded Kyra. "If you don't take care of you first, there might not be anything for Kalrapura to return to."

Kyra wrinkled her nose and sneezed. Across the room, pops and fizzes hissed at Talia's fingertips, her work moving swiftly and reminding Kyra of a mad scientist. From what Kyra could tell, Sebastian was avoiding her, and in so doing, directing all his attention on the magic being created on the other side of the room. "How long will this take?" he asked Talia.

"Not long." She turned to face them, beaker held firmly in her hands. "To create heat, I'll need to include an element of fire. I'm stepping out back for a few minutes to properly encompass the needed flame."

"Should we come with?" Sebastian shifted, as if preparing to get up and go.

She waved him to wait. "You two stay here. I won't be long." Her gaze shifted to Sebastian. "Keep her warm by any means necessary." She glanced back at Kyra. "She's starting to turn a little blue." With that, Talia left, disappearing out the back door.

In an instant, Sebastian was off the bed and kneeling in front of Kyra. He held her shoulders and studied her. She tried her damnedest not to appear or act as if she were freezing, but her teeth chattered rebelliously. "How bad is it?" he asked.

"Na-na-not ba-ba-bad." Kyra clutched the blanket around her with a white-knuckled grip.

Deep shadows filled Sebastian's eyes. An intense worry line creased his forehead. "You really are one of the worst liars I've ever come across."

Every time he'd called her a horrible liar, the delivery was accompanied with a snarky smile. Not this time. This time, he appeared particularly dismal. Kyra bit her lip to hide the chatter, biting too hard into the skin with the shaking. The bitter taste of copper filled her mouth.

"Kyra," he whispered, wiping the blood from her lower lip with a gentle brush of his thumb. He didn't take his gaze off her but continued to stare profoundly into her eyes. She saw war and conflict, sorrow and regret, and she would bet her life she also saw love. She wanted to kiss him. Her teeth chattered.

His dark pits of conflict and contemplation seemed to turn into resolve, and Sebastian pulled off his shirt and slipped under the blanket with Kyra, pressing his warm body to her skin. Together, they lay against the mattress, Kyra nestling against him, her back to his chest, her body perfectly complementing his curve.

His fire melted her ice, the thawing sending her heart to accelerate, blood to race, and a kindling to take hold within her core. She couldn't recall anything ever feeling so right. So meant-to-be. She flipped around to face him, her hands held to her chest as a barrier, and caught him off guard. For a nanosecond, his gaze had been dreamy, wistful. Now there was surprise clouding out everything else.

"You saved me, once again," Kyra said.

A humored smile almost lit up his face. "Not me. Kalrapura. Her fire is incinerating my organs."

Kyra laughed in spite of the implication. Something whispered in her ear that Sebastian could handle the heat. His office was in Hell, after all. "Regardless, she couldn't have done it without you." A silence fell between them, and it wasn't the comfortable silence they'd so often had in the past. This time was different. It was awkward and strange. Kyra wanted to burn it away, but she couldn't. She would need Sebastian's help to make that happen. "I can't imagine my life without you, Sebastian. I need you by my side." Her hands slid up and caressed the side of his face.

"I. Kyra..."

"Shhh." She softly placed her finger over his lips. "I love you. Understand?"

Almost absentmindedly, she traced his lips with her finger and felt his body respond. Her thoughts toiled between the bravery of pushing Sebastian into seeing what they could be together and fear of pushing him deeper into whatever hole he was digging to escape her. The most consuming thought—simply him. Wanting and needing and touching

Sebastian. His strong body against hers, his breath on her face. Clarity of thought was impossible.

"Tell me you don't want me, and I'll stop." Her mouth found the small space below his ear, his cheek, his jawline. His skin tasted salty-sweet, grit and greed, everything she desired. His eyes closed, and he made a sound she'd not heard before. A shiver ran through her, like a diving dragon, down below her belly. Her lips craved the taste of him, her body, the touch of him.

"I think this should do the job," Talia said, coming in through the back door.

Sebastian was up and out of the bed, slipping on his tattered shirt, before Kyra could blink. She turned around and pulled the blanket tight around her again. It was a shoddy substitute for Sebastian. She stared at him, and her teeth began to chatter. In those moments since Talia had stepped out back to create magic, Kyra had believed she was making a little magic of her own. And it might have succeeded, with a little more time. It seemed like he'd been responding. Now he was putting distance and barriers between them like a damn impossible carnival game.

"Did I interrupt something?" Talia asked, glancing between Sebastian and Kyra.

"No," Sebastian said at the same time Kyra said yes.

Talia's eyes widened before fixing her gaze on Sebastian. Kyra bit her lip and sighed, sinking deeper into the blanket and bed. Talia had definitely interrupted, but Kyra wasn't going to be the one to say so.

"No," Sebastian reaffirmed.

"Alrighty then," Talia said, obvious disbelief on her face. She walked over and handed Kyra a small vial. "Drink this and give it a couple minutes. You should feel your body temperature even out."

Kyra took the tiny bottle of glass and studied the liquid sloshing around inside. Orange with a swirl of red and murky clouds of blue—it didn't sing *drink me*, more like *toss me out*. Nor did it appear particularly significant. Burning one last gaze at Sebastian, Kyra downed the liquid and gagged. It tasted like excrement. "Gross."

"Sorry." Talia took the vial from Kyra's hand. "Not a lot I can do about the taste."

"Next time try adding vanilla," Kyra said, her lips curled into a snarl.

Sebastian plunged his hands into his pockets, his posture reeking of discomfort and need. Awkwardly, he leaned toward Talia. "Got anything for me?"

"As in what, exactly?" She regarded him with a shift in her eye that could only be disapproval.

"You know, the stuff that helps with the..." He pointed to his head.

Talia's chest rose and fell. "I think it's time you learned to deal with your talents, rather than stifle them. Don't you agree?"

His face hardened like that of an overworked and underpaid ride operator, yet he didn't argue. He merely looked away.

"Can you give us a few minutes?" Sebastian's tone was grimly grave. Kyra's heart, which had been hanging on to tether lines, plummeted to the safety netting in her gut.

"Sure," Talia said, with a hunch of her shoulders. Kyra couldn't blame her for how fast she disappeared. No one likes to witness uncomfortable situations, and Kyra sensed a big one coming on now.

"Before you say something you'll regret later—" Kyra started and was interrupted.

"Is it working?" Sebastian gazed over her from head to toe. Kyra stared back at him with a blank expression. "The potion, is it working?"

She jerked. "Oh. Not yet."

Silent fell over the room, Kyra's lecturing roll having lost its steam. There was nothing she wanted to ogle more than Sebastian, yet right now, she couldn't bring herself to, so fearful of what she'd see in his eyes. Instead, she stared at his feet, memorizing the scuff across his left boot and the wear on the side buckles.

It began with a tiny pinprick of a spark in her chest. The smallest of heat sources. The sensation quickly spread along her veins to her entire system, like a blossoming flower. Kyra wasn't on fire, but she wasn't cold anymore. She was simply comfortable.

"Listen." Sebastian began to pace the room.

Okay, maybe she was cold, after all. Kyra hugged herself and pulled her knees into her chest.

"I will admit, you are a beautiful distraction, and we did well at the friend thing."

Friend thing? Kyra shifted on the bed and narrowed her gaze.

He scratched the back of his neck. "I'm becoming a full Grim now. I'll be busy, too busy, really. And I don't have time for any of this." He waved his hand around to imply, not just Kyra, but the entire carnival. "We'll just hold each other back. And you don't want that, do you?" He stopped pacing and locked stares with her. "You don't want to hold me back, do you?"

"We wouldn't be holding each other back if we're in love." Kyra dropped the blanket and stood up.

His lip pulled into a straight line. "I don't love you." He turned and disappeared the way they had entered. He'd turned so fast, as if he were running away, and she'd almost missed it, but it had been there, an impossibly small sign of hope. And cling to that tiny hope, she would. His eye had twitched, and he had bolted before she could call his bluff.

She wanted to scream after him. Yell that she didn't believe him. But she was too stunned to squeak out a single sound. She simply stood there and watched him walk away.

34
DISTRACTION

Marcus

Weaving through traffic on highways and streets had taken longer than Marcus had hoped. It had been over an hour since they'd encountered those men on the road, since Marcus had destroyed them. And it had been over an hour since he'd talked to Rick. Not a single update had been received since. All he could do now was hope Rick had followed orders without a hitch and all the men would be waiting for him by the Market Street Bridge, because somewhere near that bridge was exactly what he needed right now.

Thankfully, the sedan was now close to the portal under the bridge, the portal that would take him to Mystic's Carnival and Bolsvck. The sedan glided down Market Street, cutting off before the bridge and dropping down to a smaller trail below. With a quick left turn, they were passing beneath the bridge and headed for the small parking lot ahead. This was where he remembered emerging from the carnival portal with Kyra. It had been a while since that day, but he was confident he could find the spot. The doorway that would return him was down here somewhere.

Hopefully, his men had ditched the attack at the Den and were already here, awaiting his arrival. Marcus glanced over Darren's shoulder out the front window. He could see the chaos and destruction that welcomed them. He exhaled a heavy breath. Somehow Davies's little band of crusaders had managed to follow them here. A battle was consuming everything. The parking lot, the park, even the little road his sedan now traveled.

"Stop here," he said to Darren. The car came to an abrupt stop.

Darren didn't need to ask why, nor would he. Marcus's men never questioned his commands. To do so would be considered subversive. Ahead, the parking lot was filled to capacity and beyond. Vehicles of all manners spilled over the paved space into the surrounding dead grass and dirt. And among the grass and metal, men warred. Beside cars, on top of cars, even using cars as weapons. And it was a damn bloody mess of a war, too.

Marcus took a deep breath and clenched his jaw. Stepping from the car, he glanced at the traffic on the bridge, then back to the pandemonium. Inside, his gut boiled with acid. His hands curled into white-knuckled fists. *Not the time or the place*, he thought. He wanted to shift, destroy all of Davies's men, but no one needed the human news reports full of dragon sightings in Nesbitt Park.

His searching stare probed the mob of men, seeking his target, the man in charge of the attack. What Davies had done, teaching his screwball collection of humans and lower-caste shifters effective ways to kill or maim dragons, was reprehensible. Comparable to telling a known serial killer where he could find your family members. Marcus ground his teeth and hissed.

With the measured composure of a man preparing for a notable meeting, he methodically removed his jacket, folded it, and set it on the seat of the car. After closing the door, he knocked on the front window using the side of his fist. The window rolled down.

"Park it here and stay in the car," he said to Darren. "I don't want anything getting on my jacket."

"Understood, sir."

Using the tip of his finger, Marcus brushed his hair into place and walked into the battle. Invisibility could have been added to his recently obtained abilities, since so many ignored him when he walked by. And even though he strode with his chest held high, there was no burden there. It bothered him not, walking within inches of men trying to kill each other, by hand or other means.

"Finally," he said between gritted teeth and grabbed the man rushing at him by the throat. The cool brush of steel slid across Marcus's side. Ice and blood and bite to the skin. Marcus grunted, squeezed, crushed the man's larynx, and tossed him aside. The blade fell to the ground.

He glanced down at his torn dress shirt. *Damn. I wanted to be more presentable when I see Kyra, but this will have to do.* Flashes of colors and clouds of dust moved all around him, a new aggressor on the attack. In a breath, Marcus threw up his arm, splintering the skin and raising thick, dark dragon scales to cover. The clash was firm, hard, and set the man's Scottish dirk to vibrate. Astonishment registered on the handler's face, and he had little time to react. Marcus's other hand was already slicing through the man's flesh with razor-sharp claws. He fell away.

"Where is Davies?" Marcus yelled and pushed on through the throng. To his right, fighting a behemoth, of all things, was Chet. Irritating behemoths, they should know where their loyalties lay, and that should not be with Davies. Marcus roared and reached for two men fighting on either side of him. Hands firmly over their heads, he dragged them across the space, smashing their skulls together. It didn't make him feel any better. Irritation ratcheted up his spine like out-of-sync scales attempting to slip into place.

Covering the distance between in no time worthy of noting, Marcus seized the behemoth wrestling Chet and tossed him across the parking lot. Chet wheezed, wiped the sweat from his brow, and pushed himself to a stand. "Thanks, boss."

"Yeah," Marcus said and tried to straighten his destroyed sleeve. "Did Davies's men follow you here?" The light of confusion and uncertainty flickered in Chet's eyes. "How did they know to find you here?"

Chet shook his head and gazed out at all the fighting. "I don't know, boss. Alls I can figure is they have a spy in our camp."

Marcus's soul felt dark, and his body burned with the angry need to crush any traitor. He buried a growl deep within his throat and shifted his gaze to the space beneath the bridge and remembered. "Have you seen Davies in this mess?'

"He was here when it all began. He killed a few of our guys and left orders with his men before disappearing under the bridge," Chet said.

Davies hadn't stayed to fight with his men. Now *that*, Marcus found more than just a little interesting. His eye twitched, brow arched, and he studied the space in which Davies was reported to have disappeared. Not the bridge, really. That wasn't what drew his gaze. It was the space beneath the bridge that interested him. The place where he would find the hidden doorway to Mystic's Carnival. And the same space, he was betting his dragon fire, that Davies had disappeared into.

From his pocket, Marcus produced a handkerchief and erased from his hands any signs of destruction. "I'm going to the door."

"Sir?" Chet tilted his head.

"Gather Rick and the men, grab my jacket from the car, and follow me through the door beneath the bridge." He neatly folded the handkerchief and slid it back into his pocket.

Chet jerked back, ever so slightly. "But the fighting, sir. How are we to—"

"This has gone on long enough. This," Marcus waved his hand, emphasizing the fighting going on around them, "is nothing more than a distraction. Either push back these morons, or destroy them by all means other than complete transformation. Understand?"

"Yes, boss." Chet started to bow and then stopped himself, as if he'd thought better of the action.

Marcus turned and walked in the direction of the invisible door. "And Chet," he called over his shoulder. Chet promptly acknowledged him. "Make it quick, will you?"

"Consider it done, sir. On it, boss."

Marcus detected a mild hint of nerves, fear, anger, and resentment rolling off the man. It was a delicious combination. One he hoped Chet would keep in check. Along his stride across the open park land, Marcus counted the dead. Not all the dead. He could care less about Davies's men. The humans and traitor shifters should have known they were signing up for their own deaths when they agreed to follow that man.

But his men, that was a different story. He counted them, quick and precise. His men had fallen, were still falling, and yet he needed them. His army to destroy Bolsvck was shrinking, and he had Davies to blame.

No matter. He didn't need an army to deal with Bolsvck. He was strong enough on his own.

Beneath the bridge, he stared at the empty spaces, searched for a hint of a door. It wasn't a door that presented itself readily. There were endless tracks in the muffled dirt from many who had tried before him. Except, he knew it was there somewhere. Kyra had taken him through it not once, but twice.

He wasn't sure what it was that finally drew his attention upward. A passing car on the bridge, maybe, that was the most likely answer. But when he looked up, from the right angle he caught a glimmer of webbing running between the massive pillars. The spider track was high above his head, yet appeared to make a nicely angled window. There was an old crate sitting alongside the column. Maybe it was there for a reason. Making sure he had firm footing and that his dress shoes wouldn't slip off the wood, Marcus stepped up on the crate and reached between the lines of the web.

Nothing.

"Dammit."

The crate cracked, and his leg plummeted through the broken wood.

"Dammit all to dragon-fire Hell." He kicked his leg clear, sending the wood crashing across to the other column. That's when he noticed it. Could be nothing, but in his experience, nothing was rarely truly nothing. And the odds of this something being the thing he sought were increasing by the nanosecond.

On the column a few feet away from him was a black line. A simple black line to the average passerby, yet when he stepped to his left the line grew wider, and with a couple steps to his right, it grew taller and faded. The line didn't fade away, only faded from black to something with depth, various degrees of grey. When he stepped within foot, he could have sworn he smelled funnel cake and midway sawdust. He stepped closer yet. Fun Zone sounds on low volume.

He glanced back and made a mental check of where his men were. Rick and a few others were putting a heated end to the battle. Men ran from the fight or died in fiery dragon breath. Chet was grabbing Marcus's jacket from the car, and Toby was only a stride or two behind him. Marcus waved, watched Chet nod and walk toward him. Chet should see what he was about to do. He should be able to copy and follow. Make sure the rest of the guys did the same.

Slowly, like the way he enjoyed exploring and savoring Kyra's lips, he pushed his hand through the darkened line upon the pillar. His hand, and then his arm, all the way up to the elbow, disappeared. The swirling pull of the portal tugged at him. Marcus scanned the men coming his way, winked at Chet, and slipped into the black.

The doorway pushed and pulled at him, twisting and twining around his body like a prehistoric snake. Everything sucked him in and abruptly spat him out.

Right at the entrance to Mystic's Carnival. His men filed through at his back, and he could feel Davies's men not that far behind in pursuit.

"You aren't supposed to be here."

An inferno of rage and lust for revenge, Marcus turned and glared at a man with glazed over white eyes. Crazy old blind codger was pointing his cane at Marcus, as if he used a sixth sense to know his surroundings. "And where is it I am supposed to be, old man?" Marcus asked. He retrieved his jacket from Chet, slipped it on, and brushed the sleeves straight.

"Not here, that's for sure." Zeke lowered his cane, placed his weight on the hilt, and stood, began wobbling forward.

This struck Marcus as funny, the idea that a broken, old man thought he could tell him what to do. A laugh bubbled up Marcus's windpipe.

“What should we do, boss?” Chet asked.

“Find both Bolsvck and Davies. They’re here somewhere. If anyone gets in your way, strike them down.” Marcus said the last part in a matter-of-fact way. As if the task were as simple as slicing bread. The roar and clatter of fighting rose behind him, the signal Davies’s men had not only reached the gate but had managed to break through to the carnival.

Marcus started toward Zeke. “It doesn’t matter what you think, old man. We’re already here. And we’re not leaving until we get what we came for.”

Something close to rage pressed into Zeke’s brows, molded to the lines of his face, but if Marcus had to describe the expression, he’d have called it parental and protective, which scratched at Marcus’s curiosity. *What is the old man protecting? The damn carnival?*

Zeke’s cane shot into the air and shook vigorously in the old man’s hand. Zeke charged. Any speck of curiosity Marcus harbored fled.

Marcus stood his ground, waiting for the rush the minor altercation would bring. Zeke swung the cane, brought it down in a cross swing.

Marcus raised his hand and stopped it dead.

Yanked it free from Zeke’s grasp.

35
FAVORS

Kyra

The bed frame squawked when Kyra sat back down. Her fingers dug and clawed at the mattress stitching, and she stared at the many boxes and bottles across the room without seeing a one. A black hole had swallowed her up for the second time today, and she searched for an inkling of fight within her, but she was coming up empty. How could she come up empty? She knew she was strong. Had always been strong. Had her strength walked out the door with Sebastian?

The tent was quiet. Talia said not a word, and Kyra suspected the embarrassingly painful situation held her tongue. Only the muffled sounds of the crowd beyond the canvas wall kept Kyra's miserable thoughts company.

"How do you feel?" Talia finally asked.

Kyra startled, stared up at her. What a stupid question. How did she feel? She felt like a rollercoaster had run loop-de-loops through her insides, torn them apart and dragged them away. She felt like she'd spun off the swirling swings and left her heart and soul behind, like she'd fallen face down in the midway sawdust and been trampled by the elephants. Her fire had blown out, and her carcass was nothing but ashes. "I'm dragon-damn*tastic*," she said.

"Sure, you are," Talia said. "I meant, are you still cold?"

It was a pretty safe bet to say she wasn't. Kyra had abandoned the blanket a while ago, and she no longer rubbed or hugged herself. Or maybe she was too stunned dumb to notice the temperature of her body. Either way, it didn't matter to her.

The countless strings of colorful buttons, charms, and trinkets marking the entrance to Talia's den of crystal ball reading clattered. "She's somewhere in here." Queen Shui's voice came from the next room. "I can smell her."

Quick as the ring in the ring toss bounces off the bottle's rim, Kyra sprang off the bed.

"We're close. We'll find her," Bolsvck said. The sounds of them shuffling through the magical room on the other side of the tent wall drew closer.

Kyra turned and grabbed Talia by the arms, panic embracing her like a long-lost friend. "You must help me. I don't want them to find me," she whispered.

Talia grimaced. "Why don't you want to see your parents?"

"I don't want to deal with them right now. Not with their pushy match-making, nor their hounding for me to forsake my Moorigad status. Besides, I want to figure out what's going on with Sebastian, and they'd rather kill him than help me."

Taking one quick glance over Kyra's shoulder, Talia motioned Kyra to follow her, and they swiftly disappeared out the back exit.

Kyra tugged at her arm once again. "You don't understand. Not only can they recognize me and have a small army to search me out, but they can track my scent."

"Don't worry," Talia said with a pat to Kyra's hand. "I got you covered. Just follow me."

And Kyra did follow Talia, right out of Mystic's Magical Market and into the Fun Zone. Like an overexcited child, Talia made their course winding, zigged and zagged in and round rides and games, sometimes backtracking. Talia told Kyra this would confuse the dragon clan members, and Kyra agreed it was a rather brilliant idea. It wouldn't stop them from finding her, but it should at least slow their progress. After circling the carousel and weaving through the crowd at the Zipper, they moved out of the Fun Zone and into the populated tents of Extraordinary Shows Defying Reality.

Here, their movements were no different. They circled or ran through tents, crossed back and forth between various passageways. When they finally came to a stop, it took Kyra a moment to determine where they were. They hadn't bothered with the stage area or seats, but had run in a silly pattern among the outer entertainment area to end up behind the stage, where the space was tightly crammed with wardrobe boxes and smaller boxes, props, hats, capes...

Kyra's body went rigid with understanding. She was standing in the domain of the creepy Magician. The same Magician rumored to keep a girl so tightly under his wing that she had no freedom. He may be magically talented, but that didn't excuse such suffocating treatment of anyone. Not ever.

"Why are we here?" Kyra asked Talia, her voice barely above a whisper. "I thought you'd be able to conjure up something to help me, like you did with the other issue."

Talia glanced around and shrugged. "I could if you wanted to wait and take the chance of being found. But why take the chance, when the answer is right here?" She gestured to the rack of clothing.

Kyra frowned. "I don't understand. How would clothing..."

The curtain pulled back with a dramatic flair, and Mr. Creepy Magician himself stepped into the back room. "To what do I owe this honor?" He tilted his head slightly. Kyra was sure the gesture was meant to show gentlemanly manners, but all she could see was sleazebag and slimeball. She recoiled a step.

Talia held her arm in a lover's link, as if she thought Kyra might try to get away. "We're in need of your assistance, if you wouldn't mind. Kyra here," Talia glanced at Kyra, "is in need of disappearing for a while, without actually going anywhere, if you get my meaning."

"I most certainly do." He strode forward, one eyebrow arched so high Kyra thought it might snap. He appraised her with the skilled eye of a sex offender; it made her skin crawl. He was old enough to be her father, possibly older. She wanted to gag. "I suppose it's the gown you seek?"

"If we could borrow it for a spell—" Talia began.

"A dress?" Kyra interjected. "How is a dress supposed to help me?"

The Magician peered down at her, slowly walked around her, moving Talia to the side in the process. "My dear, you know so little. I gather you are the reason for the change here at the carnival. The shift in balance. Mind explaining?"

Kyra balked. "The carnival is always shifting. I haven't caused any changes."

The Magician stared at her, his eyes eternally intense. "Silly girl. Not the moving and relocating." He stepped impossibly close, never breaking his glare. "The shift in power. This is the shift to which I refer. A number of powerful beings have recently entered our happy little home, and I have a feeling that isn't necessarily a good thing. Does any of this ring any bells of recognition?" Kyra bit her lip, blinked, and stared forward, avoiding further eye contact. "I didn't think so." He moved to the clothing rack and pulled a dress free from the many colorful pieces. The one he chose wasn't as wild as some of the others. It was dark forest green, which suited Kyra just fine, but it was still a dress, and she wasn't too keen on that idea. If she needed to fight Marcus, how was she supposed to manage with that big skirt strapped around her? "You want to hide in every possible way?"

Kyra hesitated, hating the idea of being indentured to this man in any way. Problem was, time was running out, and she did want to hide. She was tired and brokenhearted, and now was not a good time to deal with her family and all the dung they heaped upon her. Reluctantly, she nodded. "I want to hide. I don't want to be recognized by appearance, smell, or anything else someone could use to find me."

Creepy Magician appeared even more disturbing with a smile spreading across his cheeks. Watching him made Kyra feel downright green, just like the dress. Holding the hanger in one hand, the Magician flared the dress out in front of him. "Then this, my dear, is your answer.

Once you are wearing this, no one will recognize you. It is the perfect camouflage." His eyes twinkled. Something about them reminded her of the devil on the tarot card Sebastian had dealt her not too long ago. She shivered.

"How does that work, exactly?" She wanted to reach out and touch the fabric, see if it felt different than the average dress, but there was no way she was getting any closer to that man. Not unless her life depended upon it, and as far as she could tell, things weren't *that* desperate. Not yet.

He handed the dress to Talia and meandered to the back of his working space. Finally, after fidgeting with a few of his books and taking a sip of a drink on his desk, he took a seat and rested his gaze on Kyra again. "It's fairly simple, actually. Not to say the magic is simple, only the desired effect. What you perceive versus what others perceive. I must say, sometimes I'm rather brilliant. I astound even myself." Kyra frowned and inwardly rolled her eyes. "The dress is enchanted, you see. It took some time to get the spell just right, but now that I have it perfected..." He kissed the air with his fingers. "When you wear this dress, and only this dress, I might add, everyone you meet will perceive you in every possible way as the young lady for whom it was originally designed. So, as you can see, you will be quite safe. No one will recognize you."

Kyra crossed her arms. "So you say. Who was the girl?" He arched his brows. "The one the dress was designed for?"

The Magician leaned back in his chair. "No one with whom you should concern yourself. She has never worked here at the carnival, which makes this situation perfect for you. She was beautiful, though, with long, streaming hair of gold, and pink, pouty lips." He appeared lost in his memories, memories of a girl Kyra would bet was too young for him.

"And green eyes?" His gaze jerked toward her. Kyra motioned to the dress. "She had green eyes, right? Hence the green dress." He smiled.

The last thing, the absolute last thing, Kyra wanted in all the worlds was to look like some girl this creeper lusted after. Her lips twisted in disgust, and she took a step back toward the exit.

Dress wrapped firmly over her arm, Talia linked Kyra with her other arm and tugged her away from the exit toward an ornate changing screen. "Would you excuse us?" Talia said pointedly to the Magician.

With a smug smile, he rose and sauntered out of the room.

Talia shoved the dress at Kyra. "I know he's a bit off, but you won't have to be around him. Just put the dress on, and we'll get out of here."

Kyra sulked silently, but only a little. She snatched the dress from Talia's hold and held it up. "It's too small. It will never fit me."

"Magic, remember?" Talia gave her a gentle nudge, and Kyra moved behind the changing screen with the dress in her hands. Mounds of satin ruffled around the skirt in fold after perfect fold. A princess waistline brought a soft V-shape to the front, and the bodice was fitted and delicately detailed with colored floral embroidery. The gown buttoned up the back which meant Kyra would need help getting in and out of the garment. But at least the sleeves were short. They had a bit of a flare but would still allow her arms full mobility. The dress was so pretty, so ladylike. So not her.

Voices carried to her from the stage area. The Magician and—Kyra sucked in a deep breath—Drakhögg. She began to change her clothing at bone-shattering speed, a speed she couldn't recall ever attempting in her life. Off flew her top and pants, and into the gown she slipped. A hundred tiny buttons ran up the backside of her new outfit, and this brought her to a stop. How did anyone ever dress themselves in such attire? "Talia, help," she whispered.

Talia was quickly at her back, pushing each button into place. "If I didn't know it was you, I wouldn't know it was you," Talia said at Kyra's ear.

"It's actually working?" Kyra couldn't believe it was that simple—a change of clothes.

"Look for yourself." Talia's hand swung toward the mirror a few feet away.

Kyra moved cautiously to the mirror and beheld the beauty staring back at her. It wasn't Kyra. Not at all. A golden-haired, green-eyed girl with full pink lips nervously smiled. The dress accentuated her eyes and figure quite nicely. Her hands ran down the fabric, smoothing the lines. She was so feminine, so foreign.

"What did I tell you?" Talia stepped beside her and admired the view. Pretty amazing magic.

"I know she's back here. Stop getting in my way, old man."

At the sound of Drakhögg's irritation Kyra's stomach rolled. Talia moved toward the sound, but Kyra turned around in a quick search and spotted several small blades in a box pushed up against a pile of books and props. She grabbed one and recognized the blades as the type used in the knife throwing trick. If Drakhögg were to find her and she were to end out in the open, there was no way she was going unarmed, not with Marcus still out there somewhere. She shoved the blade in her boot, smoothed her skirt, and turned just in time.

Drakhögg barged through the curtain and stopped short at the sight of Talia and Kyra. "Sorry, ladies. I'm looking for someone. I didn't mean to bound in here all smoke and noise."

Talia giggled.

Kyra caught her breath and tried to act natural, possibly surprised at the intrusion, but her muscles were tight, and her eyes were wide. Yet, her fear was unrealized as it was quite clear Drakhögg didn't recognize her.

The lights flickered twice and went black. Even the carnival hum went silent.

Kyra gasped.

36
BIBELOT

Sebastian

If Sebastian moved at a pace matching his mood, he'd have sulked through the midway, scuffing dust beneath his feet. As things stood, he moved with a purpose, an all-out need to restore Kyra to her fully intended nature, restore her dragon Kalrapura.

The key, according to the ancient, wise Zeke, could be found in the tent of Magical Bibelots. The tricky part was finding that particular tent. It didn't always want to be found. Didn't matter, Sebastian was determined. Whether it wanted to be found today or not, that was where Sebastian headed. There was no time to waste.

After leaving Kyra with Talia, he'd taken a few minutes to stop by his own trailer and change out of his dragon-burned and battle-thrashed attire. He now darted through the carnival in his tailored tarot card reader costume. Cleaned up, he drew less attention, and he hoped, though it might be in vain, that the simple act of dressing for his business side would help him control any dragon outburst from within. Feeling excessively hot, he loosened his scarf, then shoved his hands in the pockets of his gentleman's jacket and rubbed his hands along his tarot deck. It was a simple act, but the cards often brought a sense of tranquility and purpose to his flustered being.

Sebastian's thoughts consumed him, leaving the surrounding carnival to blend into a blur at the back of his mind. All he could think about was Kyra. And occasionally, the item he would find at the end of his search. *Will it be difficult to use? Will it hurt?*

"Where are you going?"

Startled, Sebastian glanced to his side and discovered Chelsea had fallen into step beside him. It was with a heavy heart that his gaze traced the beast eating away at her body. His Reaper senses not only smelled the cancer ravaging her from within, but could locate it everywhere inside her tiny frame, or what was left of her once healthy figure. Her formerly bright eyes were now dull and carried dark baggage. Her cheeks were sunken, and her hair lay limp, having lost is usual bounce.

His footing faltered momentarily before resuming pace. He pointed to his nose. Averting her face, Chelsea slipped a hankie from the pocket of her robe and wiped. The white fabric came away red with blood. "It's nothing."

"Nothing. That's what you call your cancer?"

"I don't see any point on dwelling on sickness and letting it control me." Chelsea pulled at the front of her nightgown and robe, lifting them so that she could better keep pace with Sebastian. "Hey." She stopped abruptly.

He halted and studied her. "What is it?"

"I never told you I had cancer. Not since we met at the carnival." Thoughtfulness passed over her features. "It's because of what you are, isn't it?"

He jerked, recoiled slightly. "What do you mean?"

She lowered her head, tried to hide a meek smile, but it was no good, Sebastian saw. "I remember the night you came to me in the hospital." She peeked up, and her face was serious now. Sebastian's eyes widened. "When I was dying."

"No," he shook his finger, "if you were that sick, you were probably hallucinating."

"You came to take my soul, but you didn't."

"It wasn't me, Chelsea."

"You gave me more time." She clutched his hand in her own. Instinct told him to pull away, keep up the denial. Instead, he squeezed her hand. "Thank you," she said.

He heaved a heavy sigh. "I may not have done you a favor that night. You're not looking so great."

"I'm fine. You gave me time I wouldn't have had otherwise."

Sebastian said nothing. Instead, he studied her decaying appearance, took a deep breath, and squared his shoulders. "I'm sorry I couldn't give you more."

"It's fine. It's not like you're God with access to get-out-of-death-free cards."

Sebastian grimaced at the visual. "Listen Chelsea, I'm kinda busy right now, but you can walk with me if you want." He took up his stride again, in search of the tent of baubles and trinkets. "Was there something you needed?" He spared her a sideways glance.

Her shoulders slumped. "I'm worried about you. All this stuff going on with Kyra." She rubbed her neck, extending her head forward. "I think it's having a negative effect on you. Kyra has a negative effect on you."

"Negative effect?" He gave her a curt glance, pausing in his stride.

"I don't think she's healthy for you."

He kept his eyes on the path ahead, alert for any changes from the carnival, and this time, didn't allow his gaze to wander to Chelsea. Chelsea was a nice enough girl, but she had a bad habit of often showing up when Kyra wasn't around and trying to subtly win his affection. This straightforward attack on Kyra was a new low for her. "It's none of your business. You should be less concerned about me and worry more about your own health." He turned a sharp glare upon her face. She recoiled.

"There you are."

Sebastian rolled his eyes and paused in his step. Was he ever going to get where he needed to go? It was as if everyone was coming out of the tents to delay him. He turned an irritated gaze upon Mr. Johnson, his father's pain-in-the-Purgatory-ass minion. Chelsea shifted to the side and a foot behind Sebastian.

"We've been searching for you everywhere." Mr. Johnson stepped forward, his face tightening. A bubble of pleasure rose in Sebastian's chest, pleased that he'd irked this annoying excuse of a man, but Sebastian didn't have time to squabble with him right now. No time at all. Mr. Johnson's gaze moved momentarily between Chelsea and Sebastian before settling on the later.

"Sorry, Johnson, I've got no room for you today. Catch me on the reap later." He winked and shot between the game booths on his left. Before disappearing from view, Sebastian caught sight of another minion a few steps behind Johnson. It appeared to be Mr. Vargas. Why did his dad need so many Grims just to find him? Something nasty, ugly, and reaped with acid churned in his gut.

Never stopping to reflect, Sebastian moved through the many game booths and lit rides, heading for the area with the most tents, the Extraordinary Show tents. It was the most logical place for a bibelot tent to hide. And then a thought drifted to him out of the haze of happy screams and musical banter. He stopped and pulled back his sleeve, stared down at the marking on his arm. Talia had put the compass there to help him find the entrance to Mobürn, home of the Fire Dragons. The magical white compass on his skin had worked that day, and he wondered if it could help him find the tent of bibelots now.

Keeping a steady eye on the spinning hand within the compass, Sebastian whispered, "Take me to the tent I desire." The needle began to spin erratically. It spun and spun and spun and finally came to rest, leading the way. A victory smile inched across Sebastian's lips, but it was a dark victory. There was death in the victory, but that was a sacrifice he was willing to make.

Letting his arm lead the way, Sebastian began his trek once again.

"I thought I'd lost you." Chelsea appeared at his side, heaving.

Sebastian threw his head back. "I'd rather be alone right now, Chelsea." He spared her a glance. "Why are you following me?" He stared at his arm again and walked faster.

"I just..." Chelsea fell behind, her sick and feeble body unable to keep the pace. He knew he was being a bastard, it was only...

He groaned and slowed down. "Come on." He waved for her to follow.

He was a mess, he knew that, and he was taking it out on everyone around him. Except that wasn't the only thing at work here. There was something off about Chelsea, had been for a long time now. Her aura had changed, darkened, and her soul felt fractured. She was not the same girl he met a year ago, and he hadn't wanted to say anything. But now, his time was running out. *Should I push? Or let it go?*

They walked in silence for most of the way, Sebastian not wanting to strike up conversation, and Chelsea needing her breath to keep up with him.

It was Chelsea who finally broke the quiet. "What is that thing?" She pointed to the needle gyrating on his arm.

"It's a compass that's going to help get me where I need to be."

"And where's that?" Chelsea leaned against Sebastian, putting her weight on his arm. He could tell it was a need more than a desire. She was weak, so he helped her.

"If you insist on staying at my side, you are going to find out shortly." He could feel her smile radiate through her, a mild warmth tingling in her blood, and there was something else. Something he couldn't quite put his finger on.

The compass led them out of the exuberant Fun Zone and deep into the landscape of show tents. There were big tents and small tents, tents sized somewhere in between. Some reached forever high, while others were an average circus-tent height. Black and white and purple stripes surrounded them like prison cell bars. Red pennants flapped wildly attempting to escape. Acrobats housed a notable space on his left, tumblers and the Magician's moderate accommodations on the right.

The compass led them past these shows into an unassuming alleyway. It was desolate, untraveled. The only sound was the cheers heard from other tents. The white compass on Sebastian's arm pointed straight ahead, and then the needle vanished. "I think we're here," he said.

“I don’t see anything.” Chelsea held Sebastian’s arm tight and turned her head from side to side, her eyes wide.

“It’s here. It’s simply hiding.” Sebastian took two steps forward and stopped. He wasn’t exactly sure how the tent worked or what he should do, but figured he would follow his gut and see where that got him. Nothing ventured, nothing gained, or something like that. “Show yourself,” he demanded.

The passageway before them remained unchanged. It was disappointing, but not devastating. Sebastian remained unfurled. He squinted hard, studying the air for any signs of distortion or displacement. He detected none, and yet, the compass suggested he had reached his destination. If entrance were terribly difficult, he thought Zeke would have warned him. Having received no warning or guidance, he guessed it was a matter of knowing the right thing to say, or possibly do.

His lips twisted in deep speculation. The tent hid rare objects. Kept them safe from those wanting to use them inappropriately. He did not fall into that category. The tent was here to be enjoyed by those of pure heart and intention. Wasn’t that him? He considered his motives pure. His actions were, after all, to help Kyra, not better his own status. With a clear conscience, he tried again, this time with a slightly different approach. “Reveal.”

Above the tents before them, hovering in the sky like a cloud on a summer’s day, a shimmering tent appeared. Chelsea caught her breath. Sebastian held his. He wasn’t sure what he had expected, but this exceeded it by miles and decades. Swaying in the air as a boat would on the sea, the tent was unlike anything Sebastian had seen at the carnival before.

He wondered how secure he would feel inside something so untethered. *If* he could even get up there. He didn’t see a way up. Then, as if answering his thoughts, a set of long spiral steps descended. Not at the front of the tent, but in the center. They would be coming up from the bottom, in the middle of the bibelots collection.

“Ready?” Sebastian turned and inspected Chelsea’s physical condition, unsure if a mountain of steps was within her current ability.

"Whenever you are," she replied with a nervous smile.

"You don't have to go. You can wait here. I'll be back, you know. I really don't think that trek," he pointed to the long winding steps, "is good for you in your present state."

Her face hardened, and her lips drew taut. She studied the stairs, then glowered at Sebastian. "I want to go. You can't stop me."

"Have it your way." He wasn't in the mood to argue. He turned and headed for the steps, Chelsea shuffling behind. Ascending the steps was slow going, Sebastian waiting for Chelsea, making sure she didn't run out of breath or collapse. The steps sloshed beneath their shoes, the rail chilled under their touch. When they finally reached the top, a door in the base of the tent opened like a curtain on a Broadway show, only this one defied gravity.

Chelsea was five steps behind Sebastian. He hesitated, wanting to go inside the tent, while at the same time feeling his body flood with guilt at the idea of leaving her unattended. *What if she fell?* He'd already been foolish enough to allow her to drop so many lengths behind. He took a step back, meeting her midway, stretched out his arm, and gripped her hand in his own. Her hold was clammy and frail. Together, they took the last few steps with sure and steady footing, Chelsea's breath coming in a labored wheeze.

Sebastian hoped they would find a comfortable chair in which she could rest once they were inside. They did not. No plush, oversized chair awaited them. No seating of any kind stood in the large tent arena.

What did await them was a glistening floor in brilliant red, black, and white designs. Strings of lights streamed from the ceiling's center, cascading to the tent's outer rim, as if the lights were the canvas top, but of course, they weren't. Beyond the lighted display, the striped Big Top stretched high and wide, peaking and pointing to the sky above. In the center of the space hung a chandelier dripping in resplendent crystals of the utmost clarity, cutting the light into a dazzling display of sparkle. The walls, lush, glistening curtains in red. Everything about where they now stood was extraordinary, even in its lacking. No furniture and no curio collection. *Where are the displays housing the rare collectibles?*

Chelsea coughed, splattering blood down the front of her robe and gown. The Reaper side of Sebastian beckoned, and with his free hand, he absentmindedly fumbled with the deck of cards in his pocket. *No, not now.* He yanked his hand free. First, he would accomplish what he came here to do. When they made their way back down to the midway, *then* he would deal with Chelsea's condition.

"You should rest," he said without a glance in her direction. He tapped her hand, placed firmly on the bend of his arm. "Take a seat on the floor, if you must. Catch your breath."

"I'm fine," she said, wiping her hands on her robe. But a sudden storm of coughs snared her. She threw her hands up to cover and more splatters of blood spewed onto her palms. "Okay," she croaked. "Maybe for a bit." She lowered herself to the ground and leaned against a pole.

Sebastian studied her. She should be alright for now. He slipped away and walked toward the perimeter, confident there was more to the tent than it allowed them to see, confident he would discover its secrets. The siding resembled curtains more than the canvas of a tent, so that was where he would start. Wrapping the thick fabric in his fist, he pulled. The fabric didn't move, didn't budge, and it certainly didn't reveal any guarded secrets. And yet it was loose, wavy, clearly not the taut edge of the tent.

Left palm flat, he pressed against the curtain, pushing back an inch or two, and hit something hard and flat—he knocked on it with his right hand—and pretty big. He laid both palms against the fabric, feeling for any edges of what was hidden on the other side. An electric shock jerked his body, raised the hairs on the back of his neck, and made his knees weak. Reflexively, he stumbled back a step and started to hunch. The curtains in front of him drew back to reveal a coin-operated fortuneteller. Clicking to life, the mechanical head raised, his turban bobbing with the motion. A creepy smile appeared beneath a mustached lip, and the crystal ball between his hands swirled with turquoise smoke.

Crank, clang, clap, the mechanism rang, and a fortune spit from the big crimson box. The ribbon of paper snaked from the slot, far longer than any arcade fortune Sebastian had ever seen. He reached for the note, but paused, stared at his hand. Ghostly white skin stretched across his bones, now visible as lines of grey and oat. Since when had he become a walking corpse? Running circuits of indigo and garnet pulsed, however slight, beneath the dermis.

Did the electric shock from the box actually kill me? Sebastian shook his head. *That's ridiculous.* Whatever was happening to him, it had to do with this place, its protections. Sebastian flipped his hand front and back, wiggling his fingers. A bitter taste slithered down his throat and his stomach constricted, all while his chest fluttered with delight. Before he could change his mind, he snatched the fortune and read the message.

For all who enter the bibelot vault, pretense and disguise shall be vanquished, and truth shall be thy smock. Upon genuine-self thou will be judged, and upon genuine-self thy honor determined.

Sebastian's breath stuck, lodged in his chest, and he gawked at the paper, not sure what to make of the judgment decree. Although, it did explain his curious opaque skin. Stripped of his natural camouflage, he guessed this was what he looked like, what he *was*—a Reaper-Mara hybrid, thereby Death in the flesh.

Another note ejected from the fortuneteller with a burp. Sebastian wrinkled his nose and snapped it from where it clung, held it up to read. One silent laugh heaved through his chest. This note was considerably shorter. Six words scrolling across the thin page: *The Great Valko finds you worthy.* A quick glance at the nameplate in front of the automated carnie confirmed his identity as the one and only Great Valko.

"What now?" Sebastian asked the novelty. "Where are all the bibelots?" With a click and a clack, the box burped again, spitting out yet another note. He snatched it without a moment's hesitation and stared in disbelief.

The Great Valko finds the female unworthy.

Chelsea? The papers slipped from his fingers, fluttered to the floor, and he spun around to study the girl once more. He'd known something felt off about her. Clearly, it had been a mistake to ignore it, put it off to be dealt with later. He took a deep breath, and with it, a step toward her. Allowing her to accompany him here, to this place, exposed the truth of his suspicion.

Curled on the floor, wrapped tight in her fluffy white robe, was the dying human girl he knew as Chelsea. The same girl he'd given a reprieve from Death at her reaping several months back. Only, now... now, faintly visible was another soul hitching a ride, possibly even hijacking her body, thoughts, and actions.

Sebastian approached and kneeled before her, wiping her sweat-soaked hair from her face. "Who are you?"

Her eyes widened, and a startled expression flashed across her features. "What did that box do to you? You know who I am, Sebastian."

"I do, Chelsea." He took her hand in his, held it gently. "I'm talking to the other, squatting inside you where they don't belong." He studied her face, watched it change, and believed she had a vague awareness of what was happening. If not completely, at least on some level. "Have you experienced any loss of time?" he asked.

Chelsea glanced away and bit her lip in silence, before answering a few moments later. "Sometimes. But mostly, I listen to the voice inside my head and do as she says."

Nudging the crook of his finger beneath her chin, he turned her head to face him once again. "This voice, is it yours?"

"No." She shook with tears. "But I wanted to do everything she told me to do. All of it. It brought me closer to you, and there's no place I'd rather be." Chelsea took a deep breath.

He smiled gently. "How long has she been with you?"

"Since that first day I saw you." Chelsea sniffled. "Sometimes I'm aware when she's with me, other times, my mind is blank. When she leaves me alone, I haven't a clue how to find the carnival or you. I'm back home in a hospital bed."

Sebastian's brows pinched together. "And what kind of things has she told you to do?"

Chelsea cleared her throat. "Easy stuff, mostly. Get to know you. Get close to you. She said she needed my help to fix things, to fix her, and somehow, knowing you was going to make everything all better. But then her plan got so messy, and I didn't know what to do. Coming between you and Kyra proved to be an impossible task. At least, I thought so until I saw you today." She lowered her gaze to her lap, and tears streamed down her checks. "I messed up and I'm so weak. Too weak to make a difference."

He clutched both her hands and lowered his head to see her better. "She's hurting you, Chelsea, can't you see that? She sped up your cancer, killing you all the more quickly." He held her face in the palm of his hands and wished...oh, by all Hell's might, he wished his sincerity would be enough to cure her. "If she's broken, in need of fixing, she can never achieve any kind of mend by breaking another. Especially someone like yourself." Using his thumb, he wiped a dribble of blood from her nose.

Chelsea lowered her eyes. "You honor me, and I don't deserve it." She raised her hand and coughed, sprinkling blood into her palm. She stared, fixated on the splotches of red.

"She's murdering you, Chelsea."

"No." She met his gaze. "I did this. I am the creator of my own calamity."

The fortuneteller against the wall clinked and burped, spit out another card. Chelsea disappeared in a swirl of turquois smoke. In the last second before she was gone, after substance vanished from his hold but hints remained within the fog, he could have sworn it was the face of another he saw. A hungry, eager, and angry face, clawing to stay. Worse yet, he thought he recognized her. If only he could remember from where.

Sebastian was on his feet and spinning in a circle, searching the room, before the smoke dissipated. He was alone. His thoughts exploded like a coaster on the downhill fall, picking up speed by the second, tossing into a spin and sharp turn. Who was manipulating Chelsea? What was the big mess she'd referred to? Was the mess the reason his dad, Mr. Johnson, and all the other Grims were here?

So many Grims in the carnival. What did that mean for Mystic's? The cards could probably tell him. Like the carnival dog seeks his bone for comfort, Sebastian started thumbing through the tarot card deck in his pocket. He dealt a card—Death. His chest grew heavy. He dealt another, and Death again. The weight swelled throughout his body, the dormant dragon inside him coiled.

Another card dealt, another Death. An unfortunate Grim situation. Flipping the deck over, he found the entire deck was nothing but more of the same. With that many Death cards, it was unlikely the deck foretold his or Chelsea's fate. The fortune was for something weightier than one or two of Mystic's members. He had to get out of the bibelot tent, had to change the predictions. Sebastian didn't subscribe to the idea of a tarot future set in stone. The one the cards predicted, he was going to reap that one to Hell.

Clinkity-clankity-clunk. The patterns on the floor began to turn. Sebastian sidestepped away from the crimson circles, finding safety along the outer edge by the animated fortuneteller. The latest note lay on the floor, mocking him. He picked it up.

The Great Valko finds L. M. unworthy. Adieu.

It was a clue to Chelsea's hitchhiker. But who the Grim was L.M.?

The floor's intricate design twisted and turned like the inner workings of a clock, then, with a thundering *pop,* exploded into a tent filled with museum case after museum case brimming with rare and unique finds—the bibelots. Likewise, all around the walls, curtains pulled back to reveal displays. Everything had been here all along, only now they were finally showing themselves.

Sebastian's concerns temporarily forgotten, or at least put on hold, he jogged the perimeter of the tent in search of the necessary item. When it wasn't found framed in a curtained display, he took to a systematic search of the cases gridding the floor. His search ended at the fifth box of glass. Housed within was an ancient item of gold easily mistaken for a weapon. When studied closely, Sebastian could see it was a funnel, only built with a firm handle resembling that of a dagger.

He took a deep breath and considered its use. Dragons decorated the handle engravings and danced around the surface of the funnel. And it was a dragon this piece was going to help. The dragon soul-shifter would do what it was meant to do: shift a soul. In this case, it would return Kalrapura to her rightful owner.

"Okay, Great Valko. Help me out here." Sebastian circled the museum case, unsure how to extract what he needed.

The Great Valko chugged and burped, spit out another card, and the glass protecting the dragon soul-shifter evaporated. Sebastian felt instantly lighter, and without first checking the Great Valko's latest card, he grabbed the artifact, tucking it safely into his coat's inner pocket.

The tent shuddered, and the lights flickered. All the curtains around the perimeter dropped to a close. Museum cases slid back into the floor.

Everything went pitch-black.

All sound ceased.

The tent fell.

37
FINDINGS

Marcus

Marcus had whacked Zeke in the head with his own cane. The old man had then tottered backwards and collapsed on the ground. With an exhale, Zeke had closed his eyes and passed out. Or at least, so Marcus suspected. He was fairly certain the old geezer wasn't dead. Not that he carried.

"Damn foolish, old man." Marcus stared down at him.

The lights of the carnival flickered, went dark. The rides slowed to a stop, and the music dwindled to static, until it was nothing at all. The vibrant life Marcus had witnessed around him only a moment before was gone.

Music and laughter were replaced with grumbles and yells of concern. Even a few screams reached his ears from various ends of the park. He turned in a circle, regarding everything around him, before focusing back on the unconscious man at his feet. "Curious," he said and tossed the cane at Zeke's side.

"Boss! Boss!"

Marcus snapped around. "What is it?"

"The portal, it closed!" Darren yelled and ran toward him.

Marcus ran his fingers across his thumb. Everything got more curious by the minute.

"The portal closed with one of our guys still in it," Darren said, coming to halt, huffing and puffing.

Marcus's back straightened, and his head tilted in interest. "Which one?"

"Can't tell. When the portal closed, it sliced his arm clean off and that's all we got."

Marcus winced.

Why the heck? Zeke and the...

He spun around to the unconscious old man on the ground and kicked him in the ribs. "What's the deal, old-timer?"

"What shall we do, sir?" Darren asked Marcus.

Marcus studied the unconscious old man at his feet. "About?"

"About our men. About the closed portal," Darren responded.

"We make do." Marcus turned to face him and assess the situation. He guesstimated fifty or so of his men had made it through before the door closed, possibly ten or fifteen of Davies's men. Some fought, but most scrambled into the cover of the carnival. Likely in search of their vexatious leader. Marcus's steely eyes watched the scum disappear from view.

The carnival lacked the luster of lights, making it dark, but not unmanageable. The early hour allowed for plenty of light for him and his men. The moon was full and the stars bright. The fact that it was always night at the carnival lost some of its appeal without the illumination of a million or more lights, but where lesser beings were concerned, Marcus and his men would use the new turn of events to their advantage.

Over the discord, a scream surged. Carnival patrons stood where the portal had been minutes ago. A woman held her hands over her mouth and turned away from the severed arm on the ground, burying her face in the chest of her companion. Panic erupted in carnies and patrons alike, triggering hollering and pushing in the vicinity.

Marcus's jaw firmed. "Collateral damage is unavoidable." He

returned his attention to Darren. "We don't need to defeat everyone here today. Cut off the head, and the rest will fall in line. Eventually falling to my will or falling to dust. Find me Bolsvck and Davies."

"Consider it done." Darren ran off to relay the orders. After connecting with the men, Rick and Chet and Toby glanced in Marcus's direction with an affirming nod.

A howl cut through the night air, like dragon nails on steel. Sharp, startling, and stinging. "Damn supernatural freaks," Marcus mumbled and marched into the mayhem of the carnival crowd. He'd only been here the one time and hadn't gotten a proper look around, but figured if you'd seen one carnival, you'd seen them all.

How big could this place be?

He was the fish swimming upstream against the current. As he headed toward the attractions, everyone else moved toward the exit. After all, what fun is a carnival without any electricity to power the games and rides? Little did all these people know, there was no getting out. No portal. At least, not right now. Someone knocked into his shoulder. Marcus growled, heavy and loud. The crowd parted, offering him a large berth.

In the distance, he spied the Ferris wheel and remembered the first time he'd seen it. The day of the fire in the back lot by Kyra's trailer. His chest warmed with the memory. He hesitated in his quest. He thought he was following a logical path, one Davies would have taken, and he probably was. Except, when he peered to his right, he couldn't pass up the opportunity baiting him.

A few yards away, no longer lit yet still readable, was a sign promoting Mystic's Magical Market. He couldn't think of a better place to find that damn tarot-card-reading carnie boy. A second later, Marcus was marching down the lane between tents and trailers promising reading via palm, stone casting, crystal ball gazing, and other such nonsense.

There were fewer patrons here, probably filed out already. Marcus took a deep breath and smelled the midway sawdust, animal dung, cotton candy, funnel cakes, overcooked hot dogs turning cold, kernel corn, Polish sandwiches, candy apples, and on and on. It was a never-ending pit of flavors and scents. But of the carnie he sought, not a whiff.

A torrid of scampering footfalls raced up behind him. "I think I caught Kyra's scent back there," Chet said and dropped in beside Marcus.

"We'll get to her later." Marcus paused, noticing the sign ahead. Tarot Card Readings, it said in large, colorful letters. Cards slipped and flipped under the name. An assortment of beaded crystal drops and brass bells hung along the entrance. *Pansy*, Marcus thought and walked in with Chet at his back.

The room was dressed in dark colors with a forest of candles marking the walls, flickering haunting shadows all the way to the ceiling. A table sat center with chairs on either side, one large, worn, and overstuffed armchair on one side, and two smaller versions on the other side. The table was relatively clean of knickknacks. On the side of the table where Sebastian would sit, Marcus found a cubby hole attached to the underside. Within the hole, a deck of cards. Not knowing what possessed him to do so, Marcus pocketed the deck of cards.

"What are we doing here, boss?" Chet scanned the room with a curious ogle.

"Looking for that carnie kid; you know the one." Marcus swept across the back of the room. There were no other rooms, only an exit out the back.

"Right, that kid." Chet pushed out his chin, gangster style.

Returning a grin, Marcus slipped out the back. Behind the entertainment tent, placed somewhat out of sight, was a gypsy-like trailer. It was small and cramped, compared to the one he'd stayed in with Kyra. Guess the kid didn't need much space. He marched up the steps and threw open the door. Moonlight spilled through open windows on all sides, allowing a dim view of cramped quarters. There was a place to sit, place to sleep, even a place to store his belongings. Marcus moved into the tight aisle, though his hair brushed the ceiling.

"Find anything?" Chet clutched the door frame on both sides and leaned in.

Doesn't look like there's much to find. Marcus slowly scanned the area, then made a double-take. Beside the bed, almost hidden behind a small stack of books, was a picture of Kyra and Sebastian taken in the fun house. Heat exploded through Marcus's blood like lava from a volcano. "Nothing," he said and crushed the picture in the palm of his hand.

He was about to toss it and leave when something else drew his attention. Something shiny. And something someone had tried to hide, although not well. Not well at all. His hand slipped between two folded shirts on the shelf in front of him and wrapped around a hilt. What he pulled free was a dagger. Not just any dagger. It was the dagger the damn carnie had used against him in the Great Hall.

A deliciously wicked smile embraced his face and tingles of warmth washed over his body. "It's going to be a good day, Chet."

"Hey! What are you guys doing in Sebastian's private trailer?"

Marcus slid the dagger inside his jacket and turned to see the wild carnie girl he'd helped save the day of the fire standing behind Chet. He and Sebastian had worked tirelessly to get her free that day. Traumatized by the event, she kept causing issues with the extraction using her ability. *What was it Kyra called her? Ah, Vortex Girl, that's right.*

Chet spun around and smacked his arm down on her shoulder. "Listen, girly—"

"Careful, Chet," Marcus broke in. "That girl, she can—"

But it was already too late. Marcus's warning went unheard. Chet was swirling in a vortex into Rajũn knew where. Without fanfare or even a pop, he was gone.

"Oops," the girl said, not appearing the weeest bit sad, and took Chet's place in the doorway. "Hey, I know you."

Marcus narrowed his gaze and flashed his canines.

38
FAMILY

Kyra

"Does this happen often?" Drakhögg motioned to the lack of light while his gaze meandered up and down the ladies' curves.

"Are you for real?' Talia snapped. "The carnival never shuts down. Never sleeps."

Kyra rolled her eyes and looked away. Get away, was what she wanted to do. Standing in Drakhögg's company was one of her least favorite things. Her gaze wandered over the dark stacks of props, magic books, and costumes. Jumping near the front of her to-do list now was finding out what had happened to the carnival. She had no memory of darkness ever befalling the magical realm, not once since she'd come to live there.

Kyra rubbed her arms. She wasn't cold, per se, Talia's potion was still working, but the air had grown a tad bit nippy. Talia noticed, grabbed a wrap from the bureau, and dropped it around Kyra's shoulders. With a snap of her fingers, candles around the Magician's space sparked to life. "Magic. Don't leave home without it." She winked and delivered a hubristic smile.

"Thanks, Talia," Kyra said and contemplated what to do next.

"Don't worry, blondie," Drakhögg said, addressing Kyra. "You need not worry about a thing. I'm here, and I will protect you."

"I'm sure that won't be necessary." Kyra shot Talia a worried glance.

"Isn't there somewhere you need to be? Looking for someone, weren't you?" Talia asked with a snide smile.

"Yes." He scratched his head. "But her trail has grown oddly cold."

A massive crash resounded through the sea of tents beyond their canvas wall.

"What was that?" Kyra ran for the exit and popped into the midway, fumbling once on the skirt of her dress. Without the lights of the carnival, outside was dimmer than usual, but not disagreeable or difficult. The moon was bright and the sky, more an azure than an indigo. *Stars make the most romantic nightlights.* Kyra's heart plummeted. Too bad she didn't have any romantic interest with whom to share the moment. She bit the inside of her lip, stared at the movement of people.

A mixture of discord flowed outside the tent walls, people from all manners of life affected differently by the carnival's power outage. Among the patrons, she saw bewilderment, annoyance, alarm. Emotions that moved them at a fast walk or run toward the main exit, clearing the aisles at the not-so-moderate rate of speed similar to the kiddie zone's Express Train Ride.

Several lengths down, in the middle of the midway, as the crowd cleared, she could see the shambles of a smashed tent. Here, carnies lingered in a mumbling madness of words. Kyra's hand flew to her lips, and she sucked back a breath. It was like no tent she'd seen here before. Where had it come from?

Mere feet away, at the outskirts of the growing mass, Chelsea sat in a curled ball. "Chelsea!" Kyra called out and took a step in her direction. Talia grabbed her by the arm, yanked her to a halt.

"She won't know who you are," Talia whispered at Kyra's ear.

Kyra regarded Talia with irritation. "She might know something about that tent in the middle of the midway."

"Aren't you worried about being found out?" Talia pressed tight against Kyra, keeping their conversation private. "She'll wonder how you know her name, when she's never seen you before."

Kyra's fight lost steam and her muscles relaxed, but her anxiety did not. She stared at the small crowd collecting around the fallen tent-from-nowhere.

"What's going on? Hell of a ruckus. Anything good happening?" Drakhögg stood behind them, observing the sight over their shoulders. Kyra tensed again.

"Drakhögg! Any sign of her?" Kyra's parents and a few of their minions strolled their way, Ryhuu among them.

A flutter and pull attacked Kyra's gut. She was about to find out how well her disguise worked. Only problem was, she had no idea how to act like a complete stranger.

"Lost her trail in that tent," Drakhögg pointed to the Magician's tent, "right before the lights went out. What's going on with this place?"

Unadulterated concern illuminated Queen Shui's irises. Bolsvck, on the other hand, not the type to wear worry anywhere visible, grunted. "I don't like the way things are looking around here," he said, coming to a halt a few feet away. Turning his head to the side, he sniffed the air.

"I really don't like it," Queen Shui said. "We must find her. Leave this dreadful place at once."

"Couldn't find her, huh?" Ryhuu chimed in, a snarky expression on his face.

"As if you had any better luck, slime-licker." Drakhögg stepped forward, as if to challenge.

"Enough," Bolsvck's voice boomed. "There's no time for your dragonling games. Remember what you are. Warriors, not dragonets. We must find Kyra and leave this place. I have a bad feeling."

Drakhögg and Ryhuu lowered their heads.

Bolsvck's eyes trained on Kyra and Talia. "Friends of yours, Drakhögg?"

Kyra opened her mouth to say something.

"Just met them. In the tent, sir." Drakhögg stood tall and pointed toward the tent.

"We were just leaving." Talia linked arms with Kyra, tugged back and away from the aggravated dragon clan. Kyra allowed it, knowing she didn't belong there, not disguised as she was.

"Lord Bolsvck!" A man dressed to blend with the night—dark khakis, ribbed sweater—and loaded with weapons ran toward them.

With a grumble, Bolsvck crossed his arms and turned to face the approaching man. "How many times have I told you not to call me that?"

The man dropped into a jog, then came to a full stop.

Holy spitting fire! It was the man who had assaulted Kyra and Sebastian in the park right after they had escaped Marcus and his dragon consumption ritual. Her chest constricted, and she fought the desire to walk up and punch him in the face. Instead, she allowed Talia to guide her several steps away. Before they moved out of range Kyra pulled them to a stop and whispered, "I want to hear what's about to happen."

Talia scanned the area. "Over here." Together, Kyra and Talia moved to the shadows at the front of the next tent. They took a position facing each other so that it would look like they were chatting, yet Kyra could watch whatever transpired. Silently, she watched the man who had attacked her interact with her father. Kyra had to strain to hear, but being arrogant dragons, they didn't attempt to conceal their discussion, and their voices carried.

"Not that part, Jon." Bolsvck huffed and swung his head, as if to say the man was an idiot.

Jon leaned on his knees, hungrily inhaling the air. Drakhögg slapped him on the back. "Come on, Davies, you should be stronger than that. You used to be a dragon, once. Where did all your fight go?"

Jon Davies gave Drakhögg a sideways glance, practically snarled at the man. Kyra waited, holding her breath, for the men to clash. They didn't.

Davies shuddered, stood, and heeded Bolsvck. "Balidhug is here, and he hasn't come alone." He paused, waited for Bolsvck to say something. When Bolsvck did nothing more than stare at him with a stone-hard glare, Davies continued. "My sources tell me that while Balidhug was in his human form, going by the alias Marcus Blackall, he succeeded in the convergence. He may be impo—"

Bolsvck grunted and interrupted. "You realize, you have only yourself to blame for the way things stand today?"

"I was acting for the better good of the clan." Davies's voice hitched. "Had Balidhug been allowed to take the throne..." Davies's raked his fingers through his hair. "I had to broker the deal. Had to secure him someplace he could never do harm."

"You are a fool," Bolsvck said. "You likely created the very future you were attempting to prevent." Both he and Queen Shui glowered at Davies, discontent clear on their faces.

A howl sliced through the night; pitiful, painful, and powerful. Both Talia and Kyra threw their hands over their ears. Kyra searched for the source and came up empty. She wanted to know, wanted to see. As horrible as the sound was, it stirred more memories from her past, from the night her trailer burnt down. A woman had screamed in a similar manner that night, and she had screamed for Higgins.

The sound died away, returning the carnival to the awkward absence of music, joyous laughter, static hum, life. And this time, with a new ominous cloud pressing upon it.

"What was that?" Kyra whispered to Talia, studying her hands to see if her ears had actually bled. They hadn't.

"That," Talia began with a solid breath, "was the cry of a banshee. Nothing good ever comes from their cries."

"I've heard that sound before."

"Right before Higgins died." Talia peered at Kyra, fixatedly. "This cry was louder and longer."

Kyra's eyes widened. "What does that mean?"

A tiny V-shape pinched in the center of Talia's forehead. "Nothing good. Nothing good at all."

"What is happening here, Talia? The carnival going dark. A banshee crying. A broken and battered tent in the middle of the midway. Three things, none of them good. Are Hell and dragon fire about to clash?" Kyra clutched at her dress, desperate to tear the fabric away to something fight-worthy.

Talia squeezed her hand, and her voice came out small and wavering. "I have no idea."

Clinkity-clankity-clunk. The ground shook. "What the..." Kyra grabbed Talia's arm and dug her heels into the ground, solidifying her footing.

The busted tent in the midway shimmered and then melted into the ground. It left behind a collection of boxes, half crimson wood and half glass. They, too, twisted and jerked like wind-up toys and popped into the ground. Gone.

All that was left, one big clear box, and inside...a man.

Kyra leaped forward. *Sebastian!*

39
GLASS

Sebastian

"Shiiiit!" The ground had fallen out from under Sebastian.

For seconds that could have been an eternity, he was falling, the tent was falling, everything was falling.

His jaw muscles twitched and an ache at the back of his throat flourished. Dizzy and disoriented, he tried to grab at the museum cases for purchase. They were too slick, had no lines, no edges to grab.

What if he died here, now, not having used the dragon soul-shifter? Would Kalrapura return to Kyra? Or die with him? His throat and chest tightened, and the dragon inside him twisted in his gut. He reached inside his coat's inner pocket.

The tent spun, the curtains flashing crimson and gold, crimson and gold. He was reminded of the carousel—on caffeine. The museum cases sped away from him, out of arm's reach, and before he realized what was happening, Sebastian slammed into the chandelier at the top of the tent, the artifact fumbling in his hand. Metal and glass jabbed at his body, scratched at his skin. He tensed, wincing against the shock.

Light exploded all around him. Blinding. Sebastian squeezed his eyes tight against the sight and threw his hands up as a shield. He felt, then heard, the funnel clatter away. *No!* A tremendous crash oscillated everywhere: above, below, to every side. He bounced, then slid, jammed uncomfortably with his knee shoved in his chin. Muscles he didn't even know he had ached.

He opened his eyes. Temporarily saw double, before everything shifted into place.

What in all Grimly Hell? He was encased, as if he were a bibelot in a giant museum case. He'd slipped off his feet and now sat wedged at a precarious angle. He appeared lucky. The tent and its interior were in shambles. Walls crooked, curtains missing, flung across into nowhere. Museum boxes tilted or broken. Strings of lights hung, drooped, and lay all over the place. The Great Valko was frowning. Frowning! He had fallen on his side. His crystal ball rolled around somewhere near his turban.

Pushing against the walls, Sebastian managed to lift and right himself. His gaze focused on the dark, normal skin of his hands. The truth-seeking spell of the tent had been broken and he no longer looked like a monster. His mission, the dragon soul-shifter was wedged in the bottom corner by his right foot. He sighed, bent to pick it up, slammed his head against the glass. *Ouch!* Rubbing his forehead with one hand and running his fingers along the box with the other, he searched for a seam in the glass.

Peculiar thing, this mysterious bubble. He peered up, saw the chandelier was gone. A survey of the area identified no fallen crystal, only a barren, iron-branched frame. If he had the frame with him now, maybe he could break himself out, but the only hard item he had was at his feet, where he couldn't reach it. He moaned, dropped his head back against the glass, and replayed the events in the tent over and over in his head, trying to figure out what had gone wrong, what *he'd* done wrong, and how he could possibly fix the situation.

A banshee's fierce shriek ripped through the tent and straight through his soul. Sebastian thought surely the cry would shatter the glass. It did not. The dome vibrated, her message strengthened by the profound resonance singing up through the glass. It acted as her unseen chorus of midnight messengers, and he was the recipient.

The news from Zeke, the tarot cards, now the banshee. Could the memo be any more obvious? Somebody, probably a lot of somebodies, would die tonight.

"Hello, Dad. I'm paying attention." Sebastian kicked the glass. "Stupid Mr. Johnson." Not that any of this was his fault. Sebastian preferred to blame him, anyway. Heat pulsed through his veins, wiggled down to his fingertips, and creeped up along his neck. Pressure pushed at his back and his eyes burned. "Not now," he chanted over and over and closed his eyes, concentrated. He was dressed in his favorite gentleman's jacket. He was a gentleman, and gentlemen know how to defeat their monsters within. With a deep, down-to-the-core breath, the push of the beast subsided.

Clinkity-clankity-clunk. The ground shook.

What's happening? Sebastian turned in his tight bubble case, tried to see what was taking place. The Great Valko had righted himself, and he smiled at Sebastian. Sebastian's mind raced, he swallowed hard. The crystal ball began to swirl with turquoise smoke and the curtain slammed shut on the fortuneteller. Sebastian noticed all the curtains along the outer wall were now closed.

Crank-crank-crank. The tent's mechanical workings drummed up again. The top sprung open, exposing the darkest of nights. The space grew and grew until the top was completely gone, and yet it kept going, disintegrating the walls to the ground. A crowd of people, a mix of patrons and carnies—mostly carnies—surrounded the tent. He was on the ground. He dropped his head against the glass. "Thank you," he whispered to the universe. Someone would surely help him.

He heard his name from the crowd. But when he searched, he saw no one he would expect to call out to him.

"Sebastian!" Chelsea threw herself against the glass. Sebastian jerked. She was a wreck. Tear tracks ran the length of her cheeks, and her tired eyes were now smudged and even darker, more sunken. She clawed at the glass with dirt-packed nails.

He grinned and placed his palm against the glass. She responded in like, gazing at him wantonly.

"How'd you get in there, boy?" The Magician took short, even paces around Sebastian's glass prison.

Sebastian half watched the Magician, half watched Chelsea, wondered who the L.M. was that the Great Valko had ejected from the tent. "It happened so fast I can't really say. One minute I was standing in the tent, the next I was falling, and then I was in this." He gestured to the bubble. The Magician raised a brow, smoothed and twisted his mustache.

"You!" The crowd parted, allowing Jon Davies to rush at Sebastian. Sebastian pressed his back against the glass, away from Davies, and his will against the inner beast. "You don't deserve—"

"Easy, Jon." Bolsvck's arm swooped across the man's chest, stopping him short. "I need this one alive." Bolsvck spared Sebastian a glance. "For now. What's your *drak* with him, anyway?"

Jon Davies's eyes burned with a hatred Sebastian had never seen directed at himself. If he were a lesser being, his skin might singe. Instead, Sebastian stared right back. "Don't upset me, military man. You don't want to find out what I'm capable of." A forced laugh burst from Sebastian's lips. It might have been false bravado, but at this low point, he didn't have a lot of cards in the deck to deal. "Hell, *I* don't want to find out what I'm capable of."

Davies roared, and in the motion, the pain, Sebastian could see the beast he used to be but was no more. "That thing," Jon Davies pointed at Sebastian, "killed my men." He paused, became solemn, yet the stir in his eyes betrayed his posture. "And he killed my daughter."

Sebastian lurched to the front of the glass. "I didn't kill any of your people. Especially not Alice!" Her name withered through his mind, caused him to doubt. "She was helping me," he said more quietly and pressed back against the glass again, feeling inside his pocket, remembering the locket. It was there, as he knew it would be.

Maybe she is *dead because of me. If I hadn't been there, my father wouldn't have come. And if my father hadn't come, she wouldn't be dead.* He pressed the locket firmly in his palm, held it safely hidden. He watched the faces staring at him through the glass, like he was a prisoner on his execution day. The mix of accusations and support. His gaze locked on Chelsea. He smiled, flattened his palm on the glass before her. She was possessed, broken, and dying, but he wouldn't abandon her. Especially since a fair amount of her suffering was because of him.

That's when he saw them. Three of them. No, more than three. Hidden in recesses and shadows, there were others, their faces obscured. Mr. Johnson was among them, as was Mortifier. *Far be it for Dad to miss out on this.* Sebastian no longer believed they were here to retrieve him. Their agenda was far grimmer. His gaze locked with his father's, and he pulled the locket from his pocket, stared down at the battered gold necklace. "Your fault," he said and glared at Mortifier.

Jon Davies bellowed. Sebastian realized, too late, what he had done—openly exposed the locket. He shoved it back in his pocket and turned just in time to see Davies's fist slam into the glass.

"No!" Chelsea threw herself at Davies. He tossed her aside like a dirty rag. She toppled into another person and fell to the ground, bleeding.

Sebastian roared, anger bursting from him in waves of wings and talons. The museum case shattered into a zillion little chandelier crystals, flying into the crowd like glass missiles.

40
CURIOUS

Marcus

"Aren't you Kyra's boyfriend?" Vortex Girl leaned in the doorway and crossed one leg over the other. When Marcus remained silent, she continued. "Yeah, you're the one who helped me out of that little mess a while back." She held her hands comfortably in front of herself, except when she used them to accentuate her words, which was often. "Was that guy your friend?" She pointed over her shoulder.

There was another pause, presumably to allow Marcus to speak, but again, he said nothing. What he did do was study her with mild curiosity. His head tilted slightly to the side, a smile slowly spreading across his face with each nervous word she continued to spout. At least, he assumed it was nerves that had her rambling on. Could be she was nothing more than a babbling imbecile. Nevertheless, he found himself leaning toward her, into her drivel.

She coughed. It sounded faked. "Cause if he was...your friend, I mean...then I'm sorry about the whole zapola thing. Just can't help it sometimes. Just happens. But you know," she paused for what appeared to be effect, "he was acting kinda douchey." She stood away from the door now and took a step into the trailer. She appeared agitated and downright pissy. "Do you talk? Or are you some kind of mute?"

She was a feisty one. Dangerous and feisty. Marcus cocked a brow and didn't move. "Where did you send him?"

She relaxed, and a mild case of guilt washed across her face. "So, he was your friend?" Her hands began to knit some unseen sweater, and her shoulders swayed back and forth. Marcus wasn't sure if this was a sign of nerves or a desire to dance. "Well, he shouldn't be hurt or anything. Just relocated."

Now Marcus took one step, and one step only, closer. "Yes, but to where?" His voice was low and gravelly.

The girl jumped as if finding tiny bugs on her feet. She swiftly moved back to the safety of the doorway. "Could be anywhere, really." She shrugged. "Los Angeles, New York, 1890s London, Jupiter." She bit her lip.

"Fantastic," Marcus grumbled and pushed past her out the door.

Mystic's Magical Market was peculiarly quiet, which suited Marcus just fine. He envisioned the bottleneck of patrons at the entrance, a frenzied fear running rampant among them. He felt...nothing. Curious.

"I told you I was sorry!" she called after him. He heard her descending the few steps behind him.

"I heard. Lot of good it does me. Now get lost." He didn't glance back. He didn't have the time or desire to deal with her any longer. Fire was raging through his body, and his muscles felt like they were going to snap.

"You didn't explain why you were going through Sebastian's stuff." Her tiny footsteps rushed to keep up with his wide stride.

"Why are you still here?" he asked, nostrils flared and teeth bared.

"Were you... Are you looking for Kyra?"

Marcus's brisk, stretched stride came to a complete halt. Finally, something interesting from the girl. He turned on Vortex Girl and regarded her through a narrowed slit of a glare. "Do you know where Kyra is?"

"Sure!" Her entire body lit up, and she beamed confidence. But then her brows crinkled, and her expression dimmed. "Well, not really."

Marcus growled under his breath.

"But I saw her and Talia take off that way." She pointed toward the iron works that only minutes ago had been a dazzle of lights and moving wonders. The Fun Zone, now dark and dormant.

"Just the two of them? No Sebastian?" Marcus had no idea who Talia was, but that caused him no concern.

"Why are you so interested in Sebastian?" Vortex Girl popped her hands on her hips. "I thought you and Kyra were an item. You're not jealous, are you?"

Marcus's lips pressed together in a firm line, and his hands flexed before clasping into tight fists. "What's that way? Just rides and games?"

"There are plenty of rides and games, all right," she said with a gleam in her eye, "but if you keep going, you'll find yourself amidst the Big Top show area."

Marcus regarded her. She was young and excitable, an unpredictable combination. "Other than, 'they went that way,' you don't know anything else?"

Her body straightened, as if called to attention by a teacher. "Oh, sure. I know lots of things. For instance, did you know the first Ferris wheel was invented in—"

Marcus waved a hand, dismissing her ramble. "About Kyra or Sebastian, girl."

Her eyes widened like the full moon. "Oh. No." She shook her head.

"Then beat it." He turned and resumed his strut. Moving through the Fun Zone, he watched patrons melting down various aisles. Like a receding wave, they flushed down the midway toward the main entrance and the portal. Little did they know, it was closed.

He noticed another curious thing about the carnival. Static electricity, like lightning, every once in a while, would randomly strike, run a course along the side of a tent or across the ground. It wasn't natural, and he suspected the electricity had something to do with the carnival. Interest stirred in him, and he wanted to amass the answers to the unasked questions, like a dragon lord amasses power. What was the source? What was the purpose?

The Fun Zone eventually dropped behind him, and he entered a city of tents. Every kind of tent imaginable surrounded him. Simple tents, ornate tents, monstrous tents, mousy tents. It was never ending.

And still, the shuffle of small feet followed him. He rolled his eyes and grumbled. He didn't want to get sucked into a vortex, accidentally or on purpose.

Marcus's stomach tugged. It was a minor pinch, but it meant his insurance policy worked and Kyra was somewhere in the vicinity. His piercing gaze searched the crowd. A multitude of people filed through this section of the carnival, like herded Behemoth. They pushed toward the exit, confusion, irritation, and disappointment their companions. But not everyone sought an exit. Some drifted with leisure from show to show, or chatted with carnies, while others pressed quick and purposeful toward a ruckus farther down the row. Marcus cranked his head to see what was drawing the people like a masterful trap.

A wail, sounding much like Davies's, punched through the crowd, and the little vortex girl ran past Marcus. Feet stumbling, she paused and threw her flared hands up to her face. "Oh my beastie! Sebastian!" She disappeared into the crowd.

"Interesting." Marcus stepped to the side, into the shadows one of the tents provided. He watched with keen interest as the boy, Sebastian, morphed into some kind of beast, shattering the glass box within which he'd been trapped into a bazillion miniature pieces. "This will be more fun than I first imagined," Marcus muttered to himself. He flipped several of the stolen tarot cards in his right hand, as a dry smile squirmed into place on his face. First, he'd deal with the damn carnie boy, then he'd collect Kyra.

"Hey, boss." Marcus jerked. Rick had silently slipped up beside him. "Where's Chet?"

Marcus grunted. "Early departure."

"That's unfortunate." Rick studied the commotion in the midway. "Good news. Bolsvck and Davies, both located." He gestured to the crowd.

"Yes," Marcus said, the word slipping slow and dark from his tongue. "Where are the others?"

"Toby and Darren are around here somewhere." Rick glanced over his shoulder and pointed. "Left Darren over there only a short while ago." He straightened his shoulders and stared at Marcus. "What now?"

"We kill dragons." Marcus peered at Rick, insidious intentions gleaming in his eyes. "Are you ready?"

41
NEEDS

Kyra

Kyra vaulted toward Sebastian. He needed her. She knew he needed her. Even if he wouldn't admit it. Her heart ached to close the distance, to speed to his aid. She didn't care about the hurtful things he'd said. They'd work through that later. Right now, they only needed each other. She had to get him out of that box.

Her momentum came to a screeching halt, wrenched back at the arm by Talia. "Are you trying to ruin everything?" she hissed.

Kyra's head snapped back and forth between Talia and the mess in which Sebastian currently found himself trapped. She flung her arm in his direction. "He needs my help," she murmured.

"If you go over there now, all the effort to disguise you will have been for nothing," Talia responded. "Besides, when have you known Sebastian to get stuck in a situation he couldn't maneuver his way out of?"

Kyra's mouth dropped open to answer. No words came. She couldn't think of any, but that didn't mean they didn't exist. After all, when he'd come to retrieve her from Marcus, he'd been damn well banged up.

"Catching flies there, beautiful?" Drakhögg said as he strutted past. He spun around playfully and swatted Kyra on the butt. Kyra's mouth dropped open again, and she stared after him. He was following her father toward Sebastian. Davies was rushing the scene like a sideshow freak in need of a fix.

"Did you see that?" Kyra turned to Talia, feeling the astonishment on her face, and caught Ryhuu inspecting her with disdain as he, too, followed the leader.

Talia crossed her arms and glared at the back of Drakhögg's head. "If you mean the asinine behavior, then yes, I did."

Kyra minded Ryhuu, made sure he was far enough away, and spoke no louder than a whisper. "He's supposed to be betrothed to me, and he was just flirting with me."

A terse giggle volleyed up Talia's throat. "Rather serendipitous, the man actually making a pass at his fiancée." Her eyes twinkled with unspoken laughter.

"But he doesn't know it's me," Kyra huffed. "He thinks I'm some blonde girl he just met."

"I don't know what—" Talia stopped abruptly at the sound of loud howls and roars and shattering glass.

Kyra's heart clenched, as did her fists.

"You win," Talia said. "Let's move closer. We still need to stay out of the way, or you might be discovered." Locking hands, they moved together along the edge of the tents toward the chaos.

Ahead, wings flashed above the heads of the crowd. They were there, clear as dragon fire, and then they were gone, disappearing into the mass of people again. It was only for a moment, long enough for Kyra to know Sebastian had lost control, and Kalrapura had taken over. If only temporarily. Chelsea scrambled feebly at the edge of the crowd, attempting to push her way through, and Davies came flying backwards, as if thrown by an incredible force. Kyra's throat squeezed tight.

It was a disaster. Sebastian out of control. Her family with front row tickets to the show. And her, trapped and unable to do anything, or she'd be forced to denounce her Moorigad status, choose a clan and a man in which she held no interest. She stared at the scene, heart aching to be in the midst of the commotion.

She blinked hard. Shook her head. Her attention, nabbed by someone running at Sebastian from the other direction. Vortex Girl. Kyra's heart dropped below her gut. Well-meaning or not, that girl was bad news. Kyra couldn't, *wouldn't*, let her desire to avoid her family put Sebastian in danger of getting shifted to another world or dimension.

"No!" she yelled and pressed forward at a quicker pace, following her need to help him. Eight steps in, she stumbled against the side of the nearest tent, overcome with light-headedness. Her heart panged, and her skin turned hypersensitive. She shuddered, wanted to hurl.

"What's wrong?" Talia's hand pressed gently against Kyra's shoulder blades.

"I feel..." Kyra began and paused, feeling a wave of nausea. "I feel like I should be going that way," she pointed beyond Sebastian, toward a bend in the lane, "rather than over there." She jerked her hand in Sebastian's direction. "The feeling is overwhelming."

Talia moved in front of her, studied her closely. Her lips twisted to the side and her nose twitched. "Did Sebastian get the tooth pendant from you?"

Kyra winced. "Marcus's pendant? I haven't seen that in..." Her eyes widened, and her head jerked. "Why was Sebastian supposed to get it from me?"

Talia swayed her head to the side. "A while back I did some crystal ball gazing, attempting to get to the bottom of your condition. I saw the tooth pendant Marcus had given you. It felt significant to me. Like he was using it to control you."

"But I'm not wearing it!" Kyra's voice rose in pitch.

"Maybe. Maybe not. I saw it on you in the reading."

"You could be wrong. I've never felt this nausea before. If he was somehow using the pendant on me the entire time, shouldn't I have felt this misery before?" She raked her fingers through her hair, pulled hard as if she could pull the ugly situation out of her life with the simple motion.

An understanding smile wrapped Talia's lips, yet her eyes remained somber. "I'm pretty sure I understood the viewing correctly. I think the change in your reaction is due to the change in you and your memory or self-recovery."

Kyra blinked, became numb. "All right. But like I said, I'm not wearing the pendant."

Talia nodded, her lips drawing into a thin line of scrutiny. "I think the vile thing is on you somewhere. Would you trust me?"

"If the thing is on me and affecting my actions, by all means, find and destroy." Kyra smiled—sort of. Her smile failed even before she'd finished the delivery.

Didn't matter, Talia wasn't paying attention. She was already pulling a stone from her pocket, wrapped between her thumb and palm. She placed her hands together, angled away from each other. "A somewhat unconventional witch in my coven showed me how to do this," Talia said and silently moved her hands, shaped somewhat like a divining rod, around Kyra's body.

Kyra fidgeted and stared at the crowd, caught a few people glance their way. She didn't care. No one's approval mattered to her. No one's but Sebastian's. And as long as none of them tried to stop Talia, or were Marcus, they could gawk all they wanted.

"Found it!" Talia said, clear triumph in her voice.

"Seriously?" Kyra tried to turn, see where Talia was talking about. She couldn't. It was at her back, and Talia held her steady. "But I'm not wearing any pendant." Her voice hitched an octave higher.

"Are you a sound sleeper?" Talia's hands smoothed along a square on Kyra's upper butt cheek.

Anxiety rose like a whirlwind in Kyra's chest. "What's going on?"

She didn't need Talia's answer. Since the carousel ride, her memories had slipped back into place. Sebastian had come to take her away from Marcus, she remembered, and for some inexplicable reason, he hadn't come inside. That didn't feel right to Kyra, and her mind wrapped tight around the thought.

Maybe he *couldn't* come in. Oh Rajũn, what had she done? Marcus had forced Sebastian to leave, and she'd done nothing to stop him.

She'd even lain with Marcus, enjoyed every moment envisioning Sebastian in Marcus's place.

But then...there was whiskey, lots of it. Fighting and hitting, too. Marcus had a propensity for firewater and a heavy hand when liquored up. A vague memory of blood. Blood on Marcus's hands, blood on the sheets. She never saw those sheets again. *What happened that night?* In the morning she had been sore, so excruciatingly sore. She'd lain in bed for three days before feeling well enough to shuffle around the condo. Why hadn't she questioned it more at the time?

Talia came around to face Kyra, her face drawn and absent of color. "The tooth pendant is embedded just above your right cheek."

Until Talia's confirmation, Kyra could have gone on convincing herself it was all a bad dream. No longer. Kyra's mouth dropped open, and emotions pelted upon her like the raging storm. Anger, annoyance, shame for allowing herself to fall into this mess with Marcus. Disbelief and rage at his actions. Frustration and fear for her current situation. Strongest of all, hatred for the man who had caused this wreck.

"You have to cut it out," Kyra said, feeling a storm of conviction she had not felt in a long while. She reached down, lifted her skirt, and pulled the small blade from her boot. She held it up between them. "Use this."

Talia blinked. "Um, right." She glanced around the midway, searching for what, Kyra hadn't a clue. "Not out here. Somewhere private." Her gaze locked on a dark tent several feet away and Talia pointed. "Over there."

42
COMPASS

Sebastian

Crystals fell from the sky like rain, yet Sebastian felt not a single one. His focus was solely on Davies and Chelsea. Because of Davies's insensitive shove, the poor girl was battered, dropped to the ground like a pile of used rags. The harsh visual clawed deeper into his emotions than he had expected. No one should be handled with such severity. Especially a girl. A dying girl, at that. At the end of life's impossible road, most people deserved better treatment, an earnest adieu. For Davies to take issue with Sebastian was understandable, but to take his fury out on others, unforgivable.

Heat flushed up his neck and face, and the lights flashed on in his mind's eye. He knew. It was his job to see that Chelsea and others like her received the mercies due at the end of the path. His hybrid anomaly status was not a mistake, but rather served a purpose. Not only could he help them move to the other side as a Reaper, but as a Mara he could do so using their dreams and deepest desires to make the transition less traumatic.

The dragon inside him roared once again. Or maybe it wasn't the dragon, maybe it was something closer to home, something he didn't want to admit to, something belonging to his true identity.

Clenching his hands into fists, talons cut into the skin of his palms, and he growled with deep-seated fury at Jon Davies. Davies lunged, but was stopped cold, slammed in the chest by Bolsvck. Davies flew backwards out of sight.

"Calm yourself, boy," Bolsvck said, burning a steady glare upon Sebastian. "Such theatrics are unnecessary."

Guilt crashed upon Sebastian with the force of a tidal wave, yet he managed to bring his breath to a steady rhythm, allowing his heart to settle and blood to slow. Any regrets were his own to face, so he met the fiery dragon lord's gaze and did not dignify him with a response. Instead, he swallowed against the thickness in his throat, the upset in his stomach. Focusing on the things he hoped he could control, he breathed in and out, in and out, in a controlled metered rhythm, and gradually the wings and talons receded.

He let out one last deep breath, pulled from deep within his core. "What's going on? Why is the power out?"

"You tell me." Bolsvck glanced at the dark tents beside them, then dropped his stare to the bits of crystal at their feet. "Trouble seems to circle you like buzzards around a dying cow," he said, a new, curious appraisal in his eyes. "What species are you?"

Bolsvck's question was a kick to Sebastian's gut, and he found his sight blurring, turning to a haze. No longer did he see the man before him. Sebastian had no control over the lot he'd been dealt in this life. He was what he was, a Bringer of Death. He hated to think that meant bad luck in all things, not only for himself but for anyone close to him.

Queen Shui pushed through the crowd. "Where is my daughter?" She grabbed Sebastian by the arm and shook him, rattling his thoughts. "You still have her dragon. What have you been doing all this time?"

"Easy, woman." Bolsvck ran a tender hand along her arm, pulling her into his. It appeared to soften her storm, if only mildly.

Sebastian straightened, his face lifting slightly. He had been under the impression Kyra's parents stood on opposite sides of some unbreakable barrier, divided by clan and dragon rituals. And yet here they were, united. If only for a moment, Sebastian's heart lightened, and he had hope for Kyra's future relationship with her parents.

Bolsvck returned his arduous glare upon Sebastian. "I, too, would like to know the answer to the question. Where is our daughter?"

Sebastian realized he had been ogling the pair. With a gasp, cheeks burning, he snapped back to the moment. Only, the moment brought voices, so many voices crowding his thoughts, his head. He couldn't... He braced his head between his hands and pressed.

Need Talia's tonic.

"What's wrong with you, boy?" Bolsvck's voice cracked through Sebastian's skull like the hammer against the bell, ringing so loud it could yank the dead from their slumber.

"Sebastian."

The sound of his name was a whisper among the utterings. Still, he fixed on the source and let all others fall away. He found only mild relief, at best. His eyes burned, felt bloodshot, and when he turned his gaze to the crowd, he realized he had yet to answer Bolsvck. Except, Bolsvck didn't hold his attention. His gaze was drawn beyond Chelsea to the girl running directly for him. His heart leaped, thoughts of Kyra filling his mind. But it wasn't Kyra, nor did he want it to be. Not with what he needed to do. His gut dropped. To spare her the most pain, Kyra needed to hate him.

It was Valentina. Daughter of Destinations, or Vortex Girl, as Kyra liked to call her. Sebastian smiled inwardly at Kyra's fun quirks. Wondered if she secretly called him Card Boy.

"No!" Another voice, unrecognizable. And yet, it pulled at him.

The word drowned out everything in his mind. He swiveled and saw Talia with another he didn't recognize. A blonde, pressed against the tents beyond the crowd. The blonde stared at him with piercing green eyes, causing his insides to tingle. Odd. Something nagged him, like he should know the girl, but he had never seen her before.

Vortex. The word swirled through his head. "Hell." He spun back toward Valentina, throwing his hand up to stop her.

The volcanoes of Purgatory exploded all around him.

Or really, dragon fire fell from the sky, exploding like pyre bombs upon the ground. Murmurs distorted, transforming into shrieks and screams, wails of pain. The tent to Sebastian's right erupted in flames. In the darkening sky, Fire Dragons took to battle, fighting Marcus's incoming army with no concern for the carnival or her occupants.

"Told you Balidhug and his men were here," Jon Davies yelled over the bedlam. He was crouched low to the ground.

Bolsvck grabbed the queen into a protective hold and shoved Sebastian to the ground. Sebastian's elbow slammed into the hard-packed earth. "What the Hell—" he said, stopped short by a fireball whizzing right through the space he'd been standing moments before. Sebastian sat up on his elbows and stared at the clash commencing.

"Protect Kalrapura with your life," Bolsvck commanded, yanking Sebastian back to his feet, then turned to Davies and his own clan. "End this now. Find Balidhug."

Fighting in the air, falling to the ground. Fighting on the ground, crashing into tents. When Sebastian peered down the midway, conflict could be spotted in multiple locations. Dragons with wings. Dragons without wings. Beasts that weren't dragons at all. Sebastian searched his memory for what these others were called. He was sure he'd seen them in his research, but right now in the midst of the chaos, the species name escaped him.

"Sebastian?" Valentina stood beside him now.

"Don't touch him!" Chelsea yelped and groped at the girl's legs in an attempt to pull her away from Sebastian.

Although Valentina appeared scared, she showed no signs of being out of control of her gift. "It's okay, Chelsea." Sebastian reached down, took her hand in his, and gave her a reassuring smile. *It's time*, his mind chimed. Help her up, was what he should do, but what if she was safer on the ground? What did it matter? It was her time. Maybe she was more comfortable on the ground.

He was making excuses, and he had no idea why. He needed to ease her suffering now. But first, before he reaped her soul he needed to deal with Valentina, move Vortex Girl along. Pulling away, he scratched his temple and focused on Valentina.

"Dragons. They still exist?" Valentina's voice was full of wonder.

Through his relationship with Kyra, Sebastian was among the few aware of their existence. Long ago, they'd gone underground and stayed hidden for millennia. Now here they were, destroying Mystic's Carnival.

"They're real." He looked her straight in the eye. "Some of them want to hurt Kyra. Others want to force a change upon her she doesn't desire."

"Kyra?" Valentina's gaze flickered from him to the dragons in the sky. "She's a dragon?" Her eyes widened. Sebastian nodded. "And her boyfriend?" Valentina asked.

The veins in Sebastian's neck pulsed, and his eye twitched. Even if he didn't die this night, he didn't think he would ever find peace with the thought of Marcus touching Kyra. "A bad man who is not to be trusted," he said, his voice barely holding steady.

Valentina caught her breath. "I've made a horrible mistake." Her face flushed. "I found him going through your stuff. I even brought him here to find you." She glanced over her shoulder and Sebastian followed her gaze, saw no Marcus. "I'm so sorry."

"It's alright." At least he knew Marcus's general location. "I need your help."

"Anything." She leaned closer.

"Sebastian?" Chelsea grabbed at his arm, attempted to stand. He motioned for her to wait a moment and glanced into the crowd. Even now, fire consumed two tents and people were falling to injury, some even close to death. He could sense it, and he saw the other Reapers lingering, waiting. For all he knew, there were hundreds of them throughout the carnival, lying in wait. An arctic chill swept over him, wrapped around the dragon's fire kindling in his belly.

"You have a unique gift, Valentina." Sebastian placed his hands on her upper arms, hoping to stress the importance of the message he was attempting to convey. She stared at him, unwavering. "Whether the dragons fighting actually mean us harm or not, what they are doing here is detrimental to Mystic's and to everyone here. Do you understand?"

Valentina nodded.

"I need you to be strong and brave. Can you do that?"

She nodded again.

"I knew you could." He leaned his forehead against hers and whispered, "Send them away, Valentina. For everyone's sake, send as many away as you can."

Valentina blinked, followed it with a hard swallow. "I can do that." She turned to go, hesitated, and turned back. "You had me so scared when you appeared in that glass box." Sebastian smirked, and Valentia spun around, ran into the chaos and disappeared. Where she'd vanished, Sebastian's father shimmied into shape and approached, hand perched in his suit pocket, fedora firmly in place. Nothing like a little family reunion in the middle of Hell's welcoming party.

Sebastian grimaced, glanced down to Chelsea. He had unfinished business with the girl.

"What the bloody dragon are you doing, boy?" Bolsvck yanked Sebastian by the collar, pulled him several feet to the side. "You're supposed to be keeping my girl's dragon safe, not standing out in the middle like a big, blazing target!"

"I'm not..." Sebastian struggled against the man's strong arm.

"Exactly, you're not doing as you were told." Bolsvck tossed Sebastian to the edge of the midway. He fell onto his back, crashing into the side rigging of the nearest tent. Splinters of pain shot through his spine, and the strain of his wings pressed against his back. Pressed to be released. Scrambling to pull himself up, keep track of where Chelsea and his father were, he searched the pandemonium.

There was fighting and destruction, his home falling to ruin. Yet, with a tiny glimpse of a vortex, hope bloomed. Valentina was at work. And what was that? His gaze snapped in a new direction. The Magician was getting involved, using magic to protect Mystic's. Acrobats vaulted off one beast to the next, knocking some off balance. Carnies everywhere were jumping in to protect their home, to protect Mystic's Carnival, and they were using everything at their disposal—magic or magnificent ability.

"Where's my daughter?" Bolsvck grabbed Sebastian by the collar, lifting him till there was a mere breath's space between them.

"I don't know. I left her..." His words trailed off, and his gaze wandered to the side, to where he'd last seen Talia. She was there, moving away from him now, and still with the blonde girl. "I made sure she was no longer freezing. I had to retrieve an important item so I can return her dragon. I assumed she would find her way back to you."

"She has not." Something in the way Bolsvck spoke had Sebastian convinced he may not live to return Kalrapura if he didn't give the man what he wanted—right now. He glanced at Talia once again, and the crazy little witch, it was as if she knew he was watching her. She glowered back. Everything about her said to beware and stay silent. The message hit him in the gut like the strongman's hammer. *What is she hiding?* "What are you looking at?" Bolsvck boomed.

"I'd thank you to take your hands off my son."

Sebastian rolled his eyes and sighed. Bolsvck released him, sending him tumbling backwards against the tent.

"You!" Bolsvck said, pointing his finger at Mortifier. "I've been looking for you."

Fantastic. More dad drama. Sebastian was fairly certain, even not knowing what issue was on the line, that he would stand with Kyra's father.

Not that he had time for either at the moment. His thoughts flickered to Talia, and he slipped from the scene to follow her. But if finding Kyra would appease Bolsvck, he didn't really need Talia to accomplish the task...did he? She'd given him an extremely handy tool for such endeavors. He tugged up his sleeve and studied the compass, focusing his thoughts on Kyra. A needle appeared, spun, adjusted, and pointed. He followed, pausing when he realized it was pointed directly at Talia and the blonde.

A flutter stirred in his stomach, and he stared down at his palm, then at Talia. She shoved the blonde into a tent, glancing back at

Sebastian long enough for him to receive a full face-slap of her witchy don't-dare-follow glare. Awareness kicked him in the gut. The blonde with Talia, she wasn't Kyra, and yet she was, in every sense that mattered. His heart locked tight, then exploded with the speed of a charging were-cheetah. *The blonde is Kyra.* What manner of magic was at work, and what would be the cost?

He took a step forward, paused. He couldn't go to Kyra. Not if she'd gone to such lengths to hide her identity. He stepped back and turned away to stare into the crowd—right at Marcus.

Marcus hadn't seen Sebastian, or at least, he didn't think the evil ogre was aware of his presence. Marcus was busy barking orders at one of his cronies. The man nodded enthusiastically and then disappeared into the crowd. Marcus, in turn, strode into the mob with the strut of a man on a mission.

What is he up to?

Sebastian's gaze darted over the commotion, making note of every concern. Marcus was on a clear path for Bolsvck. No doubt, with intentions worthy of fearful consideration. And several yards away, one of his men was beating up on Kyra's mother. Sebastian's shoulders tightened, and his hand racked through his hair.

Bolsvck and his father were arguing in the midst of the crowded midway, clearly unaware of the danger lurking toward them. Not that his father had anything to be concerned with, but it was possible, Bolsvck could use Sebastian's assistance. Kyra's mother definitely could. But the true object of Marcus' obsession was neither Bolsvck nor Queen Shui. It was Kyra, and she was in the tent behind Sebastian.

He swallowed the lump lodged in this throat.

Bolsvck and Queen Shui would want Sebastian to protect Kyra so that was what he would do. He would make sure Marcus stayed clear of her.

A few steps away from making a move on Bolsvck, Marcus flinched and paused. His head turned to the side, and his back straightened.

Sebastian's mouth went dry.

With one quick spin, Marcus was heading in the opposite direction.

Sebastian's direction. Marcus was checking his hair and the fold of his lapel like his appearance mattered. Like he was prepping for a date.

Sebastian sucked back a breath. His world was spinning with suspicion and suspense and sorrow. Did Marcus know where Kyra was? If so, Sebastian had to be ready. Had to stop him.

One instant, Marcus was pushing through the midway crowded with disquieted carnies, dragons, zilants, and more. The next instant, he was glaring at Sebastian. It had happened as fast as a snap. As if a switch had been thrown, pulling Marcus' hatred directly toward Sebastian.

The heat of Marcus' animosity melted Sebastian's feet into the grown. He couldn't move. Couldn't think. Couldn't devise a plan of attack upon the man moving in on him.

Marcus's lips quivered, revealing his canines, a guttural growl rolled up his larynx, and he paused mid-stride, glaring at Sebastian.

A girl's scream burst from the tent at Sebastian's back. *Kyra.* Her name filled his head. His heart stopped, and his head snapped, angling as if to see. Wishing himself the ability to see through the tent canvas. The need—the desire—slammed in his chest, clattered and crashed against his ribcage, to follow, to run straight for the tent where he'd seen Talia and the blonde girl disappear. Marcus's attention shot past Sebastian, zeroed in and glued to the tent.

The jig is up. He knows. He knows. I need to keep him away from her.

Sebastian steeled his soul. He knew the time had come. He'd have to fight. He stepped away from the tent, toward the midway. Toward Marcus.

"Leave Sebastian alone!" A body dropped on top of Marcus. A savage assault of claws and kicks.

Sebastian stumbled back a step and blinked.

Marcus was being attacked by a blonde girl. A sickly blonde girl with wild, dark eyes. It was Chelsea.

Sebastian hesitated, stared at Chelsea and her savagery. Fingernails digging at Marcus' eyes and teeth biting into his flesh. Sebastian should help her. Only...it was clear that whoever or whatever was in control of the girl's actions wasn't really Chelsea. At least, not in that moment.

Marcus was hollering. And the thing...the thing that was Chelsea was screaming about *him*. Sebastian. Plans for Sebastian.

What did it all mean?

Sebastian turned from the scene and ran, his feet incapable of carrying him fast enough.

43
FOUND

Sebastian

Sebastian flew through the entrance of the tent and stopped dead. The two girls had their backs to him, and between them, there was a whole lot of exposed skin. Breath lodged in his throat, he turned away, stared at the chaos of the midway. With hammering heart and exasperated breath and heat flushing his cheeks, he shyly peered over his shoulder toward Talia.

She fussed over the blonde, and the blonde—Kyra—she *was* dressed, or mostly dressed, sitting on a chair looking like a wounded victim. Neither of the girls had noticed him yet. Sebastian expelled a sigh of relief. He'd seen so much skin, he'd thought she was undressing. Now, he could see that was not the case. He studied Talia and Kyra. *What in the name of Hell's admission are they doing?*

Hand laced in blood, Talia presented an object as a prize, and Kyra, in turn, lost her lunch—all over the ground. Sebastian grimaced, diverted his focus. Watching Talia toss the tiny item, which bounced off the chair beside her, it dawned on him what had taken place and the huge significance. Talia had fulfilled *his* job, the one she'd tasked him with, and one which he'd failed to complete. She'd requested he retrieve the tooth from Kyra. But in the short time allotted, he'd been unsuccessful in locating it. In the recent pandemonium, the task had completely slipped his mind.

Sebastian shifted his weight, letting guilt wiggle down his spine. It had never occurred to him that the tooth would be buried within Kyra's flesh. So bestial. Kalrapura roared, wrenched inside his chest, and Sebastian's hands clenched into white-knuckled fists. *Look out, Mystic's, bloodshed is coming.* Every one of Sebastian's nerves teetered on the edge of nuclear combustion. A Mara-reaping of Marcus would be his only satisfaction. Exposing Marcus to his deepest and darkest fears in the most painful way possible.

"It hurts. Can you magically stitch me up or something?" The words, although not in her natural voice, had come from Kyra. Of that, Sebastian was certain.

Even in her magical, made-up disguise, Sebastian knew her for who she was. All he'd needed was the proximity. Now, standing a mere eight to ten feet away, he could feel her truth, her purpose, her beauty, and his love for her swelled, rooting deeper and stronger within his core than he'd ever thought possible. His thoughts of Marcus melted into a haze, a new mission igniting inside his heart. He had to stop Kyra's pain.

From where he stood he could see Talia had cut a small incision in the small of Kyra's back. It was obvious to him, from the blood on Talia's hands and on the discarded tooth, the cut was how Talia had extracted the tooth from Kyra's body.

Sebastian ground his teeth and pushed away the murderous thoughts rushing his brain. He'd deal with Marcus soon enough. Priorities, had to keep them straight, and right now, his were inside the tent, not out. If he had understood their conversation correctly, they were in need of something for a little magical healing. Being familiar with the talker for this show tent, Sebastian had a pretty good idea how to fill their need.

Two steps to Sebastian's right, along the edge of the main entrance, was a podium by which the talker worked his forked-tonged magic, sweet-talking pedestrians into the show at an astounding rate never before seen at the carnival. An unassuming man, one would never guess the power he yielded by looking at him, thin and elderly in a soft plaid suit. The kind of man you'd expect to see sitting next to you at Sunday morning mass. Hair combed neatly to the side, every stand in its place. But this mild-mannered magic man had a habit. Not a bad habit, per se, but a habit nonetheless, of which Sebastian was fully knowledgeable.

Deep within the shadows of the wooden structure, behind the pamphlets and tickets for the show, was a small receptacle filled with toothpicks. The toothpicks were small, but they were wood, and wood was what Talia needed. Like a snake strike, Sebastian snatched the cup from the podium and spun toward the women. "Will these do?"

Both women turned on him with a sense of surprise that caught him off guard. He shouldn't have been able to sneak up on a witch and a dragon so easily. But then, Kyra was much more human than dragon at the moment, and Talia was preoccupied with her task. His gaze met Kyra's. She pulled at the back of her dress, twisting her body to hide her exposed skin.

Talia moved to take the cup from Sebastian's hand, and he met her halfway. Plucking the cup of toothpicks from his grip, Talia fished through the wooden sticks with her finger. "I might be able to make these work," she said. "Thanks."

"Great," Sebastian glanced behind him, out the tent entrance, "but I suggest you take this operation somewhere else. I don't know how long it will be before Marcus is back on my tail." Without forethought, Sebastian turned and extended his hand to Kyra. "I'm sorry you felt the need to hide. Things will get better. I promise."

Talia shook her head, a scowl turning her usual pleasant smile upside down, but Sebastian wasn't interested in her disapproval. It was Kyra who had his attention. Kyra and her bristling response to his outreach.

"You must be confused. I'm not..." She stood, pushing her chair to the side, then paused and stared him straight in the eye, her report wavering, something resembling resolve settling over her. "How did you know?"

"I'll always recognize you, no matter what form you choose to take." He spoke without reservation, his heart warming to the blossoming truth in his words.

Kyra inhaled and blinked. "But you walked away. Said we had no future." Hurt radiated from her eyes like the scorching flames of the sun.

He'd rather take the dragon dagger to the heart than hurt her, but it was true, he'd said those things. He'd seen no other option, and pushing her away had been meant to spare her heart in the end. Stubborn girl that she was, she wasn't having it. And now, Sebastian could see her feelings ran deeper than he could have hoped.

Heat flushed through his system and he averted his gaze, stared at the bottom hem of Kyra's dress, to the flares of silk and satin. He took a deep, settling breath and met her accusing glare. "It's true. I did."

"Then what are you doing here?" Kyra notched her fists on her hips. "You kiss me, you save me, and then you push me away. Could your signals be any more confusing?"

Again, he dropped his head. It was shame he was trying to hide, but in so doing he spied the tooth pendant on the chair beside them beginning to vibrate, to slide toward the tent entrance at a crawl. Sebastian snatched it, held it tight within his grasp. "You'd better go." He glanced past Kyra and met Talia's stare.

"What about you?" Talia said, taking a step forward.

"We have more to discuss," Kyra said, anger creeping into her voice. "I'm not finished with you yet."

Sebastian smirked. "I know. Later. Right now, you need to get. And I need to make everything right. Go out the back." He pointed toward the rear of the tent. "I'll distract Marcus long enough for you to get your facade back in place."

Kyra flinched, and her brows arched. "Is it slipping?"

"Your dress." Sebastian's gaze wandered over Kyra's flowing attire, pausing at the reveal of the open back.

Talia reached between them, and Sebastian shook the building emotions of the moment away. “What are you going to do with that?” Talia pointed to Sebastian’s fist curled around the dragon’s tooth pendant.

“I have a plan.”

“You better know what you’re doing.” Talia grabbed Kyra by the arm and pulled her toward the back exit.

“Do I ever?” Sebastian grumbled, shifting his gaze from the vibrating tooth in his palm to Kyra.

Kyra had stopped and fought against Talia’s tug. “I don’t like this,” she said.

The tooth in Sebastian’s hand pushed against his skin, fighting to escape. He approached her. “You don’t have to. You merely need to have faith.” He grabbed her hand and kissed it. “Now go! I need you to be safe,” Sebastian boomed, jabbing his finger toward her exit.

Kyra’s face reddened. She spun around and jogged out of sight.

“Be safe,” Talia said, following Kyra out the back.

Sebastian took a deep breath and steeled his strength in the exhale. Watching the only future he’d ever wanted disappear through canvas drapes shredded his insides like a were-cat’s scratching post. “Safe. Sure,” Sebastian said under his breath and moved to the tent siding, lifting it enough to duck underneath.

A roar came from near the tent’s main entrance. The howl was followed by the crash of the Talker’s podium being knocked sideways.

“Where are you, little carnie boy?” Marcus’s voice blasted through the tent. “Not trying to slip away, are you?”

Sebastian grimaced. “Let the fun begin,” he mumbled and dashed from the tent, letting the canvas siding fall closed behind him.

Behind him, the sound of Marcus’ snarl.

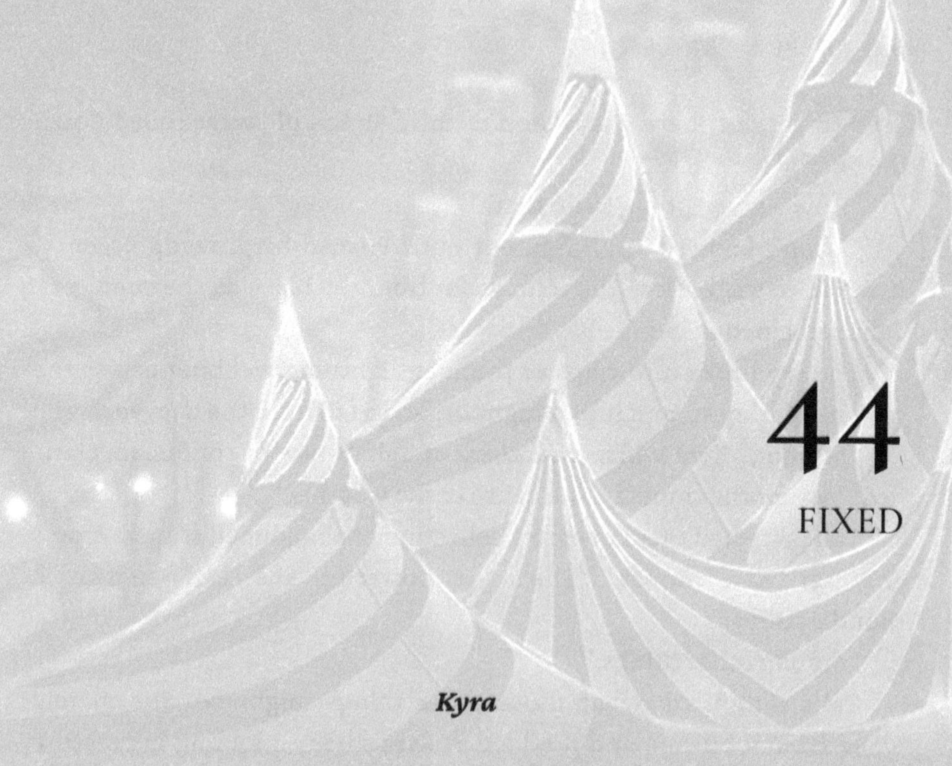

44

FIXED

Kyra

"Blazing dragons!" Kyra leaped backward, smacking into Talia. Together, they tumbled to the ground. A ball of fire exploded into the top side of the tent before them, missing Kyra and Talia by a strongman's throw of the lead weight. Black and white stripes, flapping red pennants, burst into flames. Screams erupted from within, adding to the singing chorus of the midway.

While they had been immersed in business within canvased walls, short amount of time as it may have been, the carnival's climate had fallen from tense to pandemonium. At a far distance to the west and northeast, smoke rose in angry plumes of taupe and slate.

Fire and smoke and beastly roars.

Dragons. Dragons fighting dragons. Water Clan and Fire Clan warriors fighting Marcus's traitorous dogs. Some dragons, some others: zilants. She wondered if her father or Drakhögg had taken to the fight in the sky. Or even her sister.

Kyra's heart pounded against her ribcage and she pushed herself off the ground. "Come on," she beckoned to Talia. "Let's get this done. I need to get out there. Put a stop to this." Beads of sweat rolled down the back of her neck.

"How are you going to do that?"

"I don't know, but I'll figure it out." Pushed by growing urgency, Kyra ran to the back of the tent, as far from the blaze as she could get. Talia remained at her heels.

The sky broke into claps of thunder, lightning webbing across the growing darkness, and liquid night began to fall from the heavens.

"Mother," Kyra whispered, then, at Talia's face of confusion, clarified. "My mother must be the cause of the weather."

Talia directed them over to a collection of abandoned storage crates and sat Kyra down. "She's so powerful she can control a thunderstorm?"

"Among other things."

Talia didn't ask what those other things might be. She merely wheezed and pushed and prodded at Kyra's body, molding her stature like one would a clay doll. "Don't move, or I might seal you up wrong."

The rain fell fast and hard, quenching the thirst of the fire in seconds. When flames no longer stormed, the tempest dissipated as fast as it had begun, the moon once again gliding free from gloomy cover.

Curious as the anomaly was, nothing about it surprised Kyra. Maybe it was her mother helping, or maybe she was simply showing off. Didn't matter. Kyra hadn't witnessed anything she wasn't already familiar with, and this time her, mother's ability had served a great purpose in helping to protect and preserve Mystic's. Yet despite her knowledge, her lack of awe, Kyra still ogled the sky. She found Talia doing the same.

Talia's head snapped back down, and she locked a stare on Kyra. "I thought I told you not to move?"

A scowl wrinkling her lips, Kyra returned to her former position. "I won't, if it will get us done and out there quicker."

"I know, you want to stop the dragons. You always have to rush in, try to be the hero. Have you ever noticed you kinda suck at that?" Talia snapped something at Kyra's back, and she flinched. "Aren't you the least bit worried about your own dragon?"

What kind of *dragonass* question was that? A thought flashed through Kyra's mind and she realized she wasn't feeling an outburst coming. Only a few months ago, she would have wanted to turn around and deck Talia for question stupidity. Now—now, she only wanted to move forward.

"Of course, I care about Kalrapura, but I know that she couldn't be safer than where she is right now. She's going to be fine."

"All fixed," Talia said from behind her. Dropping the toothpicks to the ground, she began the task of fastening the many buttons up the back of Kyra's dress.

"Great!" Kyra leaped off the wooden crate, an aura of zeal radiating from her soul and seeping into her motions.

Talia lurched forward, snagged the fabric on Kyra's sleeve. "Where are you going?"

"First?" Kyra studied Talia with a wide-eyed intensity. Talia waited, blinking back in response. "Back to Sebastian. He loves me. He may not know it, but he needs me. We need each other." She turned and ran around the corner.

45
SPLINTERS

Sebastian

The curtain was falling on Mystic's Carnival, or so it would appear to anyone standing in Sebastian's position. Structures collapsing beneath beasts or magic fire, flames whisking into the sky, leaping from tent to tent, and swirling black holes opening and closing throughout the midway, sucking men, women, and monsters into oblivion. Valentina was working her vortex power to the maximum, and the battle was a horrific exhibition of supernatural talent at its worst.

Warlocks, werewolves, species of all types took up the cause to protect their favorite meeting ground and sentient friend, Mystic's. The sky cracked with a resounding boom, exploding with electricity, sending wind and rain from the heavens, quelling the furor, if only temporarily.

Unfazed by elemental conditions, Reapers continued to glide among the mob unnoticed, collecting soul after soul.

Sebastian locked his jaw and narrowed a tight stare on his father. He had to stop him. Somehow revoke the Grim's work orders. This was his home. He couldn't allow it, allow her to be showered in death and tragedy. He had to protect Mystic's and put an end to all the bloody violence. But how?

Blades of crystallized ice grazed past him, frigid air sweeping through on the Reapers' wake. Memories and emotions trembled through him, and he thought of Death's whisper, fierce and frosty and fatal. Sebastian jerked and swerved out of the icy path, dropping to the ground for safety. A behemoth lay beside him, an impressive ice crystal having pinned the beast to the terrain. Rising like an iron post from where its face used to be, the ice misted and fizzed, mingling its cold with the hot, bubbling blood. Sebastian looked away—right at a jumble of feet coming his way, seconds from tripping into him.

A body fell over his back, groaning when it hit the ground. Sebastian was pushed into the sawdust of the midway, its smell of a thousand dirty trampled shoes, stale food scraps, and so many other things he didn't want to think about scratching at his nose. A swoosh and thrust followed.

"Look at that."

Sebastian twisted beneath the body to see Drakhögg's smirk beaming down at him. The warrior pulled a bloody blade free from the body draped over the top of Sebastian.

"What?" Sebastian said and shifted beneath the dead weight, pushing it away.

"Didn't think you had it in you." Drakhögg stared down at Sebastian a moment too long before offering him a hand. Drakhögg's stare was more of a glare and warned Sebastian to remain ever vigilant. A smile splintered Drakhögg's tight lips. "Tripping the bastard I was fighting before he could get away, that was quick thinking. I never expected a pretty boy like you to get his hands dirty." Their hands clasped, and Drakhögg dragged Sebastian to his feet.

Pretty boy was a curious term. One Sebastian believed did not apply to himself. Sure, he was not an overgrown, conceited oaf, rippling with bulging muscles all over his physique, but did his size qualify him as something worth mocking? He was still taller than Kyra.

He met Drakhögg's even glare and, without waver, reached into his pocket, felt the deck of cards slide between his fingers. Their energy warmed to his touch.

Without warning, the ground beneath him disappeared. Sebastian's feet swung out from under him and his hands—cards forgotten—flew to Drakhögg's tight hold at his neck, pulling and prying to free himself.

Drakhögg only squeezed tighter. "Pretty boy," he said again, hard lines pressing into his forehead. "That's why Kyra's drawn to you, isn't it?"

Sebastian couldn't answer. His vocal chords were pinched closed, his larynx crushing like an old soda can. But if he could speak, he'd give Drakhögg an earful. Then again, he'd probably just walk away before he ended up killing the guy.

"In the end," Drakhögg said, "she can't have you. She needs me."

Sebastian tried to shake his head, refute Drakhögg's ridiculous remark, but his restricted movements turned his shake into more of a bobble than a stand against Drakhögg. Someday, hopefully soon, the large and irritating warrior dragon would understand that Kyra didn't need another overprotective, overbearing man in her life. Someday all the clans would know that Kyra didn't truly need any of them.

Everything she needs she will find within herself.

Sebastian hadn't realized how true those words were until he thought them, and now he burned with the burden of such truth. Burned with a purpose and need to make her see that truth, too. Within his belly the dragon twisted, not in upset or disapproval, but in delightful understanding and impatience.

"Are you trying to burn yourself free?" Drakhögg growled in Sebastian's face.

Sebastian wrinkled his nose and blinked. It was true, his hands were in flames, although not by choice. Kyra had had her whole life to learn how to control the urges. They came to her naturally. Not for him. Not at all. And today was only his first day.

A screech accompanied by the humming of thick wings blasted from above. The sound grew closer, like a battle cry at the run. Drakhögg examined the sky, dropped Sebastian, and turned to block the zilant descending upon them. Even Sebastian could see it was too late, the zilant was too close, and soon the massive flying snake would be munching on dragon Drakhögg meat.

"OoRah!" came a warrior's cry. Leaping into frame, a dragon force wrapped in reds and coppers and hair pulled tight at the back, slammed into the zilant, pounding it with a face full of fist and knocking it off course. A pitiful pitch escaped as it flapped and lurched, attempting to return to the sky, but it found silence after one swift kick from the dragon girl's boot. "Must I always save your sorry ass, Drakhögg?"

"Thought you liked my ass?" Drakhögg retorted.

Rubbing her battered knuckles, the girl swaggered closer, a carefree pretense about her. "It's all right, when the picking is slim." She gazed at his butt and smirked. Drakhögg laughed.

Sebastian failed to share their humor. "The fight," he said and scrabbled to his feet.

"It's not going anywhere." Drakhögg grabbed the girl and pulled her to his side, slapped her on the backside, then pointed to Sebastian. "Have you met your sister's latest distraction?"

Sister—the word echoed in Sebastian's battered head. He couldn't tell if it was surprise, frustration, or anger inching through his blood—a sense of betrayal at Kyra's lack of disclosure. But she owed him nothing. He hadn't exactly been forthcoming on the topic of family...or anything else.

The girl's eye twitched, her steady gaze narrowed. "I don't know what Kyra sees." She peered up into Drakhögg's face. "But if it keeps her away from Mobürn, I'll endorse the infatuation." Her hip popped to the side. "I'll endorse anything that keeps her out of our business." Her glare appeared to be examining Sebastian, scrutinizing everything about him. "Your species is unfamiliar to me. What are you?"

"Nothing you need worry about." Chelsea, in her once-fluffy white robe, now dingy, blood-splattered, and torn, jumped between Sebastian and the two dragon shifters. Her hair a mess of tangles and knots and her voice a gravely growl, she stood in a protective stance with her back to Sebastian. Drakhögg and Kyra's sister took a step back.

"What the..." Drakhögg mumbled.

"I got this," Sebastian said, taking Chelsea's shoulder and spinning her around. Her face, usually a soft sight of delicate features, was momentarily a mask of darkness, her eyes pits into a forever void of nothingness, and then she was sweet, pretty Chelsea again. Sebastian's chest clenched, and his gut twisted. He turned to Drakhögg. "Can you temporarily forget whatever your beef is with me and do what you can to end this turmoil?"

"I'm out." Kyra's half sister disappeared in a flash of red. Drakhögg hesitated, his steps wavering between retreat and advance, his eyes sparking with a desire to strangle Sebastian. With a blink and a shake of his head, Drakhögg left.

Supervision of the dragon warriors gone, Sebastian gave his full attention to Chelsea, blocking out the world beyond, turning everything into a fuzzy array of colors and noise. Her smile, filled with sadness and remorse, was almost convincing of a genuine human girl's. Only, he knew better now, and he knew what had to be done.

He glanced away, taking in the war all around them. He hadn't realized until this moment, when he'd reached out to understand Chelsea, that he was no longer being inundated by everyone's thoughts and emotions. When had he learned to control the Mara side of himself? Didn't matter. Not right now, anyway.

Gazing deep into Chelsea's eyes, he cupped her face and sighed. "You're so tired, and you've been fighting so long."

Chelsea closed her eyes, a lone tear streaking down her left cheek, and lowered her head.

"You're ready." With the gentle compassion only possible through pure understanding and devotion to the cycle of life, Sebastian lowered them both to their knees. "Don't be afraid."

"I'm not," she sobbed, another tear running down her cheek. Her words were lies, but Sebastian admired her bravery in spite of fear. "I'm thankful to have you here with me in the end."

Soft and tender, he placed a kiss on her forehead, pulled a card from his deck, and pressed it between her palm and his, holding it there, firm.

She stared down at their hands for countless seconds and then her gaze found his face, once again. “Thank you.” Her body, ripe with cancer, collapsed into his arms, her spirit having fled in a flash. Laying her out on the dank ground, he gently wiped the blood from her nose and waited. Moments passed, possibly minutes, and there was nothing. Not a breath, a flutter of an eyelash, nothing.

The banshee wailed. And Chelsea screamed. She was dead.

“Sebastian!” The call had come from the crowd to his left.

Against all his better judgment, something compelled him to stand and turn to the sound. He needed to stay steady, confront the demon who had destroyed Chelsea. But...the voice.

Kyra and Talia were running toward him through the haze. His heart fluttered.

“Got you.” From behind him, Marcus breathed down his neck.

Pain shredded Sebastian’s insides, erupting into dragon fire across his every nerve and cell. He looked down, watched the dagger retreat from his chest.

His mind reeled. *Kyra*. Her name slipped from his lips.

He collapsed to his knees, all his good intentions for her shattered. The sounds of her screams were faint, drowned out by the thrumming, and he could no longer distinguish her form amongst the blur of color clouding his vision. Desire, need, ability—everything was draining from his body and soul. He dropped to the sawdust ground. Above him, the exploding sky was dimming. Tarot cards were everywhere, floating down upon him like falling stars.

Marcus kicked him in the ribs.

46
DRAGONS

Kyra

Kyra's heart had slammed to a full stop. Her lungs burst with protest, her screams all enveloping. Marcus had plunged a dagger through Sebastian's chest. The very dagger she'd taken from Sebastian. The one she'd hidden in his trailer. That wasn't the way things were supposed to happen.

Her world would be over without Sebastian. He couldn't die. Wasn't allowed to die.

He now lay on the ground, unmoving. Kyra's feet dragged through the dirt with monstrous effort. Talia grabbed her arm, gave her a needed tug, and Kyra's stagger picked up momentum.

Marcus tossed what looked like cards at Sebastian's broken body and followed up with a hard kick to Sebastian's ribs. Kyra's soul cried out. If only her dragon-self was intact. She'd tear Marcus into unrecognizable pieces.

Like a thundering fire ball, her family was upon the monster of a man, removing the need for her involvement. Bolsvck slammed Marcus in the chest sending the two tumbled into a brawl amidst the mayhem of fighters. Marcus burst into dragon form, and Bolsvck followed. Rushing to Bolsvck's aid, Drakhögg and her half sister, Keahi. On the other side, Kyra recognized Marcus's lackey, Toby, stepping in. They now fought several yards away, their combat constantly taking them farther and farther from where she needed to be, at Sebastian's side.

Dropping beside him, Kyra positioned herself as a barrier between Sebastian and the battle. She would serve as a wall of calm, a fortress from the chaos or further injury. Her hands hovered over his battered body, his bloodied shirt and vest, afraid her touch would cause him pain. His breath was shallow, barely more than a wheeze, and his black eyes stared up at the night sky.

"I'm sorry," he said, the sound of a gurgle in his throat.

"No, no, no. Don't be sorry. You have nothing to be sorry about." She cupped his hand in hers, kissed it.

"I failed you. Kalrap..."

"Shh." She silenced him. Kissed him. Laid her cheek against his. *This isn't happening. It can't be happening.* Closing her eyes, she breathed slow and deep, taking in the scent of him. The scent was death. Her eyes popped open, and she sat up with a jolt. "Fix him, please!" she called to Talia.

Talia stood behind her, placed her hand on Kyra's shoulder. "This is beyond me. I'm sorry."

"No!" Kyra yelled and brushed her hand along Sebastian's cheek. Fidgeting, she fixed his jacket, pulling it closed across his wound. She brushed her palms along his chest, along his arms, through his hair, lowered her lips to his, and kissed him ever so softly. "I love you," she whispered. She thought she saw a glimmer in his eye, as slight as it may have been, but whatever it was, it was gone.

"Kyra." His voice croaked. She pressed against him, snuggled close to hear his words. "Don't let them decide for you." He raised his hand, his arms moving as a weak and feeble man would move. He pressed his palm to her heart. "You know." His arm dropped, and his eyes closed.

"Sebastian," she called, her hands pressing to his arms, his shoulders, his face.

No sound, no movement came. She pressed her face to his, kissed him again. Nothing.

"No, Sebastian. No," she screamed.

The flood gates blew open, and tears streamed down her face. She cried like she'd never cried before. Like her soul was being torn away from within. Like all of creation depended on how quickly she could cover the world in tears. She cried and cried, and cried some more. Her tears fell for all the troubles they'd had, for his brilliant potential lost, but mostly, they fell for all the days they would never have. She wrapped her arms around him and hugged him to her, as if willing her life to him.

Kyra had no idea how much time had passed. Time had slowed to an incomprehensibly heavy rate.

A soft touch ran gently across her back. "I..." Talia stumbled for words. "I don't know what to say."

"What is there to say?" Kyra stood, a surge of heat flushing through her blood. She turned her back on Talia before the girl could answer and stormed toward the dragons fighting in the midway.

Bolsvck, Drakhögg, and Keahi were easily recognizable. The beast they battled, on the other hand, Kyra wasn't sure could be considered a dragon. The magic Marcus had employed had morphed him into something else, something Kyra had no words for. He tossed Drakhögg and Keahi around like chew toys. Only Bolsvck provided any kind of challenge. She wondered how her Moorigad would have fared. Would Kalrapura be tossed aside as easily as Drakhögg and Keahi? Toby was laid out on the ground, a bloody mess. Kyra had missed whatever caused his demise.

None of them had been paying any attention to her. Too caught up in their fight and completely unaware of who she was behind the disguise. The surrounding area provided nothing worthy of throwing at a dragon. Nothing she could lift, other than empty popcorn containers. Small things like those wouldn't warrant a glance. If she could lift and toss a body, now *that* might provide a chance of gaining Marcus's attention. There were several bodies to choose from. But since she was trapped with the strength of a mortal, such a choice wasn't really an option.

Fire raged in her soul, and it cried for vengeance. The longer she stared at the battling beasts, the more she wanted to destroy all them. If her father hadn't come to the carnival, none of them would have come, and Sebastian would still be alive.

Her father was trying to talk to Marcus, only he called him Balidhug. Like the guy at the club that first night. Bolsvck spoke of family and deception, things Kyra no longer cared about, so she tried not to listen. But she couldn't help but hear Marcus was blood, an uncle, torn from the family through the treachery of a faction led by Jon Davies. *Lies. All lies.*

Talia screamed. Another scream, horrific and perching, followed. Kyra spun around and came face to face with a bewitching woman with flowing midnight hair that swung in the breeze and eyes that could lead a man to his doom. She stood beside Chelsea's body and stared down at Sebastian.

"She just..." Talia stammered. "She just..." Pointed her finger at the woman.

"Rose like a spirit from the dead?" the woman said, with a wild spark in her eyes.

Talia nodded numbly.

The woman flashed a small but wicked smile and stared at Kyra. "Who did this?" Her voice was stern, harsh, and packed with anger. Her hand flicked to the side, indicating Sebastian.

Sharp pains splintered along Kyra's jawbone. She hadn't realized she'd been clenching her teeth so tight. Without a moment's hesitation, she pointed to Marcus.

The woman's face frosted over, her lips freezing in a sharp, straight line. "Then he, too, shall die."

Fury and fire, malice and ice, whatever Kyra had expected, was not what came to be. The woman moved past Kyra and approached the dragons with a soft-manner. One that made her appear as if she floated above the ground rather than walked. Her stature was solid, no trembling or pause. No visible show of fear. When she was within a tail swipe of Marcus, she dropped her cloak and spoke. “My lord, you have failed me for the last time.”

“Come on, we’d better go.” Talia was suddenly at Kyra’s side, yanking at her, trying to pull her away from the scene, but Kyra planted her feet firmly into the ground. “You don’t want to get involved in this.”

“Oh,” Kyra glanced at Talia, her brows arched, “I think I might.” She glanced back at Sebastian and choked back a sob. She couldn’t believe this was happening. Not after everything they’d been through.

All the dragons had stopped fighting and they stared at the woman’s bared beauty. Only, it wasn’t a normal, naked-woman-standing-in-the-midway kind of ogle, if there were such a thing. There was something much more sinister and magical in the way everyone was transfixed, and it set Kyra’s insides into a frenzy.

“What is she doing?” Kyra turned her pain from Sebastian to the woman and concentrated. “Why aren’t we affected?”

“Because she has her back to us. Let’s keep it that way.” Talia gave another tug. Kyra shoved her off, moved closer.

All of the dragons began to howl. They lashed out or flopped on the ground, they withered and clawed at the ground. They were in pain. That bewitching whore wasn’t only destroying Marcus, she was torturing Kyra’s family. Maybe killing them.

Before she realized what she was doing, Kyra was free of Talia and running at the whore’s back. She may not have the power of a dragon, but that didn’t mean she couldn’t tackle someone with whatever strength she did have. Kyra braced her arm out in front and slammed into the woman, square in the back. The momentum carried the two women into a drop and slide, Kyra with the advantage. She slammed her knee into the woman’s back and pressed her spread palm over the woman’s head, holding her face in the dirt of the midway.

Kyra sighed heavily and peered up to find Marcus’s beastly glare upon her. He had recovered. She had only seconds before he would kill her, or so she suspected. An even temper had never been his strong point. The other dragons would save her, maybe. She didn’t have the time to assess their situation.

"I thought you would've gotten smarter after the convergence," she yelled. "All those dragons in one should have increased your brain's ability, not diminished it."

The other dragons were beginning to shake themselves back to something that resembled normal. What had the bewitching whore done to them?

Marcus growled through his teeth, sending spittle like cannon fire at Kyra. She turned her head away. "Who are you? Why do you risk such impetuousness?"

"You see that?" She pointed to Sebastian, glimpsed at his still body lying on the ground and wiped a tear from her eye. "That," she pointed again and sniffled, "was stupid. Dumb. Reckless. Completely senseless." She tuned all her mortal fury into her words and glared at Marcus. "Or whatever other label you want to put on it. Killing Sebastian was monstrously moronic!"

Marcus roared with laughter, setting Kyra's skin to tingle. Oh, how she wanted to knock him into the netherworld. But she couldn't, not physically. Instead, she stood her ground before him, standing tall, clenching and unclenching her fists.

The woman at her feet hissed and swirled into a stance beside Kyra, snarling at her. "Don't you ever—"

"Shut it, Leila. I'll deal with you in a minute," Marcus said and turned his burning dragon eyes back on Kyra. Leila hissed but made no further moves.

Marcus showed no signs of recognition. Her guise appeared to still be in place and she would use that to her advantage. Kyra took a deep breath, let it sink down to her soul. She attempted to find calm, but there was no calm to be found in this situation. Sebastian was gone. "You want the Moorigad, am I right?" She locked a stare with Marcus. He didn't move, not a twitch.

"Who are you, girl?" His breath rolled over her, a wave or rancid meat and sweat.

She could play his game. Not twitch. So, she did. She stood perfectly still and held the glare between them. "You just *killed* the Moorigad."

Marcus jerked. Kyra would have smiled at the win if the circumstances weren't so beyond heartbreaking. Her father was already morphing into human form, moving toward the body, without realizing he was moving directly past his own daughter.

Kyra swallowed and continued. "Sebastian, not Kyra, was in possession of the dragon." She paused, took another deep breath, and then locked a steely stare on the murderous dragon. She poured every ounce of venom she could muster into her next words. "The *Moorigad* dragon."

Marcus tossed his head in the air, swinging it from side to side, and roared with the sound of a dying zilant. One flap of his massive wings, and he took to the sky and soared overhead, in Sebastian's direction.

Kyra fumbled, her heart flip-flopping in her chest. "No!" she screamed and took off toward Sebastian at a stumble-run. She was too slow. Even her father could do nothing against the mammoth beast. Marcus swooped in, collected Sebastian with his mighty claws, and flew away. Away with Sebastian.

Kyra fell to her knees, dropped her face in her palms, and let the floodgate open on a river of tears once again.

47
REAPED

Sebastian

A jolt, and Sebastian was pulled from the haze back to an agonizing reality. It had been so peaceful in the inky clouds of slumber. Had he been dead? Now, pain swam through his body like an electrical storm on holiday at a water park. But more painful than his physical state, was the knowledge that he had failed Kyra.

Or had he?

He was slipping away, but he wasn't yet dead. His body wrenched and wriggled in the clamp of a gigantic beast, and wind moved past at incredible speeds, sending his skin into shivers. The desire to close his eyes, sleep for an eternity, overwhelmingly strong. He struggled against the want, laid his hands upon the claws, and allowed the beast's emotions to seep through.

Swift, in a rush of heated lava, the rage leaped from the dragon and raced through Sebastian's nervous system. In that instant he knew—Marcus had him in his grasp. If Sebastian could muster the strength, he'd be able to scratch two things off his list before saying his final adieu: reap Marcus and return Kyra's dragon.

Sebastian struggled within Marcus's firm clench to find his pocket. His desire to succeed pushing against his desire to sleep. He thrust through. A tight fit, but manageable he'd force it to be. The deck of tarot cards brushed against his fingers. His first instinct—grab a card—but he had to be smart with his choices or neither task would be completed. Grazing past the cards, his fingers groped for the trinket, the bibelot, the item he'd stuffed in his pocket a short while ago. The bibelot was unwilling to budge. He wiggled it back and forth and back and forth and then rested.

So, so tired.

The carnival spread out below, a hodgepodge of buildings and tents. No lights illuminated the shows. Instead, fireworks exploded through the Magician's canon fire or the dragons' flames. Smoke plumed, and despair rained. Dragon-Marcus swept through the sky at breakneck speed, and they were already nearing the entrance. Soon they'd be over the lake, headed toward the tree line beyond. Time was winding down.

Everything muscle and bone wailed, begging for Sebastian to stop trying. He wouldn't, he *couldn't*. Be it out of luck or sheer will, he managed to yank the bibelot free of his pocket. It slid between his sweaty fingers, and he quickly pulled it to his chest before it could get lost to the sky. Marcus's mighty dragon stirred in his hold but kept flying.

Questions reeled in Sebastian's mind. Had they traveled too far from Kyra for the magic to work? Would Kalrapura latch on to the nearest dragon—Marcus? Did he possess enough strength to finish the task? The questions were endless. Time was not.

Sebastian had to put his faith in destiny and let everything else go. The design was straightforward, and Sebastian had zero doubt which end of the funnel blade went which direction. His hands wrapped around the carved handle of the funnel, felt the dragon designs press into his skin and, using all the might he'd managed to gather, plunged the pointed end into the gaping dagger wound in his chest.

Sebastian screamed. It was a scream worthy of a thousand bloody deaths. Torment convulsed through his soul, the essence of his being. Was the magic working? He had no idea. At the moment, he wasn't sure he cared. All he wished for now was a swift death.

The tingling began with a minute spark in his core and spread with a flash, consuming every ounce of his interior. He was turning to ash.

Marcus's hold shook, and Sebastian shifted, gazed down at the lake below. The beast's mighty claws began to squirm, loosen then tighten, then started jostling him back and forth. Left claw to right claw to left claw again. Something was happening to Sebastian, he knew that much. If heat equaled flames, then his body would be engulfed in fire. He prayed it was the magic at work, hoped Kalrapura was being released. Maybe, just maybe, Marcus felt the effects, too.

Task one, completed. Time for task two.

A mighty roar bellowed through the airwaves. Bolsvck was chasing down Marcus. The mighty king was practically close enough to chomp down on Marcus' tail.

Sebastian tried to smile but failed. He lay limp, bouncing up and down, watching the water below swish this way and that. Bile rose up his throat and his head spun. He was so hot—how was his body not consumed by flames?

He'd never thought he'd feel the way he did, but he was ready to die. With considerable concentration, he slid a card from the magical tarot deck in his pocket. The particular deck that always pulled the right card for his calling. Feebly, he reached up and tapped the dragon's claw with the card, tried to press it firmly in place.

The instant the edge of the card brushed against the beast, Marcus shivered, and his stomach gurgled. He let out a beastly howl and released Sebastian. It was liberating, and organ-drop frightening.

He was falling, card still in hand. He dropped with the speed of a rocket, headed for the water of the lake below. He crumpled Death in his palm and held it to his chest, caught sight of Marcus and Bolsvck diving after him. And then, with the whack of cement-hard water, lost sight of them. Sebastian was enveloped by the glacial tide.

48

ZEKE

Kyra

Crying wouldn't better her situation. It wouldn't bring Sebastian back. And yet, Kyra remained on her knees, rubbing her hands through the dirt and allowing the tears to stream down her face.

"Kyra!" Talia's call was insistent, urgent, and yet Kyra didn't want to look up, didn't want to face a soul. Not until she could pull herself together. Talia called her name again. This time she sounded far away, and this time, Kyra's fingers began to tingle.

She raised her head and saw the lights of the carnival blinking an erratic, pathetic flicker. The massive Ferris wheel had begun to spin again. And dangerous fingers of electricity shot from and between tents and rides and game booths. Pedestrians, carnies, dragons, and foes were vanishing like popped bubbles. The chaos turned to quiet. Talia was now gone. Her father was gone. They were all gone, and Kyra stood among the few left in the dusty midway. *Where did everyone go?*

With a kick, Vortex Girl sent a zilant away from the carnival via a black hole. Wiping a tear from her cheek, Kyra stood and turned in a circle, searching for signs of life. A metallic smell lifted off the ground and swirled around her. Tiny sparks of light ignited like fireflies, exploding all around her, fingers of electricity reached for her, and she found she was no longer standing in the midway between the many exposition tents. She stood outside the front gate, near the exit portal, now closed. *Vortex Girl didn't do that.* Kyra sniffed back her tears and straightened her shoulders. The lake spread out under a moving mist to her right, and above, in the sky, her father flew after Marcus, both of them in dragon form.

Her heart stilled at the sight of the body in Marcus's clutches.

Someone behind her groaned, and she turned to find Zeke sitting on the ground, rubbing his head. She dropped beside him. "What happened? Are you all right?"

"I'll be fine, child. Should have seen that coming." He groped at the ground for his cane.

"Seen what coming?" Kyra asked, pulling his cane to his grasp and helping him stand.

"Why, Marcus, of course." Zeke sniffed, twitching his nose from side to side. "How long was I out?"

"I don't know. I just found you." She guided him toward his usual seat, the red bench by the lake, her gaze continuously darting between him and the dragons flying in the sky.

"Of course, you did." He took a seat and peered up as if he could see her despite his blind eyes. "How long was Mystic's dark?"

Kyra's body jerked straight as a flagpole. "What does that have to do..." She stopped, realizing there was so much about Zeke and the carnival she had yet to understand. "I don't know. Thirty, forty minutes, maybe." She glanced again at the dragons. Marcus was flying strangely.

He nodded. "She should be working on the patches now."

"Patches?" Kyra asked.

Zeke tilted his head a smidge. "Mystic's has a way to go before reaching full restoration. For now, she's transporting people to the farthest corners of the park, out of harm's way. Separating foes from one another. Damage?" he asked, his face hinting he already knew the answer.

"Extensive, I think." She glanced again to the sky, and to Marcus. "Sebastian is dead," she said with a crack in her voice.

His hand found hers and squeezed gently, yet he did not appear surprised. This bothered her. The way Sebastian had acted, that bothered her, too. Even Talia, she'd known something and kept it from Kyra.

She pulled away from Zeke and stared at his cloudy white eyes. "Did you all know? Know he was going to die?" Her voice pitched, bordered on hysteria, but then something out of the corner of her eye drew her attention. Her head snapped up to the sky. Sebastian was falling!

Kyra inhaled an exasperated breath and bolted around the bench, heading for the lake. She had no idea what she was going to do, or if she could do anything, but she had to go. Something supernatural had happened. Clearly it had. The sky circled and swirled in the most brilliant array of tangerine, maroon, and indigo from the spot Sebastian fell. Maybe he wasn't dead yet, after all.

"Let it be, child," Zeke called after her.

She ignored him and kept running. The mist kept her from seeing Sebastian hit the water, but she heard it. The sound sent a wave of ice through her soul. If she'd had even an ounce of hope before that moment, how could she find any when his battered body was sinking to the bottom of the lake? She screamed senseless at the lake, at Marcus, at the situation.

The lake froze over.

Kyra wanted to drop to her knees and cry again, but she didn't. She stood strong. Watched her father dive to the surface of the frozen lake, right behind Marcus. In a thunderous crash worthy of a volcanic eruption, they collided with the ice in a mess of dragon limbs and wings.

They were far from reach—and Sebastian, he was trapped beneath the ice. She dropped and pressed her hands to the surface. It was impossible to tell where the ice ended and the water began. Or worst yet, if there was even an end to the ice. What if it simply went on and on and on...

No. Such a thought wasn't allowed in her head. She glanced back at Zeke, and although she suspected somewhere deep down inside he had the power to help, she didn't believe he would. Not this time. She scanned the shoreline, away from Zeke and toward the main gate, and saw her mother and Ryhuu.

She jumped to her feet and ran toward them as fast as her human legs could carry her. "Mom!" she screamed. "Please, Mom. Undo the ice!"

Queen Shui stared, took a step back, and allowed Ryhuu to take point and block her from Kyra's view. He drew his sword.

49
REAPER'S MARK

Kyra

"Step back," Ryhuu said. His muscles flexed, and he stood stiff and firm in defense of his queen.

Kyra froze, stopping mid step. In her panic, she had forgotten about the magic. Her own family didn't recognize her. At the time, it had been what she'd wanted, but now...now, she needed them to recognize her. Short of disrobing, how was she going to convince them of who she was? She no longer smelled like a dragon, nor could she transform into one. "It's me, Mother. Your daughter, Kyra," she pleaded, looking past Ryhuu and locking her gaze upon the queen.

"There is nothing of my daughter in you." Queen Shui turned away, implying Kyra was unworthy, but kept talking. "There is no time for such foolishness. What game are you playing, child?"

"This isn't a game!" Kyra's voice hitched. "I am your daughter."

"Enough." Queen Shui dismissed her with the wave of her hand. "Come, Ryhuu." She walked toward the ice and the dragons fighting on the frozen lake.

"No, please," Kyra pleaded.

Her mother glanced over her shoulder, her expression one of pure exasperation. But then she startled and spun around to face Kyra once more. Kyra blinked, hope blooming in her heart.

"Please, don't stop on our account," someone said.

Behind Kyra were twelve, maybe fifteen, Reapers approaching their position. Her heart sank, as did her hope for Sebastian. "We are not here for you, my queen," the tall Grim said, and his gaze flickered over Kyra and then beyond. "At least, not yet."

"That's not very comforting," Queen Shui responded. Ryhuu remained vigilant, ready to go samurai with his sword at a verbal snap.

The Grim Reaper said nothing, merely ran his gaze over Kyra again. She scratched her arm and fought the desire to scratch everywhere. Something about the man made her skin race with goose bumps. Even though this was the first time she'd come face to face with him, she was fairly sure she knew who he was. She'd had her suspicions since the first time she'd seen him on the bridge, the day she'd saved Marcus's life. A day that seemed forever ago.

Turning away from her mother, she focused her attention on Sebastian's father and the parade of Reapers he'd brought with him. "Can you save him?" she asked. "Save Sebastian?"

"It is not our place to save," he said. "At least, not in the manner in which you mean the word." Mortifier's face was void of any emotion, like a permanent state of death.

Kyra moved forward, desperation in her steps. Maybe if he saw how much she needed this, needed Sebastian, he would reconsider. "But you could if you wanted to, right?"

Queen Shui sighed, mumbled something about time-wasters, and walked toward the frozen lake again. Kyra let her go, all her hope now pinned on the Grim Reaper standing before her. He didn't appear to be much of an amenable type, but she wasn't one to give in easily.

"Mortifier, you rotting Death rep, you know you can and should." Stepping through the carnival's festive front gate, now fully lit and sparkling gleefully, slinked the dark-haired beauty Kyra had witnessed rise from Chelsea's corpse. "Mother told me all about you, before you helped her." She used air quotes around the word *help*.

The Grim's demeanor changed, however slight, with the woman's appearance. He no longer held a cold and removed manner. Kyra got the feeling he was uncomfortable, as if caught in a lie.

"You must be the child," he said, a mild rise to his brow.

"Was," she corrected. "The name's Leila, and I'm a fully-grown Mara now. Just like my mother. The woman you killed." She didn't yell or cry out, simply stated a fact.

Mortifier heaved a heavy sigh, and Kyra shifted uncomfortably in her place. She wanted—no, that wasn't right—*needed* his help, but awkward, she never had handled well.

What should I do?

Talia quietly moving toward them, around them, to Kyra's aid. Kyra's chest again warmed with hope. Then she understood the words and drew back to the conversation between Nightmare and Death. "The boy caused her slow demise."

What boy? Whose demise? The Mara's mother?

"Your mother was never meant to have a male child," the Grim said. "Allowing him to live meant her eventual end, she was fully aware of the circumstances. I couldn't allow her to kill him."

"I understand. And I used to be furious," Leila said. "But I'm not anymore. If it hadn't been for you, we never would have had Sebastian, and I do agree, he is a treasure." She stretched, smoothing her hands down the front of her gown. "Went through a lot of trouble for him, attempting to sabotage Marcus's plans."

Mortifier scoffed. "The boy is not for your meddling. Leave him alone."

"Too late," Leila said in a singsong voice. Mortifier's gaze narrowed. "I've been here a very long time, ever since you sent Sebastian on his first little Reaper mission. I've come and gone, but always in disguise, keeping watch over him. Had my claws in him fairly deep, I'd say. Until the damn human's body gave out," she grumbled. "I could have kept on with him indefinitely, if he hadn't taken pity on the stupid girl."

"Trust me, darling. If he hadn't done the deed, one of us would have been there to take care of the job."

Leila threw off his comment with a slight turn of her head. "He would have stopped you. If he didn't have the balls to do it, he wouldn't have let anyone else reap her soul."

Kyra's head spun with revelations. What was it they had said? Sebastian's mother was dead and the wicked woman who tried to kill Kyra's family was Sebastian's sister. Her chest clenched. "But he's dead!" she interjected. Both Mortifier and Leila turned and stared at her. "Dead!"

A thundering roar echoed through the sky, and the ground vibrated with one quick *thwack*. With everyone else turned to the sound, Kyra chanced a quick glance over her shoulder. What she saw had her breath trapped like a hairball wedged in her throat.

Her father was losing to Marcus, and her mother did nothing to help. Forever-loyal Ryhuu stood by her side while she appeared to play with the ice. No doubt, working the elements, but Kyra saw no rain and no thunder. It had to be the ice she was manipulating. The ice and the sky. Overhead, everything still swirled in an odd pattern of unusual colors.

"Who is this girl, and why do we bother with her?" Leila asked. Kyra glanced back, not wanting to miss a word.

"You do not recognize her?" Mortifier questioned.

Leila shook her head and studied Kyra more intently.

"Curious," he said with a tick of his lip.

Kyra had been so focused on everything going on around her, Marcus and her father fighting, her unsuccessful attempt to appeal to the Grim Reaper, that she'd failed to notice Talia's arrival at her side. It wasn't until Talia wrapped her hand in Kyra's that Kyra snapped to attention.

"What did I miss?" Talia whispered.

"Nothing, really. What happened? Where did you go?" Kyra's voice dwindled as the sound of heavy flapping came from their left.

"I don't know," Talia said. "I suddenly found myself at the back corner of the Big Top. I had to hike all the way back here."

Kyra turned, but she didn't see Talia. Not really. She looked past her, over her, and saw her own half sister, in dragon form, flying over the gaming booths. If Talia had been transported elsewhere in the carnival, like Zeke said, then maybe everyone was making their way back here, battle being an irresistible magnet.

Then, appearing out of nowhere, a zilant suddenly flew beside her, plowing into her side. Drakhögg, a mere dragon's tail-length behind, attacked from behind, and soon it was a beastly brawl in the sky. Two Reapers at the end of the line turned and walked without the slightest air of rush in the direction of the air brawl.

Kyra's hand flew to her chest. She didn't get along with her half sister, but that didn't mean she wanted to see her dead. Or Drakhögg, for that matter. "What. Why—" She stumbled for the words she wanted, weakly throwing her arms up to the commotion.

Mortifier smiled, a grimy and unsettling smile. "It is the way of things, my dear. Do not try to force change upon the nature of events. They happen as they must."

"What do you want to do?" Talia asked, gawking at the many Reapers.

Keahi, Drakhögg, her father, and Sebastian—all marks in a reaping juggling act. How many would drop? Her mind reeled between family and love, between the possible and the impossible. She turned and ran, a slow and staggered run, across the frozen lake. Her legs moved like wooden blocks with little to no agility, and her muscles seared with sharp, shattering pain.

"What are we doing?" Talia caught up and ran at her side.

"Help me," Kyra said between sharp intakes of breath, "finish breaking the magic of the dress." Her feet hit the ice and slid out from beneath her. She reached out, clung to Talia, and together, they volleyed for balance. Several feet out onto the frozen lake, they slid to a stop, still standing upright. "That was close." Kyra giggled nervously and yanked at her sleeve.

Talia frowned. "Magic of this magnitude will not be so easily broken. It will take more than a rip in the dress."

"Then what? Help me!" Kyra grabbed Talia's arms and squeezed.

"Okay. Let me think." She brushed Kyra's hold away and studied the dress. "The magic is likely coming from something woven into the dress. Or it's bound to the Magician himself. If that's the case, you're out of luck."

"How do we find out which it is?" Kyra was talking to air. Talia was already on her knees in the ice, yanking and pulling at Kyra's skirt.

"If it's woven or sewn to the dress, it's probably someplace you'd be less likely to be bothered by it." Talia threw up the skirt, and Kyra startled, catching folds of fabric in her arms. "My guess is it would be somewhere along the underside of the skirt or attached to the petticoat." She moved around Kyra, stretching at the dress's skirt.

Stuck in human form, Kyra couldn't hide the red flushing her checks, so she stared straight ahead and avoided eye contact with any dragons on the ice or any Reapers at the lake's edge. "What exactly are you looking for?"

Any answer was lost to the crash of collapsing poles and canvas. Kyra forgot her question and inspected the carnival. No longer were Keahi and Drakhögg in the sky, and a billow of grey smoke rose from the ground. Someone in or near the wreckage was screeching. In unison, the line of Reapers turned and marched toward the rising signal.

Kyra gawked at the billowing plume above the tents, her heart sinking like a stone in her chest. What had become of her sister...of Drakhögg?

Her body jerked sideways, pulled by a yank on her dress, and fabric ripped. Everything tingled. Had Talia found what she was looking for? Kyra's arms, back, torso—it all prickled with cold heat. And a shimmer ran over the dress. There for a split second, and then gone.

Talia popped up in front of her. "Deed done."

"I can see that," Kyra said. She held her hands out. They were shaking and turning blue.

"Oh." Talia grabbed Kyra's hands and started rubbing. "The magic keeping you warm obviously wore off, the dress must have camouflaged that." She bit her lip, and a narrow V-shape pressed into her brow. "You didn't feel it?"

Kyra shook her head.

"Well, dang. You're going to freeze to death out here."

“Mmmmmaybbbe,” Kyra stuttered. “Bbbut I have to make Mmmarcus see me. It’s the ooonly way to sssave my dad.”

“Right.” Talia’s eyes widened, and Kyra turned to see what she was looking at. The majority of the Reapers had abandoned their original destination.

They were now coming for her.

Kyra took a deep breath. “I don’t have a lot of time to do what needs to be done.” She turned her back on the Reapers and narrowed her sights on Marcus.

50
REVELATIONS

Marcus

Marcus slammed Bolsvck against the stone-hard ice. Ice. The lake had frozen. And had done so incredibly fast. How had that happened? He spat a mouthful of crushed ice to the ground and cleared his throat. Despite the slush that covered his body, his tumble with Bolsvck had made little to no dent in the frozen cover of the lake. A five-year winter's storm couldn't produce an ice layer as solid as concrete. Tremendous magic had to be at work.

Smoke blew from his nostrils, and his nails scratched at the frigid surface. And he'd been so close to having Sebastian in his grip. "Damn... irritating..." Marcus slammed his claw down, saw no effect. "Water Clan!" Another pound. Still nothing.

An "ahem" rose from Bolsvck. The old dragon clambered to his feet, raised his head high, and spread his wings wide. Bolsvck stood before Marcus, larger and severely more formidable than he remembered.

Marcus's lips pulled back in a quiver, displaying his ready-to-devour canines, and his claws splayed wide against the frozen ground. Marcus would have snapped Bolsvck's neck right there and then, only the elements swirling above caused him pause. He torqued his head and stared at the anomaly in the sky. Shades of red, orange, and blue whirled in a mysterious cyclone.

"Need we continue in this manner?" Bolsvck said, lowering his head.

Marcus returned his attention to his foe. The attempted show of truce was not lost on Marcus, but he wouldn't be fooled by such acts.

"Why shouldn't we?" countered Marcus. "You are my enemy. Always have been. Since the day your family destroyed mine."

Bolsvck narrowed his gaze and extended his long, scaled neck, but folded back his wings. "I had nothing to do with what happened to you. I told you this already." He paused and studied Marcus. "Have you lived with the deception for so long, you refuse to see the truth as it is?"

Marcus growled; a low, surly snarl. If Bolsvck was insinuating Marcus was stupid or an oblivious man, Bolsvck would eat those words. "I know plenty," Marcus snapped.

"I don't think you do."

Marcus refused to satisfy Bolsvck with a display of words. Things were fitting into place. It was clear Bolsvck didn't want to fight. He probably knew, as Marcus knew, the ruling Fire Dragon stood no chance at winning—or surviving. Marcus was bigger, stronger, more powerful. He lashed out, swinging his claw across Bolsvck's snout. The nails cut through Bolsvck's thick hide like razors, sent his head reeling to the side and blood splattering to the stark, white ground.

With a hiss and a huff, Bolsvck backed away. "Stop it, son!"

"I am not your son!" Marcus said, his words steeped in finality, and attacked again. They rolled and tossed in a fluctuating rhythm of shove, slash, and sting. Monstrous limbs thrashed out at each other and at the ground. Wings beat and battered.

"Listen to me, Balidhug! Your mother did not die." Bolsvck thrust Marcus away, and he dropped onto his back with a solid *creeeach*.

In a blink, Marcus had righted himself, shook the ice from his wings. "You lie. You killed them all. Incinerated the line. And banished me to grow up in the fires of Purgatory." He lunged at Bolsvck, chomped at his neck.

Throwing himself backwards, Bolsvck countered with his tail, slamming a solid hit at Marcus's side. "Neither my father nor I can ever atone for what happened to you." Claws clenched upon one another, and they rolled in a frost cloud of muscle and mayhem. "But we have tried."

They broke apart, dropped into a deadlock stare, moving foot by foot in a circle. "Stop talking," Marcus said in a raspy growl and bared his teeth. But Bolsvck kept on talking. The irritating scratch of the dragon's voice brought Marcus's blood to a boil.

"You need to understand," Bolsvck continued. "She was near death, but didn't die. Your mother lived for many long years after what happened."

"Lies. All lies," Marcus spat and swung his tail. Bolsvck took the hit, but kept staring Marcus down.

"My father had me take her as my mate, and I cared for her, kept her safe. It was the least either of us could do in the light of what Davies had done."

"Davies." The name slithered from Marcus's mighty jaw like a spilled pot of decaying snakes. He remembered Leila's words, *Bolsvck, like you, was just another pawn in a larger game. I know the name of the man who actually tossed you into that Hell. The man who helped Davies orchestrate the undermining plot.*

He didn't believe it. Couldn't believe Bolsvck could be a pawn in anyone's game. But still, more of her words rushed back. *Did you ever wonder why Bolsvck never claimed his birthright?*

Marcus' stare locked on something beyond Bolsvck. Something stirring at the lake's edge. Reapers, lots of them.

"They've come for you," Marcus said with a nod.

Above, the sky still spun in a cyclone of color reminiscent of the swirl and blur the Moorigad had created when trapped inside the glass jar. But for some reason, whatever storm brewed above, Marcus found it far less curious than a regiment of reapers slithering their way.

Could it be they were here to collect all his enemies? The edge of Marcus' lips quivered with a snarl of a smile.

Bolsvck's head spun to the shore, if only for a moment, then returned to the safe watch of Marcus. “No,” he said, taking a step back. “They were part of the deception from the beginning. They worked with Davies.”

Marcus bit the air and shook his head. Lie upon lie upon lie. His eyes burned, and he locked a penetrating stare on the monster he was soon to kill. But then...he watched the Reapers turn, focus on something other than the dueling dragons on the ice. *What are they doing?*

The Reapers moved away. Marcus hissed and swung at Bolsvck. This time, Bolsvck swung back. But neither were serious in their attack, and Marcus began to doubt himself. He wanted Bolsvck dead, didn’t he? He didn’t care about any alliance between Davies and the Reapers. He was sure he didn’t. His head snapped, a quick glance at the Reapers again. Now they moved back toward the ice. Only this time, there was a girl. A girl between him and the Reapers.

Marcus blinked. Hadn’t she been a blonde when he’d first seen her?

Bolsvck turned, his scales prickling, and pushed off the ice, wings flapping for flight.

How did she deceive me? The girl was Kyra. Marcus lunged up into the sky, dug his nails into Bolsvck’s back, and climbed the dragon, shoving him to the ground. Marcus pushed off the fallen dragon’s shoulders and took to the air, Kyra in his sights.

Wind slipped over Marcus’s wings with the force of a firestorm. Kyra was in front of him and Bolsvck was at his back. He’d burned for the Moorigad for so long, he didn’t know how to want for much else. Only her and the power. The power to destroy those who had devastated his life. His mind swarmed with words, all the things Bolsvck had said. He didn’t want to hear them, and yet he couldn’t stop. *What don’t I know?*

With each second, Kyra came into clearer view. She was watching him and didn’t appear to notice the approaching Water Dragons, or the Reapers. Her sights were fixed on him, and his on her. It was a moment of connection that stirred his belly with the sultry seed of desire. An unexpected desire that had bloomed the first time he’d seen her in action, fighting the fire in her trailer. Now, she stood upon the frozen lake, hair flapping in the breeze, curves caressed by the wind, and he longed to run his fingers through the brilliant strands of ruby. Slide his palms along her soft...blue skin?

Marcus's speed curbed, then resumed, pushing to top his fastest velocity yet. Blue. *Why is she blue?* Something dark and weighty dropped in his gut. He should have bound her with another dragon already. Or maybe not. Whatever he felt for her, his need to be accepted and desired by her made him weak. All he needed was the Moorigad. He could let Kyra die. Let her go. Problem was, he couldn't fully convince himself of such a notion enough to make it true. But if she died, it would be good, liberating, for him.

Kyra shivered and stared back at him, a moment later she disappeared from view. Damn Water Dragon. Coiling around her like a cocoon.

He dove, bringing the lake surface ever closer. Yard by yard, foot by foot, inch by inch, they all shrank into nothing in a blink. In a nanosecond, he'd have her.

Something yanked at his tail. All his momentum shifted. He went from flying forward to soaring backward and sideways. Kyra was gone, and the carnival lights swooshed past him.

51
SWIFT DEATH

Kyra

Marcus was coming for her. Coming fast. She would kill him and end all the suffering. Save her family, save the carnival, and protect all dragons, of all types and clans, from his traitorous actions.

Sweat trickled along her brow. Her palms were damp and fingers, anxious. Anxious to wrap their grip around Marcus's throat.

But that wasn't an option. She was human, and he was a dragon. In constant motion, her fingers curled in and out against her palm. It didn't make a plan materialize any faster. Time was fleeing, and she had no idea what to do, only knew what she *wanted* to do and was determined to make happen.

Without taking her piercing stare from the quickly-approaching Marcus, Kyra called to Talia. "Can you b-bestow some sort of m-m-magic upon me that will t-t-turn me into death for anything that b-b-breaks my skin?"

"What?" Kyra heard the balk in her voice.

"A bomb of s-s-sorts. Fire alone won't do. I'm not even s-s-sure venomous gas would be enough."

"Are you crazy?" Talia's voice spiked. "Are you trying to kill yourself?"

"My t-t-time is about up, anyway. M-m-might as well do some g-g-good with it." Kyra bit her lip. She had to hold strong, not show the slightest sign of a waiver.

Talia screamed.

Kyra jumped and turned to find Ryhuu in dragon form. His long, serpent body slithered past Talia and reached Kyra in a nanosecond. He moved in a circle around her, curling upon himself until she was trapped within a tiny dragon well.

He glared down at her from the top of his coil and hissed. "Where have you been, Kyra?" His head moved to and fro. "You play a dangerous game, act like a foolish child."

Kyra took a deep breath and reigned in her rage. It would be so easy to blow up in his face, punch him with her dissenting opinion. But that was not the Kyra she wanted to be, at least, not anymore. She would think her situation through and manage it by wit, not impulse. "I am n-n-not acting the f-fool," she said, opening her eyes. "I am standing up for what I believe must be done. You w-would do the same, if you b-believed in anything besides my mother."

"I believe in you, and in us," the long Water Dragon hissed.

"Would you st-st-still believe in *us* if I decided n-n-not to embrace the Water Clan?" she countered.

"You would choose Fire?" His coil loosened, and his head pulled back.

"I would ch-ch-choose neither." Kyra kept her gaze steady upon his. Felt the truth in her words. For so long, she had struggled with the choice her family pressed upon her, and all along she'd known, she always knew, all she needed to do was accept it. But she wanted nothing to do with either clan. She was Moorigad, and she wanted to be Moorigad forever, for however long or short of a time span that ended up being.

"But you would die!" Ryhuu's head motion quickened, to and fro, to and fro.

"So bbbe it, then. It's who I am, and I've decided I never want to c-c-compromise myself for someone else's superstition."

Ryhuu hissed and said nothing. With a whip of his head, he took in the surroundings and roared, his stare locked on something outside of Kyra's range of sight. She couldn't see anything beyond the big, irritating dragon wrapped around her. She pushed her hands against his body and shoved. He uncoiled with a snap of his tail and roared again.

She had expected to see Marcus and his monstrous hide blocking out the moon, bearing down on them. He wasn't there. He was... She turned to search and found him smashing into the ice—and her father. Beneath them, the ice was cracking, separating.

Her mother slipped and slithered across the changing landscape like it was second nature. Wrapping her tail around Bolsvck, Queen Shui pulled him a safe distance from Marcus and the fracturing ice. A crater the size of a small coaster appeared beside Marcus, and the 'berg beneath his feet hissed and spewed, dropping with the massive dragon's weight. In a fury of venom and fire, he lurched for her parents.

The oncoming line of Grim Reapers that held Ryhuu's attention didn't concern Kyra, even if they brought death at their touch, or breath, or however they did what they did. She figured she was as ready as she ever would be. Life without Sebastian and her dragon didn't seem like a life worth living.

Her body shivered, an uncontrollable wracking straight to the bone. She half expected to see ice crystals forming on her fingertips, but there were none, merely skin frozen stiff in a deathly shade of blue. Pounding like the rapid beat of a dragon's wings, Kyra's heart took off in a sprint. Bile churned in her belly and threatened to rise up her esophagus.

Time was running out. She had to get to Marcus.

Busy sneering at the Reapers, Ryhuu didn't appear to notice when Kyra dragged her body past him. Stiff and cumbersome, she moved forward, keeping Marcus in her sights. "Marcus," she called out. Her voice was weak, yet her soul hummed with the fire of purpose. He would hear her. She had to believe he would.

"What are you doing?" Ryhuu suddenly stood before her, no longer a tremendous Water Dragon. He grabbed hold of her as a man would a woman and peered into her eyes with glaring incredulity.

She tried to smile, a mild attempt to soften his temper. "Like I s-said. I'm putting an end to th-this."

A wisp of dark smoke whisked around them, headed straight for Marcus and her father, but then the misty substance paused and hovered on the other side of Ryhuu, directly in Kyra's line of sight.

From the smoke, Leila materialized. "I heard your thoughts, dragon girl," she said. "Proceed."

"Who is this?" Ryhuu spun around. "What is she talking about?"

"Now, now, pretty dragon boy." Leila approached him and placed her hands on the sides of his face. He stared into her dark, obsidian eyes, his face glazing over, all fight leaving his body.

Kyra stepped away, turning her back to the scene. She didn't want to think about what a Mara did or what would become of Ryhuu. She had to stay on task, no matter the cost. Taking another step forward, she called Marcus's name again. The dragon brawl had taken a turn in Marcus's favor. Bolsvck lay in a heap on the ice with Marcus standing over him.

This time Marcus heard her call, turned his head, and, in a flash, spread his wings and stood before her, stripped of his dragon form.

"Kyra, no!" her mother called out from the frozen lakebed. Kyra didn't respond, although she imagined her mother shifting into serpent form and coming to her rescue.

A breath away, Marcus stood in front of Kyra, his hand moving to caress her cheek. His eyes, his cold, blood-thirsty eyes, softening and his mouth twitching. "Kyra," he began, "I..."

She feigned a faint. Marcus caught her before she hit the ice. She hoped he didn't notice her hand slip to the edge of her boot, didn't see her pull the blade, saw nothing but her glazed-over eyes.

She blinked and met his gaze with clear deception in her reflection.

"May you have a swift death." She plunged the blade deep between his ribs.

Marcus roared and dropped Kyra to the frozen ground. Standing, he stumbled several steps back and yanked the blade from his chest.

On the ice, Kyra rolled to her hands and knees, attempted to push herself up, but her strength refused to respond. Beneath her, beneath the ice, something moved, and she peered down intently, ignoring Marcus. Down in the depths of the lake's water, below the ice-covered surface, a monster stirred, and he had shown his face to Kyra.

She gasped.

"Do you think a tiny blade such as this would stop me?" Marcus said, dropping the weapon as one might discard a piece of trash.

The blade no sooner hit the ice than Queen Shui crashed into him, dragging him away.

He was gone.

Kyra knew she should care, should follow their conflict and try to finish what she'd started, but her mind was crammed with thoughts of ginormous lake monsters. The ice shook, and Kyra fell to her side. The impact had come from below.

In those moments of chaos, multiple things happened. Marcus and Kyra's mother roared. Her father called her name. Ryhuu cried out in a blood-curdling scream, and a deafening screech came from the sky. Drakhögg and Keahi were inbound. She imagined the Reapers smiling from ear to ear at the mess she had created by saving Marcus from drowning that day. A memory she preferred to forget. Her heart raced with anger, anguish, and anxiety. *If only I'd let Marcus die that day*.

A feeble sob, Talia's, came from somewhere behind Kyra. She couldn't see the witch; her sight was abruptly blocked by the arrival of her parents. They got in her face like they had done far too often before she'd run away to the carnival.

"Quickly, Kyra. Make a choice," her mother said, grabbing hold of Kyra's hands.

"You're freezing, girl. Choose fire," her father said.

Kyra raised her gaze to them and shivered. The ground beneath them rocked unsteadily, and clinging to the ice only chilled her deeper to the bone. The surface shook again, this time cracking and breaking. Large sections shifted, lifted, and tipped at angles.

"I am dying." She closed her eyes. "And I have no dragon within me for a choice to matter." She sighed and laid her head upon her folded forearms. She wanted to fight. If only she could gather the strength.

"You are dying a Moorigad's death." Her father dropped beside her. "Make a choice, and you will live to see another day."

Was it true? Had she finally reached the point of choose or die? She didn't believe them. Dying was her fate for being dragonless and nothing more. Even so, if it were true, she refused to choose.

"I am forever Moorigad." She gazed at them groggily.

The ice cracked open, a wide hole sliced by the thump of a colossal hide cut with spurs and spikes. Glacier-like sheets skittered and flew in all directions, and the frozen surface of the lake spider-webbed with cracks, separating everything into shifting chunks—islands of floating ice. A tail swept up from the hole, looped, and disappeared below.

"Choose now!" Queen Shui yelled.

Kyra balanced on the wobbling ice and stared at the space where the giant tail had been. She'd thought she'd seen a person hanging on. Blinking the hallucination away, she glowered back at her mother and yelled, "No! Don't you hear me? I am Moorigad!"

Above, the sky quickened into a maddening swirl. Orange and red and blue blending into one muddy mess.

Zzzz*aap*, out of the sky, like a beam of light in the form of a diving dragon, the colors rocked toward the lake. Orange, bleeding with red, blending into blue; the wildly welcomed colors of Kalrapura—Kyra's dragon half. The colors slammed her in the chest. A tiny yelp escaped her lips, the glacier chunk tipped, and Kyra slipped into the water.

52
DEMONS

Sebastian

"Wake up."

The sound was weak, unwanted, and hellishly persistent.

"Wake up."

Sebastian was no longer cold, merely numb inside and out. "Leave me, I'm dying," he mumbled and swallowed a mouthful of murky lake water. He coughed and rolled on his side. The bibelot, still jammed in his chest, clanged against something solid and ungiving. Overwhelmed with exhaustion, Sebastian didn't even bother to silently curse.

"You are already dead," the voice said. "But will you let that stop you?"

At this, Sebastian opened his eyes. He was on the lake's floor. Aside from the irritating voice at his side, it was relatively calm beneath the water. The voices that had tormented him on the surface did not follow him here. And for the first time in far too long, he didn't yearn for Talia's tonic. He lived, or maybe died, in the moment.

The water around him was dirty, full of sediment, and next to him was something large and dark and impossibly deep. His eyes strained against the weight and filth of the water. What irritating thing nagged him in his death sleep? "What do you want of me?"

Crimson red, glowing eyes illuminated within the darkness. At a slow crawl, they moved closer. "To protect and restore the one you love."

A wave of warm water washed over Sebastian. It came from the direction of the thing nagging him.

Their voices sounded odd. Everything sounded odd, distorted by the water. *Come to think of it,* Sebastian tilted his head, *am I speaking or thinking my thoughts?* He was certain he wasn't really speaking at all. Not since that first large gulp of lake water.

"Why do you care about me or my love?" Sebastian asked. He dropped back and focused upward at the water's surface. He couldn't see the ripples of motion, but he knew they were there. Sure as he knew Marcus had bested him. But if Marcus had bested him, what did that mean for Kyra?

Sound rippled through the darkness of the water. "I care not for you. But she does, and that's all that matters. It's her feelings for you, demon, which will unlock the true depth of her Moorigad."

Something pitch and grotesque slithered through Sebastian's intestines, pressing against his heart, heavy and discomforting. Dead or not, he couldn't leave things the way they were. Not if he had the power to do something about it.

Sebastian yanked the bibelot from his chest, tossed it, and pushed up off the lake floor. He expected aches and pains, possibly the onset of rigor mortis. There was nothing. No external pain or discomfort. Everything he felt radiated from within. Internally, he ached to see Kyra again. To be near her. To touch her.

"That's more like it," the voice said.

"Yes, I'm moving. Why do you care, um…" He paused. "What should I call you?"

"A few call me monster. Others call me ancient. You may call me Anguis."

Sebastian stood, swayed in the slow-moving current. "Do I have you to thank for my animated death state?" He stared into the darkness, saw an underwater cave in which the massive thing dwelled. He could barely discern bits of it—or himself. It had large, protruding horns, so maybe, just maybe, Sebastian was talking to the Devil.

A low rumble responded, giving Sebastian the impression of a laugh. "I had nothing to do with your current state. That's all you, Reaper." The voice moved forward, shifting through the lake floor, causing sediment to cloud the water more than it already had. "I have waited long for a demon of your strength and desire. One who could make a difference."

Sebastian pointed to his chest. "A demon like me? What do you think I am, exactly?" He leaned forward, tried to see the devil to which he spoke.

The crimson eyes and horns inched closer. "You are a bridge between worlds. A hybrid never before known."

Sebastian scoffed. "What do you know about world bridges and hybrids? You live underwater."

A great cloud of sediment swam around them, a storm brought on by a sudden large movement. "I know many things. I have been around an eternity of years. I watch, and I listen. It has been so very long since I curled up here, determined to wait." His tail shifted. "The water has brought me many secrets and truths."

Sebastian's hands waved at the cloudy water and bubbles. "What kind of demon are you?"

Through the murk, a face began to appear, gradually taking form. "Not a demon. A dragon." The voice gave way to embodiment as the dragon moved from the depths of the cave out into the open.

Sebastian's eyes widened, but he remained silent.

"I am the first Moorigad. Pure through and through, never falling victim to the clan's absurd rituals." He lowered his mighty head to meet Sebastian. "I think now is the time to change the plight of the Moorigad forever. We start here. Today." He swept past Sebastian. "Now come. We have work to do."

Sebastian watched the massive beast swing around him, but move to work with Anguis, he did not. Instead, he thought about Kyra and her stories. It was only earlier that day, while riding the carousel, Sebastian had reminded her of a story she had previously shared. The one of Anguis the Angry, the first Moorigad. If Sebastian were to believe what he now saw and heard, this Moorigad was not cursed. Between the legend and the real dragon swimming around Sebastian, things didn't add up. He'd best stay close, keep an eye on the monster.

Sebastian locked a hold onto Anguis's tail, and the giant took off through the water at bone-breaking speed. Sheer force wanted to knock him free, carry him away with the current, but he held on with a death grip. Bubbles clouded his view, and his sense of direction was completely obliterated in the rush, wave, and froth.

Still, he could count on the compass securely tattooed to his skin, and it held steady, leading him directly to Kyra. She was dead ahead.

Sebastian's arms ached with the pain of clinging to Anguis's tail. Pain was good, a glorious thing. Pain meant life, and life meant another chance with Kyra. He wasn't going to question how he was still alive. He was a Reaper, after all. All that mattered was Kyra. For the way he'd treated Kyra, he deserved getting whipped and thrashed through the water like a battered fish trapped on a line. A line attached to a whirling, runaway speedboat.

The second time Anguis swept his tremendous tail up through the broken ice and sweet air kissed Sebastian's skin, he let go, tumbled to a stop upon the frozen surface. He bounced upright, verve zipping through his nerves and tendons. He was more than alive; he was strong, hearty, and sharp-witted.

"Shoot," he mumbled, taking in the scene. To his left, a dragon scuffle of epic proportion. A slight shift to his right, and there was his captor from earlier, the Water Dragon, clenching tight to his own head and screaming. Ahead, Kyra's parents yelled at his father. A few yards beyond, Talia flailed on the ground.

Reapers were spread out along the perimeter like a police line. And all the way at the shore was a dark-haired demon. He immediately recognized her as Mara. He'd seen her once before, in a dream. She had to be the one who'd possessed Chelsea.

He turned away, searched left and right, and found no sign of Kyra.

Not even the blonde in the dress she'd pretended to be. Maybe she hadn't come to the lake at all. But if Talia was here, wouldn't Kyra have come, as well?

His chest numbed to the thought of something having happened to her. All concept of time was lost on him—how long he'd been under the water, how long he'd been dead. Anything could have transpired during the time he was away.

Anguis moved beneath the ice at Sebastian's feet. Swimming out behind him, the beastly dragon broke through the frozen lake again, his mammoth hump of a back resembling a deformed whale breaking the ocean's surface.

"Now you've done it!"

Sebastian spun to see a wounded and blood-covered Jon Davies running toward him.

"You've undone everything I worked so hard for. You've killed us all!" Davies yelled.

Sebastian stared at Davies, something dark and noxious burrowing deep within Sebastian's soul. "What are you talking about?"

"The Ancient." Several feet away, Davies screeched to a halt. "He will devour everything. I've seen it."

"What do you mean?"

Davies dropped his head. "Years ago, I had the signs read to me. The old woman used the stars. I needed to make sure our future was secure with our rising king." His gaze wandered toward Bolsvck. The great dragon was staring at the water, after the queen's disappearing tail into the lake.

"It was not." He met Sebastian's gaze with one of a tired and worn man. "I took precautions, got the help of the head Grim, but now Balidhug has become an all-powerful, destructive force anyway. Everything we were working toward has been undone, and we must fight until we can fight no longer." He looked toward the disappearing swell.

Sebastian had concerns regarding Anguis's motives, but an old prophecy and the shouts from one man weren't going to sway him one way or the other. Was it Anguis or Davies, Sebastian needed to be leery of?

He swallowed, and a lump lodged in his throat. Ignoring the discomfort, he reached out with his Reaper senses and found he could control his ability like a skilled master. There was no craving for Talia's tonic to take the edge off, and the irritation of voice overload bothered him no more. He filed the observation away for later and allowed himself to feel Davies's thoughts, emotions, motives. What he found—no deceit, only frustration.

"Explain to me what Marcus and Anguis the Ancient have to do with one another," Sebastian said.

"You failed to reap Balidhug when you were ordered to do so. Because of you, he got his dragon back."

Sebastian frowned. He had tried to reap Marcus's soul multiple times. Davies's logic was flawed, but he followed.

"Both Balidhug and Anguis the Ancient learned of Kyra's Water-Fire Hybrid status, thus sealing this fate."

"That's the part I don't get."

Davies sighed. "Balidhug learned of her when you first dragged her out to meet him." Sebastian grimaced. *Not exactly how things transpired.* "Allowing Balidhug to bring his fight here, to the ancient's place of slumber, instilled awareness within him."

Sebastian opened then closed his mouth. His hand waved to dismiss the entire idea as absurd, but still...he clutched his hand into a fist.

"Rumor has it," Davies continued. "The ancient has been aware of Kyra for even longer. Unwilling to reveal himself, he sent magic in the form of fog to seek her out."

Sebastian's brow pinched, and he recalled the strange fog that had sleeked through the carnival during the night of the fire. The night of his fire. It had been meant to be small, contained to only Kyra's trailer, but his father'd had other plans. Sebastian had seen him that night, on the outskirts of the Backyard, an ear-to-ear grin drawn across his face.

Sebastian's plans had gone horribly wrong every time. He'd thought a small fire would have easily claimed Marcus. Kyra had been safe on the other side of the carnival, and Sebastian had used magic to suppress her dragon abilities so that she wouldn't be so eager to play the hero. He'd even used magic to keep Marcus trapped within the consuming fire. It was past his time; he needed to be reaped.

But every time he had tried to reap the man's soul, Kyra had put herself in danger to save him. She'd even lost herself in the process, landing in purgatory.

The truth, the consequences of his actions cut through his being like a Mara's web. He wanted to scream.

"You!" The sound boomed, exploding over everything and everyone, drowning out the loudest of noises and thoughts. Sebastian spun around and beheld Marcus, a monstrosity of wings and talons, storming toward him like an oncoming firestorm. Behind him, a mass of mangled dragon limbs—Kyra's sister and one of her suitors.

"He is the least of your worries, now," Davies whispered at Sebastian's back.

Mortifier stepped between the men and dragon action and keeping his back to Sebastian, called out to Marcus. "You cannot kill what is already dead."

The dragon faltered, and fire wisped from his nostrils.

"That's right," Mortifier continued. "You succeeded in killing my boy. What you failed to take into consideration was his nature. Killing a Reaper only makes him stronger." Mortifier glanced over his shoulder and appraised Sebastian. "A hybrid such as my son, who is to say what he has become?"

"Don't oversell me," Sebastian grumbled, privately acknowledging the darkness churning within his core. Reaper and Mara. Death and despair. He'd felt the change building throughout the day and had mistaken it for the dragon he harbored. The more likely truth, it was his slow death by dragon fire that had ignited a transformation into something more. Something darker.

"He's evil," Davies whispered. It was unclear to Sebastian if he was referring to Marcus or Mortifier.

"This has gone on long enough." Mortifier turned, gaze burning into Davies's skull. "I played my part, tossed your would-be devil into Purgatory, and it would seem it was all for naught."

"But..." Davies stuttered.

Mortifier spun back on Marcus, threw his hand up in his direction. "Here you are, trying to destroy my bloodline and defying your lifeline."

Marcus bared his teeth.

"You cannot scare me," Mortifier said with a slight tip of the head. "You forget who I am." He turned, glanced at Sebastian and beyond to his fellow Reapers. "Who we are."

"So, you are Death. What of it? You don't scare me." Marcus's brow creased, and his large, reptilian head pressed forward.

"You should be. We put you in Purgatory once before." Mortifier brushed a finger across one eyebrow. "We can do it again. Or worse."

Marcus growled, stepped closer. "You did that?"

"Of course. Do you honestly think," Mortifier waved his arm in an arc to indicate the present company, "anyone else could wield such power?"

Marcus's head swung to and fro, and bitter sounds of anguish exploded into the air.

"The truth hurts, I know." Mortifier's voice bled with indifference. "But I thought your little Mara companion would have helped you put your puzzle of a backstory together long ago. After all," he tapped his chin with his index finger, and Marcus paused in his approach, renewed curiosity in his piercing stare and intimidating stance, "from what I understand, Leila's been privy to the details since she was a minor."

Marcus's tail slammed against the ice with a resounding crack, and the larger glacier pieces broke. Sebastian backed up, found his balance. Everyone rocked as if standing on large rafts covering the lake.

"Stop this, Mortifier," Bolsvck said, bounding up to the conversation. "You are antagonizing the situation."

The Reaper turned on Bolsvck, grim and callous. "I do nothing more than inform. It is time for all secrets to be laid to rest." He brushed a spray of frost from his lapel. "Balidhug needs to know how Davies betrayed him, and why."

"I was working on that," Bolsvck growled. Marcus chimed in with a matching growl.

"Likewise, Davies needs to understand karma." Mortifier turned and stared down the man. "One cannot simply destroy a man and his family and not expect it to rebound upon his own." A vicious smile curved at the edge of his lips.

Sebastian's eyes widened, and he sucked back a breath. He'd never expected his father to admit to any horrible acts, and yet, here he was doing just that, albeit as vaguely as possible. He watched understanding sprout in Davies's eyes. Sebastian could pinpoint the moment Davies understood that Mortifier was using karma as an excuse to steal the Davies daughters' lives.

Everything was falling into place. Because Davies had enlisted Mortifier's help all those years ago, Marcus's family had been destroyed and Marcus had been shattered, ruined as a dragon, and forced to live his life as human after escaping. His beast-side cursed to the fires of Purgatory. In some sort of retribution or cruel lesson, Mortifier had taken Davies's family. And now he spoke of karma. Did he think he was exempt?

"Why, I'll—" Davies yelled. Marcus glowered at him.

"What?" Mortifier interrupted.

Dragons roared on all sides of them, and Sebastian fought the desire to cover his ears, let the darkness churning in his belly free.

53
BLEEDING

Kyra

Biting harder than ice, scorching deeper than fire; agony, anger, sorrow, and fever raged through Kyra's veins, moving like an unchecked dragonling. She slipped beneath the water, welcoming Death into her embrace.

But Death did not come.

I can't feel my toes.

Her dress dragged at her, pulling her like a weight. Not what she'd expected; dark, turbulent, and scratchy was the water. Frigid temperatures fought to squeeze the life from her body.

Only, life did not depart.

It lingered, struggling in a constant state of flux, causing her muscles to ache and her belly to churn with nausea.

Folds of fabric wrapped around her, confining her movements, and deeper into the lake she sank. And although she struggled for the surface, she discovered a water-free supply of oxygen she never craved. Somewhere in the back of her mind, she knew the lack of need held significance, but her mind was far too consumed with reflection.

Maybe it was her life flashing before her. Or maybe it was nothing more than obsession, her eternal desire to succeed. She had failed to defeat Marcus. The outcome nagged at her, yet she was ready, eager even, to hesitate no longer and join Sebastian in death. If only her body would comply. What had that bolt of light done to her?

The current spun her in a circle, and something hard and rough cut across her side. *Mother*. She peered after a large tail swinging around her. Except, she knew better. This creature was different, larger, and far more battle-scarred.

A subtle vibration in the water—a voice—the whisper crowded everything else from her mind.

"Child of water and fire, why do you drift to your death?"

Drained by her internal change, Kyra did not answer, and so the voice continued.

"Death is a coward's resignation. You are above such action. You are Moorigad. Choose life, and put an end to our persecution."

The word *our* rang out above the rest. Was this creature calling himself a Moorigad? His scales were old, visibly worn, and his eyes spoke of years beyond reason. *Ancient* was the term Kyra would attribute to him, millions of leap-years older than any dragon she'd ever met. If he was indeed a Moorigad, that meant everyone she knew had lied.

A choice was not required, merely *desired*. Heat exploded across her skin at a heart-stopping raw fever, and Kalrapura roared. Understanding filled Kyra and sent her blood soaring. She was on fire, internally on fire, and she loved it. Craved it, even. Scales shifted across Kyra's skin, appearing and disappeared. Her heart thrummed double-time and sudden, sharp awareness had her logging everything within her perimeter.

She had her dragon back. Kyra and Kalrapura were finally complete. And not only that, the change was still ongoing, fire and water bleeding into each other. Bleeding into one, becoming something different, something whole, something truly Moorigad. All the pain and suffering no longer felt important; it was the end result that held significance.

"You feel it now, don't you?" the old dragon asked.

Before Kyra could answer, her mother appeared and tackled the old dragon. Both dragons disappeared in a mirage of bubbles and sediment.

A scream lodged in Kyra's throat and exploded in a growl. Her body was shifting and transforming, leaving the girl behind and becoming the dragon. This time, the change was unlike any she had previously endured. Blood boiling, skin and scales shivering. The lake water around her bore the reflection and glow of the magical bleed.

Grumbles and growls in the water around her stilled, and the sense of isolation set in. Her mother and the old dragon were gone.

Kyra screamed, succumbing to her new self. Every bone, tendon, muscle, emotion, spiked with incinerating torment. Spasms took her, and red was all she saw. Red and red and spasm and red.

And then there was peace. Harmony.

Silence.

KYRA AWOKE WITH A START.

She had not died as a human, separated from her dragon-self. No. She had been reunited, made more. The water around her carried a melody she had not previously heard. The hum and beat was organic, natural to exist, and yet, her dragon-self had never been more aware of its song. Everything, for that matter, was sharper and a thousand times more vivid.

How long had she endured? Been out of touch with her surroundings and the passage of time? She peered up at the surface. Not as it should be, the lake was cluttered with a multitude of small ice masses. She remembered...it had been frozen, then broken. She'd blamed her mother.

She'd been wrong. Now, after her metamorphosis, she felt the magic coursing through the water and ice and air. The magic used to turn Mystic's lake into a frozen hazard zone had been Moorigad magic. But why?

She could melt it all, every last 'berg floating across the surface. But her gaze narrowed in on the shadows of bodies moving across the many frozen blocks above. Her mind spun with thoughts and scenarios. One swift kick, and she was rocketing through the water toward the surface, wings tucked in tight at her side.

54
CONVERGENCE

Sebastian

Everyone was tipped and tossed, as if the world had exploded. Maybe it had. Sebastian pressed his hand to his stomach to settle the churning. Where was Kyra in the midst of all the turmoil? Answering Sebastian's confusion and bursting through the ice, full body and weight, came Anguis—all talons, spikes, and teeth. He became the horizon, dwarfing everything around him. His claws scratched at the demolished bits of frozen covering, and his presence commanded complete and absolute attention.

"The Moorigad is rising, and she will be mine," he said, the words slithering off his tongue. "Will you get out of my way? Or shall we fight?"

The weight of Anguis's words were still pushing their way into Sebastian's comprehension when Bolsvck, then Marcus, rushed at the ginormous dragon. Like wasps, they were swatted away and sent careening out of sight.

He said rising.

Sebastian studied the ground. More specifically, the space between the large, floating platforms of ice.

Something was happening. The water bubbled an iridescent blue.

Sebastian shifted back toward Talia, putting urgency in his pace. She lay quietly upon the ice, as if frozen by fright. "Get as far from here as you can," he told her. She nodded, but said not a word. Instead, she began to inch away, remaining flat against the ice.

Anguis settled upon the frozen lake, his nostrils smoking venomously. "Which of you will stand for her?" He turned to Drakhögg. Beaten and worn, the Fire Dragon had his arm wrapped around Kyra's sister. It appeared they were propping each other up.

Drakhögg's eyes widened, and he shook his head adamantly. "You can have her. She never wanted me, anyway." He pulled at Kyra's sister, and together they stumbled away from the smoking beast.

Anguis laughed. "So little valor for a fire warrior." His head snapped, losing interest in Drakhögg, his gaze seeking Ryhuu.

The Water Dragon no longer screamed as he had earlier. His face dimmed, eyes turned blank, and deep wrinkles and shadows dropped across his face. He was becoming a shell of himself, and an expression that Sebastian had become all too familiar with on his reaps now owned his face. What had happened to the man?

"You." Anguis narrowed his sights on the dragon.

Sebastian went rigid and ogled Ryhuu, watched as Leila stepped out from behind him, her eyes darker than the blackest of black holes. So *that's* what had happened to him. Ryhuu had been hollowed out by the Mara.

Anguis tilted his head to the side and let loose a laugh. "Do not try your Mara tricks on me. I learned all I ever need to know about Maras from your mother."

Leila startled, blinked. "What do you know of my mother?"

Anguis sneered. "She'd broken the Mara Golden Rule, you know that. No male offspring." He narrowed his glare. "She sought refuge from her fellow Mara. Thought she might find safety in my company." A half-gargled laugh escaped. "She couldn't have been more wrong."

Leila glowered, black swamping her eyes. "You killed her?"

The beastly, old dragon grinned. It was honest and evil all wrapped up in one wickedly curved line.

Ryhuu suddenly came to life, gasped and turned to run for shore. When he started slipping and sliding on the uneven ice masses, he burst into dragon form and snaked away five times faster.

"I find the state of the modern dragon distressing," Anguis said, leering after Ryhuu. He sighed and turned on Sebastian. "It comes down to us. I know your heart, demon. Will you fight for her?"

"Why do you toy with us?" Sebastian said without waver and took a step forward.

"Don't pass over me so lightly," Leila said. "I may not give a damn about Kyra, but I definitely have a score to settle with you." Howling her attack, she ran at Anguis. He lowered his head to the ice and roared. Thundering sound and gale winds exploded, tossing her in a tumble backwards across the frozen lake.

Pleasure wrapped itself around Anguis in an undeniably excited grin. He turned to Sebastian. "I toy with you because it's fun." He reared back and then lurched forward.

Queen Shui leaped from the water, landed upon the quavering ice form, and swung wide with her tail. Anguis lunged for her throat, mouth open wide.

"Get out, demon," Queen Shui yelled at Sebastian.

Anguis is insane. Sebastian's mind reeled. Was the dragon's state of mind a Moorigad problem or something else? Either way, he was taking Anguis down.

Ignoring the queen, Sebastian raced toward the warring dragons. Ice exploded at his right. A faint hint of a dragon appeared in his periphery. He paid it no mind. The dragon was either on the same warring side, or it was too far away to stop him from his plan. He held his target steady in his sights.

The call of his name rang out over the chaos.

His pace faltered, slowed, and finally paused all with a short slide across the ice. Could his ears be deceiving him? The call sounded so much like...

His gaze followed the call, wandering in the direction of the recently arriving dragon. But no dragon met his stare. Crossing the ice and coming his direction was a scantly scaled Kyra. Her red hair flowed around her as if it were ablaze, and maybe it was. Her entire outline glowed with heat distortion while at the same time emitting a mist of frozen air. She was heart-stoppingly exquisite. The mere sight of her sent his soul flying for the heavens.

His jaw dropped, and his dead heart leapt through his chest and slammed back into his throat. Kyra and Kalrapura, one once again. And yet, clearly so much more. The vision of her engulfed him, blinded him to everything that wasn't Kyra. In that breath of a second, she was his world.

He didn't see it coming. And it happened so fast. A massive tail slammed against the ice, swept across the surface, and swept Sebastian away in its wake.

55
DRAGON SONG

Sebastian

One second, she was there, the center of his universe, and the next, she was gone. Only she hadn't moved. Something incredibly large and ungiving had smacked Sebastian sideways, away from Kyra. He landed with a twist and a thud, sending pops and cracks throughout his body. Oddly, nothing hurt. He sat up and immediately ducked.

Anguis's massive tail swung through Sebastian's path, missing him by a foot. The ancient dragon continued to fight with Queen Shui. Sebastian getting smacked sideways had clearly been an unfortunate twist of happenstance. Lying flat on the ground, Sebastian rolled clear and made sure it was safe to stand. The last thing he needed was to become the unwilling target in an unplanned game of dragon swat-n-bat.

Kyra ran toward him, and he was overcome with the desire to laugh. Laugh for all the despair he'd experienced leading up to that point. Laugh for the anger and depression and fear. Laugh because Kyra was alive, alluringly alive, and he was alive, and Kalrapura was exactly where she was meant to be. Guess he had his answer on whether a Reaper could die or not.

And he did laugh, a little.

Then held up his hand to stop Kyra's approach.

All his protective instincts kicked in. Close to destructive dragons was not where she needed to be. Plus—he glanced at his father, still standing on the frozen lake, studied him and all the men he'd brought with them. They wore their usual deadpan attire, with a few notable exceptions. Some held a hint of smile or a twinkle in the eye. They appeared excited, even eager for the outcome of the dragon battle.

He looked back at Anguis and Queen Shui. Although she held her own fairly well against such a considerable opponent, she was losing.

Sebastian glanced back and forth between Kyra and the fight. Despite his attempt to keep her out of harm's way, she now moved toward her mother. When the dark sky filled with the sound of flapping wings and echoed with a bone-jarring roar, Kyra faltered.

Kyra's sister swooped in, flew above the massive, old beast, her talons clawing at his eyes. Before Sebastian could decide on his course of action, Bolsvck crashed between Anguis and the queen.

"Hell," Sebastian mumbled. *The whole family is involved. No way of keeping Kyra out of that pit now.*

"Sebastian!"

In an instant the battling dragons were forgotten. The hair on the back of Sebastian's neck rose at the sound of Kyra's cry. He'd taken his eyes off her for mere seconds. Whirling around, he located Kyra, his blood pressure spiking. Marcus, no longer in dragon form, had his hands all over her—pulling and yanking and struggling for control. Every fiber of Sebastian's being erupted with rage and loathing.

"Let me go!" Kyra yelled. "Your stupid pendant is gone, and that stinky Serpicose won't work."

"You're coming with me," Marcus said and tugged harder.

Kyra slid on the ice and fell. She pulled herself up to her knees. "I stabbed you once. I'll do it again. Until you either leave me alone, or you're dead."

Marcus growled.

"Stop!" Sebastian ran toward them, his stomach churning and his inner cold dipping. But when he met Kyra's gaze his feet stumbled to a stop, skidded on the ice, and dropped him on his back. In a matter of seconds, her scales engulfed her body and her mighty Moorigad surged forth. Marcus was knocked off his feet with one fell swoop of her tail, and in an instant, he too transformed. Another dragon battle began.

"Isn't this exciting?" Leila swayed at Sebastian's side and whispered at his ear.

Sebastian startled, stared at her. "Who are you? And why did you destroy Chelsea's life?"

"Poor boy. Mother leaving you in the dark." Her knuckles brushed the side of his face. "I am your older sister. The true Mara in the family." Her fingers ruffled his hair, and he knocked her away. "You, the product of a Mara and a Grim, an interesting idea." She pressed her cheek against his. "For what he did to you, I would have destroyed Marcus. It would have worked, too, had a meteor shower of dragons not wrinkled my plans."

In an abrupt move, Sebastian stood up and stepped away. "Why are you here? What is it you want from me?"

"To explore you." She leaned closer. "Get to know you better."

"I think you should leave." He swung a move-along gesture with his finger, and his gaze drifted over the carnival. Dragons were taking flight from multiple locations, heading toward the lake. The lights and sounds of Mystic's now ran full-wheel. Things were spinning and blinking, and the dragons...the ones flying toward the lake were disappearing mid-flight. Sebastian's muscles went rigid. His mind reeled.

Think. Think. Think.

Valentina with her vortex ability couldn't reach a flying dragon.

Mystic's was back or repaired or whatever it was she'd needed. She apparently didn't want those dragons coming to their aid on the lake. The more he studied the occurrence, the clearer it became. Dragons who refrained from approaching didn't appear to get relocated. Kyra, Kyra's family, him, they were on their own. No help was coming.

Sebastian glanced at Kyra and Marcus, and fury blinded him. He looked away.

The wisp of a touch ran along his arm. He turned to Leila. "Why are you still here? Go!"

She recoiled, and he didn't have to see himself to know. Her reaction was telling enough. Plus, he felt the change—the darkness—take hold, start manifesting the moment he'd glowered at Marcus. That demon had used and hurt Kyra. Totted her around like a puppet.

Wide-eyed and ashen, Leila backed away. "We are not finished, you and I." Recovering her posture, she gave him a fox of a grin and vanished into the wind.

Leila's words meant nothing to him. All that mattered, all that ever mattered, was his girl of fire. His extraordinary Moorigad. For her, he would ruin worlds. An eclipse of reason flooded his veins in slow-moving ink, and he moved forward in measured steps, the darkest of thoughts manifesting around Marcus.

"I merely need your compliance, your strength. Stop your struggle." Marcus flew a foot off the ground and knocked Kyra backwards with the swing of his tail.

Sebastian's inner shadows turned to obscurity, and the remaining stars in the sky were snuffed out. He narrowed his glare, and it scorched with never-ending revulsion for Marcus, the soulless man-beast.

The beast who laughed and spewed fire like a flaming torch on steroids.

Merciful Hell. Fire went everywhere. Fire shot through the sky and shot at Kyra, and fire blew across the ice. The surface beneath her vanished, melted, and Kyra dropped back into the lake.

Talia and Valentine circled in behind Sebastian, whispering his name, but he paid them no attention. He didn't have time. Not when he stood before a fiery Marcus.

This has to stop. Sebastian splayed his hands out at his side with his palms toward Marcus. An infinity of darkness coursed through Sebastian, snaked from his fingertips, wanting and searching for a mark. Almost invisible to the non-magical eye, weaving a path across the ice, Sebastian could hear and feel the dark magic's yearning.

The ground at his feet became slick with water, his small terrain of frozen lake growing smaller by the second. And yet, the fire was subsiding, Marcus dropping, his head drooping. His scales turned brittle and his eyes grey. His wings fell limp. His life was ending. With a mere thought, Sebastian was smothering and stamping out the dragon.

Talia tapped his shoulder, and the darkness within him leaped forward, snapped at her fingers. He sensed her back away.

A crack of the ice. Sebastian ignored that too, his focus honed.

"Sebastian." Kyra's voice washed over him, tugging at his calm and unknotting his madness. She had returned to him, risen again from the frozen lake. "This is not who you are." Her hand soothed down his arm, causing him to blink and release the darkness. Marcus dropped to the ice with a *crunck.*

Sebastian's ears rang, and his gut dropped like a weight. He looked away from the destruction he had caused, sought comfort in Kyra's eyes. "I couldn't..." He sighed. "I was just so..." He paused again and stared deep into her eyes. "I did it for you. He makes me so mad."

Kyra smiled. "And you were always the calm and sensible one." Her hand caressed the side of his face. "Don't darken your soul with an ugly deed for me. I love you as you are."

"I don't have a soul to darken."

"To feel as deeply as you do, to put yourself through all that you have for me, there's no way you don't have a soul."

Marcus chortled. "So touching." He stood up. "Too bad you didn't have the guts to finish what you started. Guess I'll have to finish it for you."

"You can try," Kyra countered.

Another crack and splash.

Several yards off to their side, changes in the frozen surface were affecting another fight. Queen Shui's tail flopped in the water. The ground at her feet had broken into countless pieces and returned to a liquid state, dropping her into the lake as it had Kyra minutes before. The ice beneath Anguis and Bolsvck shifted. In a flurry of flaps, they took to flight and fight and floundered, moving chaotically toward Marcus, Kyra, and Sebastian.

"Things are about to escalate," Sebastian said.

"That's what I tried to tell you," Talia quipped.

Without a glance, Kyra swung her arm around like she was tossing a Skee-Ball at Marcus. Wind swept down from the heavens in a frenzy, dropping behind and swinging down beneath them, scooping up Valentine in its path. The current carried her like a cannon through the air.

"What have you done?" Sebastian said, his entire body tensing, fighting the desire to lunge after Valentine. Save Kyra any future regret should Valentine get hurt, or worse.

"She'll be fine—" Kyra's eyes widened.

Bolsvck and Anguis, consumed in battle, tumbled into Marcus one beat before Valentine plowed into them—or through them—and all three turned into a swirling bubble of vortex. Pulled and sucked into another-land by way of distortion, until there was nothing but Valentine kneeling on the broken ice.

Kyra's sister spiraled into the sky and roared, raining sorrow from the skies. Queen Shui thrashed in the water, an inconsolable sound venting from her dragon. Nearby dragons joined the ballad, and the water oozed heartache, while the heavens bled mourning.

56
AMBASSADORS

Sebastian

"My father. What have I done?" Kyra stood motionless, the frozen embodiment of disbelief.

Sebastian threaded his fingers between hers. "You couldn't have known your father would get in the way. At least he's not dead. Just sent somewhere unknown." Internally, his chest sank.

Outwardly, he began to actually sink, along with everyone else standing upon the frozen surface. The magic of Anguis the Ancient had been spiraled away, and with it, the ice. Sebastian and Kyra fell into the lake.

Talia and Valentine splashed and coughed, but Sebastian could see they would be okay. Queen Shui and Keahi had come to their aid.

Kyra wrapped her arms around him and dropped her head against his chest. He'd ached for this moment, but for it to happen this way was wrong. He held her tight, and they slowly sank farther in the water. Nothing he could do would take away the pain she felt, but he could be there for her now, and maybe that would suffice.

"You're a fool." Mortifier grabbed Sebastian by the collar and, in a flash of wind and water, whisked him away from Kyra into a mad dart until they stood upon the shore, dry and unrumpled, as if nothing had happened.

Kyra had burst into her Moorigad and taken to the sky. When Sebastian came to a standstill, she was already circling above the carnival.

Sebastian yanked free of Mortifier. "I'm the fool?" His voice rose to an accusatory pitch, and he glared at his father, then at the line of Reapers beyond him. Their numbers were dwindling. One Reaper, then three Reapers, all vanishing, leaving the carnival in theatrical puffs of smoke.

"You mess with things you don't fully yet understand." Mortifier shook his head, motioned to his remaining men. One of them, Mr. Johnson, had a strong hold on an unhappy Davies. "We're not here for the entertainment, boy. We have a job to do."

Sebastian rolled his shoulders. "I get that, but—"

Mortifier halted him with a sharp snap of a finger. "I don't think you do. From the very start, you were tasked with the reaping of Balid-hug, or Marcus Blackall, whatever you want to call him. And yet, you've failed time and time again." His shoulders sagged. "And the ancient—The first Moorigad..." He shook his head in silence. "You never should have talked to him."

"Okay." Sebastian waved his hand between them. "I've listened to enough of your bullcrap. Now you're going to listen to me."

Mortifier raised a brow, but said nothing.

"You may have planned out the anomaly that I am, but that doesn't mean you get to control me. And the same goes for everyone else across the worlds." He motioned to the people gathering onshore—the drag-ons, Talia and Valentine, the patrons and Zeke (sitting humbly on his usual bench). "You don't control any of them. So, if they do something that affects your collection list, changes the names or even scratches some out, you need to let it go."

"You don't tell me what to do." Mortifier narrowed his stare and stood straight, peering an inch down upon Sebastian.

"I'm not telling you what to do. I'm telling you how it is." Sebastian cocked his head to the side. "Fate is fate, but you need to let the course of events play out as they will." He pulled Alice's pendant from his pocket and gazed at it. "What happened out there," Sebastian pointed to the lake, "I didn't manipulate any of that." An image of him killing Marcus popped into his head. He blinked it away. It wasn't him. He wouldn't allow it to be him. "I simply rolled with what was taking place. It was others, people not in the know about your *precious list*, who changed the outcome."

He glanced at Talia and Valentine, and grinned. Of course, it was Kyra who had really made the difference by saving Marcus, just like she had in the beginning when she had pulled him from the water, and Sebastian loved her a thousandfold more for her actions. Instead of killing Marcus, she had sent him away. She'd reminded him life was precious. Not just a few select lives, but every life, no matter how shady they appear to others. He clutched the pendant tight. Kyra would forever stand as his reminder to be the better man, the better Reaper.

Kyra landed in an open area near the entrance portal, shook free of her dragon form, retained a modest covering of scales, and walked toward them. He couldn't help but grin at her approach.

"It looks to me like you have your priorities all in a twist," Mortifier said.

Sebastian blinked. He'd lost track of what he'd been saying, distracted by his girl. He snapped back to his father. "My priorities are exactly where they should be."

Mortifier shoved his hands in his pants pockets and pondered his son for a breath or two. "You're a Reaper. You can't escape what you are, Sebastian."

Sebastian waggled his finger at his dad. "Correction. Half Reaper. I'm not anything you're familiar with, so you shouldn't try to fit me into your Reaper mold." He glanced at Kyra. She smiled, encouraging him to continue, yet there was no denying the tang of sadness in her eyes. "I have a better handle on what I am and what I'm now capable of. Don't push me on this."

Mortifier grunted. "You think you can pave your own path? Make your own rules?"

"Not at all." Sebastian smirked. "I'm simply going to follow the course and see where it leads. I'm not going to control events or people's actions to determine who lives or dies." He gazed at the pendant again. "I'll leave that to a higher power. One higher than you."

"That's not how it works," Mortifier said.

"Are you sure about that?" Sebastian held the pendant up for his father to see. "She wasn't a victim of circumstance. You murdered her, plain and simple." He tossed the pendant at his father. Mortifier made no move to catch it. The necklace fell to the ground at the Grim's feet. "I've seen the damage you've done, exploiting and engineering individual fates. I can't believe that's the way it's meant to be. We're ambassadors, not directors, and you've been meddling. What you did—working with Davies, stealing Marcus's dragon, sending him to Purgatory for all those years on the chance of avoiding a supposed destiny...Well, that may have actually *created* that very destiny by turning Marcus into the monster he is now. So, no more. No more manipulation." Sebastian kept an unwavering watch on his father.

Mortifier's face showed deep contemplation one minute and pulled into a snide grin the next. "We shall see how it all plays out." Crow's feet spread from the corners of his eyes as his smile stretched across his face. Behind him, Reaper after Reaper disappeared, until there was only Mortifier and Mr. Johnson, with his hand clenched firmly on Davies.

"What are you planning on doing with him?" Sebastian asked.

"Nothing you need to concern yourself with. He and I are overdue for a little chat is all. You know, regarding all that stuff that has your sickle stuck in the mud." Mortifier turned to leave.

Sebastian frowned. He didn't trust his father, but it was clear a ton of debris had piled up between Davies and his father. Debris that needed to be sifted through.

Kyra now stood beside him, her gentle hand finding a home in his palm. She whispered at his ear, "We've done a lot of good today." Yes, they had. Some good. And some bad. But the good outweighed the bad. He squeezed her hand, thankful for her reminder.

Mortifier took ahold of Davies's free arm and looked back at Sebastian. "We're not finished. You'll be seeing me again." With that, Mortifier, Mr. Johnson, and Davies vanished.

Sebastian's frown deepened. Mortifier's parting had sounded eerily similar to the Mara's. He rubbed the back of his neck and stared at the empty space where his father had been standing moments ago.

"Hey, look what we found." The call came from their right.

Several yards from the lake, Drakhögg and Ryhuu marched through the carnival's main archway of lights, two prisoners in their hold. All four men resembled an amateur knife-thrower's spinning board. Cut, battered, and blood-stained. "Those are Marcus's men," Kyra said. "I recognize them. Rick and Darren." The men glared at her, and Darren spat at Ryhuu's feet. Ryhuu didn't respond. "Marcus is gone, boys," Kyra said. "Time to give up the fight."

"Marcus is gone?" Drakhögg said. "Damn. I missed a lot." His forehead crinkled. "A man takes a few minutes to recover, and the whole damn show ends without him." His face crumpled into a scowl.

Kyra huffed, and Sebastian squeezed her hand. "Last I saw of either of you, you were running away," Kyra said.

Ryhuu stood a tad taller. "I cannot speak for Drakhögg, but my actions are unforgivable. Once we were within the confines of the carnival, I realized my mistake. When I saw these two," he motioned to the prisoners, "I enlisted Drakhögg to help do some good to atone for our error."

Kyra rolled her eyes, looked away.

Dragons began to gather on the shore, wandering in from all directions. It was the low after an enormous event. Or catastrophe, however you chose to view it. Queen Shui and Keahi were organizing their returning clans. Talia and Valentine had slipped away during Sebastian's argument with his father.

Despite, or maybe because of, the way things had unfolded, Sebastian harbored a hallow pitch in his gut. He still wanted answers, wanted to understand the why behind everything. Giving Kyra a gentle tug to follow, he moved away from the beastly crowd, his destination, an old man sitting on a red bench.

57
FOREVER...MAYBE

Kyra

After everything they had been through, they were still standing, side-by-side. Kyra wrapped her hand in Sebastian's, interlacing their fingers in a snug, never-breaking love knot. Behind them, the carnival sparkled, lights aglow, rides spinning and speeding, games pinging into action. Mystic's now ran at full capacity and had begun filling the park with patrons, people unaware of recent events. Life, love, and laughter were in blissful, oblivious motion. Before them, the lake was once again a fog-hidden mystery.

Zeke sat on the usual red bench, smoking his pipe. "As it was meant to be, all things came to their proper end."

"Are you saying you planned this from the beginning?" Kyra asked.

Zeke rested his elbow on the bench's arm, holding his pipe to the side. "I wouldn't say *plan*, so much as *saw it through*." He took a puff on his pipe. "Understand, I never want any harm to befall either of you, but events were set into motion a long time ago, and history had to make a few corrections. Balancing the light with the dark, once again."

Kyra opened her mouth to respond, and Sebastian pulled her into his side, wrapping his arm firmly around her waist. "Where was the imbalance?" he asked.

"It wasn't apparent as of yet, but if things had continued to run their course, the scales wouldn't have merely tipped, they would have fallen over." Zeke's lips twisted. "And then there was the plight of the Moorigad."

"Me?" Kyra said.

"Not just you, dear. All Moorigads." Zeke sighed. "Dragon clans have suppressed your kind far too long. It's time the Moorigads be allowed to grow into their own."

"And Anguis?" Kyra tugged at Sebastian's hold, pulling him closer. There was no close that felt close enough. Not now that she had survived, he was alive, and they had each other.

"Many ages ago, Anguis lost sight of what matters most in this life. Became consumed with himself and his own power. That's what drew him to you, Kyra." Zeke's blind stare somehow found her. "You, being the same type of Moorigad mix as him. I'm not sure what he thought he could accomplish by acquiring you. A master Moorigad race, maybe." Kyra's face soured. "Perhaps now, he'll have time to reflect on his choices." Zeke took a long drag of his pipe. Kyra nodded.

"How do you know?" Kyra asked. "Where did he go? Where did any of them go? My father, Marcus..."

Zeke's lower lip pushed forward, his unseeing stare now fixed between Kyra and Sebastian. "I don't know. But I am old and have seen many things over my lifetime. I choose to have faith."

Shifting uncomfortably, Kyra pressed her lips firmly together, threw Sebastian a sideways glance.

"What about the dagger?" Sebastian asked.

"The dragon's dagger?" Zeke clarified.

"Yeah, that one. Obviously, Marcus somehow got ahold of it. But what happened to it, after he used it on me?"

Zeke tipped his head in thought. "Who's to say? It's possible we'll find it in the cleanup. More likely it went the way of Marcus, wherever that may be. Or dropped to the bottom of the lake."

Sebastian lowered his head. "Right." He gazed back at Kyra, brushed a stray hair behind her ear. "Want to get out of here?"

A smile bound to betray her giddiness began to spread across her face, even as her chest tightened with guilt over her father. Kyra bit her lip, taking a moment before answering. "Let me take care of something first."

After saying their goodbyes to Zeke, the pair moved hand-in-hand along the lakeshore to where Queen Shui waited with the remaining dragons. Since everything had come to an end, dragons had been making their way back toward the main portal gate from all corners and obscure alleys of the carnival. A somber atmosphere lay heavy over the crowd, and upon their approach, Keahi kneeled and bowed her head. Like a wave, all the other dragons, save the queen, bowed to the Moorigad.

"No, Keahi," Kyra said, touching her sister beneath the chin. "I don't want this." She prompted Keahi to rise. Kyra looked her sister in the eye and clasped her hands firmly upon her upper arms. "Unlike me, you have always been at Father's side. You understand the Fire Clan in a way I never can. You should rule. Not me."

All the dragons rose, and Drakhögg took a strong position at Keahi's side. "But you are the eldest," Keahi said.

"Maybe so." Kyra let her hands slip from her sister's side, stepped back, and grabbed Sebastian's hand once again. "But you are pure Fire Dragon, and I am not." Kyra smiled meagerly at Keahi's confused expression. "I know we haven't gotten along, but I think it's time that changes. I think..." She surveyed the scene. "It's time for a lot of change."

Keahi glanced to Drakhögg, then back again. "Are you referring to the Moorigads?"

"The Moorigads and all clans." Kyra stole a fleeting look at her mother. "As a species, we've remained hidden, immersed in our anger and complex superiority issues. Father successfully bridged the gap between many of the clans, but not all of them. Let's finish what he started." Kyra extended her hand and waited.

Keahi stared at her, her eyes wide and body stiff. Seconds melded into minutes, and Keahi didn't move. Kyra held her breath. Maybe it had been silly of her to hope she could bury years of contempt and discord with her sister in a single moment...or several long moments. An eternity seemed to pass. Keahi sighed, her entire body relaxing, and she accepted Kyra's handshake. Her sister's hold didn't burn with its usual caliber, and her eyes glistened, damp with fresh tears.

"You won't be sorry," Kyra said and pulled Keahi into a hug, hiding a sniffle for her father. She had little doubt Keahi harbored a broken heart over their father, too. As a dragon, and a warrior Fire Dragon at that, she was likely attempting to hide it to appear strong for the clan.

"You're good people, Kyra." Drakhögg patted them both on the back, simultaneously. "Too bad we weren't a better match."

Kyra rolled her eyes, stepped away. Keahi punched Drakhögg in the arm. He pretended to be hurt and grinned at them both.

Biting her lip, Kyra watched her sister, feeling pride in her family for the first time. Keahi gazed back, and they stared at each other, letting time tick by. Kyra saw confidence and uncertainty fighting for dominance in Keahi's eyes, but like Zeke, Kyra now had faith. Faith her sister would overcome her doubts and rise to become a strong leader. Turning away, Keahi led her clan toward the portal home, Drakhögg a constant at her side. *They'll make a good pair.*

"Kyra," Queen Shui said.

Apprehension squeezed Kyra's chest as she confronted her mother. Her hold on Sebastian tightened. She wasn't giving him up, not for anything.

"Your father would be proud," Queen Shui said, indicating the departing Fire Clan. Kyra blinked. "You expected something different coming from me, I know." Her mother stepped forward. "But you have surprised me today. I've seen unexpected strength in your character; choosing the righteous path over an easy one. You could have let your demon here," she said, looking to Sebastian, "kill Marcus, but you didn't. You also stood strong by your decision and heart, regardless of outside pressures. I commend you." She peered down at her hands, twisting restlessly together. "If only your father and I could have been so strong, so bold. Maybe he wouldn't be gone now." Moisture trickled from her eye, and Queen Shui wiped at her cheek. "You are no longer a child, Kyra. I can see that now. I hope your choices were the right ones and don't end up ruining your life. Regardless, you've earned the right to choose your own path." She tipped her head, then turned to Sebastian and placed her hand on his shoulder. "I wish you great happiness."

"Thank you, ma'am." Sebastian bowed to the Water Queen for the first time.

"Stop that," she said with a wave of her hand.

"Mom." Kyra threw herself at her mother, wrapping her in hug. Kyra couldn't mend all the pain of the past and present, but she could share the ache and show her mother she cared.

The queen squeezed back, sniffled, and stepped away, smoothing her royal gown. A gentle hint of a sad smile polished her features. Without a word, she turned away and led her clan toward the exit. "I do hope your idealistic future works out."

Kyra wiped at her eye and watched the small group of Water Dragons casually make their way, a mild chatter among their ranks.

Ryhuu remained behind, standing tall and straight, with his hands clasped behind his back. "I apologize for letting you down," he said. "It is not usually my nature to run from a fight."

"Like you said earlier." Kyra stepped forward. "But it probably kept you alive this time." She leaned forward and kissed him on the cheek. "And I don't blame you." She glanced back at Sebastian. "None of us do. You had a Mara in your head."

Ryhuu gave a slight nod; it resembled a minute bow. "Thank you for your kindness." He glowered at Sebastian, and returned his gaze upon Kyra. "When this infatuation fizzles out, you come find me." With an about-face, and without another word, he moved to join the other dragons.

Sebastian's fingers combed through the hair at the base of Kyra's skull. An army of goosebumps danced across her skin. "Anymore errands you need to attend to?" he whispered at her ear.

She turned into him, welcoming his enveloping embrace. He had been so patient and understanding with her from day one. Now, she wanted nothing more than to be everything he'd ever wanted or could ever want. So far, all she'd managed to do was cause pain. Pain for herself, pain for her family, and worst of all, pain for him. She pressed her forehead into his chest and closed her eyes to his radiating warmth. She'd often heard him talk of being cold, but had never found it to be true. Maybe Death was brisk and bleak on the inside, but on the outside, he was like the fires of Purgatory—a never-ending flame to compliment her own.

With a gentleman's touch, Sebastian's fingers swept her hair behind her shoulders, whisked along the curve of her back, and caressed the curve of her hips. A shiver ran up her spine and goosebumps exploded across her skin. He pulled her against him, eradicating any lingering space and molding their bodies together.

Such a simple move morphed warmth into fever. Her sorrow and remorse diminished, giving way to desire. Every bit of her ached for him, burned for him. Her heart hammered like a dragonling attempting to take flight, and from Sebastian's chest...nothing. Not a sound. She placed her hand to his chest, and still no vibration came.

"If life still blazed within me, you could be sure my heart would thrum a heavy beat," Sebastian said.

Kyra peered up at him, a crinkle setting between her brows. "You gave your life for me."

"I'd do it again in a heartbeat." He grinned at his horrid joke, then humor slid from his face. Their lips joined in intoxicating promises. Vows of endless love and steadfast devotion. Eternal courage to rise above and against all things, together. His lips, gentle and strong, tasted of sweat and embers, hope and renewal, a lifetime of awaiting memories.

Kindling burst to wildfire, ravaging her skin and soul. Never would she let Sebastian go, but rather spend the rest of her days kissing him, being one with him. Her hands slid across his sweltering skin. Every mountain and valley, every contour of his being—melted against her touch. "I love you," she whispered between kisses.

Sebastian's lingering kisses shifted to the curve of her neck. Kyra quivered, a profusion of color exploding in her mind's eye.

"Never leave me again." Her words, softly spoken, held the hint of a plead.

"Never," he kissed her deeper, stronger than he had that day in his tarot tent, or the morning in Marcus's condo, or even mere seconds ago. With his kiss he handed Kyra his soul.

Sebastian had finally shown Kyra his truth. He was her heart, and she was his soul.

58

LOVERS

Sebastian

"I love you, Kyra." He brushed his mouth along the curve of her jaw. "To the ends of my eternal being." And it was true. He loved her more than words could ever profess. More than worlds or life or any creation. She was his *it*. The only *it* that mattered in an infinity of its.

Kyra blinked, a big, deep, dreamy-eyed stare into Sebastian's soul. "Love can't even come close to the way I feel about you." She pressed forward, kissed him passionately, sincerely. Too soon, she tipped back, batted her eyelashes, and bit her lip. "Want to take a ride on the Ferris wheel?"

Sebastian caught his breath. "Are you serious?"

"Never been more so." Her lips tagged his collarbone.

"You're willing to bind your life to mine for all time?" He swept her hair back and gazed deep into her eyes.

"Without a second thought. Just you and me and a kiss at the top, as it should be. Carnie style." She nibbled his chin. "I'll be yours forever."

"Forever, it is." He sealed his words by devouring her essence once more, licking the sweet tastes of cinnamon and spice with a swirl of burning embers.

The End.

Sebastian may make an appearance in the upcoming 2024 adventures of the Royal Reaper series. Start with book one:
REAPER'S QUEST

Until that book is available, grab your next strong heroine mission with
BLOOD PROMISE, CURSED ANGEL BLOOD PROMISE

Claim your free story, **THE MYSTIC MAKER**, and be among the first to know when new stories are being released by signing up for Debra Kristi's newsletter.
https://www.debrakristi.com/claim-your-free-gift/

Dear Reader,

I hope you enjoyed the *Moorigad Dragon Collection*. Thank you so much for coming along on Kyra and Sebastian's journey. Readers and reviewers make up the foundation of our author world, and we love you madly for all you do! That being said, I invite you to post a review of the book. Not only do I love receiving feedback, but reviews also help other readers find what they are looking for.

Thanks! Until next time, keep the magic real.

~ Debra Kristi

The angel of harmony is about to become a warrior of destruction.

It's been sixty-seven years since a spell gone wrong devastated the planet. All that is left of humanity exists in the demon-ruled, sinking ruins of what was once New York and New Jersey— home to fallen angel Charmeine.

Now, by the grace of God, she has been given the chance to save the world and her angelic standing. All she needs do is work with a deplorable witch and condemn her fallen brother, the demon lord, to eternal imprisonment.

Charmaine would do anything to earn back her wings. But when she does, who will be there to save her humanity?

LOOKING FOR MORE?

THE BALANCE BRINGER CHRONICLES

USA TODAY BESTSELLING AUTHOR

DEBRA KRISTI

THE BALANCE BRINGER CHRONICLES

ORIGINS

"In my humble opinion, this is one of the best, if not the best, fantasy adventure series I have read. Each book is a masterpiece in itself and captivating and addictive."

- ***LooseBoots, Amazon Reviewer*** ★★★★★

GLOSSARY OF TERMS

- **Essence of Anodynse** – The incense extracted from the spinal fluid of dragons.
- **Balidhug** – The name by which Marcus is referred to by those not in his circle.
- **Behemoth** – Supernatural beasts, chaos monsters the size of a rhinoceros.
- **Bolsvck** – The rightful Fire Dragon King who refused to rule, Kyra's father.
- **Chaos Demon** – Destructive Demons born from the earth and out of chaos.
- **Convergence** – Merging and resurfacing of lost species with one vessel.
- **Devil's Eye** – A network of rock formations and caverns whose configuration resembles an eye dubbed that of the Devil, located at one of the most extreme depths of the ocean floor.
- **Dragonet** – The equivalent of a teen dragon.
- **Dragonling** – A baby dragon.
- **Grim Reaper** – A member of the Reaper class who has ascended to the top rank.

- **Hellhound** – A supernatural dog with black spiked fur, yellow eyes, and tremendous speed and strength thought to guard a rare, supernatural treasure.
- **Kalrapura** – The name of Kyra's dragon.
- **Minor Reaper** – A member of the Reaper class who is undergoing the learning process, working beneath a Grim Reaper's supervision.
- **Mobürn** – Homeland of the Fire Dragons.
- **Moorigad** – The blending of two dragon species. The traits of both parents clash within the host, fighting for control.
- **Purgatory** – The limbo state between Heaven and Hell.
- **Rajũn** – The first dragon and great water deity.
- **Spiritual Peace** – A witch's brew allowing a Reaper to escape his or her mental and memory gathering gift.
- **Zilant** – A winged, snake-like creature, cousin to the dragon.

ABOUT THE AUTHOR

Debra Kristi was born and raised a Southern California girl. She still resides in the sunny state with her husband, two kids, and several rescue cats. Unlike many of the characters in the stories she writes, Debra is not immortal and her only superpower is letting the dishes and laundry pile up.

When not busy drumming away at the keyboard, spinning new tales, Debra is hanging out creating priceless memories with her family, geeking out to science fiction and fantasy television, and tossing around movie quotes.

Find me online and connect!

Discover more about Debra Kristi and her books on her website:
http://www.debrakristi.com/

And join her on her Facebook author page for updates, news, discussions, and more:
https://www.facebook.com/DebraKristi.writer/

THANK YOU FOR READING

PLEASE COME AGAIN

We've enjoyed having you along for the ride.

Happy Landing!

Don't stay away long.

www.ingramcontent.com/pod-product-compliance
Lightning Source LLC
Chambersburg PA
CBHW020504310726
48979CB00016B/2783/J
* 9 7 8 1 9 4 2 1 9 1 2 0 9 *